The Vanson

David Hough

To Della

An inspiration to me and the rest of the class

David

Published internationally by BeWrite Books, UK.
32 Bryn Road South, Wigan, Lancashire, WN4 8QR.

© David Hough 2006

The right of David Hough to be identified as the author has been asserted in accordance with sections 77 and 78 of the Copyright, Designs and Patents Act 1988. All rights reserved.

A CIP catalogue record for this book is available from the British Library

ISBN-10: 1-905202-30-X
ISBN-13: 978-1-905202-30-0

Also available in eBook format.

Produced by BeWrite Books

This book is sold subject to the condition that it shall not, by way of trade or otherwise, be lent, resold, hired out or otherwise circulated without the publisher's consent in any form other than this current form and without a similar condition being imposed upon a subsequent purchaser.

This book is a work of fiction. Any similarity between the characters and situations within its pages and places or persons, living or dead, is unintentional and co-incidental.

Dedicated to the memory of
Michael Collins,
a gentle man who died in
the countryside he loved.

Author's Note

"They say the Vanson family is gonna die out for want of decent women willing to stand up to the family curse."

So runs a line in this novel. The story is pure fiction but, to the best of my knowledge, the Vanson family is now extinct in Cornwall.

My grandmother – born Myrtle Vanson – descended from a family line mostly engaged in agriculture in Tywardreath, on the south coast of Cornwall. I believe she was the last of the line, which is why I became intrigued about the Vansons. With little difficulty, I discovered where and when her ancestors were born, who and when they married and when they died. But I often wonder about the domestic detail of their lives. What sort of people were they? In particular, I am intrigued by the Vansons who lived in the early and mid nineteenth century. The historian, Dr A L Rowse, wrote about the family in *A Cornish Childhood*, but his account began with a later generation. Initially, I set about creating my own imaginary history to fill in the gaps but, increasingly, the fictitious story took over and in time this novel emerged.

The real Christopher Vanson was born in 1809 and married Anne Lanyon in 1837 in Tywardreath parish church. Thereafter, they lived, died and were buried in Tywardreath. With their distinctive dialect, the locals pronounce it *Tower-dreth*. In the old Cornish language the name means *The House on the Strand*. For the purpose of the story, I have moved time forward three years and changed the place name to Penmarith, from the Cornish *Pen-Marghas* meaning *The Headland with the Market*.

Today, Christopher and Anne are long gone and evidence of their daily lives has largely disappeared with them, but the gravestone of John, their eldest son, can be found still hidden away in the Tywardreath parish churchyard.

Although I have taken liberties with family history, I have remained faithful to the realities of time and the place. The story begins in January 1838, when:

❖ Northern Europe was coming to the end of its 'Little Ice Age' but cold spells still affected the British Isles. The winter of 1837-8 was one of the worst and became known as *Murphy's Winter* after Patrick Murphy accurately predicted the severity in his almanac. In January 1838, the temperature dropped to an unprecedented minus twenty-six degrees in Southern England.

❖ Religion was an important part of most people's lives. The legacy of Charles and John Wesley prospered in Cornwall, making the county a breeding ground for Methodism.

❖ Mining and fishing were important mainstays of Cornish industry. Farming less so. Cornish farms were generally small, mostly less than one hundred acres, employing comparatively few workers.

❖ Industrial conflict was in the ascendancy. In 1834 six Dorset men, who became known as the Tolpuddle Martyrs, were transported for swearing an oath of allegiance to a trade union.

❖ The slave trade had been illegal in Britain since the passing of the 1807 Abolition of Slave Trade Act. It was, however, only a beginning and it took the Slavery Abolition Act of 1833 to bring freedom to slaves within the British Empire. America would experience the onset of a civil war before the introduction of the Emancipation Proclamation in 1863. Sadly, none of these acts of law would totally eradicate ingrained attitudes between the highest and lowest members of society.

David Hough

The Vanson Curse

One

Early January 1838

The last of the weak winter daylight died away while the schooner, *Tamarith*, creaked and groaned against the hard timbers of an icy wharf. The slight roll of the ship in concert with the fast falling tide, the comforting shipboard sounds and the nearby fish market smells did nothing to restore Kit Vanson's confidence. Above him, a flurry of snow danced to the tune of a light breeze.

"You're gonna be alone in Cornwall. No shipmates to get you outa any tight corners," Ben Worth said in his usual blunt manner. The old sea captain jabbed his pipe stem at Kit's chest, adding emphasis to his Alabama drawl. "You still sure about goin' through with this?"

Kit shrugged, feigning nonchalance. Of course he wasn't sure, but he was not about to admit it. "Got no worries, Ben." The lie was wasted because the older man understood him better than anyone else, having treated him like a son over the years. He gave Ben his most persuasive look. "Gonna give it all I've got."

His face burned hard by sea winds, the captain nodded sagely. "If things don't work out …" He offered a handshake with apparent reluctance, releasing it quickly as if that brief clasping of hands was also a moment of loss for him.

Kit motioned to his sea chest on the deck nearby. "You'll see it gets to the mail coach?"

"Of course," Ben said amidst a cloud of pungent tobacco smoke. "Now be off with you," his voice turned hoarse, "before I try to knock some sense into you."

Kit managed a weak smile then dusted snowflakes from his jacket, pulled up his coat collar to his ears and shouldered his worn carpetbag. With a last farewell he strode down the gangway without looking back. Lingering doubts still haunted him as he crossed the slushy, grey quay cobbles, aiming into a narrow alley that led towards Plymouth town. Snow settled quickly onto his hair, and an icy chill soon ran through his frame.

Ben was right; he was on his own now. He couldn't turn back without loss of face and he was nothing if not a proud man.

In the town's darker reaches, Kit walked assertively beneath upper storeys that leaned nose-to-nose across a cobbled lane where the snow was stained with decayed food, faeces and urine. His eyes stung from the sooty blanket of chimney smoke that pressed down between the rooftops and darkened the snow gathered on the slates. Lamps glowed ghostlike from an uneven series of windows, shimmering in the hazy atmosphere. Icicles grew silently, drip by drip, from ledges and sills.

Reaching the Admiral Nelson Inn, a place he knew well from previous voyages, Kit lingered beneath its wooden signboard that rattled in greeting. The same interior lamps burned behind the glazed door, the same unsavoury smell of recently emptied piss-pots hung about the alley.

Raised voices spilled from inside the building, and Kit registered the noise with indifference. He was no stranger to fights and arguments in harbour towns. Catching a glimpse of a frail young prostitute loitering in a next doorway, he fumed: "Go home, wench!" He shook his head at the waste. He had seen too many such wretched beings, and his revulsion persisted.

She snorted at him indignantly, and tangles of black serpent's tails fell forward across her face. Before she backed out of sight, Kit registered the hollow shame in her eyes caught by a slant of candlelight.

Somewhere inside the inn, a man bellowed, a feral growl from a primitive hunter. A woman's piercing cry of pain immediately followed, curdling the blood in Kit's veins. Then he heard a harsh scuffle of feet.

"Harlot!" Furniture crashed.

The unseen situation opened Kit's mind to painful memories and thoughts of home. He peered in against the inn's mottled window glass and gritted his teeth at the sight of a woman under attack.

Appalled, he hurried into the taproom, pausing to allow his eyes to adapt to the yellow flickering lamplight while stamping heavy clumps of snow from his boots. The heat and smell hit out at him; a heady, claustrophobic mix of sweat, ale and pipe smoke.

Slamming the door shut, he scanned the room, just in time for another piercing scream to resonate against the walls. He thought of leaving and finding a quieter inn at the top end of the town, but the Admiral Nelson Inn was the hostelry he always came to in Plymouth and he was not going to be easily put off.

"Let me through!" He pushed his way forward, dragging his bag at his side and looking for the woman in distress. But she seemed to have vanished.

Hostile stares fixed him briefly then swung back to the centre of the room where two men faced up to each other.

"Stand up for a harlot, would you!"

At a glance, Kit took in the larger of the combatants who wore a rich blue velvet coat. His angry red cheeks bloomed behind splayed side-whiskers, and he aimed his riding crop accusingly to his opponent, a wasted, hollow-eyed man covered with a stained fishing smock.

The onlookers remained strangely silent, oddly detached from the conflict and that puzzled Kit. Most seafaring men needed no excuse to pitch into a fight.

"She'm a lady! You hit a lady." The fisherman, his teeth bared and fists at the ready in front of him, waited for the next move on the woman.

Lady? What lady? Kit glanced around at the spectators, expecting an explanation and getting none. He pulled at the jacket of the man nearest to him. "What the hell's going on here?"

"Keep out of this, stranger, 'tes none of your business."

Maybe the onlooker was right. Maybe he should walk away. He released the man as his stomach grumbled, louder this time. He had not eaten since the *Tamarith* berthed early that morning. His determination on a hot meal despite the commotion had him jostle his way to an empty table. He dropped his bag to the floor and slumped down into a hard settle.

The watchers budged and Kit saw the combatants circle around their makeshift arena, eyeing each other warily. He grimaced at the unfair conflict. Why had no one stopped the fight? Were they afraid of the consequences?

A buxom, rosy-cheeked serving wench elbowed her way through the crowd, ale spilling from two pewter pots. Kit rose to draw her attention. "Nell!" She jerked to a halt, and her gaze fell on him. He was glad to clap eyes on her friendly face as she approached a table nearby. He nodded towards the fight. "What's this all about?"

She paused, chewed at her ripe lips and – with a shrug and a sigh – handed the pots of ale to a pair of sullen customers. Then, without a word, she turned towards the kitchen.

"Nell!"

The girl glanced back over her shoulder. "What?"

"I need some food, dammit! And a drink."

She nodded and forced her way back through the crowd to fetch his order. Kit sat down, eyeing the plate of mutton on the next table over. Then he flinched, catching a fleeting glimpse of a woman in her twenties spread-eagled on her back.

The jostling onlookers had edged apart, giving him a clear sight of her. She sported a livid red gash across her forehead and her long, shiny black hair spilled wide on the filthy sawdust floor.

He leapt to his feet as anger forced a taste of bile up into his throat. With relief, he saw her raise herself onto her elbows then fumble with a torn shawl tangled around her arms.

Suddenly noticing that her pale blue dress was rucked up above her knees, she quickly reached down to adjust it. He didn't miss the fine, shapely knees leading down to well-contoured legs. Nearby, a sailor sniggered and instantly, her eyes radiated terror.

A stab of pain ran behind Kit's eyes. Her reaction was not one of a common whore caught up in a taproom brawl. Something was very wrong. A sharp memory flashed through his mind: the image of his youngest brother, Clem, looming over a frightened Negro woman while he beat her to within an inch of her life.

Kit fisted his hands, his nails digging hard into his palms. Hell's teeth! Not again – not here in his new homeland!

Why would only one old man come to the victim's aid? Well, he wouldn't stand aside like the rest of them. Determined to help, he powered a path between the tight-packed bodies until no one stood between him and the softly whimpering woman.

He knelt beside her. "Let me help you, ma'am." He clasped her hand, unusually firm for a lady, and eased her to a sitting position.

She mumbled her thanks with an embarrassed expression layered over an ashen skin while a red flow trickled down her face. She wiped at the blood on her forehead then froze.

"You!" A menacing shadow fell over Kit. "Leave that bitch alone, God rot you! You're in me way."

With barely contained outrage, Kit released the woman's warm hand and swung round on one knee to face the speaker. "You addressing me?"

The man grinned, but no humour reached his eyes. "Who else?"

Kit eyed him warily, biding his time. He had downed such bullies before and knew the importance of choosing the right moment to act.

The man's pockmarked cheeks quivered beneath his bushy side-whiskers as a sneer creased his face, and he slapped his riding crop impatiently against well-filled breeches. "Did you hear me, stranger? Or do I have to take me whip to you as well?"

Kit allowed a brief silence to envelop him, breathing deep in his struggle to control his pounding heartbeat. Slowly, he sought the fisherman. The old man, with rough, weather-beaten skin, cast a keen eye over the new confrontation, his arms out still at the ready to continue the affray.

With a simmering gaze aimed at the well-dressed attacker, Kit attempted to end the confrontation peacefully. "It seems to me this lady needs protection."

"Ah, a colonial!" the whiskered man slurred, adding: "keep your nose out of things that don't concern you and leave the bitch to me."

Kit rose to his feet, vigilantly. Drawing another deep breath, he squared up to the man armed with the crop while, from the corner of his eye, he saw the fisherman stand back, blood still dripping from his shadowed cheek.

"I don't mean to intrude in anyone's business here." Kit kept a watchful eye on the crop. "It ain't my way. But I take exception to men who attack women."

"None of your business." The man laughed acidly, and his eyes took on a glint of expectation. "I warned you to keep out of this." He raised his right hand jerkily then flashed the crop forward.

Kit sidestepped the blow and caught the man's forearm. With one deft move, he jerked the arm behind the man's back, forcing him to his knees, his velvet coat billowing out as he fell heavily with a laboured breath gasping from between thick lips.

Before the assailant could rise of his own accord, Kit grabbed a handful of the coat and hoisted the man to his feet. He gave a curt nod to the fisherman and jerked his head toward the door. Understanding the gesture, the old fisherman jumped ahead of them. With an ease born out of many years at sea, Kit propelled his catch towards the exit.

"Open it!" he ordered, and the fisherman grinned broadly, wrenching open the door. Kit summoned up all his reserves of strength and, with one giant heave, threw the insulted bully out into the snow. The fisherman slammed the door shut and wiped his hands together decisively.

A strange sense of elation swept through Kit, as if he had satisfied an unrecognised desire for retribution. "Reckon he'll come back for more?"

The fisherman touched his forelock. "Not straight away, sur. Ee was on his own, and I reckon ee won't come back 'til ee's got others with him. Reckon ee'll find some rich hotel for the night and lick his wounds."

"Good." Kit dusted sawdust from his breeches and sniffed with distaste. Close up, the fisherman's clothes released a heady odour of putrefying fish. Kit hurried back to the woman and thrust out a hand to help her to her feet. "Maybe he'll think again when he's sobered up some."

She stared up at him, traumatized and hesitant, before she finally accepted his grasp. On her feet, she quickly snatched her hand away, her lower lip trembling.

The mumbling customers returned to their drink and food as the excitement died away. The innkeeper appeared, a platter of mutton in each hand, seemingly unconcerned that any conflict had occurred on his premises.

"Let me help you to a table, ma'am," Kit volunteered.

"No. I'll be all right." She straightened to her full height. "You've done enough. Please don't get yourself into any more trouble on my account."

Kit caught a tremble in her voice. "It ain't no trouble. What was the commotion all about?"

"A private matter." The woman covered her face with her hands and blew a long breath, seemingly relieved. She dropped her hands and gave him a pleading look. "Please don't ask me to explain." She spoke with more than a hint of Cornish accent and yet, to Kit, it sounded so soft, almost melodic.

"If you say so." He inclined his head briefly, indicating the matter was closed. It was none of his business, but she was a pretty young thing; too pretty to be mixed up in a taproom brawl. "You got far to go?"

"No." She waved towards the stairs. "I've a room here tonight and I'll be travelling on in the morning. I'll be safe enough now."

In this place? Kit wasn't so sure. "Only as long as that man don't come back with his friends. Who is he?"

From the taproom bar, the fisherman grunted loudly: "That be Ralph Killiow, sur," he said, a slow smile spreading over his face hiding thoughts Kit could only guess at. "His father be Squire Killiow down at Penmarith. Big landowners, they be. Wise men don't mix it with them."

Kit raised a brow. "You did."

"Which makes thee an' me the only fools here." The fisherman winked while wiping a hand down his bloodied cheek.

"Reckon you're right." Kit snorted. "Penmarith, you say? Well, I guess Mister Killiow and I just might have to cross swords again one day."

The woman's expression filled with alarm. "Not on my account?"

"No, ma'am." He was in no mood to explain as his stomach grumbled, seemingly loud enough for her to hear.

"You're very kind, both of you coming to my aid." She gave each man in turn a sincere smile.

"'Twas least we could do, mistress." The fisherman sniffed loudly, and with an air of disgust, eyed the other customers. "Even if others was afraid to."

In the background, the serving wench called to Kit. He sought her with a glance, and she winked at him as she rattled a jar of ale and a platter of mutton onto his table. Her pendulous bosom heaved, as if she anticipated his intimate attention. He raised a brief smile at her then returned his attention to the intriguing woman beside him. "If you get any more trouble, you just holler for me. I aim to stay here tonight."

"I hope that won't be necessary."

"Me too. I'll bid you good night, ma'am." Kit gave her a parting nod, anxious to fill his stomach and enjoy Nell's company, but the young lady held out her hand to him awkwardly.

"Wenna. My name is Wenna Lanyon, not ma'am."

"Christopher Vanson. Kit to my friends." He took her hand lightly and released it almost immediately. Her presence here, amongst hardened seamen, worried him; she was out of place. "If you've had your supper, I reckon it's best you get away to your room. I'll buy a jar of ale for our friend here." He clapped a hand on the fisherman's shoulder. "He deserves it."

The fisherman grinned broadly, displaying a line of broken, black teeth. He ambled away to where Nellie waited at Kit's table, the stink of fish wafting in his wake.

"Mistress Lanyon!" Kit raised a hand towards her to catch her attention, but Wenna strode purposefully through the taproom, head held high, glancing neither left nor right. Barely pausing in her stride, she exited straight into the chill morning air where snow billowed on the wind. He lowered his hand slowly, stung by an apparent rebuff.

Apart from a bandage about Wenna's forehead and pallor lingering in her cheeks, the events of the previous evening might never have happened. He had an urge to chase after her, but changed his mind. Likely, they would never meet again, and perhaps it was better that way. He was, after all, a seaman saddled with a shaman's curse, and she was a lady worthy of a decent man's attention.

"Coach be waitin' to leave, Mr Vanson." The landlord lumbered up behind him, rubbing his palms together briskly. "You best be on yer way, sur."

Kit nodded and pushed aside his square wooden trencher. "Three things you should never keep waiting," he observed. He downed the last of his mulled ale and rose, drawing his cloak closely about himself. "A coach, a ship and a good lady."

The landlord eyed him keenly. "Reckon you been well acquainted with all three, sur."

"Maybe." Kit smiled.

Outside, an icy sharpness honed the morning atmosphere and a thick layer of snow lay on the cobbles. He hurried down the narrow alleyway leading to the stable yard behind the inn where the coach waited. As he strode beneath a lone tree, it shivered from the wind, which suddenly took strength, shaking loose flecks of white. He dusted himself off as he walked on while gulls squawked overhead, sharp, raucous sounds like cries of complaint.

"Be you the last one, then?" the driver called out to Kit. Did the growl in his voice betray his irritation at the weather or being kept waiting?

Kit nodded to him then scanned the sky, blowing a stream of warm breath into his cupped hands. It was time to move on.

Startled, he stopped in mid stride, one boot on the coach's step, and frowned at the sight of Wenna Lanyon already settled by a window seat, staring straight ahead as if deep in thought.

So, this was what she meant by 'travelling on'. Rapidly composing himself, he clambered aboard, slammed shut the door and took the vacant seat next to her. She snapped her gaze down to her clasped hands, as if afraid to acknowledge him.

"Sorry to keep you waiting." Kit settled back in the seat, noting a flush rise in her cheeks, coy and so endearing. Clearly, it was shyness that governed her behaviour, not rudeness. How could he persist in feeling annoyed with her?

Two other travellers occupied the opposite bench, both tightly wrapped against the biting cold air that swept down from the white-capped moorland hills. An elderly but heavily built man in clerical dress sat beside a thin, sharp-nosed woman. From their closeness, Kit surmised she was the clergyman's wife. Both had humourless faces, his red and surly, hers pale and thin-lipped. The cleric held a leather-bound prayer book open on his lap, strumming his fingers impatiently against the pages.

Kit glanced again to his side, fixating first on Wenna's faded cloak. Was she a woman of slender means? That would explain her presence at the Admiral Nelson. He chanced a longer perusal. Apart from the bandage, her head was bare and her long, shiny hair fell loose about her shoulders. Her oval face was pure as newly fired porcelain.

As if she sensed his scrutiny, she turned and smiled at him briefly in recognition, nothing more than a cursory formality, then she returned her attention to the winter scene outside the window. In one fleeting moment, he caught the straight line of her mouth as her smile died away and creases formed about her delicate eyes.

With a jerk, the coach pulled away from the inn, throwing the elderly clergyman off guard. He grabbed at his prayer book and fell forward. Kit reached out a hand to support him and pushed him back onto the bench.

"Our coachman seems in a hurry." The hint of a scowl crossed the cleric's face as he settled deeper in his seat.

Kit glanced outside. "He's noticed the storm brewing from the north. We sure don't want to be caught out in it."

"No doubt." The clergyman neatly rearranged his black frock coat. With his prayer book returned primly to his lap, he studied Kit. "Do I judge from your speech, sir, that you are from our one-time American colonies?"

"It's that obvious, eh?" Kit grinned uncomfortably. How would the English gentry react to his arrival in England? Rumours claimed they could be cold and uninviting. "I've just worked my passage from New York," he admitted.

"You're a Southern gentleman, 'pon my soul." The clergyman's affable tone and his educated accent came across easily, so out of keeping with the Cornish people's strange way of speaking. "Believe me, sir, I have the ear to recognise a gentleman, even one from so far afield."

"Alabama. My pa owned land out there." Ending the sentence abruptly, Kit clamped his mouth shut, not wanting the conversation to stray into that dangerous matter – slavery.

The clergyman leaned forward and offered a hand in greeting. "Reverend George Beattie."

Kit shook the man's hand passively, noting Beattie's unusually firm grip for a man of his age and size. "Christopher Vanson."

With a wave, Beattie then indicated the woman at his side. "My wife. If we can be of any assistance to you during your visit –"

"It's no visit, Reverend. I'm here to stay. I've inherited my grandpappy's farm."

"Vanson?" The clergyman's brow creased in puzzlement. "The name is not unknown hereabouts. There are Vansons in Tywardreath and Fowey."

"My grandpappy was John Vanson. He lived at Tregover Farm near the village of Penmarith."

"Penmarith?" Wenna gasped, swinging her head towards him.

"Yes, ma'am." Kit tilted his head towards her, fully expecting her to join in the conversation, but she shifted uneasily in her seat.

"Nothing ... I'm sorry," she replied and hurriedly turned her attention back to the scene beyond the coach window.

"I know Penmarith well, sir," the cleric added.

Kit turned to him, noting how Beattie's brows rose above podgy features while he ran his hands blindly over the prayer book, as if reassuring himself that it was still in place.

"My wife and I are good friends of old Squire Killiow, poor soul that he is."

"Really?" With no wish to discuss any member of that family in Wenna Lanyon's presence, Kit veered the conversation towards his own kin. "Maybe you've come across my grandpappy, reverend?"

Beattie concentrated, the action screwing up his face. "John Vanson? Tregover Farm?" He shook his head. "I regret to say the name means nothing to me, sir."

Again, Wenna shifted noticeably in her seat.

Puzzled, Kit turned towards her inquisitively. She held her jaw open seemingly on the verge of speaking, but she was unable to form her tongue around suitable words. A blush ran up from her neck and through her cheeks.

Covertly, he risked a longer perusal, lingering over her finely sculptured face, the delicate curve of her mouth and gentle slant of her eyes. They reminded him of portraits on broad canvas and delicate china in grand houses; portraits of women endowed with natural beauty enhanced by rich clothes and luxurious surroundings. How sad to see such beauty lost beneath a veneer of poor living.

Fearful of offending her, he turned again to the clergyman and shrugged. "I never got the chance to meet my grandpappy. Don't really know what he was like."

The coach juddered over a pothole and Beattie's body bounced, blubber-like, on the seat while his eyes lit up with sudden enlightenment. "Vanson! Yes, it all comes back to me now. His only son went abroad long ago. Yes, I surely do remember. And you'll be John Vanson's grandson?"

"One of them. I have two younger brothers back home. They've stayed to work my pa's cotton plantation."

Beattie was momentarily taken aback. "Cotton plantation?" He slammed his prayer book shut. "They'll be slave owners, your brothers? And your father before them?" His tone turned sour, judgemental. "Do you hold with that way of farming, Mister Vanson?"

Kit pressed his lips in a taut line, uncomfortable with the emerging topic. He measured his words carefully. "The truth is, reverend, I left home and went to sea at an early age."

"But your kin are still slave owners." The rector's voice dripped disdain like a mouthful of spittle. He waved the prayer book at Kit. "You'll find things rather different here. We don't hold with slavery any longer."

Drawing a calming breath, Kit answered with a deliberately conciliatory tone. "My brothers run the plantation back home. I don't claim to approve of their ways." He held back on the dark thoughts that erupted into his brain – images of violent abuse.

"But they are your brothers," Beattie stated flatly, the earlier friendliness between them fast vanishing. He drew back his head, composing the sort of pulpit expression Kit had seen in many a church and chapel. "Your kin!"

Kit leaned towards the clergyman, looking him dead in the eye. "The Bible makes some reference to that matter, Reverend Beattie. Genesis, I believe. Am I my bother's keeper?"

A vivid colour rose in Beattie's cheeks. "I'm pleased you know your Bible, Mister Vanson. But you have no right to lecture me on the words of the good book."

Kit played his next card with a cold voice. "And you, reverend, have no right to lecture me on the morality of my brother's business."

Beattie jerked back in his seat, offended and flapping his lips, as if his brain was searching for an appropriate biblical response. Finding none, he curled his facial muscles into a suspicious grimace then lapsed into silence. He opened his prayer book again and glowered down at the pages.

Kit shook his head sadly. He should have held his temper. It was bad enough his pa had dishonoured the Vanson name through his violent behaviour; bad enough he had invoked a shaman's curse upon his family; bad enough no Vanson male had any right to look kindly on a pure woman … like Wenna Lanyon. His stomach felt hollow, like a cast-aside bean pod from which all sustenance had been eaten away. Following Wenna's lead, he silently stared out at the snow now falling freely and heavily.

Two

Wenna eased herself back against the cushion and slyly closed the gap between her and the American. As the coach slipped and bumped along the icy road away from Plymouth she then allowed her thoughts to play mischief with the man beside her. Would Christopher Vanson notice her arm now touching his?

He loosened his coat, and the unmistakable warm tang of male perspiration escaped. Her interest aroused, she glanced at him and felt a flutter in her chest. His features were rugged and handsome, but that was no conclusive reason for any woman to set her cap at him.

If only she could attract the American's attention without shaming herself. She shuddered at her sinful wish. Why should a worldly man like him pay attention to a poor farmer who had never travelled beyond Plymouth? If only she were not on the verge of bankruptcy.

Ruin.

Her reverie darkened into sadness, reliving the condescending expressions of the Plymouth bankers as they refused her a loan. 'You have no parents? *You* run the farm?' they had queried, aghast at her audacity in presenting herself at a bank.

She consciously conjured up memories of her long-dead mother and images of her more-recently deceased father slipped along in their wake. Then the odd circumstance of his death brought forth a shiver. Who had fired the bullet that pierced her father's back? Why would no one tell her? Against all reason, she still blamed Pastor Pengorse, the itinerant union agitator, and her hatred of him grew even more.

A niggling headache began to creep deep behind her newly formed scar. Maybe she blamed too much on the pastor's interference in her life. Maybe she was at fault for not heeding Thomas Roskilly. The parish constable had warned her about Pengorse's ways the day he came to her farm looking for him. The very same day her father was murdered.

"You ain't gonna let me in then?" Frustrated at her blunt refusal, Roskilly leaned over the lower half of the kitchen door, his tufted black brows creased together above the bridge of his nose as he visually searched about the room.

"You'll get in my way." Wenna gave him a sour look and then turned her back to the constable, resuming her vegetable chopping at the table. Pure obstinacy had induced her to close the lower half against him, leaving him prey to the cold wind. She had never pretended to like him and wasn't willing to start now. Vegetables done, she moved on to dissecting a scrawny rabbit.

"'Tedn't very friendly of you. When your father comes home –"

At the obvious threat about to be spilled, Wenna whipped around and stopped the constable with a glower.

Clutching his stovepipe hat to his chest, Roskilly reconsidered then stabbed a finger at her. "You tell him as how I called. Tell him as how I was askin' after Pastor Pengorse."

"What do you want with the likes of him?" She hoped her tone hid her fears well.

"You know of him then?"

"Of course I know *of* him!" She risked a wide glance beyond the constable, across the yard towards the barn. "Most folk round here know of Pastor Pengorse. That's no crime, is it?"

The constable shrugged then patted a bulging pocket. "I has a warrant for him from the magistrates. Squire Killiow named Pengorse to the justice at Fowey. 'Tes said ee travels the country stirrin' up trouble amongst the labourin' classes with his fancy words and how ee even knows them Tolpuddle men by name. And there be many as reckon ee was responsible for them riots up at Bodmin."

Wenna lowered her knife on the table. "Why are you telling me all this?" She wiped her hands in her apron, deliberately extending the action for some time. "And what's my father got to do with it?"

The constable eyed her with suspicion. "Your father, Mistress Lanyon, has been seen meeting with Pengorse over at St Austell. Oh, yes," he said nodding with glee, "and more lately ee's been seen meeting the pastor in the Cross Keys Inn here at Penmarith."

How had Roskilly gathered so much detail? Wenna let go of her apron to fold her arms in defiance. "I know nothing of this." Had the tremble in her voice gone unnoticed? Beneath her bodice, her heart raced.

"Really?" Roskilly's eyes flickered in the face of her defiance. "There even be stories goin' about that Pengorse has been seen here at this farmhouse."

"Nonsense!" Suspecting he was fishing for yet more details, she went on the offensive. "A Methodist preacher here? Why, you see me in church taking communion every Sunday, don't you? Would I allow a Methodist preacher in this here house? Well, would I?"

Roskilly considered her words for a spell. "'Tes true, I do see you in church. But not yer father. An' ee be the one seen with Pengorse. If I find Pengorse in this house ..."

"I wouldn't allow my father to bring trouble into our home." At the lie her heart palpitated and ached.

"That be just as well." He wagged his finger yet more sternly. "I wouldn't want to see a nice young maid like you sent to prison. Just you remember this: the militia be out lookin' for Pengorse. And when they find him you know what they'll do." Wenna held her stance. He gave her one last perusal, jammed on his hat and turned away. His back held straight, he stomped towards the lane, puffing loudly.

She hurried to slam shut the top half of the door and leaned against it, relieved yet shuddering. Eyes tight shut, she sighed deeply: Dear God, don't let them discover the truth!

The kitchen was quieter but much cooler, a gloom permeating the heart of her home. A new ache racked her forehead. Oh father! What trouble are you stirring up now?

She should never have allowed her father to shelter the likes of Pengorse. Other places were available; Methodist places, where the itinerant preacher would surely be welcome.

Now shivering from cold, she reached for and threw two lumps of coal into the constantly burning fire. On a whim, she added a turf of dried peat she had dug out from the bog below the bottom field. The flames licked round the fuel and mellow warmth slowly spread out across the kitchen. But her tense headache remained. She stifled a sniffle with the back of one hand then washed her hands in the cold water tub before tending to her rabbit stew.

She did not have time to fully rid herself of the stress before the kitchen door swung open and young Jimmy Rudge, their labourer, stomped in from the yard. "I heard ee talkin' to Mister Roskilly, mistress. Be it trouble for us?" Concern laced the thin drawn lines in his white face.

"I don't know. But I ought to speak to the pastor. Go and tell him to come and see me straight away."

"'Ess, mistress." Jimmy eyed her with hope. "Be ee goin' to send him on his way?"

"I'd like to, Jimmy. I'd like to very much. He's been hiding in our barn for three weeks now. I want to know what his plans are."

"The likes of him bring nought but trouble."

"That's as maybe." Wenna waved the boy along. "Just tell him 'tes safe to come to the kitchen."

She went to the window and followed Jimmy, her only farmhand, with sadness in her heart as he lolloped off across the yard to the barn on skinny legs. Wenna hoped proper food would one day fill out his emaciated body.

The boy went out of sight into the barn. With the stew simmering on her range, Wenna pulled a three-legged stool from beneath the table and sat down. She cupped her forehead and rubbed it with the heels of her palms. Hadn't she problems enough without Pengorse's rabble-rousing behaviour?

She raised her head when the pastor opened the kitchen door and bent his frame to enter.

A powerful man close up, he held his shoulders well back as if nothing could ever drive him to fear, not even God. She was unsure of his age; was he young and prematurely grey, or did he hide greater years with consummate ease? For a fleeting moment he took on the mantle of an imposing beau, handsome and dashing. Ridiculous! She quickly wiped that idea from her mind.

"What's the trouble, Wenna? You look upset." He approached her with long strides, leaned across the table and clasped a hand beneath her chin. "Have you tears in your eyes?"

Wenna quickly wiped a backhand across her face and drew away from him. "You've got to leave as soon as possible, Mister Pengorse. The constable was here and he's a warrant out for you."

"I saw him." The preacher remained irritatingly calm, seating himself at the end of the table as if he were about to intone the grace. "I overheard much of your conversation. You were wise not to let him into the house."

Wenna stabbed an accusatory finger at him. "He thinks you're the real leader behind those rioters being tried in Bodmin. You're the only one with the education to be a leader."

"Since when was education a crime?"

"It all depends upon how you use it, don't it?" The pastor laughed heartily at her comment and it offended her.

"You're a clever woman, Wenna. Do you think I ought to be on trial also?"

"If 'tes true," she said grimly. "If you're as guilty as they say."

He gave her a bleak look. "You're wrong and you do me a great injustice. I was preaching in Truro when the Bodmin riots began."

"Even so …"

"Wenna, believe me." Pengorse gave her a surreal smile.

She bit at her lip unsure of how far to press the matter. She had seen deception in other men. And yet laughter lines sprouted from the corners of his eyes, as if … as if he was taking her for a child.

"I had *no* part in those riots."

"That's not what the constable thinks. And the Squire's named you to the justice at Fowey." She took a deep, worried breath. "You mustn't be caught here or it'll bring trouble to all of us."

The pastor spread his hands philosophically. "It was inevitable, I suppose. I'll talk to your father."

"No!" She swallowed, fighting to bring her voice down to an even tempo. "I want you to go now. Please leave us alone. You frighten me."

"I frighten you?" His dark eyebrows lifted in unison. He rose and with two strides towered beside her. He clasped her upper arms with his huge hands, drawing her to her feet. "How can I believe that?"

"You do!" She froze momentarily at having spilled the emotion foremost in her heart. She freed herself from his grasp and snapped a hand to her mouth. "Please go away!"

"Not until your father gets back," he stated with icy calm. "It was *he* who invited me into this house." Pengorse grabbed at her hands, trapping them between his. They were hard, with a fierce, insistent grasp. "Trust me, Wenna. Wait until your father returns from Bodmin."

The liberty he took increased her fear of him. "Leave me be!" She thrashed against his grip. But Pengorse held her firm.

"Don't run away from me, Wenna. I hold you in very high regard. Who knows, one day I may have need of a wife like you to support me in my work."

A wife! She blinked, shocked. Her head began to whirl. Panicked, she jerked on her hands, yelling: "No!" Having finally freed her hands, she looked at him dazed while his eyes feasted on her body, ultimately resting on her heaving breast. "Good heavens! I could never marry the likes of *you*!"

"Why not? You're a fine young woman."

How dare he! She took a step backwards, pressing her palms flat across her chest to still her beating heart.

Unperturbed by her reaction, he continued his ogling. "You're twenty-four years old. Without hope of a husband. Yet any decent man should have dreams of a wife as fulsome as you."

She gaped at his audacity. Such blatant rudeness and such obvious leering intent. And him a preacher! She clenched her teeth, suppressing the urge to hit out at him. "That's enough! There's been no time for me to wed, Mister Pengorse." Her voice came out hoarse. "Too much to do here on the farm. Now, please go. Please."

Shaking his head sadly, he stepped back. "All right, Wenna. We'll talk about it again some other time." He swung on his heels and headed out of the kitchen.

He was midway to the barn when she realised the implication of his words. "No. Never!" she shouted after him, but he seemed not to heed her.

When he was out of sight, she slammed the door, and the catch caught with a loud clunk. She stood with her back to the rough-hewn oak, pressing her hands hard against the surface, and let out a groan. The thought of marriage to such a domineering man sent shivers of alarm vibrating through every fibre of her body.

She staggered towards the kitchen table, leaned her hands upon it and hung her head, her breathing shallow, hoarse gasps.

Wenna gasped and shifted sideways against the American, trying to avoid a flurry of snow that blew into the coach through the ill-fitting window.

"Trouble, Miss Lanyon?" he enquired, making no effort to add space between them.

"Just snow. I'm all right. Thank you." She dusted off her cloak and resumed staring out at the snow drifting into barrow-like mounds. Hedges were buried so deep, only their upper twigs poked out from the ground like aspiring buds. Trees, black and skeletal, waved their branches in a weird parody of flimsy arms dancing to the tune of white death, but her head throbbed, dulling her vision, the dazzling snow blinded her and the rocking and bouncing seat unsettled her stomach.

"You *sure* you're all right there?"

Christopher Vanson's warm, comforting voice penetrated her weakened state. She hesitated. "Yes. Perfectly all right," she lied, afraid to initiate any deeper conversation. What would the rector think of her?

The coach juddered against a rut adding to the pressure of his arm against hers. Still, he made no attempt to move aside. Was that a sign of his interest in her? Her shyness with young men was often misconstrued as an air of coldness, but perhaps Christopher was more intuitive than others. Dear God, she was so much in need of a friend such as him. She turned again towards the window and rubbed a hand over the condensation.

The coach rumbled on over the uneven slushy road, wandering past a small farm heavily coated in snow, so like her own. In an instant, painful memories resurfaced, focussing on Crabtree Copse Farm and her father.

The whinnying of his horse warned Wenna that her father had returned. She grabbed her cloak and rushed out to him, a lantern held high in front of her. His face bore an ashen weariness and his shoulders were slumped forward. He had barely dismounted before Pengorse ran out from the barn.

"Well, George?" Pengorse's words were sombre and filled with anxiety. He grabbed at the horse's reins. "How did the assizes go?"

Her father leaned against the horse's flank. "There be real trouble abroad, pastor," he reported, shaking his head. "Them union men won't get much justice. You'd think the magistrates would have learned after what happened in Tolpuddle."

Pengorse met Wenna's gaze. "Things are bad for me also, George. The parish constable was here today, asking for me and in possession of a warrant."

"That so?" Her father rounded on her.

"'Tes true, father." At her confirmation, his face turned cold and hard.

"Put the horse away, girl." He threw the reins at her, drew a deep breath and wearily waved the pastor towards the warm kitchen.

Would she ever be more than a slave in her father's house? Frustrated, she led the horse to the stable, settled it down for the night with hay and water then hurried back to the kitchen to find Pengorse standing in front of her Cornish range, warming his hands.

Her father looked up. "Did the constable know the pastor was here?" he snarled at her as she closed the door.

"I don't think so." Her jaw clamped tight, she strode across the room and removed the stewing pot from the hob. She would not cower to his bark, her dignity would not allow it. She swung round and met her father's glare with her own. "He's been seen with you, father."

Pengorse pulled out a chair and sat down heavily. "I overheard bits of the conversation. What she says is right, George."

Wenna breathed a silent prayer of thanks. She stared straight into her father's grey face, noting the droop of his mouth, the distant expression in his eyes. He had been drinking.

The itinerant preacher sighed heavily. "I'll have to find somewhere else to hide out for a while. Somewhere off your land."

"Dunno where you'll go, pastor," her father mumbled, lumbering towards his scrumpy barrel. He juggled a tankard beneath the tap and let out a generous measure of rough cider.

"What about Tregover Farm, John Vanson's place? Couldn't I hide there until the trouble dies down? It isn't far away."

Her father raised the tankard to his lips and drank, swallowing half the measure in one go. He wiped his mouth then gloomily shook his head.

"What better place to hide than on a dead man's property?"

"I dunno, pastor. Old Jacob Padder be living there at present." Her father sucked in a rasping breath as he considered the possibility. He exhaled loudly and took another deep draught of cider. "The village gossips say Vanson has a grandson who'll take over the land."

"But not yet. Right?" Pengorse's expression brightened. "You can lead me over there tonight."

"What about Padder?" Wenna cut in, concerned for the welfare of the labourer living alone on the Vanson farm. She swung her gaze between the two men. "Do you never think of other people around here? Is it only yourselves you care about?"

"He doesn't have to know." Pengorse sent her a pointed look. "The fewer people who know where I am, the better."

"There be an old barn out in Vanson's ten acre field." Her father refilled his tankard and drew up a chair opposite the preacher. "Reckon as how ee could hold out there for a while. We could send food over to ee. Wenna could take it."

"Me?" Wenna fumed at her father's assumption. "But that would put my own freedom at risk."

Her father glared at her. "Ee'll do as I tell ee!"

"I will not!" She crossed her arms in defiance.

"Yes, ee will, girl!"

No good would come of arguing the point in front of Pengorse; she would raise it again later when her father was sober. At least the preacher would be leaving their land. Wenna held her tongue and turned away while her father took another drink to fight off the cold. Shortly after the two men set out into the night.

Desperate to take her mind off her worries, she fussed about the kitchen long after her father and Pengorse had left for the Vanson barn. Shortly after midnight, a scuffle of footsteps in the yard broke the eerie silence. Moments later, she heard a rap at the kitchen door. Her father wouldn't knock; he'd just walk in.

She stared at it with rising fear. "Who is it?" The hesitation in her voice was unmistakable.

A muffled, gasping voice called out to her. "Pastor Pengorse. Hurry, Wenna."

With a feeling of dread, she opened the door, drawing back as

Pengorse stumbled in alone. Seeking an explanation, she glared at the preacher. At Pengorse's silence, she pushed past him and panned about in the darkness outside.

"Get back inside, girl!" When she didn't obey, Pengorse grabbed at her elbow and dragged her in, slamming shut the door.

Wenna stared at the preacher, a bout of shivers raking through her body. "Where's my father?"

He released her and clasped at his still heaving chest.

Dread crept into her heart. She searched Pengorse's eyes then switched her worried glance to the closed door. "Where's father?"

"We were ambushed."

"Ambushed!" she wailed.

Dear God, her father had been captured! The militia could force him to reveal that Pengorse had sheltered at their farm. What would happen to her? She shuddered, remembering the constable's warning.

"Militia men were waiting for us over at Tregover Farm," Pengorse panted, "maybe they guessed I was here and I'd be moving out after Roskilly's visit." He slumped into the nearest chair. "Or maybe they just got lucky. They opened fire on us."

Wenna gasped then an invisible hand clutched at her heart. She struggled for breath and fell into the chair next to his. "Father's been hurt?"

He nodded silently.

"Did the militia men take him to the gaol?"

Pengorse averted his gaze. She grasped at his frock coat and shook him to gain his attention. "Answer me."

He laid mournful eyes on her. "He was shot, Wenna. I saw him hit the ground. There was nothing I could do about it." His voice was heavy and sombre.

Icy fingers reached into her soul, searching for her lifeblood. Her field of vision narrowed into a shoulder-width tunnel. "He's dead?" she squeaked.

Pengorse's nod was filled with finality.

"Dear God, no!" She released her grip on the preacher to hug her waist and rock in her chair.

"I'm sorry, Wenna."

"You!" Wenna jumped to her feet, pushing back the chair with such force it fell over. "It was all your fault!" Blackness filled her heart, pure hatred for the itinerant preacher. How she loathed the man. The room began to swirl about her. "Oh, dear God. Father's dead!" Her last parent was gone. What would happen to her and the farm?

"Almost certainly dead. I saw his arms fly up when a bullet hit him in the back. He must be dead."

At the sudden realization that she was on her own, she fell back again into the chair. Her father, that irascible, impossible old man, was gone forever.

"I'm sorry, Wenna." Pengorse rose and pulled her up roughly into his arms. "There was nothing I could have done."

She hated him more than ever because his assurances sounded insincere, conjured up for the occasion – the words of a speech, not a heartfelt condolence. She thrust him aside. "Leave me alone!"

Pengorse stumbled back a couple of steps, adding: "I'm sorry, Wenna."

"Are you?" She eyed him with disdain. He had left her father behind to die alone. "Are you really sorry for what you've done?"

"Sorry for what *I've* done? Do you blame me?" Shoulders slumped, he looked the part of a man maligned. His face turned deathly white. "I did nothing wrong."

But she could not bring herself to believe him. "Get out of here now. Quickly! Before the militia arrive to search the house." She sniffed and wiped at her eyes, determined she would not weep. Not yet. The militia and the constable would surely arrive here soon, and she must play the part of innocence. In time, the constable would tell her formally of her father's death, then she would weep. But not before.

"You're right. The militia will surely be coming here to investigate. I must have somewhere to hide."

"Yes, they'll be coming here, searching for you! You must go away now." She pressed his bulk toward the kitchen door, anger and fear knotting her insides.

"Where can I go?"

"I don't know and I don't care. Get out of this house! You've brought us nothing but trouble. Get out! Get out!"

Pengorse lumbered towards the kitchen door. "I'm sorry, Wenna. I really am sorry."

"Get out! I don't want to see you here ever again."

Kit brightened as the journey progressed. Wenna Lanyon seemed keen to remain tantalisingly close beside him on the seat cushion. Better still, she had an alluring appeal, despite her silence. Unlike Nell, she had an air of purity about her, virgin as the snow on the far heath. Even up close in a bouncing coach, she exuded the fresh, clean scent of a woman who washed regularly.

Why had such a woman lodged at the Admiral Nelson?

The reason was none of his business, and he reluctantly chased the matter from his mind. Instead, he turned his attention to the scene beyond the coach as it lurched and rolled down the sloping approach towards the new Saltash floating bridge over the River Tamar. Tall-masted ships lay at anchor in midstream, some offloading into lighters, others waiting for the tide to turn and carry them on up river to Morwellham Quay.

The river threw up a choppy surface as the coach was pulled onto the floating bridge platform. Kit lowered the window sash and leant out to marvel at this innovation. How Ben Worth would chuckle at the idea of a ferry being dragged across the river by steam engines and chains. He was firmly of the opinion that no steam engine could ever replace sails for efficient water travel.

Hearing a moan, Kit drew back inside the coach. The clergyman clutched his prayer book against his stomach, his wife fussing about him. His face had turned puce as the float chugged noisily into the fast flow of the river, yawing against the tug of its heavy chains. Wenna Lanyon took Kit's place at the window, setting her face to the cold, damp air. By her smile, she seemed to be relishing its sharp sting, but she shivered and eventually pulled the leather strap to raise the sash. Barely five minutes later, the float bumped against the slipway at the Cornish side of the river and the horses heaved the coach ashore to continue its journey.

Just beyond the limits of Saltash town, the coachman called the passengers outside while he cajoled his team up a slippery incline. He swore at the dark clouds that scudded low across the sky, cloaking the trees at the upper limit of the hill.

Kit spared a glance back over snow-covered fields to where the Hamoaze, the St Germans River and the Tamar wound together like slithering silver snakes in endless mating. Striding close beside him, Wenna let out a verbal shiver.

He shifted his pace to match hers. "You look distressed, Miss Lanyon." The bottom of her gown was now thickly layered with slush and it dragged against her ankles.

"Distressed?" She kept her focus on the lurching coach in front of them.

"You look cold. May I lend you my cloak?" He offered his arm, uncertain how she would react. Was it right for an English lady to accept his offer?

"Thank you, but I think that would be unwise." She spared him the briefest of glances with her answer. Now her eyes rigidly focussed on the slush and mud churned up by the horses.

"Unwise?" Kit laughed aloud. "It's only my cloak I'm offering, not my attentions. Did the talk of slavery offend you?"

She angled her head in his direction. "Oh, 'tes not that."

The coach halted at the top of the hill, and the coachman turned in his high seat to call them aboard.

Pausing at the step, Kit offered her his hand, hoping she would accept. "I swear to you that I have no part in that offensive trade. Nor would I deliberately cause offence to a lady like yourself."

A deep, searching expression drifted across her face. She hesitated and then, with one smooth swoop, took his hand and climbed back into the coach. Kit smiled inwardly; it was a moment to savour, the touch of her hand in his.

He was last to climb aboard, wary of Beattie's sharp expression of distaste aimed directly at him. The coach pulled away, and he settled into an uncomfortable silence.

A heavy snowstorm delayed the coach several hours on the high ground near Liskeard. Darkness was falling fast when the mud-caked wheels slipped and rattled on the cobbles as the coachman reined to a halt outside an inn at the lower end of Lostwithiel.

He hopped down from his icy perch. "Out you come, all of you.

We have to stop here to change the horses. There's food available inside."

The Reverend Beattie rose first and squeezed his bulk out of the coach, mumbling: "We'll not get any further tonight, I'll wager." He hurried towards the inn, his wife scurrying along behind.

Kit jumped to the ground behind them and reached out a hand to help Wenna descend. "Mind you don't slip. I reckon it's going to ice up good and proper this night." She took his hand, and again he sensed that warm inner glow while he helped her down. He would have been happy to retain her slender hand in his, but she jerked it away as the horses whinnied, their steamy breath lit up by the flickering light spilling out from the inn's bay windows.

"I was hoping we'd get farther than this," she said, drawing away from the team.

Kit wished he could hear more of her mellow, husky voice. How could he have missed the warm timbre of her speech earlier? "Are you travelling far, Miss Lanyon?"

"I had hoped to reach Penmarith tonight." She shivered and drew her cloak tighter around herself as they walked together towards the inn. "'Tes little more than an hour's ride from here on a good day, but I'm sure the Reverend Beattie is right; we'll not be able to continue any farther in this weather."

Penmarith? Kit felt a light apprehension. Why hadn't she mentioned earlier that she was destined for Penmarith? "We're headed for the same place."

"Same place, same weather," she stopped and faced him, "probably the same problem."

"Problem?"

"Ralph Killiow."

He studied her face in the light spilling from the inn then grinned. "I can handle him."

She answered his statement with a laugh without humour while her lips remained straight. Her eyes were such an intense shade of blue, strongly contrasting with her deathly pale skin. "Will you travel straight to Penmarith, Mister Vanson?"

"Not immediately, ma'am." He nodded towards the inn, and they resumed their walk to the entrance. "I've business in St Austell first. I reckon I'll stay the night here and travel on tomorrow, whatever the weather."

"Then I hope the business goes well for you."

"I expect it will." He stopped in the stone arched doorway and cast a wary gaze about him. "What we need now is a warm supper to keep out this cold. I sure do hope the landlord's wife is a good cook."

Beattie was right; no one would travel farther this evening. But Kit was in no hurry, not now. He was almost home – his real home, that place he had sought without even knowing where it was.

He had come very far since that day he'd left the plantation shortly after his fifteenth birthday. Pa had been angry. They had argued bitterly over the morality of slavery right up to the moment he rode away from the house. Rode away? No. He might as well face up to it; he had *run* away because he could not cope with the truth.

He had shouted unkind remarks to his pa and that had been so very wrong. For all that he had brought the shaman's curse upon the Vanson family, Pa was due some respect. Kit chewed at his lip. Was that why he was here? Was this a path of atonement, a journey to Pa's roots?

Or was he, once again, running away?

Three

Kit awoke suddenly, jerking upright to the wail of wind whistling through the eaves. Or was it a banshee invading his mind in some ghastly nightmare?

In those first few minutes after waking he could not separate reality from the dregs of a night vision. Age, the very stuff of Grandpappy's native land, came to life in the creaking of the floorboards and the rattle of the ceiling joists. He settled back on his pillow. Painful memories returned, filling his mind to bursting and focussing on his last homecoming, in Alabama.

Leaning back in the saddle, he wiped his necktie across his sweating brow. The house remained exactly as he remembered it; the white frontage shimmered beneath the blinding sun, with its high stone pillars standing to attention at either side of the main entrance. His perusal slowed on the ornate veranda running across the entire width of the façade. He visualized his ma and pa seated in their favourite rocking chairs, watching the sunset as it faded over the carpet-like spread of their cotton fields.

He nudged his horse into a trot. How would they greet him? He'd left home a puny boy sitting at the tail end of a buckboard watching the house disappear around a bend in the avenue. Now he was a hardened man, six foot tall, well muscled and – he hoped – infinitely wiser. Maybe, with age, Pa would have changed also, mellowed enough, perhaps, to accept him back without recriminations.

He reined-in directly in front of the main door. A young slave ran forward and reached out to take the reins. The boy was painfully thin with deep-set eyes and glistening black skin.

Kit dismounted. "Is the master at home?"

The boy eyed him warily, edging backwards to the barn.

"The master." Kit nodded towards the house. "Is he at home?"

The boy stopped and kept his eyes downcast. "Massah Pasco

Vanson, he'm out in the fields, suh." Hesitating, he added in a subdued voice: "Massah Clem Vanson, he gone off to town."

"No, boy. I mean your old master and mistress? I want you to go and tell old Master Vanson he's a visitor."

"Only Massah Pasco here, suh. Massah Clem, he –"

"I heard you." Kit took off his hat then rolled his head to loosen the tight muscles in his neck. When he was done, he eyed the boy once again. "Look at me, boy. The old, old Master Vanson, where is he?"

The slave's eyes widened in understanding. "Old massah, he died suh. So they say. An' old Missus Vanson, she died too, suh."

Kit froze. Ma and Pa were gone! Yet everything else seemed much as it was all those years ago. Only a single word rasped out from deep inside his throat. "When?"

The boy shrugged. "Afore ah came here, ah guess."

A heavy thumping surged in his temple and his eyes drifted out of focus. He sucked in a cleansing breath. "All right, boy. Get someone to fetch Master Pasco. Tell him Kit's home."

"Yes, suh." The boy backed away, pulling on the reins in no apparent hurry. When he finally turned, Kit shuddered at the sight of angry red wheals criss-crossing his back, some barely healed, others still oozing.

He winced, a sick feeling churning inside his stomach. Dear God, it was still going on, even with Ma and Pa both dead. He dragged himself up the steps to the cool veranda.

A black woman hustled out of the house, a wary look in her eyes. She set her thick hands on her more-than-ample-hips and asked: "Who'm you, suh?"

Who was he? A stranger at the door of his father's home – his dead father's home. "I'm Kit. Christopher Vanson. I've come to see my brothers."

The woman's eyes opened wide, and her hands flew up to her cheeks. "Massah Kit! Why, we all heard about you, suh. They say you done run off long time since."

"Well, I'm back again now." He scanned about. Back to what? He licked at his crusty lips.

"Yes, suh." A strong hint of surprise chased the earlier caution in her expression. She motioned him to a cane chair. "You just take a seat right there, suh. My, oh my!" Chuckling throatily, she hobbled away into the house, and he sank down, the throbbing in his temple increasing.

The black woman returned with a lemonade in one hand. "Just you take this, suh."

He looked up, surprised at her keenness, and took the filled cup. He guzzled thirstily, clasping the cup between sweaty palms. He then let out a satisfied sigh, stared at the glass and smiled. "Just like Ma used to make."

"My boy, Sam, he done gone to fetch Massah Pasco back from the fields. Massah Pasco, he sure be glad to see you, suh."

"He'll be surprised, that's for sure." Kit closed his eyes, dismissing the servant.

He set down the cup onto the table by his chair and stretched out his legs. Immediately, exhaustion set in. A deep draining sensation coupled with the sun's warmth carried him off into a light doze.

"Goddammit, it is you!"

Kit awoke with a start, eyes blinking away the dregs of sleep and focussing on a rider reining-in by the veranda steps.

Pasco nimbly jumped down from his horse and bounded up the steps. He jerked a hat off his mop of straw-coloured hair and threw it on the nearest chair while a broad grin washed over his sun-tanned cheeks and square jaw. Wonderment flashed from within his deep blue eyes.

Kit took in the trademark features of the three Vanson brothers; a copy of the face he had seen recently only in mirrors. He reached for the brawny outstretched hand and was pulled to his feet. "It's so good to see you, Pasco." He clasped at his brother with warmth born out of years of separation.

"Real good to see you too, Kit. You sure have filled out since ah last saw you. By golly, wait 'til Clem sees this."

Easing the tightness of his clasp, Kit retained a hold on Pasco's hand, now hard and firm from years of cotton farming. "You and Clem both well?"

"Sure, we are." Pasco pulled his hand away.

Kit noted the speed with which the delight in his brother's

expression faded away. "Spill it, Pasco." He asserted his demand by raising his hands to his hips.

Pasco hunched his shoulders. "Well, Clem hits the bottle at times, but I guess you don't wanna hear that now." He straightened himself. "Business sure is good, though."

"Heard as how Ma and Pa died." The words choked out from his throat, hoarse and painful.

"Yeah." Pasco lowered his head. "Pa, he took real sick with a fever an' there was nuthin' we could do fer'n. I guess Ma just gave up once he was gone. One day she took a fever as well. Died within a year of each other, they did. Buried out there on the hill." He pointed towards the blue-green slope marking the southern boundary to the plantation. "It was done all proper like, with a preacher an' all. Pa always said as we was to bury 'em both out there."

Pangs of guilt stabbed Kit deep inside. He never would get to settle his differences with Pa. "I'm real sorry I didn't see them again."

Pasco flashed him with a broad grin. "Hey, we gotta celebrate now that you're back."

"Yeah. Guess we must." The house was quiet, too quiet. Kit had expected little ones running in and out, shouting and playing in the sun. He nodded to the front door. "Say, you and Clem, you're not married are you?"

Pasco gave him a sheepish look. "Not yet. But I got me an understandin' with Emma Bayne. You remember the Baynes?" Kit nodded and Pasco added: "They own that big plantation beyond the Blueback Hill. Me an' Emma figure on gett'n hitched soon."

"I'm pleased for you, Pasco. I surely am." Kit was genuinely happy for his brother until a dark memory usurped his joy. He forced a tight smile across his face for the benefit of his brother, who seemed not to notice his discomfort.

"Needs a woman in this house again, and Emma, she sure is a purdy li'l thing." His brother suddenly eyed him warily. "What's wrong?" Kit averted his gaze, embarrassed. "You're wonderin' if she's pure, right?" Pasco said pushing the matter.

"The curse, Pasco. That damned Vanson curse." He sighed deeply then eyed his brother. "Forget it, I shouldn't have mentioned it."

A grin lingering about Pasco's lips failed to reach his eyes. "Aw, darn it! I ain't worried about the curse. It's surely just a load o' superstition anyways." He reached for his hat and slammed a fist into it. "You don't need to worry none about me, big brother. Clem's the problem." Pasco wound an arm around Kit's shoulders. "I'm glad you're back again 'cos he sure needs a bit o' handlin' since Pa died."

"You'd better tell me about it." Kit turned on his brother, brushing aside the friendly gesture.

Pasco let out a deep sigh. "When he gets hisself drunk, he takes a fancy to them slave women. An' when he wants one, he just goes in there an' takes his choice. Just like Pa did. I just can't reason with him any more."

"And he gets drunk often?"

"Pretty much."

"He always was a wild one." Kit reassured his brother with a pat on a shoulder and a promise. "I'll talk to him."

Pasco dredged up a genuine grin. "I'd sure appreciate that. Reckon Emma's pa'll be none too pleased at the idea of her comin' to live here with Clem carry'n on like that."

"You mean we gotta look after the family name?"

"That's right." But the cynicism was lost on Pasco. "Hey, you remember how Pa used to tell us about our family owning land in England, saying how the Vansons was once real wealthy folks until they had themselves a civil war over there. All they had after that was some farmin' land, but that was better'n bein' poor. You remember that? Pa even thought of going back there, you know. Anyway, Grandpappy died."

"Grandpappy Vanson?"

"Died and left his farm to Pa. Guess we should've written him after Pa died." Pasco paused to reflect. "Reckon it belongs to you now, bein' the eldest. That's the way the law goes in England. What do you think? You fancy ownin' a farm way over there?"

Kit shaded his eyes and panned around the land. "Dunno, Pasco. I figured it was time I came home. Just to see how things stood. I've no thoughts of settling in England."

"Sure. I know. This here place is your home 'n all. Clem 'n me, we need you here now with Ma 'n Pa both gone."

Rubbing his jaw, Kit grabbed on the easiest option. "I'll stay a while and think on it." But even then, his doubts loomed ominous. Little had changed, despite his parents' death.

The chill in the Cornish air drew a shiver from Kit. His stomach rumbled; an indication morning had come. He crawled from his bed and placed a palm against the window, melting the hoarfrost which had turned the mottled glass opaque white. Smoothing his hand across the pane, he enlarged the peephole and checked on the weather. A bitter wind blew along the road and across the nearby fields, lifting up handfuls of dusty snow and sending them swirling through the air like miniature ghostly whirlwinds.

He dressed and strode down to the taproom where the landlord brought him a substantial breakfast that warmed his belly but not his limbs. After the meal, he sat before the fire, alternately rubbing his hands and holding them out to the flames.

"Not used to this weather, sur?" the landlord asked, rubbing a ragged cloth over the gnarled oak tabletop.

"It ain't like Alabama weather, that's for sure."

The landlord guffawed, as if Kit's discomfort amused him. He turned away to take stock through a front window. "Reckon as how the snow'll continue a while yet."

Kit grimaced. "That sure ain't no comfort." He returned to his room and stood at the window. In the street below, his erstwhile travelling companions boarded an early coach for Penmarith, Trevisco and Fowey. The St Austell coach was timed to leave an hour later.

He packed his carpetbag and spent the rest of his wait beside the fire in the taproom until the landlord gave him a knowing nod. Finally, he pulled up his collar and walked out into the cold air.

He threw his bag on the roof of the waiting coach. "Many passengers on this trip?" he called up to the driver.

"Only thee." The man thumbed his pipe and bent his head into the wind.

Kit climbed inside the coach and the team of horses lurched forward. He peered from the window at a barren landscape rolling by, occasionally broken by a small thatched cottage unprotected from wind or blizzard. He fretted as the horses lumbered ahead, and the coach bumped over hidden stones and potholes along a barely discernable trail.

In the distance, standing stark and lonely as if the world had passed it by, he discerned a cluster of mine buildings sprawled across the landscape like unhealed scars. Smoke puffed steadily from tall chimneystacks and quickly melted into a low, grey cloud. Protruding from the engine house like a giant mechanical arm, a metal beam rose and fell in slow time, pounding a long column of timber rods down many fathoms into the unforgiving ground. A smaller beam in the nearby whim powered a winding wheel. Was it a tin or copper mine? Kit frowned. It was impossible to tell from a distance.

As on the previous day, at each hill he disembarked, pulling his collar tight against the cold wind. He trudged behind the coach and its struggling team of four horses, looking down at the churned up snow. Did Wenna Lanyon tramp these same hills only hours before? How easily his mind drifted off to that young woman. Maybe too easily.

Shortly before noon, the coach trundled through St Blazey and Mount Charles before the short drop down into St Austell town. The horses drew to a halt outside a busy coaching inn. Kit jumped down to the slushy road with cold, aching joints and a keenness to finish his business as quickly as possible.

A brisk walk brought him to the office of Charles Tapper, Notary and Commissioner of Oaths, at the west end of Fore Street, where the Bodmin Road met the turnpike from Truro. A gaunt-looking junior clerk showed him up a creaking stairwell to the notary's office.

Tapper, a grey-haired and weighty man, beamed at him through narrow-rimmed spectacles. "Come in, Mister Vanson." His voice had a cold, hard quality, but Kit was thankful that Tapper's Cornish accent was not too strongly marked. The notary remained seated, his red cheeks puffed out to give him an owl-like appearance. He waved Kit towards a worn leather chair. "Do have a seat, my dear sir."

Heated by a blazing log fire, the office was pleasantly warm. Settling in the chair, Kit's gaze fell on the puddles of water pooling around his feet as clogging snow melted from his boots.

"It's not normally as cold as this in Cornwall, of course. Even in winter," the notary said, but his words held a wary tone. Kit surmised he was unused to dealing with an American. "Two of our Cornish rivers are frozen solid, just like the Thames in London." He picked at a plate of sweetmeats without offering any to Kit, hiccupped and snapped a hand to his mouth. Finally, he took on an air of business. "I've been expecting you this past week or more. Your letter was none too clear about when you would arrive."

"Storms on the crossing from New York made the journey long and tedious." Kit watched Tapper guardedly. Why did the English seem so inscrutable to him? He was, after all, a descendant of the same stock.

Tapper nodded curtly. A veiled look crept through his dark eyes. "Now, about the extent of this inheritance." He shuffled through a mass of papers on his desk, picked out one or two documents seemingly at random and, after a quick perusal, discarded them. "Had the deeds all ready for you as soon as I knew you were coming. Dashed if I can find them now. Ah, yes. Here we are. Tregover Farm."

He ran his eyes down the first page of a parchment-coloured document then lifted his gaze beneath bushy lashes. "You realise your grandfather was not a wealthy man, by English standards. He kept his head above water as long as he was able. But that's about the most of it."

A doomed feeling invaded Kit's chest. "Did he saddle me with any lasting debts?"

Tapper lowered the page. "Well, no." He picked up another sweetmeat, again without offering any to Kit, dusted his hands together after swallowing the tantalizing treat and then returned to his official stand. "Nothing serious. But towards the end, he sold off most of his cattle to pay outstanding bills and had to let his hired labour go. You'll need to invest money to get the farm back to its full potential." He gave Kit a questioning look. "If you need an introduction to Waterson's Bank, I'll be happy to oblige." His manner was oddly stiff and unbending, as if he had something else to say but could not bring himself to say it.

Kit kept his feelings well hidden. He had not anticipated any hefty investment. Could Tapper be holding back other hidden impediments to later throw at him? Or was the notary fishing for information as to his financial status? Kit didn't bite. "I'd better have a look at the place first."

"Naturally." Tapper released the parchment which floated down to the desktop and settled. "You'll find Jacob Padder still tending the farm. He's worked there since your grandfather first took him on, oh, must be nigh on forty or fifty years ago. Rumours say he's been mixing with the dissenters so you'll need to watch him carefully." Tapper leaned over his desk, his expression conveying a warning. "And there's been talk of farm hands wanting to form a union in these parts. It's bad enough the trouble we get from the miners without the farm labourers stirring things up."

Mentally storing away the list of problems he expected to face, Kit rubbed at his aching shoulders. "You've been paying this man, Padder?"

"I've been paying him out of the residue of the estate until now. It was your grandfather's wish." He picked up the deed papers, flipped them around and pushed them across the desk for Kit's perusal. Easing back into his seat, Tapper popped another titbit into his mouth and sighed with satisfaction while Kit began to read.

After a few lines, he raised a glance to Tapper. "It says here," he pointed to the paper, "the farm is one hundred and ninety-five acres. How does that compare with others in Cornwall?"

"Above average. It's mostly good quality, arable pasture and down-land with about ten acres given over to woodland. At one time, your grandfather had a sizeable dairy herd as well as a herd of pigs, and he was wise with his crop rotation. I suppose it's not much by Alabama standards, but it's enough to give you a good living, if you can get it all productive again." Tapper shrugged. "But the place has been run down since your grandfather died. If there's anything I can do to help set things to rights, any introductions …"

Kit straightened in the chair, detecting a further hint of deviousness in Tapper's tone.

"Or should you decide to sell the property, I'm certain I could soon find you a buyer."

He'd sensed something else was coming at him, but he'd certainly had not expected this option. How cold and confident Tapper's words were, as if well rehearsed and well hidden behind that mellow voice.

Kit adopted a doubtful expression. "Sell it? No." He shook his head firmly to assert his mind could not be changed at present. He would store away the offer, but had no immediate intention to take advantage of it. It would be tantamount to giving in before he started. Besides, he did not entirely trust Tapper. He wasn't sure why; he just didn't.

"And your plans?" The notary seemed overly curious.

Kit shrugged. It was no secret. "For the moment, I aim to get to the farm and find out exactly what I've let myself in for." He rose to his feet and stepped ponderously towards the frosted window. The snow fell heavily once again. He stood with his back to the notary, searching for the right words before he swung round. "There is one thing you can tell me, Mister Tapper. What do you know about a man called Ralph Killiow?"

The question ruffled Tapper; it was obvious from the time he took to compose a reply. "Mister Ralph Killiow is the only son of old Squire Killiow. The Killiows own Studmore Manor, near Penmarith."

Kit detected something unsaid behind the notary's words. "And ...?"

Tapper shifted in his seat. "Old Squire Killiow is a local magistrate. He owns a wide area of land from Polkerris almost up to Golant, except for Tregover and Crabtree Copse farms, that is. Most farmers thereabouts are the Squire's tenants." Tapper paused and pursed his lips. "His son, Ralph Killiow, runs the estate, and it's no secret, he'd dearly like to get his hands on those two farms to give him a tighter grip on the whole area."

Kit fixed the notary with a dark look. "Is that why you offered to mediate, if I decide to sell my farm?"

Tapper leapt to his feet, flustered. "Oh, no. Don't get me wrong, Mister Vanson. I've only your best interests in mind. I have a feeling the Killiows will soon get control of Crabtree Copse Farm anyway. It's only sixty acres and owned by a woman. You know how women are: totally incapable when it comes to men's work."

Fixing the notary with a lengthy stare, Kit struggled with his instinct. What was it about the man that made him feel so uneasy? "If that farm were sold to the Killiows, wouldn't it leave me as the only owner not beholden to them?"

The official wound his fingers tightly together. "Near enough."

"You don't approve of small farms like Crabtree Copse?"

"They cause a problem for the real landowners." The notary forced a ragged smile. "It's the way things are here in Cornwall. Small farmers are a hindrance to progress. The big landowners, like the Killiows and the mine owners, are born to rule, and that's the best way of it. The workers are there to do what they're told. If they don't," he said, wiping at his sweating brow, "there are ways of dealing with them. Coming from a plantation colony, you'll know all about that."

Kit's stomach hit his heels. "Have you slavery over here?" Even if he tried, he couldn't have avoided the acid tone in his words. He shook his head in disapproval.

Tapper smirked, eased himself back into his chair and tented his fingertips together. "Not in the way you understand it, but we have a way of dealing with the lower classes when they cause trouble. We get rid of them. A few years ago in Dorset, six men were transported to the colonies for taking illegal oaths while forming a trade union. They had to be put in their place."

Kit shook his head again, this time in disgust. "Reckon the squire's son would make a good plantation owner."

"The Killiows are natural born rulers. Common folks over in Penmarith wish the squire's daughter would inherit the estate, but it's Mister Ralph Killiow they'll be looking to as their new master one day. My advice to everyone is to try to get on with the man now and avoid trouble later."

"I came here to be a farmer, Mister Tapper. Nothin' more than that. Who owns Crabtree Copse Farm?"

Tapper paused, a sweetmeat halfway to his mouth. "Didn't I tell you? It's owned by a woman called Wenna Lanyon."

Kit forced back the smile that threatened to break out and nodded grimly at the news. He had half guessed already, and it gave him a brief moment of pleasure to call her image to mind.

Less than an hour after his arrival, Kit was shown out of the office by the same clerk and stood, buttoning his coat in the outer doorway. Now why hadn't Mistress Lanyon told him she owned a small farm? Why didn't she own up to being his future neighbour? Interesting and mighty puzzling. He pulled his collar tighter against the billowy snow that settled irritatingly on his eyelashes. Another vision of Wenna

Lanyon crept into his mind unbidden, and it pleased him more than he could imagine.

The coach from St Austell to Penmarith had long since departed. The Fowey mail coach – the next best thing – was late leaving and might not have left at all but for his persuasive insistence. The journey was tortuously slow. Snow still fell heavily, and the road leading out of St Austell lay hidden beneath several inches of muddy-coloured slush. Either side of the trail, distant hills stood out bleak and uninviting.

Shortly after four o'clock, the coach rumbled across an old stone bridge and came to a slippery halt near the dockside at Trevisco; the closest it would pass by Penmarith. Kit dismounted and recovered his carpetbag from the snow, where it had landed, thrown down from the roof by the coachman. He resigned himself to walking the rest of the way to his farm.

He took stock of his surroundings. Nearby, three men unloaded a clay barge moored at the dockside. Kit counted more than a dozen workers in their heavy working clothes congregating farther along the quay. Standing tightly packed, they stamped the snow and blew into cupped bare hands to keep warm. As Kit prepared to move off, a strident voice bellowed out across the icy scene, wafting away on the chill air. More men tagged on to the back of the larger gathering.

Odd disjointed words drifted back to Kit: "Decent wages … union … fair treatment … exploitation …"

Intent on the orator's message, the dockworkers nodded to one another in agreement. Unable to see the focus of the gathering, Kit mingled at the rear of the group and the speaker's words took on coherence.

"Four years ago, the Tolpuddle men were transported to the other side of the world. But we fought for them and they were pardoned. Are you not yet ready to stand up against your masters on your own account?"

Kit craned his neck to better view the orator. He stood tall and erect, an imposing, grey-haired man in a black cloak. A preacher of some sort.

The cleric raised his hand up towards heavy, fast-running clouds. "Are you going to allow the owners to get away with such treatment again? Right here in Cornwall?"

"Them were Dorset men." A ferret-faced man near to Kit spoke out, and the group turned to acknowledge him. "What do ee expect us down here to do about it, pastor? 'Tedn't none of our business."

"It *is* your business. And you must unite, my friend!" The pastor lowered his arms in a wide sweep and sought out the ferret-faced man. He spared him a brief glance then panned the crowd. "All of you must fight against oppression or you will be the next convicts on the transportation ships. Unite and tell the government they cannot transport all of you. Unite because it is the only way to fight back. Clay miners, tin miners, dock workers, farm labourers, you must all unite!"

"They do say ..." Heads turned towards another speaker at the rear of the group, on the far side from where Kit stood. Being the centre of interest, the man went on: "... that the Tolpuddle men were led by a preacher. I heard as how ee was party to drawin' up the oath, and ee was the real power behind the union. What do ee know about that, Pastor Pengorse?"

"Idle rumour." The pastor snorted, his eyes darting from man to man before settling his stare on the heckler. "If such rumour held any truth, then the authorities have been somewhat lapse in not finding this preacher. But you should be wary of rumours, my friend."

The speaker continued unhindered. "They do say it were a Cornish travellin' preacher that were behind it all. You be a Cornishman, pastor, for all your fancy words.

The crowd hushed, as a deep grin spread across the pastor's face. "Yes, my friend. I'm Cornish through and true. And I'm here as one who's passionately dedicated to the betterment of the common man, but –" He stopped speaking abruptly, his gaze searching far beyond the listeners.

"Scatter!" The command came from the rear of the gathering. Instantly, the group dispersed. The dockworkers lolloped through the snow towards the clay storage buildings, while many others merged into the activity about the barges.

A few moments later, Kit was the only one standing in a patch of well-trampled slush watching a dinghy pull away from the dock and steer into the gathering darkness. The Cornish pastor sat hunched in the stern, wrapped in his dark cloak. He stared back at the meeting place and, for a second or two, his eyes settled on Kit.

At the dull clumping of horses' hooves, Kit swung round to spot Ralph Killiow approach with half a dozen mounted men behind him. This was one man he had no wish to meet. Pulling his hat low over his eyes, he hurried away until he came to the lee of a snow and clay-covered building where he chanced a glance back.

The horses and riders continued towards Polkerris and, within minutes, the Trevisco dock labourers sluggishly resumed their work as if nothing untoward had happened.

Kit wrapped his cloak tighter about himself and strode away towards the town. Amidst the narrow, snow-bound streets, he found an inn with a roaring fire in its taproom. Glad to be out of the weather, he bought a jug of porter and warmed himself in front of the flames.

The innkeeper approached him and eyed him suspiciously. "Ee'll be a-wantin' a bed this night, sur?"

"No. I'll just spend a while thawing out my freezing bones and then I'll be on my way. Can you tell me how to get to Tregover Farm?"

"Tregover Farm? Up near Penmarith?" The innkeeper scratched his bulbous nose. "Oh, ee don't wanna go up there, sur. Not this night. 'Tes all snowed up, for certain. Besides, old Vanson be a-died this year or more."

Kit rubbed his hands together briskly. "He was my grandpappy." He noted how the innkeeper's jaw sagged at the mention of the family connection.

"Oh? Begging yer pardon, sur. I should've known who ee was from the way ee talks. American, ain't ee?"

"That's right."

"I heard as how old Padder was a-waitin' for ee."

With warmth returning to his fingers, Kit asked: "Can you lend me a lantern? I'd like to get to the farm tonight."

"Ah, reckon I can, sur. Reckon I can. But 'tes a long way ... an' in this weather!"

"I'd be mighty obliged to you."

He took another ten minutes to warm himself completely before pulling his cloak tight around his shoulders and setting out to walk to Tregover Farm. He followed the innkeeper's directions out of Trevisco and along a narrow lane bordered on both sides by six-foot banks topped with white-painted living hedges. He held the lantern high to better illuminate the deep, virgin snow ahead of him.

His legs soon grew weary, and his thoughts began to drift without cohesion until he came to a junction, neither branch seeming to take precedence. He took a blind guess and set off along the right hand fork. The cold burrowed deeper into his muscles and his legs stiffened. With another hour of steady trudging behind him, he came to a collection of farm buildings, silent and forbidding in their ghostly mantle.

Had he come the right distance for this to be Tregover Farm? He strained to hear a loose, rhythmic sound almost drowned beneath the wail of the wind: The burbling noise of a fast flowing river. Many times Pa had told him grandpappy's farmhouse sat alongside an old bridge over a river. *Tre-gover*; in the old Cornish language, meant the farm by the stream. In days long past, Pa had affirmed, the best Cornish farmhouses were always built close to a reliable water supply and Tregover Farm ranked highly in the local community. Kit shaded his eyes from the fast-blown, stinging snow and stared at the house. Smoke billowed from the chimney, quickly whipped away on the wind, and a light burned at one of the windows.

Kit shivered then thought of the fire burning inside the house. Certain this farm had to be his inheritance, he mustered the strength to reach the front door. In a brief moment of reflection, he noted the rotten wood, warped with age. He paused only to gather his breath before pushing it open with frozen hands.

An atmosphere of warmth and comfort immediately enclosed him as he stepped inside. He snuffed the innkeeper's lantern and closed the heavy front door with a firm thrust.

"Padder!" He stamped the snow from his boots. "Jacob Padder! Are you at home?"

No one replied. The only sound came from the wind blowing beneath the eaves. He removed his cloak and hung it on the nearest hook. "Are you in here, Jacob Padder?"

A door creaked directly in front of him and then swung open. Expecting to find a sixty-year old farm labourer, Kit gaped in astonishment. Instead, framed in the doorway, Wenna Lanyon stared back at him.

Four

With unbearable tiredness digging into her bones, Wenna dropped to her knees before the dying flames in her back parlour. Her cotton dress was no protection against cold draughts.

She worried a great deal; she had little fuel to spare, and in a few more days, she would have none.

Shivering, she knelt back and fingered the bandage covering the slice to her forehead, half hidden beneath the fall of her long black hair. It itched something terrible.

"Mistress?" At Jimmy Rudge's call, Wenna pivoted on one knee. He approached her with a lowered gaze, his face reddened.

She was in no mood for vacillation. "Out with it, lad!"

Getting no response from him, she pushed a log onto the fire and rose to her feet. "I've heard rumours," she snapped. "People in the village are talking about you and Jenny Tinder from up at Studmore Manor."

"'Ess, mistress."

At the boy's mumbling, she lost a bit of her temper. "Is that all you have to say?"

"Mistress …" He shuffled from foot to foot.

"If you won't speak up now, go away and think about it. And don't come back until you're ready to talk."

"'Ess, mistress." Jimmy spun on his heels and hurried away.

Wenna shivered, sat down and pulled her shawl closer round her shoulders. Hadn't she enough problems with the hay barn roof badly needing repair, the meagre supply of winter fodder dwindling fast and no money to buy more? Then she recalled how Waterson's Bank in St Austell had refused to lend her money, relying too strongly on the support of the Killiow family. The Plymouth banks had turned her down on purely commercial grounds.

A tear trickled down her cheek. Maybe the banks were right; maybe she was beyond help. Scratching at the itchy bandage then at the tears, she prayed she would at least survive the winter.

She left the parlour to fetch a bowl of skilly still warming on the kitchen range and, on returning, inched her chair closer to the fire. The skilly was hot and nourishing, albeit only a mixture of scalded milk and bread, but she ate with exaggerated care. As each mouthful stung the inside of that cheek, she caught a lingering memory of Ralph Killiow's vicious attack.

The front door opened and a blast of cold air ran through the house. Wenna frowned, expecting no visitors. She jumped to her feet and shuddered in fright when a man's voice called out, the words barely audible behind the parlour door.

She reached for the only weapon available to her; the thin iron poker she stoked the fire with. Wielding it above her head, she tiptoed to the door. A jelly-like wobble gripped her legs at the thought of Ralph Killiow and his henchmen returning to pressure her into selling. She gripped the poker tighter.

The intruder called out again, sharper and clearer. Something about the voice triggered off a hint of recognition. She partly pulled open the parlour door and gaped at the giant figure standing in the narrow stone-flagged passage.

"You!" An unseen hand held her rooted to the floor while she struggled to recover her composure. "Mister Vanson, isn't it?"

The American stared back, perplexed, his hair and trouser legs caked with snow. "Ma'am? Ain't this here Tregover Farm?"

"No." Her tension drained away, and a giggle came to her lips. "You've come to the wrong place, Mister Vanson. This is Crabtree Copse Farm."

"I must have taken a wrong turn back at the fork in the road."

"Not so surprising in this storm." A tingle of uncontrollable excitement ran through her and she felt the blood rushing up her neck. "Is your horse outside?" she asked, prepared to take the animal into her near empty stable.

"No, ma'am." His teeth chattered. "Ain't got no horse. I walked from the village."

"In this weather?" She raked her gaze up and down his muscular frame. Although hunched over from the cold, he was still every inch the young man who had come to her aid in Plymouth. "You'd better come in the parlour and warm yourself before the fire."

He obeyed, ducking his head beneath the low lintels.

"Where's your cloak?"

"I thought this was Tregover Farmhouse, so I hung up my cloak by the others."

Wenna nodded. "Sit yourself down here." She indicated the chair she had occupied only moments before. "Perhaps I can get you something hot."

Wracked by spasms of shivering, he by-passed the chair and knelt before the flames, holding out blue hands. "Please, Miss Lanyon, don't trouble yourself on my account. I'm sorry to have barged in and inconvenienced you like this."

"'Tes no trouble. You must stay a while and warm yourself." She quickly wiped a wry smile from her lips. She couldn't recall when she had last entertained a man such as the mysterious Christopher Vanson. Probably never had. She would fetch him warm food in a moment, after first savouring his presence.

He turned and grinned at her, warmer colour slowly returning to his skin. "Your head is still bandaged, were you badly hurt?"

"I'll soon get over it." She sat down near the fire, close enough to him without actually touching.

"I surely hope so." He went silent for a moment then rose from his knees and sat where she'd indicated, directly facing her. "I wonder," he paused uncomfortably, "are you ready now to tell me why that rogue Killiow struck you?"

She averted her gaze. It was so tempting to confide in him. "'Tes his way. Mostly, it was because he was drunk. But also, he made me a proposition and was terribly annoyed when I refused him."

"He wants to buy your land. Isn't that what it was all about?"

She gaped at him. "How did you know?"

"The notary, Mister Tapper, mentioned it." At her quizzical look he added: "He was the business I had to attend to." The young American leaned towards her, his brow furrowed, his expression intent. "Is Killiow putting pressure on you to sell? Physical pressure?"

"'Tes his intention to force me to sell, one way or another." Wenna sighed. If Christopher Vanson was to survive here as a farmer, he might as well know what Killiow was really like. She drew in a deep breath then forged ahead.

"I'm in difficulties, Mister Vanson. Financial difficulties. I need money for repairs and I went up to Plymouth to find a bank willing to help me. But none would. However someone passed on word to Ralph Killiow. I booked a room at the Admiral Nelson because I couldn't afford a decent hostelry. Killiow waylaid me there and said he would buy me out and find me alternative work in the manor house."

"What sort of work?"

"Menial work as a ... servant." She chewed nervously at her lower lip. How could she hide the lewd suggestion others had so clearly heard? "He wants me to," she paused for breath, "to be nice to him."

Christopher shook his head in confusion. "You've lost me somewhere."

"He's the squire's son, Mister Vanson." At his blank look, Wenna turned away, pretending to run her fingers across her bandaged brow as if it itched. Her visitor was unfamiliar with the behaviour of less honourable members of the English aristocracy. She glanced back at him and lowered her voice to a hush. "He considers taking young girls to his bed at his whim to be his prerogative."

Christopher faced her square on. "And the local people allow this?"

"What can they do about it?" She shrugged. "Most girls accept it because they know the consequences of refusing. If they don't make too much fuss, they get paid off. I imagine you must have similar problems in Alabama." Watching his reaction from beneath half-closed eyelids, she noted how the colour drained from his face.

"We do. But mostly it's the plantation owners taking advantage of their female slaves."

"Same problem, different races." The American couldn't miss the bitterness in her tone. A pained expression flitted across his face, as if he understood the problem better than she had expected.

"What will you do?"

She jutted her chin, her blood rising. "Stick it out. I've worked on this farm ever since I was a child. I intend to go on working here. Meanwhile, I certainly don't intend giving myself to Ralph Killiow. The man disgusts me!"

"Mighty angry at him, hey?"

"That damned impossible man!" Her hatred for Killiow was boiling over, and she didn't want her new neighbour to think her a harridan. "I'm sorry if I've allowed my anger to show. Mister Vanson, it really is too bad outside for you to continue your journey. Perhaps you'd better stay here tonight." Silently, she pleaded with her eyes.

"That's kind of you, ma'am, but …"

He moved to stand and she quickly rested a hand on his arm. He felt strong and muscular beneath her touch. To her delight, he settled back down again.

"What would other folks round here say about me staying here? I sure wouldn't them to talk unkindly of you."

"They'll do that anyway, with us being neighbours. And I'd take it as a favour if you'd stop calling me ma'am. I told you my name is Wenna."

He smiled. "Cornish?"

"'Tes, for sure. And you're Christopher, grandson of John Vanson."

"My kinfolk call me Kit."

"A common enough abbreviation, but I prefer Christopher. 'Tes a noble name, the name of a saint and an explorer of the New World. May I call you Christopher?"

"As you wish."

He sank further back into his seat, as if he had already accepted her offer. She noted the outline of his broad shoulders beneath his jerkin, the square cut of his chin, the appealing match of his blue eyes and the way his straw-coloured hair set off his wind-blown complexion. Then she shook herself back to reality.

"I'll get Jimmy to make up a bed for you in his room." She rose and took a step towards the door, but then thought better and turned around with an explanation. "He's my labourer and he can show you the way to your own farm in the morning."

"Your labourer sleeps here in the house?"

"Yes." Had she just admitted to her fears? Perhaps. She shrugged her shoulders, adding: "I don't feel safe when I'm alone in the house. Not with Ralph Killiow living just the other side of the village."

"It's uncommon decent of you, Wenna." Christopher settled closer to the fire, his eyes already glazing over from fatigue. "My grandpappy's man, Padder, he'll be wondering what's become of me."

"Maybe. But one more night on his own isn't going to do Jacob Padder any harm. Besides, he's little more than the buildings to look after since your grandfather sold off most of his stock."

Christopher raised his head and forced his drooping eyelids wider. "Tapper told me about him selling most of the animals to pay bills. Do you know what's left?"

"Time was he had eight horses and nigh on ninety head of cattle as well as his herd of swine. Now, there's a horse in your grandfather's stable and one milk cow."

He raised a weak grin. "Not much, is it?"

"Not enough to keep the farm going." She considered him wryly. "You'll need to buy new stock and hire more men."

The front door opened again and the wind whistled through the house. Jimmy Rudge came into the room, his arms laden with wood. He froze when he spied the American.

"Beg your pardon, mistress. Didn't know ee had company."

Noting the enquiring expression in the boy's eyes, she went ahead with the introductions. "This is Mister Vanson, new owner of Tregover Farm. He lost his way and thought this was Tregover."

"'Tes a wild night to get lost." The boy spared Christopher a tight smile and dropped the split wood alongside the fire.

Wenna ran a quick mental contrast between the lean boy and the hard-muscled man. "I've told Mister Vanson he can bed down in your room with you tonight."

"'Ess, mistress." The boy's worried expression switched to deep-felt relief. "Maybe 'tes as well for him to be here. Word's got round the village about what ee did in Plymouth. Reckon Mister Killiow already knows who hit him." After he'd stacked the wood, he faced Christopher square on. "Squire's men will be on the lookout for ee, Mister Vanson."

Christopher's dubious gaze went from Jimmy to her then back to Jimmy. "Are you telling me I'm not safe on my own farm? On a night like this?"

"Mister Killiow sends his men out in all weathers." Jimmy nodded towards the door. "I'll go make up a bed for ee, sur."

Wenna stood up, warmed by the prospect of saving the newcomer some trouble for this night. Deeper feelings also nudged forward; starkly uncomfortable feelings coupled with exciting emotions that had been hidden away far too long.

When Jimmy was gone, Christopher focussed his attention on her face. His fleeting expressions told her he was trying hard to figure out what was happening in this community. She shifted in discomfort.

"How long have you lived alone? Apart from the boy, that is."

"Since my father died last year." She clasped the shawl about her shoulders.

"Has Killiow struck you before?"

"He came to the farm a while back with two of his men. They beat Jimmy and held him down before they set on me."

"Has he …"

At his pause, she shot him a confused look.

"You know …"

"Raped me?" she asked. His deep sigh told her she'd guessed right. She shook her head. "He was sober then and wanted me to go to him willingly. I'll never do that."

She shuddered at the memory, hesitantly seeking approval in his eyes, but all she saw was how much anger they emitted.

At that moment, Jimmy returned to the parlour and she was glad of the interruption. Excusing herself, she left with a curt comment about heating up some food. In the kitchen, she filled three bowls with hot skilly, cut up some additional chunks of crusty bread and took them into the parlour on her best platter.

"At least we're not starving." She set one bowl into Christopher's hands. "Not yet, anyway."

Christopher let out a hollow laugh. "Not with a spirit like yours, Wenna."

She gave the second bowl to Jimmy and settled down with the third. Aware of Christopher's gaze still fixed on her, she smiled back at him, but her heart was drained of all pleasure. The memory of Killiow's most recent attack had driven out all sense of warmth. When the food was eaten, she fought back a yawn, gathered up the empty bowls then noticed Christopher's drawn look. "You'll be tired now. I'll show you to the attic room."

"It's been a wearying day." He smiled, rising.

He followed her up the stairs, his heavy tread bringing squeals of complaint from the bare boards. On the upper landing, she opened the door to his room, wished him a good night and tip-toed back down to the parlour where Jimmy knelt before the fire, busily damping down with rough slack.

"Leave that. You can go to your bed now." Fatigue wracked every part of her body. Her attempts at saving the farm and the stress of being attacked had drawn so much of her strength.

"'Ess, mistress." Although he acknowledged her order, the boy stalled, kneeling in front of the fire. "Can I talk to ee now?" His voice shook.

Wenna tensed up, wary of what was to come. "What about?"

"Got me a problem, mistress." He kept his head down, eyes focussed into the dying flames.

She sighed inwardly. At least he'd admitted to a problem.

"'Tes not that I don't appreciate workin' here."

Wenna slumped into a chair. "But you're planning to leave me, aren't you?"

He swung round, still on his knees. "Mister Killiow sent a man to talk to me father. Ee wants me to go back and work at the manor. An' ee says ee'll pay me seven shillin's a week if'n I go back to me old job."

"Seven shillings!" Remembering she had lost her previous labourer to Killiow at this high wage, Wenna clasped her hands tightly in front of her and tried to keep calm. "Mister Killiow pays seven shillings only to his best men, the rest get barely enough to live on. Jimmy, he's using you to get at me. Once you've left me, he'll sack you again. Have you forgotten how he dismissed you only last autumn? He'll do the same again."

"Dunno about that, mistress, But I need to get more money." He threw some loose, damp dross onto the back of the fire. "I'm gettin' wed."

"I heard it in the village. Why didn't you tell me about it before now?"

The boy hung his head. "Thought ee would be angry with me. Knew ee would be upset about it."

"Jenny Tinder is having your baby. That's what they're saying in the village."

"'Tes true, mistress." He rubbed black dust from his hands and rose to his feet. "That's why I need more money an' Mister Killiow says ee'll pay me seven –"

"Where will you live?"

"Mister Killiow says ee'll rent me a room in one of his cottages."

Silence fell on them until Jimmy turned to leave the room. As he neared the door, Wenna called after him. "You and Jenny can have a room here if you'll stay. A room of your own here in the house."

His face lit up. "A room here? Are ee sure, mistress?"

"I want you to stay, Jimmy."

"But I can't afford to pay for Jenny's keep. Ee knows that. Are ee quite sure? About the room, I mean?"

She raised a wry smile, fighting against her inner frustration. "I'm sure, but most likely mad to be saying it." She turned serious. "As for money, I can't pay you any more than five shillings, but at least you'll all get a roof over your heads. You, Jenny and the baby."

Jimmy rushed back towards her, his face beaming. "You'm a real good lady, mistress. I always thought that. A real good lady to work for."

"Don't rush so fast with your compliments. Jenny can help out in the kitchen and the garden to pay for the food you all eat."

He nodded several times. "Thank ee, mistress."

"Go to bed, Jimmy. We'll talk about it more in the morning."

After he had gone, she sat on for some time, disturbing memories saturating her mind. Eventually, feeling drained, she climbed the stairs to her own room and tucked herself beneath the blankets in her shift. An hour or more passed before she drifted off into a light doze.

She awoke and sat up with a start, sensing someone shuffle in the darkness near her bed. She tensed further. Had Killiow's men broken in? Remembering her state of undress, she pulled her bedclothes up around her neck. "Who's there?"

"Hush ee, mistress." She let out a huge sigh of relief at Jimmy's words. "There's noises outside the house. I came to warn ee."

Wenna concentrated to hear what had roused Jimmy. The wind howled through the numerous gaps around the old farmhouse: rattling doors, shaking loose boards and squealing through narrow cracks in the walls. She strained to hear sounds that didn't belong; manly voices drifting around the house, and heavy boots crunching through the thick, crisp snow. The occasional, unmistakable sound of frozen leather clothes creaking with movement.

"Mister Vanson told me to come an' wake ee," Jimmy whispered. "Ee said as how you ought to come with us 'til we see what's goin' on."

"Tell Mister Vanson I'm coming." Wenna swung her feet out of bed and shivered in the bitterly cold air. "Give me a moment to dress."

She had no intention of being caught by intruders while still in her shift. She waited until Jimmy scurried away and searched about for her outer clothes. When fully dressed, she crept along the upper passage to Jimmy's room. Christopher met her in the doorway, his outline just visible now that her eyes were accustomed to the darkness.

"We have some unwelcome visitors," he whispered.

"I heard them. It must be me they've come for. They can't know you're here."

"Maybe that's just as well." He brushed his hand lightly against her cheek. "It gives us an advantage. Stay here with Jimmy while I investigate downstairs."

"You take care," she ordered.

"Of course."

He slipped away down the staircase into the deeper darkness, creeping step by step down the creaking stairs. She could do little against Killiow's henchmen – the confrontation in Plymouth had emphasised her vulnerability – but she wished she could have followed and assisted Christopher instead of hiding.

Jimmy leaned closer to her ear. "Maybe I should go with him, mistress."

She grasped at his arm. "Stay here." Against determined thugs, the boy stood as little chance as she.

"But mistress ..."

The front door squealed on its iron hinges and Wenna tightened her hold on Jimmy's arm. She forcefully shook her head. Was that Christopher opening it or the intruders making their way into the house? Shivering, she stepped back into the deepest recess of the bedroom, pulling Jimmy with her.

Another burst of howling wind confirmed the front door had opened again. Loud, angry cries filled the air, followed by the crashes of falling furniture. She felt another cold blast.

"We got to help him!" Jimmy wrestled free and ran towards the stairs. Wenna ran after him, hoping to catch hold of him before he bounded down the stairs. But her effort was for naught.

From the landing, she peered down the stairs. Lanterns waved, throwing grotesque shadows across the walls and voices bellowed then, amongst them, Christopher Vanson cried out in pain.

Five

"Mister Vanson, can you hear me?"

The voice seemed to come from far off as if from another dream. Kit awoke slowly, his conscious thoughts oozing into a world turned upside down.

Strange lights flashed and swam in front of him, twisting and weaving like fireflies on a dark Alabama night. A loud whistling noise invaded his head, growing louder and louder, seemingly determined to drown out his every coherent thought.

"Christopher, are you all right?"

He clasped at his aching brow, clenching his teeth as he fought against a blinding headache. His vision came slowly into sharper focus, but nothing made sense. He was in a soft bed, in a strange room, and an out-of-focus figure hovered nearby. Where was he? He closed his eyes in an effort to filter out the pain stabbing through his head directly behind his eyes. The ruse failed.

"Mister Vanson?" The indistinct figure leaned over him and wiped his face with a damp cloth. "Christopher, can you hear me?"

The voice ... the silhouette ... the gentle touch ... could only be that of a young woman. But who was she?

"At least ee be awake, mistress." Another voice, manly, floated in the middle distance.

"Christopher, if you can hear me, remain still." The woman's voice sounded nearer, liltingly soft and comforting. "Just lie still and relax."

Relax? Was she mad? With pain running like red-hot pokers through every muscle in his body! Firm, small hands clasped his. Warm, callused hands of a woman used to manual work. For no obvious reason, he conjured up an image of a girl he had met in Rio: dusky skin, black hair, firm breasts, warm temperament ... a soft bed. Was he back in Rio?

He forced open his eyes once more and blinked. "Where am I?"

The effort to speak triggered yet another stabbing pain, but this time through his jaw. He closed his mouth and a sharp jolt vibrated through his teeth.

"Thank God you can speak," the woman said, "you're at Crabtree Copse Farm. Do you remember what happened?"

What a stupid question. Of course he didn't remember. He forced his shaken mind to concentrate. Memories trickled back to him in flashes. A farmhouse … crisp snow outside … heavy figures lying in wait. A fierce struggle to barricade them out then a sense of defeat when a violent gang beat him back.

There must have been at least three or four heavily-built, well-armed thugs. He had knocked more than one to the ground before they overcame him, before they knocked him unconscious.

Hazy curtains drifted away as she leaned over him, her lips slightly parted, allowing a glimpse of her well-tended teeth. And that soft, fresh smell. He stared up at her milky white face, concern marring her expression. Then clarity of vision returned. Why had she a bandage about her head? She most certainly was not the girl from Rio, but looked equally beautiful.

"My God, but I was so worried about you." She smiled. "You've been delirious, slipping in and out of consciousness."

Suddenly, he recalled her name. "Wenna?"

"Lie still." Her face was deadly serious as she ran her fingertips through his head of hair.

"Wenna." He winced at the pain in his jaw. "Did they hurt you?"

"No. You must have put the fear of God into them, Christopher. They fled after you tangled with them."

He closed his eyes briefly, sighing aloud. "Gee, they sure had me licked."

"You did well enough."

Her demeanour relaxed visibly; the shocked expression faded to be replaced by … a smile? He blinked. Yes, there it was again; a smile that washed gently across her lips. Such a genuine smile as he had not seen in many a year. If only his body would stop aching so he could enjoy it.

Her bandage still worried him. When had she incurred her injury? "You're sure I beat them off?"

She eyed him with an I-don't-tell-lies expression. "Of course I'm sure. Most of the blood staining my floors is theirs. You almost certainly saved me from another beating."

Then the earlier conflict in Plymouth came back to him. "There were too many of them." He raised himself on one elbow, and Wenna instantly coaxed him back down to the bed.

"Lie still, Christopher. You mustn't try to move."

He liked the way she called him Christopher, just as his ma used to when he was a kid in trouble. He shuffled in the bed to find a comfortable position and groaned loudly as another sharp pain attacked his ribs.

"She'll look after ee, sur."

He quickly recognised Jimmy Rudge peering from behind her and holding an earthenware bowl of water.

"What's the damage, other than my ribs?" He stretched one hand down beneath the bedclothes, searching for injuries and finding bare skin beneath a coarse nightshirt.

"Cuts and bruises, mostly, so far as we can tell," she said quietly. "You've been badly beaten and you'll be sore for some time."

Kit grimaced. "Sore as a coyote on a cactus. But worse things happen at sea. Take it from a seaman."

She snapped her fists to her hips. "I was so worried about you!" The admission had barely left her lips before she lowered her eyes as if ashamed.

"It's nice to have someone worry over me." He tried to smile to put her at ease, but winced instead. "It's been a long time since any woman took this much trouble."

Wenna averted her head to one side. "We all need someone to care about us."

He shifted in the bed, and a fiery stab shot up through his trunk. "Just one thing troubles me. This night shirt –"

"Belonged to my father." She grinned ruefully. "It just about fits you."

He ran a hand over the coarse calico. "Yeah, it fits near enough. But who took my clothes off and put the nightshirt on me?"

A scarlet flush ran up through Wenna's neck and cheeks. "Jimmy … Jimmy helped me."

Curbing his embarrassment, he closed the one eye on the side where the headache hurt most and squinted at her with the other. "Guess that makes it all right, then."

The flush persisted in her cheeks while she ordered him to rest and straightened the bed covers. Then, pushing Jimmy ahead of her, she left him. He quickly fell into another uneasy sleep. When he woke again, the late afternoon light was fading fast while a blizzard howled outside and snowed-up the panes of the bedroom window. Inside, candlelight flickered off the walls and a fire blazed in the hearth.

The aches returned to his body, but duller than before. Kit groaned as he straightened the nightshirt, which had raked up into painful lumps. The headache was also making its presence known, back in the area behind his eyes, but this time less blinding.

Wenna came to him a while later, a shy grin breaking out across her face. "Are you hungry?"

"Not so's you'd notice." He sighed ruefully. "Guess I'll feel like eating later on."

Despite the refusal, she hurried away and returned with a steaming bowl cupped in her hands.

"But I'm —"

"Hush, now. You must eat something." She sat at the bedside and calmly spooned hot broth into his mouth, giving a little smile of satisfaction when he swallowed.

The broth warmed his stomach and the glow spread through the rest of his body. "You sure are a good cook and you look good as well."

She smiled coyly, and he admired the straightness of her milk-white teeth. "That's not a proper thing for you to be saying, Christopher." She tapped the spoon over his knuckles as a warning to keep his tongue in check, despite his state.

"That hurt!" He shook his hand with exaggeration.

"You're strong enough to take it." She ladled more broth and spooned the measure into his mouth then carefully wiped away a dribble from his chin with her finger, lingering as if enjoying the touch.

He studied her through half-closed eyelids. "You and me could get along well, if you promise not to hit me again. Become good neighbours, maybe?"

She frowned as if gauging the offer. "I surely hope we become good neighbours, Christopher."

What a contrast between Jimmy's voice and Wenna's. Hers sang to him in a sweet melodious lilt, unlike the boy's coarse drawl.

"Well, I guess that would be one good reason for being here in England." He raised his hand to her cheek, feeling a tingle of excitement in the way she inclined her head gently to better enjoy the touch of skin on skin. Most respectable girls would draw away from him.

When he withdrew his hand, she turned serious. "Why are you here, Christopher? Why did you really come to England?"

He shrugged his shoulders and the pain of bruising shot across his back. "I inherited a farm."

She spooned more broth into him then paused. "But that isn't the only reason, is it?"

"It's enough." He stretched his lower jaw then went on: "My grandpappy left the farm to a Vanson, and I don't intend to let anyone else get their hands on it. I aim to make a go of it."

"But you could have helped your brother make a go of your father's plantation in Alabama, couldn't you?"

"I could." Her questioning was a mite too close to the mark. "But it wasn't the life for me."

"Because of the slavery? Was it really the way you told the Reverend Beattie?" Her persistence was too sharp now, and he wished she would stop.

"I felt for the suffering of the slaves," he said coldly. "We've won our independence over there, but I'm not so sure that we deserve it just yet. One day the blacks are going to say 'no more', and when that happens, blood will flow right across those cotton plantations. There's enough slaves over there to set the South ablaze."

"There'll be a war?"

"I reckon it'll happen. Maybe not for some years yet, but it'll happen. And when that day comes, I'll feel obliged to take the side of the black man."

"But that'll mean going against your own brothers?"

He grunted at a sudden spasm of pain. "Maybe that's why I had to leave. My brother, Pasco, ain't as bad as our younger brother, Clem. Maybe Pasco'll see the right path when the time comes. Clem sure won't."

"I see." She levered more broth into him then dropped the spoon into the empty bowl. "Pasco and Clement. Your father surely had an ear for Cornish names. Pasco now owns your father's slaves?"

"God help him."

"You're a man with a conscience." Her whisper sounded much like some kind of prayer.

"We all have our problems."

"Is that *all* you're running away from? Slavery?"

He gave her a shocked look. "You think it ain't enough?"

A defensive expression rose on her face. "I sense there may be more. After all, a man like you would normally be married."

"You sure are forward, Mistress Lanyon." He hoisted himself up in the bed, and a sharper pain stabbed through him. He groaned, easing back down. "You want to know why I ain't married?"

"I'm sorry. I had no right to pry."

He dismissed her apology with a curt wave of his hand. It was in his mind to concoct some story, some lie that would leave him in favour in Wenna's eyes, but they were to be close neighbours. He would have to tell her the truth one day and it might as well be now.

"There's a curse on us Vanson men." At the lack of surprise on her face, he carried on. "'Tis a curse I wouldn't want to pass on. You see, when my pa first went out to America, he took advantage of a Negro woman. Many white men did so to satisfy their needs, but this young woman belonged to a shaman." At her questioning look, he explained: "A sort of Negro witch doctor who put a curse on Pa and all his seed. We Vanson men will never again find virgin wives: that was his curse. Any woman figuring to marry a Vanson man is fated to first lose her purity."

She gasped. "That's a terrible thing to have hanging over you."

"There's more."

"More, you say!"

"Word of the curse got round amongst the local plantation owners.

They say the Vanson family is gonna die out for want of decent women willing to stand up to the family curse."

"And you believe that?"

He shrugged. "I dunno. But Pa sure did." Keen to turn the discussion away from his revelation, he nodded towards the bowl. "Any more?"

"You've eaten the last of it."

He wiped a hand slowly across his mouth. "You're wondering what sort of man you've got here in this house."

"Was I?"

"It's plain in your face, Wenna." He settled deeper against the soft pillow. "If we're to be neighbours, I guess I might as well set the record straight. It ain't a pretty story."

"I'm used to difficult tales. Go on."

He grunted and obliged her. "Pa and I didn't see eye to eye about slavery so I went away to sea for some years. I went back to the plantation hoping things would be different. But they weren't. Both my parents had died."

Nights dragged overly long on the plantation. Probably always had, but when he was younger, he had run with it. Took it for granted.

Home for two days and already the agony of seeing things just as they always had been was getting unbearable. Not just because of the arguments with his brothers over that and Clem's abuse of the coloured women, it was the odious smell of the place – the oppression. He must either learn to accept this way of life, or he must leave.

A long, pitiful cry pierced the hot Alabama night.

He snapped up to a seated position in his bed.

A new cry ripped the night air, rising and falling like the howl of a wounded wild animal. It came from somewhere inside the house. As abruptly as it began, it fell into silence.

Just as he began to relax and entertain the thought of settling back down, the cry returned ten times more plaintive; someone suffering and reaching out for help.

Kit flung the bed sheets aside, tugged hard to get his pants on and raced into the passage just as Pasco shuffled out from his room next door, holding aloft a lighted candle.

"What in tarnation was that noise?" Kit tightened his belt, now ready for whatever was happening in the house.

His brother raked fingers through his mop of hair. "Best you go back to your room, Kit. I'll deal with it this time."

Kit gave Pasco a don't-patronise-me look. "Like hell you will. It's Clem ain't it?"

Pasco nodded.

"We'll both deal with it." Kit grabbed Pasco's arm and coaxed him forward. While they marched towards Clem's room at the far end of the passage, he winced at the shrieking cries interspersed with the sound of a cane forcefully connecting with someone's flesh.

Pasco held him back at the bedroom door, clutching at his upper arm. "You sure you wanna see this?"

"Open it," Kit growled, his tension poised ready to snap.

Pushing him aside, Pasco swung open the door. "Suppose it's time you learned the truth."

The two men barged inside the room. The door crashed back against the inside wall and instantly the beating and cries ceased. Eerie silence hung over the macabre scene in front of them while flickering lamps cast ghostly shadows across the walls.

Clem loomed over the bed, brandishing a knife in one hand, a thin stick in the other. A naked black girl lay face-down on the bed, spread-eagled with her wrists and ankles roped to the bedstead. Her back glistened from massive blood loss as she let out a frightened whimper, her back arching and twisting with pain.

"What the hell is this fool doing?" Kit shot the question at Pasco, but didn't wait for an answer. Damn stupid question, it was. He crossed the room in two steps and plied the knife from Clem's grasp then tossed it to Pasco. "Cut her free, Goddammit!" Without waiting for a response, he whipped back to confront his youngest brother.

Clem glared at him – a look of intense hatred through eyes widely dilated with teeth bared. He'd seen this look in numerous sailors while in port. A cocktail of alcohol and opium had so pickled Clem's brain the boy had no idea what he was doing.

Kit held out his hand. "Take it easy, Clem. Give the stick to me, boy. There ain't gonna be no more beating this night. You hear me?"

In an instant, anger fled from Clem's face. He was a little boy once again, frightened, staring into space. He swung his gaze between his two brothers. "She wouldn't …" His words came out thick and distorted. "She wouldn't … come to bed with me. Said … said I was a bastard. Said we Vansons was all cursed to hell."

"Okay, Clem." Kit held him aside while Pasco led the whimpering girl from the room. Once the door was closed, Kit coaxed his brother down onto the bed. The expression on Clem's face mellowed. He stared into emptiness, sinking fast into a deeper stupor.

"Reckon you need to sleep, Clem," Kit said with conviction.

"That you, Pa?"

"Sure is, boy." Kit wrapped the bloody counterpane around his brother. "You just sleep, we'll talk in the morning."

"Don't take the light away, Pa!"

"Course not, boy. You just close your eyes, now." He knelt down beside the bed and clutched at a tightness across his chest. How could things have gotten this bad?

His brother sank deeper still into his drug-induced stupor. Half an hour passed, and Clem's eyes finally closed. Satisfied he could do no more for him, Kit walked slowly and deliberately down the long staircase. Pasco was waiting for him in the library, a whisky in a shaking hand, his face glowing ghostly pale in the dim candlelight.

"You seen to the girl?" Kit asked.

"Got O'Hara to take her back to her cabin. He's a good overseer, knows how to keep his mouth shut. I'd better see how she is in the mornin', though. Might have to fetch us a doctor."

"Reckon you might." Kit grabbed at the whisky bottle, his own hand also shaking. "What about Clem? Has he done this often?"

Pasco gave him a grave nod. "I did tell you he was a problem." Then he took a deep swig from his glass.

"He ain't fit to be here on this plantation. We gotta do something about him, before he kills someone and one of them slaves takes revenge."

Pasco focussed on his brother, his eyes terrified. "Trouble is, I can't handle Clem alone. You see now why you gotta stay here. You gotta help me."

"We'll talk about it tomorrow." Kit panned slowly about the familiar room where he had grown up; the place he had learned to read and write. Childhood and innocence were long gone now.

"You just gotta stay, Kit." Pasco wiped at his mouth with a backhand.

"Sure." Kit examined the whisky bottle through unfocussed eyes and then slammed it back on the table. "You get back to bed, Pasco. I'll look in on Clem again."

Kit slept no more that night. Shortly after daybreak he looked in again on Clem who was asleep and snoring loudly. Then he walked down to the slave's compound. The Negroes were awake, sullenly eyeing him while they fetched water and prepared their food. No one spoke to him. Silent, brooding resentment followed him along the dusty path between the huts.

He found the girl's hut at the edge of the compound, just where Pasco had described. A ragged drape hung across a single window, the door opening was shielded by another torn and dirty cloth. A long pitiful moan broken by gasping sobs confirmed he was at the right location.

Kit pulled back the cloth and peered into the gloom. At first he registered only the abject poverty of the inside, the few broken scraps of furniture lit by shafts of daylight running down through holes in the ceiling. He followed his hearing. The moaning came from a bundle of clothes lying on a cot in a dark corner. He edged farther into the room. A naked black figure lay face-down amongst the rags. She turned her head towards him, her anguish highlighted by a shaft of daylight.

Adequate words eluded him. "I'm sorry. I only want to help you." Inside, his belly churned, roughed up by uncontrollable anger towards his own brother.

"You can't do no more here." A strong male voice came from the doorway behind him. Kit turned. A tall slave carried a bucket of water and placed it by the bed. "I'll take care of her now."

It was a brush-off, but Kit couldn't leave, not yet. He wanted to know more about her, help in some way. "You related to her?"

"No, but you best leave it to me."

He was a muscular young man, but it was his authoritative manner and confidence that impressed Kit. He wasn't the least bit afraid of the white man in the hut with him.

"If she needs a doctor, you'll tell me."

"We know how to treat this sort of thing. We had to do it before." The Negro's voice held no trace of deference, no 'Massah' in any of his sentences.

Kit nodded in acceptance. "It won't happen again. I promise you."

The Negro shook his head in disbelief. "It will. It already happened too many times." He then knelt down beside the bed and soaked a rag.

"But not on this plantation. Not again!" Kit swung on his heels and left the hut in a blaze of anger, his hands bundled into tight fists.

He stormed back up to the house with the sun breaking over the shacks' roofs and certainty flooding his senses. Pasco was nowhere in the house, depriving him of the chance to vent his feelings with an argument. The anger persisted, through the day, chewing away at his innards.

Pasco returned early that evening, and by then, Kit was firming up his plans. He could not stop the cruelty on the plantation; neither could he stay here amidst such horror in such a beautiful location, but he had to do something. Later that evening, sitting alone on the veranda, he silently composed himself for what had to follow.

He blamed his Pa. It was he who took advantage of the shaman's woman all those years ago. Wasn't this all tied up with the curse?

Why did you do it, Pa?

Finally determined on his plan, Kit gritted his teeth and marched into the dining room where Pasco was having his supper.

His brother looked up, a soupspoon half way to his mouth. "Kit, you seen Clem this evenin'?"

"I sure have. He's a mess, Pasco. I missed you earlier, you took off for the fields before I could tell you of the girl." It was in his mind to add that his brother hadn't even asked about the victim, but he put that aside. "She's badly hurt."

"She's only a black. No one fetched me to get a doctor so I figured she'll get over it."

Only a black! Kit halted in mid-stride and ripped his brother out of his seat, drawing his face inches to his own. Pasco's spoon clattered to the floor.

"What in tarnation you doin', Kit?"

"Only a black! She's a human being!"

"All right! All right! Let me down!"

Kit released Pasco to fall back into his seat. "Clem is leavin' here. I tell you, he's gotta go!"

Pasco's eyes held a stark look of surprise. "But where's he goin'?"

"I know a ship which'll take him."

His brother gasped in astonishment. "What good will that do?"

Kit straightened. "God alone knows if it'll do any good at all. Clem can do the same as I did; sail the seas and see the world. It'll either make a man of him or it'll kill him. I'll pray it'll make a man of him."

Pasco's face held instant doubt. "You think Clem could take it?"

"I dunno. It might be the death of him. But I don't see any other way."

His brother stared down at his soup bowl in obvious reflection then sought Kit. "You sure the ship will have him?"

Kit replied with a curt nod. God, he hoped he'd made the right decision. "The captain owes me a favour."

"And what about you, Kit? You're staying, right? I really need you here, you know."

Kit squeezed his eyes tight shut. Was Pasco ever going to get the gist of this? Was he ever going to understand why his own brother could never be a party to slavery? Probably not, and there was no more point in arguing the matter.

He gave Pasco a saddened look. "I couldn't stay here. You know that. Even with Pa dead, I couldn't be a part of plantation life. Took me all day to see the truth of it, but I've finally made up my mind. The plantation is your'n. You can work it with Emma. I wish you well, brother." At the questioning look on Pasco's face, he went on. "Me? I guess I'll sail to England and settle on Grandpappy's farm. See what it's like."

"Should be very different to this." As if he had dismissed the problem already, Pasco picked up his spoon, wiped it and resumed eating.

"I hope so, Pasco. I sure do hope so." But he'd whispered the words as if he was trying to convince himself.

But was it any different here? Kit laid still, eyes closed, while Wenna's imprint on the mattress confirmed that she was silently watching over him. What dark thoughts ran through her mind?

Eyes still tight shut, he prodded: "Do you want to throw me out now?"

"Because of what your father and brother did?" Her voice held a strangely thoughtful lilt. "You're not responsible for their misdeeds."

He opened his eyes. "So I get to stay?"

"For the time being."

He let out a sigh of relief. At least she didn't appear to hate him. And if she did, it was not so much as he hated himself at times.

"Do you think the curse is all superstition?"

She shrugged. "If it is, we get enough of it around here." She laughed, and he was more attracted to her then ever. "You obviously don't know much about Cornwall. 'Tes all Celtic land, a place steeped in myths, legends and superstition. I'll wager most Cornish people will believe in your curse."

"And you?"

She wouldn't meet his eyes. "Whatever I think about it, Christopher, I intend to keep to myself for fear of starting a disagreement between us."

"In which case, I won't ask again." It was time to change the subject before he spoiled their growing relationship. "Tell me about yourself, Wenna. How do you cope in this harsh and superstitious place?"

"I manage as best I can." She accepted the abrupt change of subject easily and cast her gaze out of the window, her eyes focussing on some far distant spot. "I've worked this farm all my life and I intend to go on working here until I die or Killiow gets the better of me." She returned her attention to him with a tortured look about her. "My father was shot helping a Methodist preacher escape from the clutches of Killiow and his kind. One day I imagine they'll try get me also."

A stab of anguish speared his heart. "I'm real sorry about your father, Wenna. But they don't shoot people for no reason. Surely?"

"They had reason, so they say. The truth is, Christopher, we have oppression here also. Employers are constantly reducing the wages of their workers until 'tes now almost impossible to survive on a labourer's pay."

"Sounds like the English treat their labourers nearly as bad as we treat our slaves." As the words came out, a cold certainty set in. He had run away from a problem back home in Alabama, and found a similar problem here in Cornwall. Would his conscience sooner or later force him to turn and take a stand?

Wenna nodded curtly. "You're right at that, Christopher. The working men here are not slaves, but they might just as well be. Some round here are shackled to the land or to a mine, just as surely as if they were in irons." She closed her eyes tightly, and the subsequent silence weighted heavily between them.

"Will you be able to hold out against this mighty landowner, Killiow?"

Wenna opened her eyes and seemed to compose an answer before replying. "I don't know. Only a few of us still fight him now. If I lose the farm, I don't intend to go down easily."

"You sure are a brave woman." And damned good-looking, though he would not trust himself to say so again. "One way or another you'll win in the end. We both will, together."

"I hope so, Christopher. I really do hope so."

She left him shortly after and total darkness fell on the farmhouse. She came back later and sat with him throughout the evening, quietly holding his hand while they talked. Before she left him for the night, she leaned marginally closer as if ... as if she might kiss him. But she didn't, of course, because no respectable young woman would do that so early in their relationship.

That night he slept uneasily, waking at various times for no apparent reason. He awoke just as daylight began to lighten the room, announcing a lull in the storm. He rose painfully from the bed and stumbled across the cold boards to the window. The landscape was unbroken to the horizon. A watery sunlight fell upon a panorama of fields merging into one all-embracing and gleaming white sheet.

"Time I was on my way," he muttered to himself and was pleased that his jaw ached less. He dressed with difficulty, grunting as spasms of pain shot through his muscles. He tackled the stairs slowly and found Wenna busy in the kitchen amidst a glorious smell of cooking. Hunger pangs hit his stomach.

At the sound of his boot steps on the cold flagged kitchen floor, Wenna stopped stirring a pot and stared at him. "Heavens be, Christopher Vanson! Are you well enough to be up and about?"

"Sure, I am." He grimaced despite his bravado. "The storm's broken, and I have to be on my way to see what Grandpappy left me in his will."

She let out a sigh of resignation. "Jimmy will show you the way …"

"Better he stays here with you in case of trouble."

"If you say so." Wiping her hands on her apron, she studied him. "But you still look weak. Before I let you leave, you must have some bread and a bowl of skilly."

Kit smiled and took a seat at the kitchen table. Under Wenna's watchful gaze, he ate until he could swallow no more. Contented, he wiped at his lips and rose. It was time to go and nothing, not even Wenna Lanyon, would detract him from his intent. She helped him with his cloak, giving the direction he should take, and he hobbled to the kitchen door, a sharp pain piercing his leg muscle where one of his attackers had brutally kicked him.

"You'll take care, Christopher." She stood close behind him as he gingerly opened both halves of the thick, oak door.

Outside, the biting coldness still held sway, and he clasped his arms about himself as a few light snowflakes swirled about in the wind. But, for the moment, the worst of the storm had passed by. A virgin white bank was piled up at the side of the house and some of it fell into the kitchen.

"You be sure of it." He latched the lower half of the door between Wenna and himself then smiled.

He turned around and began clumping his way through the snow then stopped abruptly when his foot struck against something solid. He had dislodged a dark object from its hiding place beneath the crisp white mantle. Frowning, he bent to pick it up, a tremor invading his entire being.

A pistol.

Gritting his teeth, he checked the chamber then whipped around, holding up the gun by the handgrip, the frozen metal gluing itself to his skin.

"What is it?" Wenna asked still holding the upper door halfway open.

"It's a pistol. Killiow's henchmen meant business, Wenna. And it's loaded. They came here ready to do you some real harm."

"Come inside again. Show me." She opened the lower door and he stepped back into the house, closing both halves behind him.

"Let me see it." Her tone belied great concern.

He set the pistol down on the table, and the clunk of metal on wood echoed around the room.

She stared at the gun, her face turning ashen. "They ... wouldn't have ... shot at me." But her shocked look told him she was uncertain.

"Wenna, people don't carry these things unless they mean to use them. Your father was shot dead, and now they're after you!"

She suddenly pulled herself together and hurried towards her cooking pot. "'Tes just as well they didn't get the chance to use it."

"Right. But what about next time, Wenna? What about when they come back?" In that moment, his determination to reach his own farm dissipated, blown aside by this new discovery. He had to stay here a little longer while he considered Wenna's safety.

Six

Wenna's hands still shook as she served the mid-day meal, her attention constantly flashing back to the gun now lying on her dresser. Hunched over the kitchen table, his eyes focussed on his plate, Kit seemed unaware of the extent of her horror. He dipped a hunk of bread into the bowl, soaking up the last of the hot vegetable stew. His expressions throughout the meal ranged from warm smiles to concentrated deliberation.

"Will you leave for Tregover Farm now?" She brought into the open what she guessed was his private dilemma. "Jimmy's suggested he show you the way."

He paused, his chunk of bread half way to his mouth. "That'll leave you here on your own. Not keen on doing that." A straw-coloured lock fell across his wrinkled forehead and he brushed it aside.

Did that mean he really cared about her? She studied him reflectively, searching for more clues. "Jimmy knows the quickest route. After he leads you homes, he'll hurry back." She threw in an invitation. "And you can come back again in a day or so. That's if you want to, of course."

She held her breath. Would he want to be with her again? The memory of putting the injured Christopher Vanson to bed infused itself into her mind and she hid her shaking hands in her apron pockets.

She had been upset then, but not blind. With Jimmy's help, she had stripped off his clothes and bathed his wounds and shivered with excitement at the sight of his naked body. So muscular and ... well endowed beneath his canvas broadfall trousers. Dear God, how could she think such lewd thoughts? And him with a terrible curse hanging over his family line.

"Of course I'll come back." He confirmed with an honest smile. "But I don't like to leave you here while Killiow has these evil intentions towards you."

"I appreciate your concern." She sat beside him, determined to savour the pleasure of his company while it lasted. "I've grown used to looking after myself since my father died. I'll manage."

"Then again, I can't stay much longer if I'm to get to Tregover Farm today. There's another storm a'brewing in the sky and I ought to leave well before it gets dark."

Disappointment fell into place as easily as it had when previous young men had taken their leave, never to renew a budding relationship. She hoped she covered the hollowness inside her. "It isn't far if you follow the path across the fields and through Low Meadow Woods. Jimmy will have you home inside half an hour." She bit at her lip. "You mustn't worry about me. I can cope."

Christopher sat back in his seat and eyed her intently. "You'll keep your front door firmly bolted and you'll keep that pistol near you and loaded?"

She sighed out of slight irritation. "I promise. I don't want you to worry unduly, Christopher. 'Tes unlikely those men will be back again after the beating you gave them." She studied him from beneath lowered eyelashes and was startled when a dark look marred his face.

"Of course I'll worry!" He flung his arms wide. "I'd rather stay here and help protect you."

"And I want you to stay," she quickly added, wondering how far she should go. Impulse urged her to snatch at whatever might grow between them. "But you must get to your own farm while this break in the weather lasts. I thank you for your concern; it means a lot to me." Resigned, she fiddled with a dirty spoon.

He placed his hand, strong and warm, over hers, stopping her fidgeting. She sensed a deep intensity behind his now calm expression and wished he would bring it out into the open. Only then would she express the emotions uppermost in her mind.

"Okay, then. I'll return in a day or so." He rose slowly, still smarting from his injuries. "Until then."

"Until then." She jumped to her feet and, moving closer to him, she wagged a finger. "You must rest and recover properly from your beating. And I'll think of you fondly."

"And I'll …" He grasped both her hands.

Why did he hold onto her overly long? Her heart thumped at the intensity of his warmth. "You'll see me again?"

He smiled at her, and she dared to wonder what lay behind those rugged good looks. Could it be that his life of manly hardship harboured a boyish need to be accepted and loved? She could fill that need, if only he would give her the chance. She lowered her gaze to the floor to hide her blushes as the implications sank in. Those were dangerous thoughts.

"I'll see you again soon." He confirmed his intention with a curt nod.

"And I'll be waiting for you." She reluctantly broke apart their clasped hands. For the moment, his words were enough.

Wenna shivered as she stood at her door, watching Christopher and Jimmy trudge away through the deep virgin carpet covering the ground as far as the horizon.

The storm had abated, but low, steel-coloured clouds scudded fast and angry across the sky, a sure sign of more havoc to come. An unaccustomed emptiness engulfed her and swirled inside her heart, disorienting her. She closed the door and tried to busy herself inside the kitchen.

To her dismay, almost two hours passed before Jimmy entered through the kitchen door, his face and hands bluish with cold. Wenna ordered him to sit in front of the blazing parlour fire while she reheated a bowl of stew for him.

She placed the warm bowl into Jimmy's hands, fished a spoon from her apron pocket then pulled up the nearest chair by the fire. "Was Mister Vanson pleased to get to his farm?"

"Oh, 'ess, mistress. Delighted, ee was. Ole Padder had the place all warmed up for him. Mister Vanson said as how it were like home from home."

A tinge of unreasonable sadness drifted into her mind. Home from home sounded too much like somewhere he would want to stay. How wonderful to have him living so close to her and yet he would remain in his own home while she struggled on in hers.

The expected storm announced itself shortly after nightfall with a long, bellowing rumble of thunder, reaching out through the dark night air like a portent of what was still to come. Moments later, a brilliant flash of lightning lit up the farmhouse with an eerie silver-blue light. Further rumbles turned into crashing roars as the storm blew overhead and more snow fell.

Wenna ventured to a window, hands clasped to her cheeks. Lightning flashed brilliantly all round like angry, arthritic fingers spurting down at the open landscape. She gasped at its intensity and quickly withdrew to her bedroom where she hid, fully clothed, beneath her bed covers.

A howling gale lashed the house for several hours, driving in snow through any crevice available, under doors and through the ill-fitting window casements. It whistled into Wenna's bedroom where she shivered at the sight of fluffy white flakes billowing across the floor. Finally, distant rumbles allowed her only short punctuated periods of vivid dreams interspersed with much longer periods of waking.

She arose before dawn, stoked up the fire in the kitchen range and brushed aside the snow blown in during the night. The first signs of daylight lit up the dim plaster walls, gradually easing the distress of the long night. She peeked out through the kitchen window.

A light was already burning in the cattle barn, which meant Jimmy was milking the cows. She prepared breakfast for both of them and midway through she couldn't stifle a deep yawn. When she was done, she sat down at the table for a rest.

The front door slammed open then shut, startling her. Jimmy rushed into the kitchen, his eyes wide with alarm.

"Mistress! Come quick!"

Hairs began to prickle on Wenna's neck. "What's the matter?" She swallowed hard. "Have Killiow's men come back?"

"No, mistress. I was comin' back across the yard when I saw somethin' wrong with the hay barn. I went to look and the roof be fallen in!"

Wenna groaned aloud. The roof of the old hay barn had been unsafe for some time, and she had been meaning to get it fixed. She jumped to her feet and followed the young man to the front door where she donned her cloak.

The snow fell lightly now, an ethereal eddy of dancing flakes. They trudged across the yard at an angle from the main house to where the old barn sat. Just beyond, the newer cattle barn had survived the two storms. But in the grey morning light, the old barn looked all wrong. The centre roof section was gone, an enormous jagged hole looming.

They negotiated their way inside where the remains lay broken and twisted on the dirt floor. Wenna let out a stream of bleak whimpers. Soon the wet would seep through and her crop would be ruined.

Jimmy dug an arm into the snow, gauging its depth on top of the hay. "An arm's length, mistress. What're we gonna do?"

"I don't know, Jimmy. I just don't know." Without hay, without her small reserve of winter food, she was ruined. Even if the barn was repaired, she could not afford to replace the crop. A line of dampness trickled down her cheek and she hastily brushed it aside.

Everything was now against her: Killiow, the weather, even the fabric of the farm was falling apart about her.

She had to salvage what she could. "Come on, Jimmy. We'll move what we can into the new barn. Hitch up one of the horses to a sledge."

The boy scampered off across the yard while Wenna worked her way towards the rear of the barn where the roof was still intact. A small mound of straw and a few bales of hay against the back wall looked salvageable. Clambering over a mountain of snow, she found a few sacks of fodder not touched by the catastrophe.

She took stock of everything and told herself this disaster was really nothing worse than she had already suffered, but the truth was inescapable and her heart sank. This could be the end.

She was walking away when a sudden movement froze her dead in her tracks. "Who's there?" She heard shuffling behind the low wall of hay. An animal perhaps? "I said who's there!" The shuffling stopped. Her fingernails bit into her palms and she winced.

A tall figure eased out from hiding and rose to its full height.

"You!"

Pastor Arthur Pengorse shook his head at the devastation, dusted off his coat and stepped towards her. He castigated her with one look. "You should pay more attention to the upkeep of your property, Miss Lanyon."

Her blood boiled. "What are you doing in my barn? You were asked never to come near this farm again."

"Hiding from the storm and the magistrates." He drew himself taller, as if he meant to remind her that he was a man of the cloth, but his clothes, crumpled and dirty, detracted from his once imposing stance.

"In my barn?"

"I had to find shelter someplace. There are too many people after my blood, and I thought it would be safer here." He cast a wary eye to the roof's ruins. "I was wrong."

"How long have you been in my barn?" She crossed her arms undaunted.

"A few days. I took only what food I needed from your winter store. I'm no thief or vagabond."

"A few days!" she gasped as realization set in. She jabbed an accusing forefinger at his chest. "The night before last, men broke into my house. They were searching for you, weren't they? It wasn't me they were after, it was you!"

As if the matter was of no account, he shrugged his shoulders. "Most probably."

She gaped at his heartless manner and recovered with a quick swallow. "And you did nothing to help us. When Mister Vanson tried to protect me, you did nothing!"

Pengorse wiped more straw from his rumpled clothes then cast a surprise look at her. "You mean he needed help? He didn't seem to. It was fortunate for me your new neighbour has an iron arm. He made a good impression with the intruders." Pengorse sighed long and deep. "Well, now that you've found me, are you going to invite me into your house?"

He'd been watching, doing nothing to help while Christopher was being beaten. Anger tumbled inside her and spat from her mouth. "In my house? No." She shook her head with vehemence. "Never! I want you off my land. And don't ever come back here again."

"Surely not?" Pengorse gave her a wry look. "You're a hard-hearted woman, denying shelter to a man of God."

"You're no man of God. Get off my land."

He raised a finger towards her. "Your father –"

"My father died because he was taken in by your fine talk, Pastor Pengorse. But I won't be taken in by you. Not me. Get out!" The barn door creaked open behind them.

Jimmy Rudge stood at the open door, a pistol in his hand. "You heard the mistress." Pengorse's face whitened with outrage at the pistol aimed steadily at his heart. "You leave here now, Mister Pengorse."

The pastor shook his head at the turn of events and stepped purposely towards the farmhand. "Would you have the courage to pull the trigger, boy?"

"Reckon as how I would. For a man like you."

"You'd kill me? Me, a man of God!"

"'Ess, I'd pull the trigger on ee." Wenna had never seen Jimmy's face so white, but he held his hand steady. "'Tes up to God whether the bullet would kill ee."

Pengorse cursed. "We'd better not give you the chance to find out, had we? For the sake of your soul, boy." He drew back his shoulders, dusted down his cloak once again and strode on out.

The boy lowered the gun and wiped a backhand across his glistening forehead. He reached out a hand to help Wenna down from the snow-covered hay. "I heard him arguin' with ee, mistress. So I ran into the kitchen to fetch the pistol."

Wenna's gaze followed Pengorse out from the yard. "Well done, Jimmy." The pastor strode away across the fields without looking back, his footsteps trailing behind him in the thick snow.

Jimmy suddenly grabbed at her arm and pointed to an adjacent field. "Look, mistress! There be someone else up there!"

She shaded her eyes as she looked up. A dark figure stood in the lee of a small copse; a well-wrapped man huddled beneath a tree, silently watching the farm.

"Do ee recognise him, mistress?"

"No. But, whoever he is, he must have seen the pastor walk away." Wenna let out a long breath, which condensed in the cold air.

"'Tes a fair bet that he's one of Ralph Killiow's men. And if I'm right, he'll go straight back to the manor and report that Pastor Pengorse was here."

"That don't look good for ee."

"No, it doesn't."

It was obvious in hindsight. If Killiow's men had been searching for Pastor Pengorse, they would have left a spy to watch the house. He might have been hiding nearby for some days. Wenna shivered; she had every reason to fear what Ralph Killiow would do next.

"Reckon they'll catch him, mistress?"

"One man won't catch the Pastor. I'm more concerned about what they'll do to me, Jimmy. I've been seen harbouring a wanted man."

Wenna turned towards the damaged barn. She faced an impossible situation even without this new development. She had no money to repair the roof or replace the ruined crops and no banker would advance her one penny.

She dragged herself slowly back to her kitchen, fetched a tin box and sat at her scrubbed table. She opened the box containing all her documents. No matter what way she read them, the message was clear; she was now bankrupt. A tear rolled down her cheek, gathering strength as it dribbled, just like the sad facts dribbling through her mind.

An hour passed before she thumped her palm on the table and stood up. Determination rolled into place. She had only one option, and it wouldn't be an easy one. She would have to bluff her way through the bartering with that blaggard, Ralph Killiow. But in the end, she would have to give in to him and sell her land.

That alone and no more.

She would not work for Killiow and she certainly would not give in to his carnal desires. Neither would she throw herself onto the mercy of Christopher Vanson, much as her instincts told her she ought. A brazen hussy might go straight to him, offer intimate attentions in return for his help, but Wenna was no hussy. She had far more self-respect than that. If she had to, she would leave Penmarith and find work elsewhere.

She walked sternly back out to the barn where Jimmy struggled to salvage some of the winter fodder. At the sight, any lingering doubts quickly melted away. On a final note, she decided she would not allow Killiow to take the animals. She would have Jimmy drive them over to Tregover Farm where Christopher could use them as a foundation for his own new stock. It would be one puny way of hitting back at Ralph Killiow.

"Jimmy!" She called out through the open barn door.

The boy turned around. "'Ess, mistress?"

"Come here."

The boy came shambling out, scratching his head and looking puzzled.

She coughed to clear her throat. "I've some bad news for you, Jimmy. I won't be able to offer you and Jenny Tinder a room here."

Jimmy's jaw dropped open. "But, mistress –"

"No 'buts', Jimmy." She faced him sternly, struggling to keep her voice firm. "I've lost too much hay and fodder and, besides, Mister Killiow will soon be after me for sheltering Pastor Pengorse. I can't fight him any longer, not now. I've no option but to sell the farm. Mister Vanson will have to take on new workers so you must ask him for a job."

The boy's jaw dropped even further. "But what are ee gonna do, mistress?"

She pulled herself together. "Never mind. I have my plans." Like it or not, already those plans were firm in her mind.

Later that day Wenna stood at her kitchen window, daydreaming about the meeting she'd have with Killiow. Her thoughts were already gloomy and grew darker still when she spotted Thomas Roskilly, the parish constable, riding into her yard on an aged nag. As he dismounted, she anxiously went out to confront him. "What do you want with me, Mister Roskilly?"

"I heard as how Pastor Pengorse were here." The constable gave her a shifty gaze. "Came to see if you were hiding him."

"Oh you did, did you? Well, you can search as much as you like, Mister Roskilly, but you'll not find that man here on my land!"

Roskilly seemed unperturbed by her outburst. "You know where ee's gone, do you?"

"No, I have no idea. Who told you he might be here?"

"I er …" Roskilly ran his tongue round his lips. "Well, actually, Miss Lanyon, it was Mister Killiow who suggested I search your barns."

Damn him! So it *had* been his man watching the farm.

She flung an arm towards the barns. "Search all you want. You'll not find him here." And she stormed back into her house.

Seven

The weather moderated the following day. Sure that Jimmy was busy outside, Wenna filled a bowl with warm water, stripped off and stood naked in front of the parlour fire to wash. She would later don her best clothes and she would approach Killiow with pride, not shame.

Closing her eyes, she conjured an image of Christopher Vanson. She ran one hand down between her breasts and over her flat stomach, and allowed it to come to rest at the apex of her thighs. A tremor gripped her. She was twenty-four years old and no man had yet visited that private part of her body.

Maybe no man ever would.

Her mother had been much younger when she'd lost her virginity. Pregnant at seventeen, she was forced into marriage with the first man who would have her. Why else would a well-educated and articulate, young woman like her marry such a rogue as George Lanyon, and bring with her enough dowry money to buy the farm? But her mother had died of consumption when Wenna was barely eight years old and memories of her faded with the years. Wenna had known her mother such a short time, but she remembered her with affection.

For her father, who she had understood better than she ever let on, she had long harboured only distrust. Night after night, year after year, she had sat up late waiting for him to stagger home from the Cross Keys Inn in Penmarith, sometimes barely able to stand. As a frightened, motherless child she had learned to follow him up the stairs, collecting his discarded clothes, supporting him when he seemed about to fall.

How incongruous that her final failure had come so soon after meeting Christopher: a strong, dependable man who might have changed her life, given time. Was this what fate had planned for her all along?

If so, fate was too cruel.

Still naked, she knelt down in front of the fire and began to laugh long and slow at the terrible irony of her situation. Not much more than an exaggerated giggle at the start, it grew into a loud, frightening bellow. She laughed until tears streamed down her cheeks. Then she clasped her hands about her face, not knowing whether she was laughing or crying. She raised her hands to her eyes when it became clear that they were not tears of mirth; they were tears of grief. Her laughter was no laughter at all.

An hour passed before she was dressed and ready to leave the house. She stood by the kitchen door, straightened her blue dress, wiped all trace of dampness from her cheeks and left the house, her head held back defiantly.

She arrived at the village and stopped a while, her determination flagging. Why should she not pause to chat with the villagers she'd known all her life? Why must she rush on to the Manor? Why? Because she was putting off the inevitable and feared approaching Studmore Manor. Might as well face up to it, she was nothing short of scared. But that was no excuse; she had to confront Killiow, bargain with him for a decent price. She had no other option.

But she tarried even longer in the village.

Kit blew into his icy palms and rubbed his hands together vigorously, bringing them back to life while his breath condensed in the freezing air like ghostly ectoplasm floating in front of his face. He strode across the fields – *his* fields – savouring the pleasure of being alone in winter scenery so at odds with the heat of Alabama. He could have ridden but chose to walk, to feel the land beneath his feet. Land he owned.

He came to a sloping headland where gulls clamoured furiously at his approach. Breathing hard after a steep climb, he stopped at the highest point of his land and stared out at angry waters where the English Channel bumped up against the Atlantic Ocean. He swung his gaze left and right, savouring the barren sweep of the hills along the Cornish coastline, satisfied by his sense of belonging. This land was once his ancestor's place and now it was *his* place.

Feeling the wind's bite, he tore his attention from the sea view and turned inland. He trudged steadily across a five-acre field adjacent to Low Meadow Woods, his footsteps the only visible violation in the crisp snow. Ahead of him, a wisp of smoke rose up beyond a thatched barn just visible above a small copse.

Jacob Padder had told him the building was once an open-fronted linhay where cattle were fed in racks away from the farmhouse, but Kit's grandfather had installed wooden doors to keep out the winter storms. The smoke caught the light northerly breeze and drifted languidly towards the English Channel. Kit paused, puzzled. The barn belonged to Tregover Farm, so who had lit a fire on his land?

He angled towards the building and, as he neared it, singing floated down to him, carried on the northerly breeze. A rich baritone voice sang a hymn that, at first, sounded quite out of place in the white landscape. The melody lacked a whole range of voices to do it justice, a choir or congregation in full flow such as the rousing hymn-singing fervour of the Alabama slaves gathered early on a Sabbath morning before his father drove them towards the fields. Pa held no truck with slaves keeping holy the Lord's Day, claiming the laws of God didn't apply to darkies.

Kit listened intently but did not recognise the tune. He focussed on the words, strangely haunting and relevant.

I feel Him in the soil,
In my daily work and toil.
I glory in the strength of His command.
In the rain and in the snow,
He's beside me as I go.
Yes, I feel Him in the hardy land.

The voice swelled into a rousing chorus.

Power in the land!
Power in the land!
There is power in the hardy land.

The hymn stopped abruptly, as if the singer had heard Kit's approaching footsteps. Kit rounded the open barn doors and came upon a shadowy figure sitting crouched by a struggling wood fire just inside.

He drew back his shoulders and walked up to the intruder. "What in tarnation are *you* doing here in my barn?"

"Your barn?" The man stood up, his gaze sweeping furtively from side to side. When he finally focussed on Kit, his face broke into a broad expression of recognition. His manner became instantly apologetic. "My dear sir, I do beg your pardon. You must be the young American they're talking about in the village. I'm –"

"Reckon your name is Pengorse, ain't it? Saw you on the docks at Trevisco some days ago." He gritted his teeth for effect. "And I heard as how you were responsible for Miss Lanyon's pa being shot."

Pengorse raised both hands in rebuke. "Me? Now, just you be careful of what you accuse me, young man." Kit took note of the hands, more fleshy than muscular and clearly unused to manual work. "George Lanyon was shot while helping me, but he wasn't shot *by* me."

"He died because of you and your rabble-rousing. That's what I was told."

"You're new hereabouts and you probably haven't learned yet just what you're up against." Through heavy, lowered eyebrows, the pastor paused and put an emphasis to his next words. "George Lanyon was shot in the back by a man called Ralph Killiow."

Taken aback by the revelation, Kit blinked. "Killiow? Are you certain of that?"

"Absolutely. I was there," Pengorse added in a subdued voice. "I haven't told Miss Wenna of this, it would serve no useful purpose, but you can be sure of it."

Kit raised a hand to his forehead and rubbed at a throbbing temple. If Pengorse was speaking the truth, Wenna was in dire danger. She needed his help. He lowered his hand and cast his gaze about the barn to assess the pastor's hiding place then he eyed Pengorse with an accusatory expression. "Wenna claims you led her pa into trouble."

The preacher had returned to his fire and now knelt beside it. He picked up a stick and poked at a blackened pot sitting in the flames then raised his gaze to Kit. "He helped me of his own free will, whatever Wenna may have told you."

"That so? Well, whatever the truth of the matter, Wenna figures that you're big trouble. So, I want you to leave."

"But the barn is unused and I do you no harm." Pengorse pulled the pot from the fire, using the stick. "Will you not allow shelter to a man of God?"

"Genuine men of God can always find shelter with their followers.

It strikes me there's few folks about here willing to offer you a bed or a meal."

Pengorse stirred the contents of his pot and a warm smell of broth rose into the air. He sighed then shrugged. "They're frightened of possible retribution from employers like Ralph Killiow. Are you frightened of the squire's son, Mister Vanson?"

"No, and I ain't afraid of you either," Kit said, stabbing a finger at the preacher. "From what I hear, I figure you're big trouble and right now I just don't want any of it on my land. I'll be back here tomorrow to check on my barn. Make sure I don't catch sight of you here."

A wry smile creased the pastor's face. "They say in the village that you hail from the Southern States, a place where black men and women are kept as slaves. Is that right, Mister Vanson?"

Kit curbed his reply.

"The villagers claim that you don't approve of slavery." Pengorse kept his eyes averted from Kit. He reached a finger into his broth, sucked it dry and then nodded with satisfaction. "Some say you told the Reverend Beattie you left Alabama because of your family's involvement in slavery."

"Maybe I did."

"Well, I also don't hold with slavery." The pastor searched about for a spoon. "I don't hold with any philosophy of a man being subjugated by another. In this country it's the employers who subjugate the working labourers and deny them a decent wage. I champion the poor man's cause. I stand up for them against the likes of Ralph Killiow."

"You rouse them into a rabble, so I'm told."

Pengorse challenged Kit with a penetrating gaze. "I encourage them to stand up for themselves. Whatever Wenna Lanyon may have told you I did not harm her father. Like me, he felt for the poor working man. And he died for his conviction. If you turn me out of this barn, I'll be at risk of my life. If a man championed the cause of the slaves in Alabama, would you turn him off your father's plantation?"

The preacher's words hit a raw nerve. Kit ran his hands down his face, a hint of remorse already watering down his intentions. "Okay, you half convince me. Only half, mind you. You can stay provided no one gets to know that you're here. Or until I hear you've caused someone real harm."

"I'm obliged to you, sir. Most obliged."

"If Ralph Killiow finds you here …" Kit left his sentence unfinished. He had no need to spell out Killiow's reaction.

Pengorse smiled at the favourable turn of events. "He hasn't found me yet." He blew a cooling breath over the pot and spooned some content into his mouth.

"He'd better not." Kit gave him a curt nod then headed off down a shallow hill extending as far as the distant English Channel shore. Silence followed him as he walked away but the wood smoke and the cooked food lingered on the breeze tickling his stomach.

Kit's spirits fell. Could he ever escape the oppression of his fellow man? Maybe he should have stayed back home in Alabama, facing up to his father's wrongs. Maybe Cornwall was *not* his rightful place. He hunched his shoulders, jammed his hands into his pockets and continued on his way back to his farmhouse.

Tregover Farm – so much bigger than Crabtree Copse farmhouse – sat in a small hollow with a ring of elms to one side and long sloping fields to the other. Built three hundred years ago on a grand scale, it displayed a strange lopsided look to it as if it were unfinished when in fact, Cromwell's soldiers had destroyed two thirds of the original huge edifice in 1645. Only the west wing of the original house remained.

Kit had often drooled over and gaped at his father's rambling accounts of their lost riches, accounts that grew more incredible with each telling. Lantregover was the family's grand estate, and Pa had patiently explained that, in the Cornish language, it meant '*the enclosure of the house by the stream*'. Before the civil war, the Vansons were wealthy on a par with the Rashleighs and the Grenviles, but the Vansons were Royalists, supporters of a lost cause and fated to forfeit most of their land. With Lantregover for the most part in ruins, they retreated into the single surviving wing. No one was too sure when the remains of Lantregover House became Tregover Farm. The barns and stables – built from the ruins long after the civil war – surrounded a cobbled yard that was hidden from his view as Kit approached through a thick copse.

Shivering from cold, he was relieved to see smoke wafting out from the farmhouse chimney. He rounded a bend in the worn path skirting the copse, taking in the full sweep of his farm buildings, and stopped abruptly. Something was wrong, something serious. Men, horses, an apparent argument in his cobbled yard! Kit shielded his eyes against the snow's glare.

Jacob Padder, his leather jerkin flapping open despite the cold, stood at the centre of the dispute, surrounded by strangers well wrapped against the winter chill. A tall man wearing a heavy brown cloak over his riding coat and breeches sat astride a black stallion while three riders stood by their mounts, holding the reins. Kit took in the rest of the scene; a herd of cattle huddled together in one corner of the yard, agitated by the disturbance and tramping the snow into a thick brown slush. What in tarnation were those animals doing here?

He quickened his pace.

Faces turned towards him as he hurried through the farmyard gate. The tall rider swung his horse round, face-on to Kit. The animal whinnied and protested, but the horseman easily kept his seat. Kit halted, recognising Ralph Killiow.

"Ah, Vanson," the squire's son said with a satisfied grin.

Despite a nagging fear of more violence to come, Kit approached the group. "What do you want here, Mister Killiow?" A calm ring to his voice revealed he hadn't lost his poker skills.

"Came to talk to you, Vanson. Came to give you a fair warning."

"Warning?"

Killiow gave him a curt nod. "A certain renegade preacher by the name of Pengorse was seen making his way towards your farm." He paused then continued through bared teeth. "If you catch sight of him, you'll let me know."

"Will I?"

Leaning back in his saddle, Killiow glared down at Kit, daring a contradiction of his orders. "You will, if you know what's good for you." When Kit refused to take the bait, he shifted his attention across the yard towards the cattle, grimacing. "When did you get the new stock?"

"That's my business." Kit noticed Padder edging towards him. He gently signed the old man to hold back. He could handle this alone.

"Mark my words, Vanson. You'll not make a go of it here. Cattle or no cattle. You Americans don't understand our farming ways."

"I can learn."

"It would be better if you sell me the farm." There it was – not a warning but a threat. The first step in Killiow's attempt to take over Tregover. Sweeping a hand about the entire land, Killiow boasted: "I understand this earth, you see. Gentlemen landowners are born and bred to it."

"I said I can learn."

Gritting his teeth in frustration, Killiow leaned forward in his saddle. "Maybe I didn't make myself clear, Vanson. I said it would be better if you sell me the farm. Better for your health all round, if you get me meaning."

The walk had been exhausting, and Kit had yet to recover fully from his injuries of two nights ago, but he understood. "Don't threaten me, Mister Killiow. The last time you and I met, you came off worse. Remember?" He jutted his chin in emphasis.

"Ah yes," Killiow snarled, "but this time I brought some moral support with me."

The henchmen, their faces leering with obvious evil intent, advanced perilously close to Kit to reinforce Killiow's words while Padder hovered in the background, his crusty old face creased with worry.

Once again Kit signalled the labourer to keep away. It was no fight for an old man. Then he squared up to Killiow's men.

When his henchmen got within striking distance, Killiow called them back with a sharp order. "Not this time, men. We'll give the American time to think things over. Time to come to his senses."

"I already gave you my answer," Kit said firmly.

"You'll see sense in time." Killiow smiled, slapped his horse's haunches and swung round to the farmyard gate. He rode off at a canter, the horse's hooves digging up a flurry of snow.

Immediately, the henchmen jumped on their own mounts and followed after their master. Kit waited until the sound of muffled hooves receded into the distance before he turned to his labourer.

Padder lifted his cap and scratched his bald head, muttering: "That were a nasty business, sur."

"We can handle the likes of them." Kit jerked his head at the new cattle in the yard. "Where on earth did that herd come from?"

"Ah, them." Padder's tone brightened markedly. "Young Jimmy Rudge were over earlier an' ee brought Miss Lanyon's cattle over this way. All of them. Ee said as how she was givin' them to ee, sur."

"Giving them to me! But why in tarnation should Miss Lanyon send her cattle over here to me?"

"Summat about the roof on her hay barn fallin' in."

"The hay barn?" Kit studied the strange lines of the animals, quite unlike the Longhorns he was used to seeing back home. "But that don't explain it. She's another barn for her cattle, I saw it."

"P'raps ee should go over and see her, sur."

"I will."

Kit stayed only long enough to warm himself in the kitchen before he mounted the only horse from his stable and led the aged mare across the white fields. Drawing near Crabtree Copse Farm, he sensed a change in the place.

A few stray rays of weak sunlight fell on the snow-covered buildings, sparkling on the icicles hanging from the eaves. The old barn – at the opposite side of the yard from the farmhouse – took on the mantle of dereliction. The closer he came, the worse the damage appeared.

Jimmy Rudge emerged from the barn, wiping his hands on a small bundle of loose hay, and walked quickly across to meet him.

Kit dismounted and hurried towards the damaged building. "Came to see if I could help."

The boy waved a hand urgently over the damage then his shoulders sagged. "The weight of snow brought the roof down on top of all our winter feed. Mistress be right put out about it."

"I'm not surprised. Is Miss Lanyon in the kitchen?"

"Mistress edn't here, sur."

"Oh! When will she be back?"

"Dunno." Jimmy stared down at his boots and kicked at the hard earth. "She's gone to see Mister Killiow at the manor." His words were delivered in a hushed whisper, as if it were a message of great importance.

"Why on earth has she gone to him?" He shook his head and groaned. It took little imagination to guess what Wenna now planned after the loss of her winter feed.

"Not supposed to say, sur." Jimmy coughed then raised his head. "She said she were gonna settle some business with him." He clamped his mouth shut as if afraid to say more.

Kit gritted his teeth, alarmed. "Is she going to sell the farm?"

The boy didn't respond, confirming his suspicion. Kit gave him a sharp stare until he relented. Jimmy nodded, his eyes turning dull. "Reckon so, sur. Said she couldn't go on any longer. Not with the barn damaged. Besides, Pastor Pengorse were hidin' out in it without the mistress knowin'. She ordered him off her land, but one of Killiow's men saw him walk away. Mister Killiow'll be right put out about that. Could make real trouble for her."

Pengorse again! Wenna was afraid for herself and Jimmy because of the damn preacher.

"What will your mistress do when she gets back?"

"Dunno, sur. She said as how her visit might take some time an' I wasn't to worry about her if she was late."

Kit groaned again. Looking for a solution from Killiow could be downright dangerous; the man had no conception of mercy. He raced back to his horse, calling over his shoulder: "What time did she leave, Jimmy?"

"'Bout an hour ago, I suppose, sur. Mebee more."

"How do I get to the manor?"

"'Tes the other side of the village, sur. You just follow the road and you can't miss it." Jimmy hunched his shoulders. "Before ee goes, I has to talk to ee, sur."

Kit mounted his horse and looked at Jimmy. "Can it wait?"

"Suppose so, sur," he muttered.

"Leave it 'til later."

Cantering off towards Penmarith along the narrow lane, Kit followed a single set of distinctive footprints in the snow at the side of the road. They faded as he approached the village, becoming lost in a general mess of trampled snow. At the far side of the village, a mish-mash of slushy hoof marks ran along the centre of the road, almost certainly left by Killiow and his men returning from Tregover Farm. Kit rode on, anger festering inside him.

Damn that man! He had to stop him from buying Wenna's farm. For her sake. Or was it for his own sake? He urged the horse on and after rounding a bend in the road, he spied a three-storey, square shaped building faced with stone and roofed with Welsh slate. Studmore Manor. Ivy covered the front wall and surrounded the imposing main entrance, almost obliterating the painted coat of arms.

He dismounted when he reached the high, wrought iron entrance gates and immediately two imposing men in leather jerkins, each bearing a heavy wooden club and a menacing look, confronted him.

Kit squared his shoulders. "I'm here to see Squire Killiow or Mister Ralph Killiow."

One guard stepped directly in front of him, smacking the club against his open palm. His broad face cracked a smile to show lines of blackened teeth. "You can't."

"Why not?"

"Ee just can't," the same man growled. "Mister Killiow said as how ee's not to be let in."

"Then you know who I am?"

"We know," the other man said, stepping forward and aping his companion's menacing gestures. "Go away, Mister Vanson."

Kit considered his next move. He didn't relish another beating. There had to be another way. He remounted and turned the horse away from the manor. "Have you seen Miss Lanyon?" he called back over his shoulder.

"Go away!" both men shouted in unison.

Kit's body ran tense as he rode slowly away from the estate. Without stopping, he kept his glance over his shoulder. Was Wenna inside the house? If so, was she safe? Somehow, he had to find out.

Eight

Once out of sight of the guards at the gate, Kit dismounted and, leaving the horse tethered to a tree, he pushed his way through a tall hedge into the field beyond. He now could spy on the rear of the manor house. Well wrapped against the weather, a lone woman strolled across a flat, white rectangle he guessed to be a snow-covered lawn. Two pointers lolloped along beside her, their breath condensing in the cold air. He edged his way towards them.

Certain neither the woman nor the dogs had seen him yet, Kit crouched in the shadow of an overgrown bush and waited for them to move on. Instead, the woman changed direction, now walking directly towards him. As they came nearer, the dogs paused and sniffed the air suspiciously. They went into a barking fit and suddenly sprang across the field towards him.

"Down Hector! Down Apollo!" At the woman's command, both dogs froze as if paralysed. They sat on their haunches roughly three hundred yards in front of his hiding place, growling softly.

"You there! Who are you and what are you doing on this estate?" The woman marched up to the bush. She looked about Wenna's age but wore an expensive coat that Wenna could never have afforded. Her fair hair was tucked tightly into a warm bonnet and her blue eyes had an appealing intensity about them.

Kit rose slowly to his feet. "Gee, I'm sorry to trouble you, ma'am. I guess I didn't realise I was on someone's private land."

The woman eyed him keenly. "You're American, I can tell by your accent. You must be the man who's taken over Old John Vanson's farm."

"Yes, ma'am. I'm Christopher Vanson, his grandson."

"That's no excuse for your behaviour."

Kit flinched. Who was this woman who spoke with such authority?

"What are you doing, hiding like a hunted fox?"

"It's rather a complicated story." Kit took a moment to compose his words. Whoever she was, his gut feeling told him he should trust the young woman, nothing more than intuition. But was mere suspicion enough? "Can you tell me, ma'am, if Miss Lanyon is up at the manor?"

"If she is, I'm not aware of it. Why? What is it to you?"

He stared into her eyes then trusted his intuition. "Thought she might be in some sort of trouble."

"Trouble? At the manor?" She humphed loudly, coyly flattening one slender hand against a pale cheek. "Don't be ridiculous." But her expression changed to doubt. "What sort of trouble?"

Kit shrugged. "Not too sure. Just a thought, I guess."

"So you came galloping to her rescue?" The young woman's eyes sparkled as if laughing at him. "You're obviously mistaken. I haven't seen Miss Lanyon at the house today or, indeed, for some time. Will you walk with me?"

Kit quickly stifled a gasp of surprise. It was more a command than a request. "Well, I ..."

She fixed him with the look of one who would not take kindly to a refusal. "You were up to no good on our land, were you not? And I would so hate to have to tell my brother what you were doing out here."

Our land? The woman had to be the squire's daughter, Ralph Killiow's sister. She had the family trait as well – an inclination towards intimidation. A memory flashed through his mind. Tapper had said local tenants would prefer that she succeeded the old squire as owner of the manor. Maybe his intuition to trust her had been right after all. He forced a smile to his face. "I beg your pardon, Miss Killiow."

"As well you should, Christopher Vanson." Her stare radiated undiluted confidence. "Now, will you walk with me? Or will I tell my brother an American has been prowling about our land?"

"Do you leave me any choice?" He bent his head with some exaggeration.

"No." A pout creased her lips.

"Then I guess I happen to be going in your direction."

"Good. You can keep me company while I exercise the dogs." She waved a hand at the two animals, releasing them from their stay and watched them bound off across the snow. "You will address me as Beth and I shall call you Christopher."

"Is that proper, ma'am?" Kit frowned at her air of familiarity. He caught the hint of devilment in her eyes, far more subtle and effective than the blatant sexuality of Nellie at the Admiral Nelson Inn.

"Probably not, but I insist on it. I like the look of you, Christopher Vanson."

"If you say so, ma'am ... Beth."

The woman was openly flirting with him, of that he had no doubt, but he found the experience strangely enjoyable. She had the aura of that attractive woman in Rio, free with her favours but far more refined. The real reasons for his presence at the manor began to slide into the background, and he gave himself a mental shake to remember that his first priority was Wenna.

"Tell me about yourself." At his hesitation, Beth Killiow insisted: "I want to know all about you."

"All?"

"Of course." She drew her head back, and Kit noticed the revealing line of her long, slender neck. "That's what I said and that's what you will tell me."

He was getting nowhere with his search for Wenna, but he felt a growing certainty that this woman might be able to help. She might even give him access to the manor, if he didn't upset her. He would oblige her, for the moment.

"You know where I come from," he began. "My pa had him a cotton plantation in Alabama." Then he briefly told her of his life in the Deep South, omitting any detail painful to his memory. And, for good measure, he added some of his adventures at sea. While he talked, they tramped through the white fields and across the lightly wooded hills surrounding the estate.

"You're a very interesting man, Christopher," she said, smiling at him in a way he found hard to resist. Her beauty extended beyond her face, spreading over into the way she behaved, the way she spoke. He could not recall when he had last met someone with such clever social skills.

They stopped at the top of a steep slope leading down into a dense wood. Beth swept her arm across the view of snow-covered hills that stood out white against the dull grey sky in front of them and said: "That's the extent of our land, Christopher. As far as you can see, all the way to the horizon. Makes your little farm look puny, doesn't it?"

"And your brother aims to add to it," he added dryly.

She grinned at him sideways, sly and yet appealing, as she headed on down the slope. "Most landowners want more. They get addicted to being lords of their estates, rulers of their tiny kingdoms. Ralph is no different. But let's not talk of that. Come –" Her words were abruptly cut short as she fell. One moment she was upright and the next her feet slid and crumpled beneath her. She tumbled forwards, sliding and rolling over in the snow, crying out in pain.

Not stopping to think, Kit leapt after her and grabbed at her flailing arms. He dug his feet into the ground, but his boots slid forward uncontrollably. In desperation, he wrapped his arms about her and flung himself on his back. He came to rest lying half way down the slope with Beth stretched out flat on top of him.

"Oh, my God! Help me up!" she wailed.

"Hang on, Beth." He sat up, helping her to her knees as he did so. They were both caked in snow, and Beth had lost her bonnet. Her long, fair hair blew about untidily across her face. "Can you stand?"

"I don't know." She eased her weight onto one leg then the other and cried out, wincing. "My ankle! It hurts!" Her face was screwed up with pain as she slumped down again and hugged her left leg.

Kit shook snow from his head and rose to his feet, testing his limbs first. No major damage, just a few more minor bruises to add to the multitude he had already suffered at the hands of Killiow's men.

"Beth, can you move your foot?"

Her cheeks turned noticeably paler as she tried. "I can wiggle it, but it pains me."

"Then it most likely ain't broken. Are you hurt any place else?"

She checked herself. "No, just my ankle. It's hurting badly though."

"But can you stand on it?"

"Of course I can't, you fool! You saw what happened when I first tried to stand." She gritted her teeth at the pain. "There's nothing else for it, you'll have to carry me. Are you strong enough for that, Christopher?"

He nodded. "Reckon so, but –"

"Then do it!" Her tone broached no argument. She stretched out her arms towards him.

"If you say so, ma'am." He took a deep breath, swept her up into his arms then relaxed. She was but a featherweight compared with many women he had carried. "Reckon a slim young woman like you ain't gonna cause me no trouble."

Her face transformed instantly from pouting to beaming.

He climbed back up the slope and trudged towards the manor with Beth snuggled down against him, resting her head on his shoulder so that her face was close to his. Her ragged breathing tickled his cheek like a long, tantalising kiss.

While her ankle was undoubtedly hurting, Kit sensed that she was taking every advantage from the situation. Why did that not surprise him? He took her straight across the flat lawn and in through the kitchen entrance.

At the sight of the squire's daughter looking hurt, a buxom woman raised her hands in shock and ran to them. "Oh, my heavens! What's happened, my lady?"

Kit glanced at Beth who was simpering, her head still resting on his shoulder, stray wisps of her hair now glued to his face.

"Don't fret, Mrs Trevose. I've hurt my ankle."

Kit set her down in the closest easy seat and stepped back while Beth wallowed in the cook's attention. He quietly melted into the background, silently appraising the surroundings.

The ministrations and cries of pain as Mrs Trevose tried to remove Beth's boot brought Ralph Killiow to the kitchen, cursing angrily. "What's going on here?"

"Miss Beth's fallen and hurt herself, sur." The cook pointed to the ankle with the boot still in place.

Ralph Killiow snorted loudly then his expression darkened at the sight of Kit. "What the devil are you doing here?"

"Calm down, Ralph," Beth called to him. "I fell and sprained my ankle while I was walking the dogs and Mister Vanson kindly carried me home. If it were not for him, I'd still be lying out there in the snow."

Killiow's expression turned darker still. He advanced on Kit. "Found you by accident did he? How did he come to be on our land?"

"It's of no consequence." Beth let out a painful wince. "I'm most grateful to him for bringing me home. Now, run along and fetch Doctor Cuxholme."

"The devil, I will!" Killiow bellowed and bared his teeth.

"Ralph! Do as I say!" Beth's voice cut sharp into the air, the compelling tone of one who would be neither contradicted nor ignored.

Killiow stopped in his tracks, glared at Kit for a spell then turned his glare on his sister.

"Before you go, Mister Killiow …"

Killiow swung back to him. At Kit's hesitation, he snapped: "Well?"

"Has Miss Lanyon been to see you today?"

"Miss Lanyon? Here?" Killiow's face broke into a stupid grin. "Whether she has or hasn't visited the manor is no damned business of yours."

Kit clenched his fists at his sides and adopted a sincere look while doubting its effect. "I need to find her."

Beth shot a black look at her brother. "Tell him, Ralph."

Ralph Killiow scowled at his sister then relented. "No, she hasn't been here, damn her hide." He stormed from the room, roaring at the closest manservant to fetch the doctor.

Relief flooded through Kit. Likely, Wenna had tarried in the village, and he might yet stop her from reaching the manor. He turned back to Beth, anxious to search the village, inch by inch until he found Wenna. "I guess I'd better be going."

Beth flashed a dashing smile at him. "I shall want to see you again, Christopher Vanson. You will come and see me again, won't you?"

"Sure, I will." He took the instruction easily. This young woman could be of use to him, and it amused him to pander to her.

"Good. I think you and I could get along so well together."

On Beth's instructions, a wizened old servant in a black uniform escorted Kit to the front of the house. Before closing the front door, the manservant glanced around anxiously. "T'would be best if you went straight home, Mister Vanson. The master edn't himself today."

Kit glowered at the man. "What do you mean?"

"Best ee go straight home, sur." On that warning note, the manservant shut the door firmly behind him.

Kit walked away with deep misgivings. He had yet to discover what had happened to Wenna and, at the back of his mind, was a lingering memory of the Vanson curse. Was Ralph Killiow foolhardy enough to treat the villagers as badly as Alabama slave owners?

Wenna had run out of excuses and people to visit. It was time to get to Studmore Manor and deal with Ralph Killiow. She stopped at the edge of Penmarith village, where a bank of hedging overhung the road, to compose her thoughts and rehearse her words.

A rider approached fast from the direction of the manor, the striking of hooves muffled by a trail of snow and slush where numerous horses had passed before. Anxious to avoid any confrontation, Wenna stepped back behind the hedge, pulling her skirt clear from the ground. The horseman swept past, his attention fixed on the village. She gaped.

Christopher Vanson.

What business would he have had with the Killiows? Wenna hugged a snowy bank behind the hedging and waited until he rode well out of sight before she took to the road again.

How fortunate he had not seen her. Just a few words from Christopher might have dissuaded her from her intent.

She stepped cautiously along the tree-lined lane. Icy cold dampness seeped into her boots, and when it reached her feet, she quickened her pace, pausing only when Studmore Manor came into sight. An imposing edifice from the outside, it also oozed an invisible aura of malice.

She still had time to change her mind, time to turn away and ask Christopher Vanson for his help. How could she do that when her pride would not allow it? Neither would her imminent bankruptcy.

She walked on.

Two of Killiow's henchmen waved her through the main gates,

heckling her with lewd suggestions. Frightened by their behaviour, Wenna hurried on and paused only when she came near the house.

What now, the front door or the rear one? Determination forced her teeth tight together. She would enter the house at the front as a neighbouring farm owner and not at the back as a mere tenant.

The footman opened the door and frowned at her with an air of disdain. "Yes?"

"Hello Binner, I want to see Mister Ralph Killiow." She swept past him into the entrance hall before he could bar her way.

"Is he expecting you, madam?" His last word came out with a note of contempt.

Wenna glared at him. "No. But I'm sure he'll see me. 'Tes a matter of business."

"The master is resting in the drawing room. I'll see if he will receive you." Binner walked away.

Wenna cast about the dark interior and hugged herself. Doubts surged about inside her head; doubts mixed with intense fear. Too late now, she had to go on. She focussed her attention down the hallway.

Cobwebs anchored to the dark oak ceiling beams shimmered and bowed. Plaster cracks ran haphazardly from one end of the passage to the other. Stains of dampness rose up from floor level like creeping intruders clutching at the walls. The old Squire Killiow was a rich man and had hosted magnificent balls in years past. So why was the place decaying? Was it because of the Squire's evil heir?

Distant footsteps echoed hollow, like ghostly sounds from an empty tomb. Wenna started as a door near her flew open and a slight female figure bumped out noisily, knocking against her. The young woman flailed and her walking stick clattered to the floor.

"Damnation!" she cried out, grasping at the doorframe. She bent awkwardly and gathered up her walking stick. Once in control of her stance, she glanced at Wenna. "What are you doing there, Miss Lanyon?"

"I'm so sorry, Miss Killiow. You're hurt."

"It's nothing." The woman smiled ruefully then let out a long exasperated breath. She teetered, and Wenna quickly offered her hand for support.

"Can you stand, Miss Killiow?"

She waved the hand aside. "Yes. Don't fuss. I suppose I was in too much of a hurry. Father says I'm always being too hasty." She drew herself upright. "I've hurt my ankle and don't walk too straight."

"How is your father?" Wenna asked.

"Father? Why, he's just the same. Very frail. But thank you for enquiring, Miss Lanyon." Beth Killiow's expression turned sombre. "I was so sorry to hear about your own father. Such a terrible loss. I thought of calling on you at the time. But, you know how things are with my brother; it could have turned nasty."

Wenna blinked, suspicious. The Squire's daughter should not be speaking to her like this – too much familiarity with a peasant farmer. "Why would that be, Miss Killiow?"

"I'd like to feel I could call upon a neighbour in time of distress." Beth Killiow rested her hand lightly on Wenna's arm, as if it were the most natural thing to do. "And we are neighbours, are we not?"

"Yes." Wenna's tone mellowed. "But why should things turn nasty?"

Beth withdrew her hand and rested it against the wall, easing the weight from her injured leg. "It's not easy for me to explain. My brother has said such terrible things about your family. It makes things dashed awkward for me."

Wenna could think of little to say in reply, nothing that would be agreeable to Beth Killiow, so she simply nodded.

Further along the corridor, Binner coughed to draw Wenna's attention. He stood impatiently outside the library door.

"I must go." Wenna backed towards the footman. "I have business with your brother."

"That sounds ominous." Beth grimaced and then quickly followed it up with another smile. "Take care, Miss Lanyon."

"I'll try to." She turned away and strode down the long corridor to the servant.

Binner knocked hesitantly, opened the library door and coughed. "The lady to see you, sir."

"What lady?" Wenna couldn't mistake the bellow from inside the room.

Binner stood aside and ushered her inside. "Miss Lanyon, sir."

"The Lanyon woman!" Killiow sat up suddenly from his slumped position before a blazing fire, nursing a glass of amber fluid, and swung round. "Dammit, Binner! I thought you said it was a lady. Must you let every damned farm wench into the house?"

With her heart hammering inside her chest, Wenna stood inside the doorway, biting at her lip, stamping down on her anger. She had not come here to take abuse from Ralph Killiow, but neither would she allow him to provoke her into an argument unnecessarily.

Binner shuffled from the room and the door creaked as he closed it, leaving Wenna alone with Killiow.

"Well, what do you want, woman?" The squire's son sank back into his seat, facing away from her and taking a deep gulp from his glass.

"I came here to talk to you on a matter of business, Mister Killiow." Her rehearsed words set the scene. But she had another matter to clear up before she got down to the nature of her business. "Why did you send your henchmen to my farm a couple of nights ago?"

Killiow downed another mouthful of liquid and glanced at the ceiling. "What makes you think I would send anyone to your puny farm?"

Wenna kept a lid on her emotions. "You've reason, and we both know it. Mister Vanson was with me at the time. He was badly beaten up."

"So?" The word came out slowly, cynically.

She took another step into the room, asserting herself. "I think 'twas all your doing, Mister Killiow. No one else around here would send out ruffians to beat up an innocent man who was defending me and my honour."

Killiow laughed out loud. "Your honour, madam?" But he made no attempt to deny the accusation. Instead, he leapt to his feet, swung round and took a few steps towards her. Whisky fumes wafted across the short span between them. "Your *honour*? I think you have high ideas above your station. People like you do not make use of the word *honour*. That is the prerogative of your betters. Besides," he waved his hand in a wide arc, spilling whisky onto the carpet, "by your own admission, you were entertaining a man in your house. How can you talk about honour?"

Wenna persisted. "But for Mister Vanson, your men would have attacked me."

"Pure speculation." He reached down to refill his glass from a crystal decanter. "Did anyone actually lay a hand upon you?"

"Not on that occasion, no. But they would have done."

Killiow righted himself and waved his arm unsteadily. More drink slopped from his glass. "No one attacked you, so you cannot but speculate what might or might not have happened. You've no complaint."

"You had no right."

The squire's son came closer, stabbing his own chest with a forefinger. "I had no right?" She recoiled at the stench of foul breath mixed with stale sweat, but he seemed not to notice. "Remember where you are, young woman, and who you address. No one questions my authority in this house."

Wenna drew herself together. She thrust her chin forward. "Really?" This was no time for subservience. "I think 'tes about time someone did. Why did you send your men to Crabtree Copse Farm?"

"You dare question me?" Ralph Killiow glared at her, his eyes blazing with anger. "Let me put you straight, Miss Lanyon. Rumours abroad say that Pengorse has been hiding on your property. If it's true, you'll pay the price for harbouring a criminal. Mark my words. I'll come down hard on any man or woman I find sheltering that preacher."

"I've no dealings with Pastor Pengorse. Besides, he's yet to be formally charged by a magistrate." Her heart still thumped, but she resisted the temptation to clasp at her chest. She would not give him the satisfaction of seeing her fear. For a moment the air hung with tension then Wenna pressed on. "Was that why you sent your men? To look for Pastor Pengorse? 'Tes not a very polite way of looking for a preacher."

"Don't criticise me, woman."

"I will do so. You're an evil man, Mister Killiow."

Oh God, she had lost her patience. How could she have been so foolish? She waited for the reprisal surely to come.

He loomed over her frail body. "Evil? How dare you! Evil, indeed." Killiow emptied his glass, belched and refilled it. "That's enough from the likes of you." He downed another gulp of whisky, and grabbed the bell pull beside the fire. The door opened almost immediately and the footman came into the room, his gaze shifting uneasily from side to side.

"Fetch Pengwidden." Following his employer's command, the footman bowed silently and backed out, leaving the door open.

"About my business –" Wenna began.

"Business, be damned! You need a lesson in civility." His voice now had a distinctly slurred edge. He advanced threateningly on her. "In this house we don't tolerate insolence from the likes of you."

"You don't frighten me," she lied, while mounting terror ate away at every fibre of her. She had handled the meeting badly – that was now patently obvious – and this was no longer the right time to bring up the sale of Crabtree Copse. It was the time to bow out, quickly.

"So, I don't frighten you, eh?" Killiow curled back his lips. "You're a damned trouble to me, Miss Wenna Lanyon, and I think it's time I put paid to your stubbornness. You'll not leave here 'til I show you how to behave."

She took a step backwards, alarmed. "Don't threaten me! I came here of my own free will and I'll leave under the same circumstances."

"The blazes you will!" He threw his glass aside where it shattered on the floor. "Why did you come, anyway? To accuse me of attacking your visitor?"

"Yes."

He frowned suddenly, as if remembering her earlier words. "You said you came here on a matter of business. What was it?"

Wenna edged back towards the door. "It can wait 'til you're sober enough to reason with."

"You insolent wench!" He raced after her and raised his fist to her face. "How dare you address me in that manner!" Then he lowered his fist and smiled, as if he had been dealt a sudden revelation. "Is it the farm? Are you ready to sell or do you need some further persuasion?"

He had somehow read between the lines, but Wenna couldn't respond as a hesitant cough had her swinging around to a thick-set, coarse-featured labourer who had come into the room. He bowed his head, clasping his cap tightly to his rough shirt.

"Pengwidden, put this woman in the empty bedroom next to me own. Lock her in and bring me the key."

The labourer's brow rose in shock. "But, sur –"

"You can't lock me up!" Wenna turned to Killiow, a sharp tightness gripping her chest. He couldn't do this to her. He couldn't imprison her as if she was an outlaw.

"We shall see, madam." He laughed and a gob of spittle rolled down his chin. "You'll find I can do whatever I like with you."

Her brain went numb, not silently numb but screaming as if in physical pain. "The magistrate will hear of this." Even to her own ears, her voice was hoarse, strained. But her words were a weak threat because Ralph Killiow clearly held the upper hand. His father *was* the magistrate.

"You're a damned foolish woman. Where will you find anyone of importance to listen to your lies?" Killiow filled another whisky glass and drank from it heavily. Belching loudly, he turned his back while Pengwidden grabbed at Wenna's arm and pulled at her.

"Leave me alone!" Wenna struggled against his grasp. Surely other servants would hear her cries and let Beth Killiow know of his brother's machination. She must hold out until then.

"Sorry, mistress." Pengwidden tightened his grip and led her from the room. "I has to do what the master says. Me job depends on it." He propelled her up two flights of a darkened stairway, seemingly deaf to Wenna's constant sobbing cries to be released. When he pushed her into the appointed room, he claimed: "I'm sorry to have to do this, really I am." But his face betrayed the truth of his words.

Wenna glared at him as he backed out of the room, avoiding eye contact with her. Then she heard a key turn in the lock and a final click. She closed her eyes and breathed raggedly as the servant's footsteps faded.

How could Pengwidden do this? Surely, no honest man would imprison her, even if it cost him his job. This could not be happening to her. If she remained calm this nightmare would fade away and she would awake in her bed back at the farm. She took a deep breath and held it before releasing the air in one long, low gasp.

Nothing had changed.

Struggling against her rising panic, she crossed to the window and looked out. Her faint hope of escaping vanished. The room was three storeys up facing the well-guarded front of the house. She sank to the floor, her back against the wall and wiped tears from her eyes. Damn you, Ralph Killiow. Damn you! And a curse upon her own poor judgement. She could not have handled matters worse.

Dusk fell, pulling in frightening shadows. Wenna clasped her arms about her waist, fighting a violent shiver. It was all her fault; she should never have come here alone. If only she had spoken to Christopher Vanson when she had the chance. If only she had told him where she was going. But she had told no one except Jimmy, and he would not venture here. She rose from the floor and lay on a hard bed against the opposite wall. Full darkness soon fell, and she drifted into a light sleep out of exhaustion.

She came instantly awake when a key rattled in the lock. The door swung open and Ralph Killiow stood within the surround, a flickering candle lamp in his grasp. It cast an eerie light about the walls, sending dancing shadows up and down the uneven plaster. He reached out a hand to the doorway to steady himself. Wenna detected the potent stench of alcoholic breath.

"Well? Have you have you c… cooled down, madam?" His slurred words more than confirmed her suspicion. He tottered towards her and she came to her feet, squaring up to him. "You have no right to hold me here."

"Rights don't … don't come into it. You're here and … and you'll sss…stay here until you come to your sss…senses." Killiow staggered closer, each reeling step sending the candle on another wild lurch.

Killiow was astride that narrow ledge between drunken incapacity and drink-enhanced desire. How far would he go? How far would the drink drive him? Her heart thumped hard against her ribs.

"Please stay away from me."

"Why?" He leered at her. "Don't you f…find me in the … the least bit attractive?" He slid the lamp onto an old tallboy and reached out to clasp her. "Let me h…hold you."

Wenna drew back instinctively, shrinking back unknowingly towards the bed. "I said stay away from me!"

"And I asked you why. All it will t…take is a bit of co-oper… cooperation from you and ... and we can both go away from this happy."

"Keep away." She wrapped her arms about her waist, knowing Ralph Killiow would not listen to anything she had to say.

Yellow front teeth gaped between his thick lips and spittle dribbled down his chin. "I've had me eye on ... on you, Miss La...Lanyon. I've a mind to ... to take you right here and ... and now."

"No, please. I'm not like those village girls you've seduced." She wouldn't lie abed with him even if he paid her handsomely. A painful tightness in her throat impeded her voice. "I'll not give in to you. Stay away, please."

"Don't pr...pretend, woman. Don't act as ... as if you haven't known a man before." He snapped out a grabbing hand. Caught, she struggled. But, even in his drunken state, he was too much for her. His fingers twisted in the folds of her dress, pulling her body tight against him.

"Let me go –" Her words were cut short by the sudden tearing of her dress. In one long movement, he had ripped her bodice away from her chest.

The sound of her own screams pierced into her head, and she gripped at her throat, hearing her pitiful cries erupt spasm-like from her windpipe.

Dear God. Surely he would not dare. He mustn't! Someone would come to her aid. They had to! But her hopes were dashed immediately. No one had even peeked into the stairway earlier when she was dragged to her prison. They would not help her now.

Killiow was beyond reason, his hands flailing at her, ripping her shift. The more she fought the more he threw himself into his sport. She threw her arms across her bare breasts, hiding her nudity. He laughed demonically while her protective gesture allowed him to pull her dress fully down to her waist. Still laughing, he forced her arms aside to inspect what lay beneath while Wenna screamed again; a long, wailing cry that came straight from her heart. In response, Killiow guffawed with a stupid lop-sided grin across his face.

"Always thought you ... you had a good b...body beneath them clothes. Was right, wasn't I?"

"Master!" A voice called from the doorway, cold and firm.

Killiow broke off his attack, his jaw drooping, eyes dilated. He turned towards the intruder, glaring. "Get out!"

Pengwidden, white-faced, wilted against his master's grimace. His earlier firm voice melted into a whimper. "Beggin' yer pardon, sur, but –"

"Get on with it. Can't you see I'm busy?"

"Beggin' yer pardon, sur. We, that is the rest of the servants an' me, we heard the screamin' an' we wondered ... that is –"

"The servants? Damn you man, get out!"

"But, sur –"

"OUT!"

Pengwidden retreated, closing the door slowly, and Wenna's last hope of rescue disappeared with him. A long, cold shudder snaked up her spine and raked through the rest of her body. The room spun about her, faster and faster. Focus, she had to focus, if she were to resist him.

Killiow ground his teeth together and, strangely, the noise reverberated inside her own head. "Now we will f...finish our business."

He loosened his belt and his breeches fell to the floor, anchored round his ankles. He stumbled out of them and kicked them free. Wenna pleaded to him, silently hoping he would be too drunk to carry out his threat. His left hand came out to her face, and he slammed her backwards. She lost her footing, her head connecting hard against the bedstead. On the rebound, flashing stars marred her vision, and a buzzing sound filled her ears. And death stared her in the face. The certainty of it hit home. She could think of nothing else.

"Don't you d...dare move from th...that bed." Without warning, he punched her jaw with his fisted right hand.

She slumped onto the bed, greyness melting into black.

Tumbling waves of consciousness crept back slowly. Spinning lights. Foul breath. Stabbing pressure in her loins. Grunting. Then an intense pain which radiated throughout her body. Her consciousness waned ... back into darkness.

She came around with no idea how long her brain was numbed. After a while, vague, horrible notions briefly surfaced. They died as quickly as they rose, leaving her dulled mind blank for seemingly long periods.

She woke to a heavy weight pressing her against the mattress. A stinking, blubbery weight. She reached a hand to her head where it throbbed. Further consciousness returned painful. Slowly, coldness tingled her skin. She opened her eyes. Daylight flooded the room then dimmed when she briefly closed her eyes again. Cold air drifted around her skin, cooling her. She reached down, her hand searching for a bedcover. She was naked! Panic rising, she pushed against the mound of flesh pressing down on her stomach and chest, and Killiow moaned.

His mouth was close to hers and each foul breath raped her sense of smell. Nausea rose deep inside her. On the verge of retching, she screamed: "Get … away … from … me," then she tasted bile in her throat.

Killiow rolled off to one side until he lay on the bed alongside her. "You're awake again." He sat up and then belched loudly. "I always knew I would have you one day. The whisky didn't hold me back this time, eh?" He belched again, fouling the air around them.

Wenna pushed herself onto her elbows and a sharp pain shot up through her lower abdomen. Feeling a trickle of warm fluid – perhaps blood – running down one thigh, she fell back heavily against the bed and lay rigid.

Please, God, let it all be a dream! Don't let this be real. Please God! And all the while, she held the certainty that her situation *was* real.

She stuffed fisted hands against her mouth to stifle her whimpering. When she drew her hands away, her sorrow came out like the pitiful cry of a lost kitten, a helpless animal. Her chest heaved in time with her sobbing.

A door opened, not in here but in some far off place, and boots scuffed against floorboards. Pengwidden's voice cut into her consciousness. Not a real voice – nothing would ever again be real. It crept out from a dark nightmare; a disembodied voice that merely sounded like Pengwidden.

"Beggin' yer pardon, sur," the voice said. "The rest of the servants is getting upset about the young woman. They was wonderin' –"

"Tell the fools to go about their own business!" The bed creaked as Killiow shifted away from her. "I've finished here, anyway."

"We was wondering if Miss Killiow might help the young lady, sur."

"The devil she will! Anyone who says a word of this to me sister will answer to me. Now get out!"

The servant's footsteps shuffled away. Killiow grunted and heavier footsteps echoed across the floor, uneven and accompanied by a loud belch. Wenna clamped her eyelids tightly together until the door slammed shut. Thank God, Killiow was gone. But the stench of his drink-soaked breath lingered.

She lay flat on her back, her naked chest heaving. Unclean, she was unclean – horribly unclean – desperately filthy. She had to wash herself; scrub the filth from her body. She rubbed a hand roughly across her stomach then froze. What was the point of washing? She would never again be worthy of any man's attention.

While she composed her thoughts, her lower lip trembled; an uncontrollable, unstoppable quivering, as if it was destined to continue until … until she died. So this was what it was like to lose her purity. This was the shame and horror of abuse. No trace of pleasure, no trace of joy in knowing that she was attractive to a man, nothing but nausea and repugnance and … and hatred of herself.

Time passed, she had no idea how long before she pulled her torn clothes about herself and fell into spasmodic bouts of convulsive weeping. Immeasurable time passed – maybe it was an hour or more – before she was able to drift off into a light sleep.

The dreams, when they came, were violent but no more violent than reality. Huge rats scrambled over her, noiselessly gnawing at her flesh. Eating … eating … devouring her body … defiling her soul. She shuddered, and in that instant a scrambling, scratching sound burst into her brain.

She awoke, jerking her body upright. Her muscles shrieked in pain. She hugged her arms about herself, shivering. The room swam into focus.

No rats in sight. Just someone fiddling with a key in the door lock. A sharp pain piercing through her stomach and a dull ache irritating her jaw. Daylight lit up the dull walls around her. She pulled together the torn remnants of her dress across her body and anxiously waited.

The door creaked open.

Pengwidden shuffled into the room, his eyes averted to the floor. "Master wants to see ee downstairs."

Could she follow the labourer down the stairs with a measure of dignity? Did any dignity remain inside her? She held her bodice tight against her chest to prevent it falling and followed him out, each step bringing more pain to her defiled body.

Ralph Killiow sat at a long table in the refectory, calmly eating his breakfast.

Calmly eating!

Wenna stepped hesitantly into the room and stood facing him while Pengwidden hurriedly backed away. The ache in her jaw intensified; she was grinding her teeth together, hard and noisy.

"Well?" Killiow picked at his food, keeping his eyes focussed on the plate. "Have you come to your senses, woman?"

"Come to my senses?" Wenna stretched her lower jaw that ached so badly and flinched. Could it be broken? "Will you please let me go now?"

"You're free to leave whenever you wish." He laughed and reached out for a wine goblet. "Or perhaps you'd like to spend tonight in the comfort of me bed? Now that you've got yourself a taste of what I can offer, eh?"

A blinding pain flashed across Wenna's forehead. Struggling to fight off a bout of giddiness, she pulled her eyes tight shut. "Mister Killiow, I would never give myself to you willingly, whatever the cost."

He sneered, drawing in a long breath through his nose. "Don't flatter yourself, madam. It's your farm I want, not your skinny body. Quite frankly, I could find a better woman than you in the Truro brothels."

Finally, but too late, they had come to the real reason for her presence in the manor. She stiffened, knowing she could so easily lose everything at this point. Determination; she needed determination. A determination not to give in easily.

"My farm is all I have left. If I lose that, I have nowhere to go, nowhere to live."

"That's your problem, madam. I'll give you fifty guineas and I'll let you go free provided you leave Cornwall. I don't want you wandering about homeless on me land or anywhere near it." At her gasp, he added: "It's me last offer. All you have to do is sign over the farm. Now, Miss Lanyon, what is your answer? Now!" He slammed the table top with a palm and Wenna started.

"For fifty guineas?" It was a pittance. Far less than she had intended to ask. Less than one year's rental paid by Killiow's tenant farmers. "But that's robbery!"

He turned a gruesome stare at her. "You think you can do better by staying? You think you can make the farm pay?" He shook his head. "I know about your barn roof falling in and I've witnesses who'll swear before a magistrate they've seen Pengorse on your farm. I could have you locked up in Bodmin gaol this very day. Take the money, madam, and let's be done with this damnable business."

Wenna's mind swirled. Killiow's threat was very real. For all her intention to bargain, she had little choice but to agree to Killiow's terms.

She had but one final card to play before she would finally give in to his offer. "What about Tregover Farm, are you going to ..." Her voice faltered. "Are you going to take Mister Vanson's land also?"

"The American?" Killiow snorted. "He'll not last long; he doesn't know the way we work. That farm won't pay its way under him any more than it did under his grandfather. And when he finally goes bankrupt, I'll buy Tregover at an even lower price. I don't need to lay hands on him."

"Would you swear to that?"

"What do you mean?"

"If I sell you my land on your terms, would you give me your word that you will not try to take Tregover Farm for as long as Mister Vanson lives on that land?"

"Would it persuade you to sell?"

She gritted her teeth. "It might."

He grinned and waved a hand at her, dismissing the matter. "I'll give you me word, Miss Lanyon. I'll not put pressure on him to sell. And you can rely upon it."

"You'll not put pressure on him?" she choked out against a raw dryness in her throat.

"That's what I said." He turned towards the door. "Pengwidden!"

The coarse henchman shuffled in. "Sur."

"Get a dress from one of the serving maids and give it to the Lanyon woman. She looks like a whore with her own dress torn."

"'Ess, sur." Pengwidden hurried off to do his bidding.

Wenna turned away so that Killiow would not see her look of dejection. In his moment of triumph, she would not give him that satisfaction.

"Now, to the sale of the farm." He pushed back his seat and crossed the room to a sideboard. "I had a contract drawn up by Tapper some time ago. Thought you'd come to your senses sooner. You can sign it now, and I'll get Tapper to fill in the niceties later."

Wenna crossed the room, her head hung low. While she glanced over the first page of the contract, Killiow sneered: "Don't take too long at it. And don't concern yourself about the empty spaces. They'll be filled in later."

Her hand shook as she turned the first page aside. Much of the second page was blank. How could he get away with this?

"It'll look legal enough by the time Tapper finishes with it." Killiow pushed a pen into her hand and stabbed a podgy finger at the bottom of the page. "Sign here."

Wenna took the pen and held it over the paper. Was there no other way out of this?

"Sign it, woman!"

Wenna flinched at his threatening tone. She could find no other way. She barely shook her head at losing her entire inheritance as she signed the document. It was her final defeat. She turned around, totally dejected, and saw Pengwidden with a coarse calico dress draped across one arm.

He handed it to her, his gaze lowered towards the floor. "It belonged to young Jenny Tinder. Reckon as how it won't fit her much longer now that she be havin' a babby."

Wenna took the garment silently and backed away towards the door.

"I want you away from here, woman. Away from Cornwall so that

I never have to see your face again. And put on that servant's dress before you leave. I'll not have you walking out of here with your scrawny tits showing through."

Wenna paused with her back to him. "Then provide a place for me to change my clothes, if you please."

"Hell, no! Put on that other dress now or, by God, I'll do it for you."

Wenna sighed, casting aside the last of her dwindling measure of self-respect. Keeping her back to Killiow, she removed her own torn clothes and changed into Jenny Tinder's coarse garment. It fitted tightly because Jenny was a more slightly built girl, but it covered her with some small decency.

"May I leave now?" she asked, her back still to Ralph Killiow.

"Get out of me house and get out of Cornwall." Killiow grunted with satisfaction, and Wenna heard the cutlery being picked up. Killiow had already dismissed her, returning his attention to his breakfast. She shuffled from the room.

"Don't ever let me find you again inside the county boundaries." Killiow's last warning echoed in her mind as she hurried down the long, cold passage.

"Miss Lanyon! Is that you? Stop! Wait there, Miss Lanyon. I can't run after you." A female voice called out from behind her. She stumbled to a stop and turned slowly. Beth Killiow was hobbling out from the library, one hand firmly resting on a walking stick. "How nice to ... My God! What's happened to your face? There's bruising around your eye!"

"A little mishap." Wenna averted her gaze. She stood to one side, her face in shadow.

"What sort?" Beth asked in a caring but firm voice.

Wenna ignored the question and changed the subject. "I see your ankle is still paining you, Miss Killiow."

"Oh, tush." Beth waved her free hand. "It's easier today. I fell yesterday while I was out walking with Mister Vanson, that beautiful American gentleman. He carried me home in his arms."

A shudder ran through Wenna's body. She had assumed that Christopher had completed some business with Killiow as he'd rode away from the manor the day before. What was he doing out walking with Beth Killiow? Her already black depression sank even deeper.

"Now, Miss Lanyon, tell me what happened to you. My God, what a mess your face is! Who did this to you?"

"'Tes best you don't ask."

Beth drew back, realization evident on her face. "I came out to investigate Ralph's shouting. It was directed at you wasn't it? My God! He got into one of his drunken bouts and he hit you! Didn't he?"

Wenna brushed at her damp eyes. "My quarrel is with him, Miss Killiow, not with you. Please don't involve yourself on my account."

"Miss Lanyon … Wenna." Beth's hand reached out and touched her arm. "I had intended that we would become friends. If my brother has harmed you, it is most certainly my business. I'll speak to him on it."

Wenna gasped. "Please don't. I must be away from here." She shook herself loose from the solitary spot on the cold passage floor and walked away with as much residual composure as she could muster. She had lost everything: her decency, her farm and even the potential close friendship of Christopher Vanson. Her only option now was to leave Penmarith as quickly as possible.

Nine

An uneven rapping noise rattled around inside his head, someone or something banging against solid wood. Kit yawned, stretching his arms. He blinked, scanned his surroundings then shook his head. He had fallen asleep in a wooden chair in front of a Cornish range that had gone out. He was cold and in someone else's kitchen, someone else's home.

Dull, frosty daylight peered at him through a small window in the opposite wall from where he sat, barely lighting up the big kitchen. He stretched out a leg and a sharp cramp shot up through the calf muscle. As full consciousness came flooding back, he remembered why he was here at Crabtree Copse Farm – waiting for Wenna's return. He had searched the village without success and this was his last hope of finding her. Surely she would return to her own home?

The rapping noise continued.

"Who the hell is that?" he called out, rolling his shoulders to bring back life to his stiff muscles.

The rapping ceased and voices echoed beyond the door in the narrow passageway that ran through the house. The kitchen door swung back, and Jimmy Rudge edged into the room, pulling a thin, pasty-faced girl tightly wrapped in a heavy shawl. Her gaze darted about the kitchen, as if afraid.

"Are ee awake now, sur?"

"Reckon I must be." Kit wiped his eyes, shook his head and blinked again. Sudden realisation set in: *Wenna had been missing all night!* He jumped to his feet and grabbed at Jimmy's arm. "Your mistress; you haven't seen her?"

"No, sur." The boy drew back, placing the girl behind him.

"Your mistress didn't return from the manor!"

"Nothing I could do to stop her goin' there," he protested. "Jenny has somethin' to tell ee, sur. About the mistress."

"Jenny?" Kit pushed past Jimmy to better see the girl hiding at his back.

Jimmy gently coaxed her forward. "This be Jenny Tinder, sur. She and I be goin' to wed."

Kit studied the girl. She had a gaunt, unhealthy look about her, eyes large and staring, as if perpetually begging for something she could never have. She worked her mouth nervously, pursing her lips and then relaxing them. A perfect match for Jimmy Rudge, he guessed.

"You know something about Miss Lanyon, Jenny?" Kit fought a rising feeling of dread in his heart.

The boy prodded his future wife. "Tell him, Jenny. 'Tes all right, ee won't hurt ee."

The girl composed herself by clasping her hands in front of her chest and coughed. "'Twas like this, sur. I heard as how Miss Lanyon was at the manor last night. Things like that do quickly get 'round the house amongst the servants. We was all a bit worried 'cos the master were in a real bad mood, like. But 'twere the screamin' what really upset us most."

"Screaming?" Kit felt the colour drain from his face and a muscle in his jaw ticked. "She was there all night?" Dear God, don't let this be true.

"Yes, sur. Mister Killiow had Miss Lanyon locked in one of the top floor rooms, right next to his own. Then later ee went to her. When ee was real drunk."

Kit closed his eyes. The damned curse. He prayed silently until he felt sane enough to speak. "What happened then, Jenny?" He coaxed her with a pained expression.

The stark look of fear across the girl's face eased somewhat. "We heard this terrible scream. Then a loud crash. Reckon ee must have been doin' somethin' ... somethin' real bad to her. You know what ee's like, sur."

Kit slumped in the nearest chair. "Yes, I know what he's like." He cast a hopeful glance at her. "Did no one try to stop it?"

"Stop it?" Jenny shook her head vehemently. "You don't do anything to stop Mister Killiow, sur. Not if you wants to keep yer job." She backed away towards the door while staring into his eyes.

"Mister Vanson? You understand don't you?" At Kit's silence, she added: "Reckon I'd better be goin', sur. I knew I ought to tell someone here about it, but I has to get back again before they find out I'm gone."

Jimmy folded his arm protectively round the girl's shoulders. "Jenny wants to leave the manor, sur. When we get wed. At first, Miss Lanyon said Jenny could come an' live here, but now the mistress says we has to find somewhere else." He looked pleadingly at Kit. "Will there be any work at Tregover Farm, sur. We'd both work hard for ee."

Kit sighed. He had failed Wenna when she needed him most, just as he had failed his father's slaves. It was that damned curse all over again. Wearily, he forced a false tone of composure into his voice. "Will it mean real trouble if you're found out?"

"Might get beaten, sur. But I don't like it there anyway. T'will be all right just so long as the master don't find out."

"Don't let him beat ee, Jenny." Jimmy cut in, squeezing her tight against himself. "Mustn't let him beat ee in your condition."

Her condition? Kit studied the girl more closely. If she was pregnant, it was yet to become obvious. "Are you with child, Jenny?"

She nodded.

Kit filled his lungs with a strengthening breath. "Killiow ain't going to beat Jenny in her condition, Jimmy, you can count on that."

The boy dropped his gaze to the floor. "Thing is, sur, we ain't exactly sure about when we'll get wed. Don't have nowhere to live yet."

"Well, Jimmy Rudge ..." Kit shook his head at the young couple's situation while still struggling to come to terms with Wenna's fate. At least he could do something to protect Jenny Tinder. He put a hand to the boy's shoulder. "With Jenny pregnant, it sure looks like you're good at something."

"'Ess, sur." The boy raised a ragged smile.

"What was your work at the manor, Jenny?"

"Kitchen maid, sur."

Kit swung round to Jimmy. "Take her over to Tregover, boy, and tell Jacob Padder I sent you. You can both work for me, if that's what you want. Tell Jacob to sort out some place for you both to sleep."

Jimmy's eyes lit up. "Thank ee, sur. Oh, thank ee very much, sur."

Kit then turned back to face the girl. "Can you cook, Jenny?"

"Oh 'ess, sur. I bin workin' in the kitchen at the manor since I were twelve." For one so young and so painfully thin, she had a strangely haunting smile that spread directly from her big, round eyes.

"Good. Tell Padder you're the new cook."

She beamed back at him. "Thank ee, sur. I'll do me best for ee."

"Jimmy?"

"'Ess, sur?"

"Keep your pants on, boy! Save your strength for working my land."

Jimmy nodded awkwardly, and Jenny blushed as they both edged to the kitchen doorway.

Kit pulled on his leather boots. Hunger rattled in his stomach, but he had no time to eat. If Killiow had ... Dear God, was there no limit to what he might have done? Damn the man.

"You goin' to see Mister Killiow, sur?" Jimmy asked from the open doorway.

Despite his fears and brewing anger, Kit kept his voice calm. "Guess so. I have to find out what happened to Miss Lanyon."

"Shall I come with ee, sur?"

"Not this time, Jimmy." He shot the boy a grim look. What could such a puny lad achieve against the weight and political power of Ralph Killiow? "Reckon you've done enough for your mistress already. Saddle me a horse and then be on your way."

The air hovered bitingly cold over the farmyard. Languid grey clouds drifted across a mottled grey and blue sky. Jimmy's breath condensed into streaming puffs as he led a horse from the stable.

Kit rubbed his hands together. "Is it always like this in winter?"

"No, sur. We don't normally get snow like this." The boy handed him the reins. "Don't normally get snow at all. They say in the village that 'tes God's punishment on us fer all the smugglin' that goes on along these here coasts."

"Smuggling?" Kit shook his head. "You certainly do lead interesting lives." He mounted the horse and set off at a canter along the narrow lane.

Confusion set in as he rode away from Crabtree Copse towards

Penmarith. Yesterday Beth Killiow had flirted with him at the manor and it had tickled his ego. Then guilt hit at him hard once again. In all probability, Beth's brother had later abducted Wenna in that same place. What were Beth's motives? She was, after all, a spawn of the Killiow line.

Having failed to find Wenna in the village yesterday, he had returned to Crabtree Copse in the vain hope she would be already there. He had spent a restless evening waiting for her, wondering what she had been doing at Studmore Manor, trying to tell himself her life was not his concern.

Not his concern.

Just as the slaves on his father's plantation were not his concern. Just as Clem's behaviour was not his concern. Dammit. His feelings towards Wenna had deepened over the past two days, and her troubles were *very much* his concern.

Suppose Wenna had been attacked by Killiow? In one brief flash of anger, the Vanson curse raised its ugly head. If she had been raped, could he have been responsible? Could his interest in the young woman have been the cause of her downfall – all because of the curse Pa had brought upon them?

He rode into Penmarith village, and shielding his eyes, he peered towards a flurry of activity at the far side of the frozen duck pond, outside the Cross Keys Inn. The snow-splattered coach from Lostwithiel stood at the front entrance. The driver led one team of steaming horses away while an ostler backed a fresh team of four into position. Passengers, heavily wrapped against the chill air, stamped their feet in the muddy slush.

Kit scanned around the rest of the village, taking in the bleakness of the shuttered schoolhouse, the heavy pillar of smoke rising from the rectory chimney, the glow of the foundry fire inside the smithy's wooden barn. A sudden shudder raked his frame when he spotted a lone figure walking hurriedly across the village green, towards the inn. Even at a distance, he recognised Wenna's distinctive way of walking.

Thank God he had found her.

He called out to her, but she walked on as if her ears were deaf to the world. He coaxed his horse into a trot until he was close enough to call to her again.

"Wenna!" He jumped to the ground.

This time she stopped and turned to him, her manner immediately cold. "What are you doing here, Christopher?"

"Your face!" he gasped. Heavy bruises and bloody scars disfigured her cheeks. He grabbed her by the shoulders. "Oh, Wenna! What happened to you? Did Killiow do that?" Horror swept through him, bringing a rush of warm blood to his face.

She brought a hand up against one cheek, hiding the bruising and averting her eyes. "'Tes of no consequence now. I'm very sorry, Christopher, but I cannot talk to you. I must go. I'm leaving on the coach."

Anger erupted deep inside and spilled out in his raised voice. "Tell me first what happened at the manor. Why did you go there without talking to me first?"

"That's my business!"

He breathed deeply and calmed his tone. "Wenna, I'm sorry. I didn't mean to raise my voice. I'm very concerned."

"I have to be on that coach, Christopher. I can't stay to talk to you."

"Can't stay? But why? What's happened?"

Her voice turned tight and snappy. "Whatever has happened, whatever I've done, it's none of your business. So leave me alone, Mister Vanson." She turned on her heel and hurried towards the coach.

Kit stood frozen to the spot, stunned by the outburst. Was this the same Wenna Lanyon who had gently tended to his injuries? He shook himself alive, ran after her and grasped at her arm, pulling her up with a jerk. "Please, Wenna, tell me what happened. What did Killiow do to you? Tell me! For God's sake, woman, I care about you."

"I told you to leave me alone." She swung her face violently away from him. "Leave me be. You know nothing of our ways so don't get involved."

"But I *am* involved, damn you!"

Waiting passengers turned towards them, faces frowning at the confrontation. Kit bit anxiously at his lip. If only he better understood the English character.

He released his grip. "Goddammit, Wenna. At least tell me where you're going," he said with a hushed urgency.

She settled her gaze back onto him. "I'm simply going away. I'm leaving the area. For good. So don't try to follow me."

"Because your barn roof caved in, or because of Killiow? For heaven's sake, talk to me. Tell me what's going on."

She let out a long sigh. "It's all got out of hand, Christopher. I've lost all my winter feed, it's true, but there's more to it than that." Her sad, distant eyes met his. "Pastor Pengorse was hiding out in that barn and one of Killiow's men saw him walk away from my land. Killiow has threatened to use his witness against me and anyone who tries to help me. The magistrate will say I was harbouring a wanted man. They could send me to gaol."

"Gaol? No, not you!"

She nodded, and her face suddenly lost its firm set, crumpling into tears. He threw out his hands to hold her, but she roughly pushed him away. Dampness trickled down her cheeks, scouring trails from her liquid eyes.

"Ralph Killiow would see to it and don't you believe otherwise," she mumbled behind the tears. "I can't take any more risks here. I've sold up and now I'm leaving." She jabbed the heel of one hand at her face, dragging it down her cheek.

"Sold?" Kit fought to control his anger, hissing through tightly clamped teeth. "You sold your farm to Killiow?"

She glanced back at him, just a brief look but enough to betray her naked fear. "'Twas the only way."

He snorted loudly. "You mean you gave in. After all you told me about standing firm, you gave in to him?" Kit rocked on his heels. If only he had been able to stop her from going to Killiow. "He must have attacked you, forced you to sell. Is that it?"

She set one palm flat against his chest and spoke in a soft, husky voice. "I really liked you, Christopher. But now you must make your friendships elsewhere. With people like Beth Killiow."

"Beth?" His mouth hung open. "Why Beth Killiow?"

"It'll help you to be a friend of the Killiow family. You and I must never meet again. It would go badly for you with Ralph Killiow, if we were ever seen together."

"This is just plain nonsense. I can handle Ralph Killiow without help from his sister. And I'll be seen with whoever I choose."

"Get aboard if you're coming." The coach driver's hollow voice called to the passengers.

Kit darted a quick glance at the coach and then sought Wenna's hands. "I'm begging you not to go. Believe me, I can handle this."

"Can you?" Wenna asked, her shoulders sloping in dejection. She pulled her hands free. "I'm leaving, Mister Vanson. There's nothing you can do to stop me. It's all over." Clasping her bodice tight against her chest, she turned and headed towards the coach.

"Don't go, Wenna. Let me give you a ride back to the farm." He called out to her, but she didn't respond, and Kit was certain she had turned a deaf ear to him. He tried again to reason with her. "We can talk. You take the horse and I'll walk."

She continued directly towards the coach, silent and unmoved.

"Wenna?" He hurried after her and shuffled into step with her. "I won't let you go."

"Don't be silly, Mister Vanson," she cast him a quick glance, "you don't own me and you can't stop me. Go back to your own farm. Now, please leave me alone." Then she broke into a run, her feet kicking up the powdered snow.

Kit slowed then hung back. That same empty feeling from seeing the abuse of slaves on his father's plantation overcame him. The feeling he experienced when he backed away from the problem instead of doing something about it. He stared at Wenna's back, and for just the briefest moment, her worn coat became the mutilated skin of a coloured slave. He shuddered, remembering the whimpering young woman lying face-down on her bed in her tiny hovel. More anger surged inside him, threatening to consume him entirely. He had to fight it.

The fresh team of horses was in position, pawing at the ground and snorting, steam rising from their hot flesh. The coachman pulled himself onto his perch and took the reins. He cast a glance around the village, bellowing: "Anyone else wantin' to get aboard?" He paused, then added: "We be ready to leave."

Wenna was last to board, a vulnerable figure clambering into the coach without a backward glance. Kit expelled a sudden burst of breath.

He had to stop her.

He bounded forward. But the coach was pulling away, the team of four straining to cut a path through the slush and snow. He ran beside it, shouting her name. She slouched by the window seat and looked the other way. "Wenna, wait!" But she only shunned him.

He stopped and kicked angrily at the thick snow, sending up a cloud of white. Then he ran back to his horse and heaved himself onto it. Still shouting her name, he pushed his horse until he was alongside the coach again, bouncing wildly in the saddle. Bereft of all reason, he released the reins to wave both arms while crying out to her. But his words had no effect.

He had failed her.

He followed alongside the coach until it reached the St Austell road, where it slowed to take the sharp bend. At that point, Wenna leaned against the window and waved him away, a wild angry look in her face. Such a look would haunt him for many a night. It was all over; he had lost her. Sadly, angrily, he reined in.

Killiow would pay for this! The bastard! He sat astride the horse for a while, his emotions bubbling inside. To control his racing heartbeat, he breathed deeply, but still it thumped fast and loud beneath his jerkin. Finally, he turned his mount and set off along the road towards Studmore Manor.

At the manor gate he cantered past the two guards, ignoring their shouts for him to give way. He was almost at the front door when he jumped from the saddle and rushed inside the house before the two men could stop him.

He was making his way down the long corridor when a servant approached. Kit stabbed a hand at him. "Where's Ralph Killiow?"

The man thrust back his shoulders beneath his tawdry uniform and eyed him frostily. "I beg your pardon, sur?"

"Ralph Killiow," Kit bellowed. "Where is he? Tell me, man!"

"Who shall I say wants him, sur?"

"Don't bother, just tell me where he is." At the man's silence, he thundered on down the hall.

Behind him, the front door burst open, and one guard cried out: "Stop him!" Kit turned to see two henchmen armed with wooden cudgels, bounding along the corridor after him.

He pushed past another servant who had rushed into the corridor and ran towards the only open door at the far end. He found himself in the kitchen and recognised the buxom cook, Mrs Trevose, standing at the sink. He slammed the door shut behind him and turned the key in the lock.

The cook turned around, her eyes wide with alarm. "What's the meaning of this?"

It had been a mistake to come here alone, a stupid mistake born out of uncontrolled anger. Kit ignored her and ran fast across the room to the rear door and ripped it open. With cold air breezing into his face, he plunged out to draw up sharply in the next moment.

"Christopher Vanson, why I do declare!" Beth Killiow stood at the edge of the snow-covered lawn, leaning heavily on a walking stick. She smiled at him, but her expression turned quickly to one of puzzlement.

He looked to his right then his left, sudden indecision hitting him hard in the stomach. Should he continue his flight, or enlist the help of Killiow's sister? He startled at a splintering crash behind him. The two thugs had smashed open the locked door and now blundered through the kitchen.

He took a hasty step closer to Beth. "I'm sorry about this, ma'am. Can I talk to you?"

"Of course." As the two henchmen emerged from the house, her face turned to cold anger.

"Hey, you!" one man shouted at Kit then stopped abruptly at the threatening glare from Beth. The other man pulled up sharply, bumping into the first.

"I guess I ain't exactly welcome here." Kit smiled at Beth, nudging up beside her. Would she now help him or throw him to the wolves? He held his breath, waiting, hoping.

She took a moment to consider the conflict and then raised a stern finger towards the two men. "How dare you burst around my home like this? Leave us alone." Her tone was one of authority, a mistress exercising firm control over minions.

The men hesitated, eyed one another and reluctantly turned away. Kit released his pent-up breath in one low, long sigh.

She linked her arm through his and leaned heavily upon him as she led him on across the lawn. "Now tell me what this is all about."

"Did you know Miss Lanyon spent the night here?"

"I saw her this morning." She froze, a confused expression spreading across her face. "I didn't know she was here all night."

"Your brother kept her prisoner here."

"The devil, he did!"

"It's true enough." He studied her face. Throwing aside caution, he related all he had learned from Jenny Tinder. When he had finished, Beth remained silent for some time.

"It all fits. I saw Wenna last night and again this morning. I didn't realise ... How stupid of me. She was hurt and I guessed Ralph must have hit her. But to keep her here ... He's a very difficult man."

"You can say that again."

"Christopher ..." Beth paused as if considering her response. "Thank you for telling me this. Trust me and let me see what I can do about it."

Caution crept into his mind. Could he trust her? "Is there *anything* you can do?" He studied her face to get the full impact of her response.

"Maybe."

She led him back into the kitchen where the two thugs stood in anticipation. She drew back her chin at the sight of them. "Anyone who stops Mister Vanson from freely entering or leaving this house will answer to me." Then she took his hand in hers. "Goodbye, Christopher, and thank you for coming to talk to me."

Kit judged it prudent not to disabuse her assumption on his reason for calling. It was enough that he would get out of the building in a fit state to tackle Ralph Killiow at another opportunity. He mounted his horse at the front door and left Studmore Manor under the frustrated gaze of the two thugs. Neither man approached him, but one silently tapped his cudgel against his leg, in warning.

Frustrated at failing to confront the squire's son, Kit set his mind to solving another problem. Instead of going straight home to Tregover, he cut across country from the village until he reached the five-acre field from where he could see the roof of his old barn. The late morning air was piercingly cold and the light shimmered on the snow. He drew back on his horse's reins as he came in sight of the barn. Just as before, a flimsy trail of smoke billowed away on the cold breeze.

"Pastor Pengorse," Kit called out as he dismounted in front of the barn. One of the tall doors opened and the preacher peered out.

"Come in out of the cold, Mister Vanson."

Kit went in. A small fire crackled just inside the door, the smoke whipped away by the wind to disappear fast into the frosty air. Across the other side of the barn, a small bundle of bedding lay against one wall with an open bible atop it.

"You look cold, my dear sir." The pastor bent over the fire. "Let me offer you a taste of hot tea."

"Don't intend to stay. Fact is I'm here to tell you to go."

"Go?"

"Yes. Killiow's men saw you leaving Crabtree Copse Farm, and it's caused a whole lotta trouble for Miss Lanyon. Now she's gone from the village. Forced to go. And she's sold her land to Ralph Killiow."

The preacher frowned, chewing at his lower lip. "I'm sorry to hear that."

"You better be, pastor." Kit gritted his teeth. "'Cos I want you to leave here before you cause any more trouble."

Pengorse spread his hands wide. "But I only aim to do God's work. I preach his word and look to all men to act in the way of his teachings. Can't you see that?"

"Sure, but I guess God's asking you to figure it out some other way 'cos your way sure ain't working. Be off this land by tomorrow, pastor."

"May God forgive you, young man."

"I sure hope he does." Kit retreated outside, the pastor's piercing gaze burrowing into him. Was he doing the right thing? And what sort of mess had he landed himself into when he took on this damned Cornish farm? Things had been so much more clear-cut when he was at sea. Maybe he ought to go back to it.

Tired and dejected, he rode slowly back to Tregover. He threw off his coat and dropped into a seat in the parlour where a warm fire crackled in the grate. He removed his boots and twisted his toes in the heat, praying Wenna would find a comfortable place this night.

Jacob Padder came into the room, touching his forelock. "Them two young people came, sur."

Weariness washed over him and he yawned. "Good, Jacob. They'll be safer if they stay here in the main farmhouse until we sort out this business with Ralph Killiow."

"Beggin' yer pardon, sur, I reckon as how ye're right. I done as ee said and got them settled. There's an attic room where the dairymaids used to sleep back in yer gran'father's day. I thought as how the young woman could sleep up there. So I took the liberty of suggestin' she might go up an' tidy the place a bit. As fer Jimmy Rudge, ee can sleep in with me fer the time bein'."

"Good thinking, Jacob. Where's Jimmy now?"

"Dunno, sur." The old man scratched his chin. "P'raps ee's with the young woman."

Kit heaved himself out of his seat. "I need to talk to him." He climbed the bare wooden stairs to the attic, weary after his exertions. He pursed his lips at the sound of voices and movement inside the attic bedroom. Suspicions filled his mind as he reached the door, and he adopted a severe frown before walking in. Barely inside the room, he stopped dead in his tracks.

Two naked bodies writhed on top of a cot beneath a south-facing window. In plain sight were Jimmy Rudge's bare buttocks pounding up and down in time to his gasping grunts.

Kit coughed. If he wasn't so tired and so worried about Wenna, he'd laugh hysterically.

The two figures stopped their conjugal movements and both turned to face him, aghast. The girl flushed and clasped a hand across her face, leaving the rest of her slender body exposed. Jimmy remained mounted on top of the girl, seemingly unsure what to do next.

He worked up a guilty grin. "Oh. Sorry, Mister Vanson, sur."

"Jimmy." Kit crossed the small room with one giant step. He sat down on the end of the bed and weighed his words carefully. "I'm sure you're aware that I need about a dozen workers on this farm. But I really can't wait for you to father every single one of them." The girl giggled.

"Sorry, sur," the boy repeated, but he remained locked between the girl's thin thighs, awkward and crestfallen.

Kit rose and folded his arms across his chest. "I'm a God-fearing man, Jimmy, and I don't intend to see you taking advantage of Jenny. Put your pants on and take her to see the vicar of the church in Penmarith. As soon as you come back, you can tell me when you'll be wed. Is that clear?"

"'Ess, sur." When Jimmy saw that Kit wasn't leaving the room, he lowered his gaze. "Now, sur?"

"*Now!* Where do your folks live, Jenny?"

Her fingernail coyly tucked between her lips, she replied: "In the village, sur. Near the inn."

"Okay, both of you. On your way back from the church, you just call and tell them about the wedding. And you be sure to tell them that I'll be letting you live here. Maybe one day I'll give you the use of one of the old farm cottages – once we've sorted things out with Mister Killiow."

"Really? Thank ee, sur." Jimmy flashed him a grateful smile and rolled to one side preparing to rise, but still covering Jenny's nakedness.

Jenny beamed at Kit. "'Tes awfully kind of ee, sur." Her face still brightly flushed, she sat up covering her breasts by coaxing her long hair over them and forcing Jimmy off the bed.

Kit sighed. "Jenny, for heaven's sake, hurry up and put your drawers on."

Ten

Beth Killiow feathered her fingertips on the squire's cold hands. They felt like death. His skin, a pale parchment colour, hung from his face in loose folds, disquieting her. "Father, can you hear me?"

She sat on the edge of his bed, pangs of conscience pulsating through her thoughts. Should she spare her father the pain of further suffering, or was her duty to the local community more important? But for her father's failing health, she would have spoken up long ago of her brother's foolishness with women.

Jolyon Killiow lay prone against his pillow, raspy breaths gurgling from his open mouth. Beth warmed his clawed, venous hands between her palms. His weak heart would not hold out much longer. With each passing day, he sloughed off more muscle control, more coherent thought, more will to live. His demise would bring no tears of sorrow to her brother's eyes, of that she was certain. Only then would Ralph inherit Studmore Manor and the title of squire.

The old man's eyes flicked suddenly wide open and he smiled. "Beth, my child, 'tis damn cold in here."

Beth cast a glance at the roaring fire burning in the grate. She rewrapped the shawl tightly about his shoulders, but her father still shivered. He tugged at the loose sleeves of his nightshirt and pulled down his woollen cap. It still seemed a meagre compensation against his failing heart.

"I'll get Mrs Trevose to prepare a bowl of broth for you," she replied in hushed tones. "You must have something hot inside you to keep this damnable weather at bay."

"You can be a good girl when you put your mind to it." He patted her hand and the skin of his palm reminded her of old, worn leather. "You take the trouble to care for me. Not like Ralph." His voice turned surly. "Hardly see the boy these days."

That was her opening, her opportunity to broach the subject weighing so heavily on her mind. "It's Ralph I want to talk about, father. There's been some trouble."

"Trouble?" Failing eyes glistened as Jolyon Killiow struggled to sit upright.

"Lie back, father." Beth leaned forward, rucked his pillow and gently pressed him back against it. She nodded sombrely. "There's been trouble, and I must tell you about it. I hope this doesn't upset you too much. Ralph kept a local woman locked up here overnight. Wenna Lanyon of –"

"Lanyon? You mean George Lanyon's girl?"

Beth drew a deep breath and nodded vigorously. "According to the servants, Ralph got himself into a drunken stupor. He locked her in a bedroom on the third floor and …" She bit at her lower lip. "He may have raped her."

"The devil, he did!" The old man's twisted fingers grasped at her wrist, his nails digging into her skin. He squirmed again, pushing aside his daughter's hands as he sought to get upright.

Once again Beth gently coaxed him back against his pillow. He complied begrudgingly. "It's not the first time we've had this sort of trouble. There's been talk in the village. Some say he was also involved in George Lanyon's killing. And you remember that business last spring when one of the kitchen girls was with child. They claimed it was all Ralph's doing. He's no good, father."

"The devil take him," the old Squire hissed between well-gapped teeth. He drew back his thick lips and the family resemblance became clear to Beth. "That damned boy will be the ruination of us. Should have drowned the scoundrel at birth!"

"There are less drastic measures." Beth ran her fingers lightly down the length of one of his hand. "You could put some sort of pressure on him to change his ways. Can you not discuss it with Tapper, seek his advice?"

Her father shook his head. "Rogues like Ralph don't change their ways." He stared across the room at the mullioned window overlooking the drive. "You didn't hear anything last night, did you? You didn't hear all this happening?"

"No, father, but you and I wouldn't hear anything anyway, living here in this wing. The servants over in the west wing heard the woman screaming, so they say. And this morning I came across Wenna Lanyon in the main hallway. She had heavy bruising about her face, as if she'd been beaten. I don't think there's much doubt about it."

The squire slumped against the pillow. "No, there wouldn't be much doubt, would there? We've both known for a long time Ralph was no good. A bad apple. I hoped he would grow out of it, but I had me doubts he ever would."

"Bad apples only get more diseased with time, father."

"An apt observation, girl." The old man grimaced and wrapped his crippled fingers about hers. "You're right, of course, you usually are. Best you send for Tapper. I may have to disinherit the boy. Truth is, sad to say it, but the matter's long been in the back of me mind. I should have acted before now. Can't have the name of Killiow going down in history as the name of a tyrant, can we?"

Beth began to worry; she hadn't anticipated such a drastic response. "If you disinherit him, the Killiow family will cease to be associated with Studmore. Is that what you want? Do you intend to sell the manor?"

The old man beckoned her closer. "There's still time for you to find yourself a husband, a decent man who'll take over as squire. Someone I can trust, not like that gambling fellow you were so keen on a year or so back. What do you say to that?"

She flushed. Her father had touched on a difficult subject. The gambling fellow had filled a period of her life she had enjoyed to the utmost. It was also a time for which she harboured reluctant regrets. Shame walked hand in hand with her enjoyment of sultry nights in bed with that loveable rogue. Where would she find a decent man in these parts, unless she set her cap to the likes of Christopher Vanson?

"I'll ask Tapper to come and see you, and you can talk to him about Ralph. Maybe find another way to handle him?"

The old man coughed then leaned over towards a nearby pot and spat out the phlegm that bubbled in his throat. "Talk to him yourself, Beth. Explain it all to him, though I'm sure Tapper knows most of it already. These people usually do. I'll speak to him when we're ready to do something."

"All right, father." She pulled the counterpane over his chest indicating she was about to leave. "If the weather is no worse, I'll ride into St Austell and call at his office tomorrow morning."

The old man settled against his pillow. "It's a good job I have you, Beth. Need you to handle things now that I'm on me last legs."

"Tush, father. You'll be up on your feet again when the spring comes. You just see if I'm right."

He lowered his eyelids. "Maybe. Maybe not. But I thank you for the kind thought. Always had a soft spot for you, Beth. Wish you'd not turned out so self-willed, but there, can't have everything the way we want it, can we?"

She pushed aside a solitary white hair dangling over his forehead. How much longer could his heart stand the cold and the strain of life at Studmore Manor? "I am what you moulded me into, father. You and mother, God rest her soul."

"Nonsense. You are what you always wanted to be." He paused to gather his breath. "At your age, a girl should be wed. You would be too but for your foolish liaison with that gambling fellow. Sir Harry's son would have taken you, if you hadn't disgraced yourself with the gambler." He sighed deeply, the breath now hollow inside damaged lungs. "Why did you do it, Beth?" His eyes begged for an answer. "Why did you behave like a common whore? Even the servants knew the damned fellow had bedded you."

"That's unfair, father." Beth pouted, stung by the sharp edge to his words. "I am what I am, and if that's not good enough for Sir Harry's son, then the devil take him. Didn't like the fellow anyway. His eyes were set too close together."

"Hah! It's not his eyes you should have been thinking of." The squire laughed though no smile crossed his face. "That family has money and breeding, and that's what counts."

The family boasted money and breeding for the having, that was true, but Sir Harry Philimore's witless son would never have measured up to her ideals as a husband. No, never. Not after she had tasted the reckless lovemaking of the gambler.

"I'll choose my own husband when the right time comes, father."

"You're too strong-willed by far. You should have been the eldest son, Beth. With that strong will of yours, you'd have made a good squire."

"Rest, father." She winced as she rose to her feet. She had dispensed with her stick, but walking was still painful. She hobbled down to the kitchen and fetched him some hot broth. When she returned to her father's room, he was fast asleep so she quietly placed the bowl onto his bedside table and crept away.

She returned to the kitchen where the aroma of freshly chopped vegetables greeted her. Mrs Trevose stood hunched over the big, well-scrubbed table, her attention now on kneading bread dough. At Beth's noisy entrance, Mrs Trevose raised a glance at her.

"I didn't see a sign of Jenny Tinder, Mrs Trevose. Has she not come back from wherever she went?"

The cook wiped the sweat off her forehead with the back of one hand. "No, my lady. I think we may have seen the last of her."

"Really? Are you sure?" Beth reached for the table and steadied herself. "Have you any idea where she might have gone?"

"Reckon so. If you don't mind me speakin' plainly, my lady." Mrs Trevose straightened her back and wiped her hands on her apron with a terse, deliberate movement. "Rumours say young Jenny is in a family condition. And 'tes said that Jimmy Rudge is responsible. He now works up at Crabtree Copse Farm with Mistress Lanyon. Like as not, you'll find Jenny there."

"I see. Thank you, Mrs Trevose." Beth averted her gaze. The rumours had reached her ears also but floundered in her dilemma. She was concerned about all the female staff, including Jenny Tinder, but this was no time to bring up the subject of Wenna Lanyon in the Studmore kitchen.

An hour later, she hobbled across to the oak-lined dining room where Binner, his eyes focussed straight ahead, stood at the ready to serve. "Lunch is ready, ma'am."

"You may serve me now, Binner." Beth took her seat. "My brother will eat when he's ready."

"Yes, ma'am." Binner brought the serving dishes, one by one, from the sideboard and waited while she transferred the food to her plate.

She started to eat and stopped abruptly as the front door burst open and Ralph's voice bellowed through the house. Beth felt her senses tingle; she hadn't seen her brother since Christopher Vanson's visit and had no idea where he'd spent his morning.

He ambled slowly and unsteadily into the dining room as she studied him intently. When he ignored her, she continued eating. He slumped down at the end of the table farthest from her and still his breath of belched-up whisky fumes stank up the air. Was he sufficiently in control of himself for discussion?

He snapped his fingers at Binner. "Well! Where's my food? Come along, man."

Binner hurried to the sideboard and returned with a fully-laden plate, which he placed on the table.

"Now get out while I'm eating." Ralph reached for the claret and poured himself a full glass.

Beth glanced at Binner standing well off to one side, chewing his lips, obviously afraid of leaving in case Ralph required something else. "Your manners still leave a lot to be desired, Ralph." She nodded to the servant, confirming he should leave the room. When they were alone, she set down her knife and fork and stared her brother down. "We must talk."

He snorted loudly. "What do you want now? More complaints about me drinking?" He gulped down a mouthful of wine, lowered his head and picked at his food.

"There's been some bad gossip about you." Beth paused and wet her lips with her tongue. "About you holding a woman prisoner here last night. Talk about you beating her and raping her."

Ralph snapped his head up. "Drivel! Who's been talking?"

"The servants."

He let out a loud, explosive laugh. "The servants! Let them talk, damn them. They're nought but paid lackeys. We both know how to handle servants."

"Father thinks things have gone far enough." Beth studied his face, hoping for a sign that the situation, compromising as it was, had sunk into her arrogant brother's mind. "Assuming what's being said is true, it's not the first time you've brought dishonour to the family and it won't be the last time unless something is done."

"Done? What do you mean?"

"If it's true – about you raping the woman – father intends to disinherit you."

"Disinherit me!" Ralph's knife clattered on the table, and he sprang to his feet, his cheeks flaming. "He can't do that."

Beth felt a spasm of alarm sizzle up through her spine. Ralph could be violent when roused. She grasped her knife and fork tightly, her gaze fixed on her brother's face. If he came towards her ... "He *can*, Ralph. If the coach is running to St Austell in this weather, I'll be seeing Tapper tomorrow. I'll ask him to come here and discuss the matter with father before any decision is taken. There's still time for you to mend your ways."

"How dare you! You can't threaten me like that. Father? Disinherit me? Ridiculous."

"It's no idle threat, Ralph." No doubt now remained in Beth's mind; he had attacked Wenna Lanyon. How could she avoid the obvious? "It's a serious warning, brother."

He swung unsteadily on his heels, waving his arms like windmills. "Hell! You're all against me. Damn you. Damn all of you!" Finally recovering his balance, he stormed to the door, roaring: "You'll regret this, damn you." Without a backward glance, he left the dining room, the door swinging heavily on its hinges. Beth shivered with unaccustomed fear.

That night, she locked her bedroom door and slept uneasily. Twice during the night she ventured out, creeping along the corridor to her father's room to check that he was safe. Her father hadn't long to live, she was resigned to that, but she didn't trust her brother not to expedite the matter.

The following morning, she first checked the weather. Snow was falling only lightly, a gentle flurry settling onto the white countryside without a murmur. Beth dressed hurriedly, satisfied herself that her father was comfortable then walked quickly away from the house before Ralph appeared. She could have taken a horse from the stables, but that might have alerted Ralph. Besides, it was only a short walk to the village where she would catch the St Austell coach.

The road down to Penmarith was strangely quiet with no sounds coming from the deathly white woodland except the occasional thump of snow dropping from the branches of overloaded trees.

Halfway to the village, Beth spied a young man striding purposefully towards her. Damn, she should not have come here alone; these roads were too dangerous for a lady of her breeding. She glanced round hurriedly, praying he would not accost her. Highway thieves had a knack of finding women at their most vulnerable time. Still berating herself for not having asked one of the servants to accompany her, she anxiously edged in towards overhanging trees.

The stranger trudged closer, breathing heavily, puffs of exhaled breath misting the air in front of him. Dressed in a thick, navy-coloured coat, he had a strangely familiar appearance. Certain she should recognise him, she was equally sure she had never before met him. Was it his straw-coloured hair, capped with a thin layer of snow? Or was it the square-cut jaw and deep blue eyes? The touch of recognition was too compelling; it dispelled her initial fear. He was both familiar and yet, too young. As she passed him, she nodded in vague greeting. The man paused, surprised by her gesture, then touched his hat.

"'Morn'n, ma'am." Even the voice held a familiar ring, an exaggerated form of a familiar accent. "I'd sure be obliged if you could direct me to where I'm head'n."

"And just where are you heading, sir?"

"Tregover Farm, ma'am." He stamped his feet in the snow, as if trying to keep warm. "The coachman told me it's some place hereabouts, but I can't seem to find it."

She smiled as understanding dawned. "You'll be kin to Mister Christopher Vanson."

"Surely am, ma'am. Name's Clement Vanson. Clem to my friends." A wide grin split his face, a strangely enticing grin, almost too much to resist. "Kit's my older brother."

Beth held out her hand. "How do you do, Mister Clement Vanson. I think I shall be a friend and call you Clem. You're heading in quite the wrong direction for Tregover Farm. It's the other side of the village. Come, you can walk back towards it with me."

"I'd be glad to, ma'am."

A tremble tickled inside her chest. Was it wise to take so quickly to a complete stranger? Doubt crept briefly into her conscious thoughts, but she brushed it aside. He was no complete stranger; he was the younger version of a man she would gladly set her cap to. He was the image of a man with whom she had already flirted.

"You know my brother, ma'am?"

"We're neighbours, of a sort."

"That's real nice. Didn't catch your name." His eyes held a hint of amusement.

"I didn't give it." She rucked up her nose. "My name is Miss Elizabeth Killiow. But you will call me Beth."

"Why, that's a real nice name, Beth."

Flattered, she gave him a fleeting smile in response then pursed her lips. "Tell me about yourself, Clem."

He studied her with a puzzled expression. "You wanna know about me? And we only just met."

"Most certainly." She beamed a smile at him, and his eyes sparkled in return.

"Well, I hope I don't bore you." Then he chuckled.

"I promise you I won't be bored." She edged closer to him as they walked, nudging her arm against his.

Their conversation continued until they arrived at the village where the St Austell coach stood outside the inn, its wheels caked in slush and mud. A single set of wheel tracks wound along the road past the frozen duck pond while numerous trails of footprints criss-crossed the area. Thick snow muffled the inn's roof, icicles dangled haphazardly from the eaves and condensation misted the windows. An ostler led the steaming horses towards the stables while the coachman engaged the innkeeper in conversation.

"This is where I must part with you." Beth pointed to the far side of the snow-covered village green. "Your road is over yonder."

He took her hand and guided her towards the coach. "Oh no, Miss Beth, I must insist in keeping you company until the coach leaves."

"It'll leave very soon." She looked up at the clock on the church tower. "I really must say goodbye to you." Impatient to get on board, Beth pulled back her hand and scuffled up to the coachman who was now leaning against a wheel, puffing on a clay pipe and rubbing his hands together vigorously. She frowned at the lack of replacement horses. "Coachman, when do you leave?"

"Beg yer pardon, Miss Killiow." The coachman touched his forelock. "The coach is cancelled for today. The snow's too deep."

Beth threw him a scathing stare. "I intend to get to St Austell and back today."

He touched his forelock again. "That'll not be possible, my lady."

"Too deep." Beth snorted. "It hasn't snowed all night, except for this light flurry."

The coachman shook his head. "But, Miss Killiow, it snowed farther west. Real bad it was. We had some trouble gettin' here. The road between St Austell and St Blazey be quite blocked up with snow drifts."

"Surely not."

"I'm sorry, my lady. There's no chance of gettin' this coach back to St Austell today. You ask the young gentleman there." He motioned to Clem.

"Reckon that's true enough, Miss Beth." Clem slapped the coach's door. "This here is yesterday's coach, not today's. We had to stop half way and spend the night near a place called Poldruid and finish the journey this morn'n. Not that it was so easy just comin' this small way, you understand."

Beth clucked her tongue. "Well, that puts paid to my plans." She reached out a hand to Clem's arm. "When you see your brother, you must tell him I have plans to get to St Austell to discuss a mutual problem with Tapper. Christopher will want to know."

Clem raised a brow inquisitively. "You seem to know my brother real well, ma'am."

"Well enough. You're very much like him." Too much like him. How could she avoid the truth? She had a fascination for the young American who had inherited Tregover Farm and that fascination was now spilling over towards his younger brother. She would need to keep a tight rein on her emotions if she was to avoid making a fool of herself once again. The sort of fool she became in the gambler's bed.

"Well," he grinned, "I really should be on my way."

"If you must, Mister Vanson. As I said, Tregover Farm is about half an hour's walk in that direction." She pointed again along the narrow, snow-bound lane. "But I live along this other road and I must make my way home again. Alone."

"If there's anything I can do for you …" the American began, leaving the important words unsaid.

Beth recognised the opening. That old familiar tug resurfaced: the choice between what she wanted and what propriety demanded. It would be wise to walk away from this man. Right now. She chewed at her inside cheek, hopping from one foot to the other. Damn it, no. She *would* allow her private wishes to win the day.

She put together her best interpretation of a beaming smile. "Actually, I'd be most obliged if you would walk with me. Keep me company for a while."

Clem drew back his head, seemingly caught off guard. "Walk with you, ma'am? But you're goin' in the opposite direction and I aim to see my brother this day. I ain't seen him since we both left Alabama."

"Is he expecting you?"

Clem stared along the road towards Tregover Farm then switched his gaze to her. "No. I guess not. But I aim to surprise him."

"You can surprise him later, can you not? In the meantime you can come back to Studmore Manor with me, and we can take tea together. Then we can talk."

Before he could protest, she threaded her arm through his and turned him away from the road leading to his brother's farm. She liked the feel of his strength and also the gleam in his eye. This man could be interesting.

"Well, ma'am. It's a long time since a lady was so keen on tak'n my company. I surely can't refuse."

This was outrageous; she was behaving as badly as before. She kept her pace deliberately slow so she could savour the young man's company.

As they walked, she told him about herself – enough to whet his appetite without destroying his interest. "Christopher didn't tell me much about you." She pouted for effect. "He told me about Pasco taking over the plantation but said very little about you."

"Most likely he don't talk about me to anyone." Clem avoided eye contact with her keeping his attention on the road ahead. "I'm the sort of relative folks don't own up to havin' for fear of disgracin' themselves."

Beth stared at him quizzically. "What exactly have you done wrong?"

He rolled his eyes. "Oh, just about everythin' a man could do wrong. Got drunk. Mixed with bad women in bars. Kit made me leave home and go to sea. He thought it might make a man of me."

"And did it?"

Clem snorted. "Ma'am, I been at sea for nigh on six months now an' it ain't done me one ounce of good. I still drink just like I used to. I got drunk in a bar in Bristol while I was mixin' with some bad women, an' by the time I woke up, my ship had sailed."

"I can see you're going to be a worry to your brother."

He shrugged. "Well, see'n as how I was stuck in England anyway, I figured on visitin' him. But I reckon he might not be too pleased about seein' me."

She glanced sideways at him with a grin. "You could try renouncing the drink."

"That would be a desperate remedy, ma'am. Have to be a real good reason for me to do that."

Clem hung back at the manor drive, but Beth was determined to extend their meeting. The attraction was growing fast, and she never allowed opportunity to slip through her fingers. She hustled him into the drawing room then hurried along to the kitchen to call for tea and biscuits. A new servant girl announced that Mrs Trevose was out in the hen run collecting eggs, but she assured Beth that the tea would soon be forthcoming.

"By the way, where's Mister Ralph this morning?" Beth asked, hoping he'd been seen. "Is he about yet?"

"'Ess, my lady." The servant girl curtsied. "I was takin' the old master's tea upstairs, and Mister Ralph met me on the stairs and said as how ee would take it up."

Dread welled up inside her, driving all other thoughts from her mind. Ralph never took the trouble to tend to father, quite the contrary. She hurried back to the drawing room and beckoned to her visitor. "Come with me, Mister Vanson. I may need your help." She led the way as they bounded up the stairs. The door to the squire's room was shut, but Beth threw it open with barely a pause and burst into the bedroom.

At the horrific sight before her she stepped back, a startled cry bursting from her lips. Clem came up behind her, bumping into her retreating form.

The American looked beyond her into the bedroom and gasped aloud. "Oh my God!"

Ralph Killiow knelt on the bed astride his father's limp body. He held a pillow in his hands while glowering down at his father, his face crossed with a wretched expression of intense hatred. He froze at the intrusion, turned and threw Beth and Clem a withering stare.

"No!" Beth rushed forward to help her father, but it was clear at first glance that he was dead.

Clem heaved Ralph off the bed, dragging him away from his victim. "My God! What've you been doin' here?"

Weeping uncontrollably, Beth fell to her knees at her father's bedside and grasped an icy cold hand. How could Ralph have done this? It was inhuman.

She whipped around to her brother. "You murderer. You cold-blooded murderer!"

Late that evening, Beth peered between the flickers of two candles at opposite ends of her dressing table and studied the reflected image of deep wrinkles across her forehead. Her face was pasty white. She gently combed her fingers through limp hair draped about her shoulders, sighing so deeply her breath condensed on the mirror.

Her maid stood wide-eyed beside her, frightened, as if the house was now haunted.

"I look a mess, don't I?"

"If ee say so, my lady."

"I do say so." Drained almost beyond endurance, she lowered her head into both hands and wept silent tears, which dripped onto her dressing table, while her breast heaved and heaved again.

Weeping might temporarily drive out her sense of despair, but she knew the feeling would return tomorrow. Ralph would see to that. She wiped angrily at her eyes, sat back and sniffed loudly before running her fingers through her hair, fluffing it out around her shoulders. Reflected in her mirror, the maid stared and waited.

They both started when the bedroom door burst open, and Ralph staggered into the room, Beth catching his entrance through the mirror. She also caught the thrust of his fist at the maid, a determined expression on his face.

"Get out. I want to talk to your mistress." The girl staggered back from Ralph's blow. Cowering, she eased around him and closed the door behind her.

"Still beating women, Ralph?" Beth wiped her damp eyes with the backs of her hands. "What do you want?"

"Natural causes," he said smugly. "The doctor has confirmed father died of natural causes. Not surprising. We all knew he had a weak heart."

She drew her gown tighter while studying his mirror image. "You killed him." The hatred she felt for him threatened to overwhelm her.

He furrowed his brow. "Prove it. All you saw was me trying to revive him after his heart failed." Ralph stabbed a finger at her threateningly. "And that's the way it's going to be told. You hear me."

Beth narrowed her gaze at Ralph's reflection. "You're evil, Ralph. Pure evil."

"Bitch!" Ralph swung on his heels, reached for the doorknob then paused. "If you try to spread lies about me, I'll make sure your name is blackened in every court in this land. You're no saint, Beth. You've done things you're ashamed of, and don't you forget it."

"I've never killed anyone." She turned in her seat and stared at him, surprised at her ability to hold back further tears.

"Who's going to believe that? If there's any suggestion father was murdered, you'll come under investigation first."

She gaped at him and quickly recovered from her shock. "Why?" Beth cowered as her brother's eyes squeezed into slits, an intimidation he used often.

"Because you're the slut who whored her way into the bed of a worthless gambler," he hissed, darting his head forward like an ugly cobra. "Need more money, do you? Father's money?"

"No one will believe that."

"Don't count on it." He stormed from the room, pushing aside the maid waiting outside.

Beth slumped over her dressing table. He was right, of course. With her background, who would believe her?

Eleven

Mid January 1838

From the moment she first arrived, Wenna disliked Tregonissey; a dirty mining village lying in the shadow of enormous, conical waste-tips rising ghost-like from the snowbound landscape. She stayed around only because she had found work as a bal-maiden in the Old Treverbyn Mine and lodgings nearby in Polly Kellow's cottage. A job and a room; enough to keep her alive.

She shivered as she battled the cold while hurrying into Ezra Roskilly's shop, next door to Polly's simple cob-walled cottage. The shop owner was nowhere to be seen, but the air hung heavy with the constant potent smell of his tobacco smoke.

Polly Kellow, small boned and bent with age, sat behind the bare wood counter, silently knitting. She raised her dull grey eyes as Wenna entered.

"It's going to be a cold evening for certain." Wenna smiled, took two coins from her purse and pointed to a tea chest beside the counter. "Just tuppence worth, Polly." She could ill afford the luxury, but it raised her spirits and reminded her of better days.

"Ee do look right worn out, me dear." Polly set aside her knitting and measured out a meagre portion from the chest, wrapping it in a twist of brown paper. "Reckon they work ee some hard up at the mine." She hesitated for a moment, as if unsure whether to speak her mind, and then added: "And ee bein' a cut above the rest of them women."

Wenna ignored the probing remark. "The others cope well enough with the work. I'll do the same." She turned away and bit at her lip. If she could blend in with the other women, she might be able to live out her life without drawing Killiow's attention. The alternative was to heed his threat and flee Cornwall.

Reaching the door, she pocketed her tea and then halted in her tracks as Ezra Roskilly came into the shop. Tall and pot-bellied, he had a dark face set with a perpetual scowl around his sagging jowls.

He raised his head to stare down his nose at Wenna. "Have ee got all ee wants, then?" His voice held the sharp, confident tone of one used to giving orders or abuse without rebuke.

"Yes, thank you." Wenna gritted out her response with a measure of forced respect far beyond her wishes.

"Mistress Lanyon, edn't it?"

"Yes."

"I heard about ee. Lived at Penmarith, didn't ee?"

Wenna edged around him, too tired and stiff to continue the discussion. "Yes." She had revealed that much to the mine captain and tittle-tattle would pass quickly enough through a small community like Tregonissey.

Roskilly considered her for a moment. "My cousin, Tom, he's the parish constable over at Penmarith. Tom knows all that be goin' on over there. All the trouble they farm people be causin'."

Wenna stiffened. "Really?" Roskilly was a common enough name and she had not thought to link the shop owner with the Penmarith constable. A dangerous oversight. Maybe she had been a fool to remain in Cornwall, defying Ralph Killiow's orders.

"Word is that ee sold yer father's farm to Squire Killiow. Made a pretty packet, did ee? Got lots of money?"

Wenna clasped her coat tighter against her chest. Could she never escape the influence of the Killiows? She stretched herself to her full height, still short of eye to eye with Roskilly. "It was *my* farm, Mister Roskilly, and what I did with it is my business."

His lips curled, exposing chipped and yellowed teeth. "Don't take that tone of voice with me, maid. I don't take no lip from the likes of ee."

"No offence intended, Mister Roskilly." Wenna gave him a dry smile. "Now, I'll be saying good day to you."

Roskilly's footsteps followed her, step for step. "You plannin' on stayin' long round here?"

"As long as I have work here." But how long could she stay here once Ralph Killiow found out? How long before the Roskillys divulged her presence here? In the space of a few minutes her hopes were dashed, and she knew she would soon have to move on.

"Got friends, have ee? Round these parts?" Roskilly's voice took on an even harsher note. "Young women need friends. Especially up here, and havin' money to spend. More especially when ee's been warned to stay out of Cornwall."

Wenna's heart thumped, but she canted her head at him. "I'm sure I don't know what you mean, Mister Roskilly." She turned suddenly and, without looking back, she pushed open the shop door and stepped out into the icy, damp evening air.

She let herself into the bitterly cold cottage next door, hanging up her bonnet and coat but keeping her shawl about her shoulders. She prepared a small fire in the kitchen, blowing into it to encourage the flames until they grew strong enough to throw some semblance of a cheery glow around the room. With flames and heat, she brewed herself a small portion of tea, following it with a couple of potatoes boiled over the fire.

An hour later Polly came into the cottage, shuffling and bent. She set a small, badly wrapped packet on the bare table. "Here ee are, me 'andsome. I managed to snaffle a bit of Roskilly's cheese. 'Tedn't much, but it will help fill ee up."

"That's right kind of you." Wenna slumped her shoulders and hesitated, wondering how she could take food from the old woman. Then self-preservation kicked home. With hunger rippling through her stomach, she lifted the cheese gratefully. In return, she offered a small share of her own precious tea.

"That'll be nice." Polly fussed as she stoked up the small fire. "I don't mind tellin' ee that a cup of tay would go down very decent."

"'Tes the only luxury we have, Polly. And it helps perk me up a bit."

"Does the same fer me." Polly stole a knowing look in Wenna's direction. "At least we got a roof an' a fire, an' a bite to eat." She threw a small piece of coal onto the embers then eyed Wenna with caution in her gaze. "There be one thing I should warn ee about, though. Them Roskillys. They're a rough living lot. Hard-drinking, hard-fighting and hard-swearing, all of them. So take care now, you hear me? Especially when ee goes into that shop. That Ezra Roskilly's up to no good."

Wenna kept her eyes averted. "How do you mean, Polly?"

"Fancies young women. And ee has a way of gettin' what ee wants."

Wenna drew a deep breath. It was not a new problem, just a new perpetrator. "I can handle things," she said with a false air of confidence. She clasped her hands tight together to stop them shaking.

Later that evening, she sat on her bed and ran her fingers around the hem of her skirt. Forty-six of her fifty guineas, mostly in five pound notes, were sewn into the hem for safety. Satisfied the money was still intact, she folded the skirt carefully and laid it beneath her bed. Often tempted to buy nourishing food and warmer clothes, she held herself in check. Better to save the money until she had no choice. If her circumstances worsened, she would have no option but to spend it. If circumstances improved, saving it would no longer be important. In the meantime, she used no more than was necessary.

The following morning she rose early and tramped across the frozen land towards the mine. The air was unusually still and thick with damp. Cold fog lay like smoke in the hollows. She reached her work in the air dries before sunrise, busily scraping at dried blocks of clay when daylight came and the fog lifted. She pulled her coat tighter about herself. The work was arduous, leaving her hands rough and scarred, and her body weakened.

Not far off, working alongside a diverted slurry stream, a group of men hacked away and broke up the decomposed granite using their Cornish 'dubbers'. Their work was dirty and tiring but the shift captain, Gryffyn Lugg, a stout, balding man with piercing eyes, kept the men firmly in check. A composition of sweat and clay dust always caked his face, smoothing out the crevices that lined his features.

Captain Phineas Prideaux, the clay works captain, strode out from a nearby hut and paused to inspect Lugg and his team. Heavily muscled with thick black hair and rough-hewn features, he had a quiet way about him, urging the men on through persuasion rather than harsh words. Minutes later, he turned away, seemingly satisfied.

Midway through the morning Lugg came striding fast towards Wenna. "Mistress Lanyon!"

Wenna set down her scraper and wiped her hands on her apron. "Yes, Captain?"

"You'm lodgin' with Polly Kellow, ain't you?"

"Yes, sir."

The shift captain stopped close to her, an agitated expression about his face. "You been upsettin' my pal, Ezra Roskilly, have you?"

Wenna suppressed an urge to shout her answer. Instead, she replied calmly: "No, Mr Lugg, sir."

"Well, Ezra says you don't treat him proper. You'd do well to make a friend of Ezra, you would." He leaned towards her menacingly. "That's if you wants to go on workin' here."

Wenna nodded and picked up her scraper. "I'll remember what you say, sir." It was in her mind to claim a right to fair treatment, but she held her tongue. In this place, she had no rights. No rights at all.

"Do that, me girl." The shift captain turned abruptly and strode off towards the breakers. The other women working nearby eyed Wenna suspiciously, but no one said a word. They all knew that to argue with Gryffyn Lugg was to risk losing your job.

"What's a shivaree, Polly?" Wenna sat before the cottage fire and wriggled her toes inside her damp boots. The Saturday afternoon shift had stopped early for a village wedding celebration. "We never had the like over at Penmarith."

"Then you never seen a real weddin'." Polly smiled. "Dancin' and drinkin' and singin'. That's what a shivaree be. Everyone has to be there."

"If there's going to be drinking, I'll give it a miss." Wenna shifted in her seat. "I don't fancy fighting off the likes of Lugg and Roskilly with drink inside them."

"They'll come lookin' for ee. Just watch yerself, Wenna. They don't take a refusal from any woman." Polly's stare now held no warmth, only a cold warning.

Wenna returned to her room, more determined than ever to avoid trouble.

Darkness began to fall, and a noisy rabble of villagers gathered in the narrow main street outside. Curiosity got the best of her, and she peered out of her window from behind her ragged curtain.

Two bearded men, dressed up to impersonate the bride and groom, led a procession of loud music and dancing into a field across the road from the cottage where a bonfire already blazed and a hustle of miners drew beer from a immense barrel.

She didn't like the look of the sky any more than the drinking. Dark, low clouds drifted overhead, threatening more snow. A sharp frost chilled the air, and the bonfire lit up the breath condensing from a hundred chattering mouths.

Beyond her walls, she could hear the merrymaking growing louder and rowdier until, a later peek revealed, the women had begun to leave the men to their drunken celebrations. Wenna retreated into the deeper shadows of her room, the reflected glow of the bonfire dancing on the uneven cob walls. Fully clothed and ready for any trouble, she lay down on her bed and wrapped the blanket closer about her.

Raucous laughter now echoed across from the field, interspersed here and there with the loud belligerent sounds of arguments and fighting. Eventually the celebrations slowly petered out as people drifted back to their homes.

Wenna awoke with a start. Loud, beer-slurred voices broke the night outside the cottage while her room was now in almost total darkness, the bonfire having died down.

"Are ee in there, Wenna Lanyon?"

She recognised Roskilly's voice. He was close by her window. She huddled beneath the blanket, the cold hand of dread creeping through her. Please God, she prayed, make them both go away.

"Don't you be upsettin' old Ezra Roskilly, now." Another man chimed in. It was Lugg. "Come to the window, me 'andsome. Remember what I said."

"I got some beer in me house if ee wants it." Roskilly continued. "Do ee want it, then?" She didn't respond.

"If you don't come out, we'll have to come in an' get you." Lugg sounded much more insistent this time. Not so much a taunt as a threat.

Why did God ignore her prayers? Wenna wiped at tears forming on her lashes. As long as the two men stayed outside the cottage, they were no more than a nuisance, but suppose they came inside and caused trouble? Polly would be obliged to ask her to leave. Resigned, she slipped out of the bed and fumbled her way to the window.

"Mister Roskilly. Captain Lugg. Please go away, will you. You're causing trouble for Mrs Kellow."

"Causin' trouble, are us?" Ezra Roskilly hissed back. "I'll have ee know that Polly Kellow's in no position to complain to me about trouble. By God, I'll have her out of me shop tomorrow if she do complain."

"Please, Mister Roskilly. Leave us in peace." Wenna pulled the blanket tighter about herself as if it alone could protect her. "What is it you want?"

"We wants ee to let us in, Mistress Lanyon." Roskilly belched. "Mebee ee can use some of yer money to buy us a drink." His sentence ended abruptly.

"What the hell!" Lugg's cry was also terminated suddenly and followed by a loud scuffle.

Wenna peered out into the moonless night beyond. Amongst the confusion of voices, one stood out more sober than the others.

"Get along there, both of you. Don't you know better than causin' trouble for honest people?" She sighed with relief at the raised voice of Captain Prideaux.

"Mind yer own business." She cringed at Roskilly's blatant threat.

"You want trouble, Roskilly? You've got it." Now Prideaux's voice betrayed his angry mood. More scuffling noises told Wenna a fight had broken out between the two men.

Wenna's heart raced with fear. Polly must surely have heard the commotion, but she seemed determined to remain in her own bedroom. Was she also filled with stark fear? Wenna ran downstairs to the front door and unbolted it gingerly. Just a few yards away, a single lantern illuminated a violent tussle. Roskilly struggled with Captain Prideaux while Lugg stood to one side, leaning drunkenly against the cottage wall.

A well-aimed blow from the mine captain sent Roskilly reeling to the ground. Lugg staggered upright and backed away while Roskilly rose to his knees and crawled after him.

Captain Prideaux came towards Wenna, wiping his hands together in a gesture of satisfaction. "You'll have no more trouble with them two. But mebee I ought to stay a while in case they come back."

With cold perspiration trickling irritatingly down her forehead, Wenna stood her ground in the doorway. "Thank you for coming to my aid, Captain. I can look after myself now."

"Don't you want me to wait around? Just to be sure there's no more trouble."

"No, sir. I'll be all right now. They won't bother me again tonight."

Prideaux stepped back, somewhat reluctantly. "'Tes no bother, me 'andsome. We could have a cup of tay together and a cosy chat, mebee?"

"Please, sir." Wenna lowered her voice until it was almost begging. "Please let me be. I want no trouble here."

"Well, if that's the way ee feel." She picked up Prideaux's tone of exaggerated hurt. He turned to walk away. "I'll see ee Monday mornin', Mistress Lanyon."

"Yes, sir. Thank you, sir."

Wenna waited at the door until the night enveloped the retreating mine captain. Nearby, Roskilly and Lugg shuffled noisily back to the shop, hurling threats and insults in their wake. She bolted the door and scrambled up to her bedroom where she closed the door firmly and levered a chair back beneath the handle. No real protection against a drunken miner, but better than nothing.

She slept little that night, constantly on guard for the possibility of the men returning. She awoke to the distant peal of Sunday morning church bells drifting along on the breeze from St Austell town. The ragged timing coupled with the unholy clatter of the tenor and treble bells reminded her of the ringing at Penmarith church. Perhaps the ringers had yet to recover from their Saturday night celebrations.

Yawning, she dressed slowly to the sound of Polly moving about downstairs and tunelessly singing a Methodist hymn. Wenna waited until the singing abated before she crept down the creaking staircase. Polly stood just inside the front door, dressed for a service at the local Wesleyan chapel.

"Mornin' to ee, Wenna." Despite the greeting, Polly's voice seemed somewhat cold this morning, almost hostile.

Wenna saw no point in avoiding the issue. "Did you hear the spot of bother last night, Polly? Ezra and Mister Lugg were here. But

Captain Prideaux came along and sent them both packing."

"Captain Prideaux, eh? Well there be no love lost between Ezra Roskilly and Captain Prideaux, I can tell ee." Polly stared at her long and hard. It could have indicated anything, but Wenna chose to take it as a warning.

That afternoon Wenna walked down to Charlestown Harbour. She could ill afford to buy food in the shops in St Austell without making inroads into her capital, but she had high hopes of bartering for fish direct from the boats. Farther west into Cornwall, the Methodists held strong feelings against landing fish on the Sabbath, but the Charlestown fishermen had no such misgivings. Wenna haggled the price for a pair of mackerel from a boat newly tied up in the outer harbour, careful to display only a few pennies in her hands.

Despite the long uphill journey, she walked home with a pleasant anticipation of sharing the fish with Polly. A crowd of churchgoers gathered outside the Primitive Methodist Chapel at Mount Charles, the men wriggling uncomfortably in their best suits, the women eyeing Wenna and her two mackerel with prim, unforgiving reproach. None of them would go hungry this day, Wenna judged.

Polly's cottage door was ajar when she reached Tregonissey. Her heart full of misgivings, Wenna hurried towards it. Polly would never leave it ajar in winter.

"Polly?" she called out, blinking as her eyes adjusted to the gloom inside the cottage. She then paused and listened for a reply.

Footsteps shuffled overhead in her bedroom. An intruder! Wenna climbed the stairs, wary of losing her money but determined. She pushed open the bedroom door and stopped dead in her tracks.

The room was in total disarray and Ezra Roskilly knelt on the floor beside her bed. Her best skirt was roughly draped across her only blanket, torn from hem to waist. Her money was spread between the blanket and Roskilly's hands.

"That's my money!" Wenna threw aside her fish and rushed at him with no thought for her safety.

Roskilly swung round to face her, a wide evil grin across his face as he stood up. "Maids like you don't have this sort of money."

"Put it back," she wailed, her fisted hands raised as if about to hit out. But her body betrayed her and went suddenly rigid with fear. "That's from the sale of my farm."

"Who'd believe that? I reckons as how ee stole it." He grasped the notes tighter. "This don't belong to ee, and I'm takin' it."

Wenna shook one fisted hand at him, stretching for the money with the other. "Give it to me. It's mine. You mustn't take it. It's all I own!"

Roskilly laughed acidly. He pushed her aside with a single swipe of his arm. "My cousin, Tom, will be wantin' to hear about this. He'll know who's had money stolen in Penmarith." Roskilly paused. "Mebee ee'll ask Mister Ralph Killiow who this was stolen from."

"That's my money!" She reached out to him again, determined to retake possession of her notes.

Once again, he swept his arm wide, knocking her back with one heave. She crumpled onto the floor with her legs twisted beneath her. Whimpering with the pain of his blow, she sat up and threw out her hands to him. "Please. It's mine!"

"Not any more, it edn't." He bumbled his way down the stairs and out from the cottage, his laughter trailing behind him.

Still smarting, Wenna sat on the bed and let her grief spill out. That money had been her only safeguard against poverty, how would she ever recover it? In the back of her mind the implied threat that Roskilly's cousin in Penmarith would have words with Ralph Killiow scared her even more. Everyone and everything now conspired against her. The more she thought about the entire mess, the stronger her tears flowed.

Beset with anguish, she slept little through the following long, dark night.

She was at her job before six o'clock the following morning, hoping to start without drawing Lugg's attention. As always while the workers arrived, he stood outside the shift captain's hut, arms folded. Spying her, he strode across the frozen, white ground, fixating her with a scowl.

"You'm not wanted here, maid. You'm sacked." The shift captain's harsh words were out before he reached her. The other bal-maidens stood nearby, watching silently, empathizing.

"But why?" Wenna felt dampness begin to well in her eyes.

"'Cos we don't employ thieves here, that's why. Now, get along and don't be lettin' us see you here again."

She held out her hands, begging. "But I've stolen nothing. I was robbed."

"Don't you come on with them lies. Ezra Roskilly told me all about it. You'm a thief and you'm not wanted here. Now, be off with you."

Twelve

Clem sat silent and uncomfortably upright in his English saddle, scowling at the grim weather. The wind had abated and a few stray shafts of yellowish morning sunlight pierced the grey, drifting clouds.

"Still want to stay around?" Kit pulled up his coat collar and glanced across at Clem. "I ain't keepin' you a prisoner." At his brother's continued silence, he added: "I can find you a ship going somewhere warmer."

"See how things pan out." Clem kept his attention forward, eyes focused on their destination.

Kit followed his brother's gaze. Studmore Manor had a remarkably calm appearance with a light flurry of snow drifting down onto the virgin white lawns. How could such a peaceful scene hide the evil deeds of Ralph Killiow?

"Heard in the village that the River Thames in London froze over," Kit said, tempting his brother into conversation again. Urging his horse over a snow bank bounding the Studmore estate, he added: "Worse winter in living memory, according to some folks. Not really your sort of weather, is it?"

"Said I'd wait and see, Kit," Clem insisted, setting his jaw defiantly.

"Don't take too long about it." Kit followed his words with a sharp glare, put out by his bother's stubbornness. He would have more to say on the subject some other time. "Beth doesn't know we're coming?" His horse slowed, panting while heavily laden and ready for a lengthy journey later in the day.

Clem spared him a glance. "Figured it best not to worry her unduly. If she knew we was comin', she'd only fret and worry." Kit nodded, a fair enough assumption.

Beth had become a frequent visitor to Tregover Farm in the two weeks since the funeral of the old Squire, arriving at odd times in her pony trap and almost always monopolising the attention of his younger brother. Often they sat beside a blazing fire in the parlour's open hearth and talked at considerable length, not involving him in their discourse. And when Beth left the farm, she invariably took her leave of Clem with a lengthy holding of hands, sometimes a stolen kiss on the cheek.

"Is she still distressed about her father's death?" Kit asked, still trying to prompt his bother into conversation

"Course she is." Clem's sullen tone hinted at some inner anxiety. "Beth and me, we both know Ralph Killiow killed his pa. But there ain't nothin' either of us can do about it 'cos we can't prove it. That man's evil, and I'd string him up myself if I could."

"Guess I'd be obliged to help you," Kit replied evenly, then fell into silence.

He'd been angry when his brother first arrived at Tregover Farm. And suspicious. If Clem resorted to his old ways here in England, it wouldn't bode well for his own reputation. He studied his brother furtively. Could he control Clem's excesses with drink, drugs and women? Kit had to admit he'd also recognised a change in his brother's behaviour. Away from the influence of the Alabama plantation, Clem was mellower, calmer. But would it last? Taking no chances, he'd emptied out all the alcohol he could find on the farm.

One conversation still troubled him.

"How's Pasco?" he'd asked Clem minutes after his arrival. "Has he married Emma Baynes?"

"Sure," Clem replied, eyes averted. "But they had themselves problems right from the start. Seems as Emma weren't so pure as she made out. She's been bedded by the Baynes's overseer. Story was, he weren't the only one she'd slept with, and that was why her pa allowed her to marry a Vanson. What with the curse and all, old Abe Baynes just wanted her married off to any man who'd have her. Pasco was right cut up about it."

"It's the damned family curse," Kit hissed.

"Guess so."

Neither brother mentioned it again.

They trotted to a halt at Studmore Manor's front entrance and swung down from their horses. No Killiow henchmen greeted them. Instead, an aged servant opened the door and anxiously reassured them. "Master weren't expecting visitors." Nevertheless, he escorted them down the long corridor to the library.

Kit dismissed the servant just outside the door and barged noisily into the room, keen to make his presence felt from the start.

Ralph Killiow raised himself from being hunched over his wide oak desk, an open whisky bottle to his right and a half-filled glass still in one hand. At the sight of them, a deep, angry scowl spread fast across his face. "Who let *you* in here?"

"Guess we invited ourselves in." Clem took a supportive stance right alongside Kit.

Killiow swung his incensed gaze between the two brothers, his expression flitting from anger to suspicion to fear. He emptied his glass in one swallow and jabbed out a hand for his whisky bottle. He poured a full glass with a single unsteady movement, spilling much of it over the desktop. "Well, what do you want?" Then he threw the drink to his lips.

Kit folded his arms across his chest. "We came to confront you, Killiow. Reckon it's time we sorted out one or two matters face-to-face. Can't let things go on as they are."

"You impudent whelp!" Killiow's voice squeaked with astonishment. He gulped again at the whisky.

"We've had the courtesy to wait a while." Kit sighed loudly in exasperation. "We've had the courtesy to wait a while out of respect for the death of your father. Now it's time to get a few things sorted out."

Killiow recovered from his original surprise. "Big words, Vanson." He slammed down his glass, stood up and drew back his shoulders, his bushy whiskers bristling with indignation. "Come to the point."

"I will." Kit shifted his feet apart to shoulder width, hoping his stance would tell Killiow that he wouldn't be put out. He would remain in his library until he got what he came for. "But first, I want to know the truth about what happened to Miss Lanyon. You forced her off her farm and there's rumours flying about that you assaulted her."

"Forced her?" A drunken twitch invaded one eye. His body waving precariously, Killiow sought support by leaning a palm on his desktop. "That little fool came to me, begging me to buy her land." He narrowed his gaze at Kit. "What happened between her and meself is none of your concern so keep your nose out of other people's business."

Killiow hadn't flatly denied the accusation. He was guilty as hell. With every muscle twitching to grasp the man's neck, Kit forced himself to speak calmly. "There's good evidence you kept her locked up against her will. And evidence you treated her real bad."

"Evidence?" Killiow drew back his thick lips in a lengthy sneer. "What evidence?"

"People gossip even in places like this. Servants let slip what they know."

"Spying on me, were you?" Killiow threw a flabby hand into the air and then quickly returning it to the desktop for support. "Upset because the wench spent the night here?" Killiow aimed an idiotic smile at Kit. "Had an eye on her yourself, did you?"

Clem took a threatening step towards the new squire, his fists tightly bunched, but Kit reached out a hand to restrain him. If the rough stuff started, he would have little chance of getting more information from Killiow. He planted his palms over Killiow's desktop and leaned forward. "What happened that night between you and Miss Lanyon?" Even to his own ears, he sounded surprisingly calm.

"Didn't she tell you?" Killiow laughed in derision. "You poor fool. She sold me her farm, that's what happened. She sold it willingly after a little – shall we say – a little friendly persuasion."

Kit's blood curdled. The urge to strike the man was fast draining his self-control. He stabbed the squire's shoulder with his forefinger. "You're despicable. Men like you don't deserve to live on this earth."

An incipient scowl blackened Killiow's face. "You, sir, are going to feel the force of me whip across your back."

Seething to the limit of his composure, Kit straightened to his full height and added some distance between Killiow and himself. "Where did Miss Lanyon go after she left the village?"

Killiow snorted, grabbed at his glass and noisily gulped back another drink. "God's teeth! How the hell should I know where she went! Besides, 'tis none of your damned business." His pockmarked cheeks and brow were now flushed a deep crimson. "Truth is, that young woman had trouble coming to her."

"Had trouble coming to her?" In a moment of vivid recollection, Kit conjured up an image of the overseer on his father's plantation walking away from a young black woman's cabin and guffawing: "She sure had that comin' to her!"

Killiow flared his nostrils. "She's no more than a common whore," he sneered. "A harlot."

Wincing at the pain stabbing through his heart, Kit closed his eyes. It all came back to him like a lurid nightmare. The harlot became the terrified slave girl crying out while the plantation owner brought his whip down across her blood-soaked back. Then he recalled another weeping girl holding nought but her torn dress in front of herself as she staggered away from her master's bedroom. And a distraught child being dragged from her parent's cabin to serve her master's whim.

He glanced sideways at Clem. Could he ever forget his brother's appalling behaviour? That poor girl in the slave hovel, she'd be scarred for life.

Sending Clem to sea didn't solve anything. Others would carry on with the abuse. He should have stayed to deal with it. He should have been there to put a stop to it, once and for all. Instead, he had run away to England. Dammit. He had run away from the problem.

But not again.

He should have helped Wenna despite her pleas to leave her be. God forgive him. He had stood by while she fled her village in distress. Guilt gobbled through him, devouring him, over-riding all cogent thought.

Not again.

Worst of all, he could have been the real cause of Wenna's terrible ordeal. Had he not taken a keen interest in her? And was he not a carrier of the Vanson curse?

Damn the curse and damn this man Killiow.

Clem reached out and clasp Kit's arm. "You okay, brother?"

Kit brushed him aside and rounded the desk towards Killiow. The squire's eyes widened in fright and, in that same instant, Kit lashed out at him with a tight fist, catching him a slanting blow across his gaping mouth.

Ralph Killiow fell back against his chair with an astonished look across his face, as if he had never considered the possibility of being attacked in his own home. Even before he could cry out, Kit swung another blow at him, this one catching him full on the temple and knocking him senseless. The squire's limp body slid off the chair onto the floor.

Clem moved towards them, but Kit waved him back. "This is my business. I'll handle this my own way."

His brother nodded then jerked his head at the prone figure. "He's gonna be mighty upset when he wakes up."

"Yeah. I sure do hope so."

The door opened behind them, and the brothers swung on their heels. The same aged servant stood in the doorway, his mouth gaping open.

Kit stomped towards him. "Tell your master, I look forward to meeting him again. When he wakes up."

He was half way to the library door, Clem a pace or two behind him, when a henchman stepped up behind the servant, a tall, brutish figure raising a heavy flintlock pistol. He swung his ugly gaze between the two brothers then focussed on Kit. "Should have killed you the first time."

The first time? In a flash of understanding, Kit recalled the night he was assaulted by Killiow's thugs at Crabtree Copse Farm.

Before he could react, his brother had leapt ahead and grabbed at the man's gun hand, forcing it aside until the barrel aimed at the far wall. Clem let out a cry of rage as he struggled to overcome the man's strength and disarm him. While Kit wondered whether to join in the fracas, a sudden explosion filled the room, followed by a loud thud as the weapon fell to the floor, useless once its single charge was spent.

Still the two men were locked in close combat. Clem was easily dwarfed by his opponent, but quicker and more agile. He sidestepped a blow, grabbed a forearm and deftly swung it round the man's back, thrusting it upwards to inflict pain and control his opponent. Trying to escape from the hold, the henchman ran blindly face-first into the wall. The brute dropped to the floor, concussed, with his face heavily bloodied.

"Nice one, Clem." Kit patted his brother on the shoulder. "Thought I might need to lend a hand, but I see you sure can look after yourself."

A sudden squeal of shock startled the brothers. They turned around in unison and stared out through the door. Beth stood frozen still on the staircase, clutching a shawl to her chest and staring at them, wide-eyed.

"What's happening?" she cried, suddenly continuing on down the stairs.

Clem rushed to the bottom of the staircase. When Beth reached the ground floor, he clasped at her shoulders, blocking her view into the library. "Sorry, Beth. We didn't want you mixed up in this. It started as a private argument with your brother, but one of his henchman decided to join in."

She put her hands to her cheeks. "Why? What's it all about?"

"Kit wants to know what happened to Wenna Lanyon."

Eyes dilated, Beth sidestepped around Clem and bustled into the library. At the sight of Ralph Killiow sprawled unconscious on the floor, all colour drained from her cheeks.

"Oh no!" She turned on Kit with a painful look. "I can understand your anger with my brother, but this is not the way to deal with it. Can't you see this is going to make things much more difficult for me?"

At her last words, Kit felt his stomach tighten up with worry. "Does he threaten you, Beth?"

She ran both hands down her face, letting out small choking noises. "Yes. He …" Her voice momentarily failed her as she raised an anxious look at Kit. "Yes, of course he does. Isn't it obvious? I saw Ralph murder our father and I'm afraid one day he'll want to silence me." She fell into quiet sobs.

Hell! He'd never thought of her position. "Surely there must be someone who can stop him."

"No," she wailed, her lips a pale pink line within her pallid face. "Yesterday I took the coach into St Austell and spoke with a lawyer.

He told me I've no real proof. He warned me that I mustn't make any accusations I can't substantiate."

Clem put his arm about Beth's shoulders and sought Kit's eyes. "It ain't just a matter of evidence. You see, Kit, Ralph Killiow carries a load of weight with the local gentry. Even though both me and Beth saw what happened, we figure there ain't a local magistrate who'll even consider chargin' Ralph Killiow with his father's murder."

Kit focussed on Beth. "You really do fear he might attack you?"

She nodded vigorously. "I lock myself in my room at night and pray that Ralph will drink himself so senseless that he won't bother me." Heaving a deep sigh, she gave Kit a desperate look. "I'll have to leave this place and find somewhere safe."

A grunting noise behind him caused Kit to whip round so fast he stumbled. Ralph Killiow had come to and was staggering to his knees, groaning loudly. Blood dripped from his nose and mouth, while a half closed lid was a good precursor to a black eye.

"I'll have you thrown into gaol for this," Killiow hissed, using his desk to lever himself upright.

Beth stepped up to her brother. "No, Ralph, you won't have anyone thrown into gaol. There's been enough violence and it has to stop. You're a cold-blooded killer. If you bring these men before a magistrate, I'll tell everything I know about you."

He flung a hand wide in Beth's direction. "Lies. All lies!" Beth stepped back, narrowly avoiding a blow to her face.

Beth menacingly narrowed her gaze at her brother. "A magistrate might feel obliged to *say* it's all lies, Ralph. But father's good friends will know the truth. They all know what sort of man you are." She wagged a finger at him. "You'll be an outcast, Ralph, an outcast with no friends and no place to go except the four walls of this house." She straightened to her full height. "Let there be an end to this, and I'll go away from here and not bother you again."

"Go away?" Killiow sneered. "Where will you go, woman? *I'm* squire now, and *I'll* decide what happens to you."

Clem stepped between brother and sister and set his arm around Beth's waist in show of support. He glared at Killiow in defiance. "She's more than welcome to come with us to Tregover Farm, ain't she Kit?" He whirled around to his brother.

"Of course she is. It only pains me that I didn't persuade Miss Lanyon also to take shelter in our home."

"Miss Lanyon? Damned whore. If you want to find the Lanyon woman, you'd better start by searching the brothels in Bodmin."

Before Beth or Clem could stop him, Kit rammed his fist once more into Ralph Killiow's face.

Kit was still uncertain how far he could trust his brother, but he had no other option. "You'll take care of the farm, Clem." It was more of an instruction than a request.

"Me and Beth will see your farm safe," Clem assured him from atop his mount and Kit nodded in response.

When they came to the crossroads in Penmarith village, Beth and Clem bade him farewell and rode on towards Tregover. Kit waited until they were specks in the distance then clucked his horse onto the narrow, muddy track that cut across the fields towards the St Austell Road.

One way or another he had to find Wenna. It was more than just neighbourly concern; it was a matter of personal honour. Even more than that, he'd come to realise how deeply he cared for her. But such powerful emotions were new to him, difficult to understand.

Darkness had fallen when he arrived at the outskirts of St Austell town, tired and hungry. He quickly secured a room at the Duke of Cornwall Inn and ate a hearty supper. The next morning he hurried through miserable streets to the office of Charles Tapper.

According to the notary, Wenna had called to see him, anxious to settle the sale of her land and be on her way, as if – so Tapper claimed – she were afraid someone might force her to change her mind. But to Kit's intense annoyance, the notary was unable to shed much further light on Wenna's whereabouts, except that she had hinted she might head off north of the town. Tapper had chosen not to question her too closely on how she would survive or where she would live.

Leaving the office, Kit made a mental note to employ another notary should he ever again have need of one. He spent much of the day treading the snow-bound streets of St Austell asking traders and travellers whether they had seen any woman answering Wenna's description.

One labourer raised Kit's spirits. The man thought he might have seen a woman of that description up in Tregonissey, but he couldn't recall her name. Other townspeople were more emphatic; they had seen a young woman leaving the town on the St Blazey Road. Two riders claimed to have seen her walking along the snow-bound highway.

But was it Wenna? And, if so, where had she been heading?

It was fully dark once again by the time he interrupted his investigations and sought a second night's shelter at the inn.

Thirteen

Late January 1838

A scuffle of rats woke her.

Wenna sat up in darkness, an icy draught whistling across her face. She raised the blankets to her chin, focussing her attention on the scampering noise. The rats prowled across the attic floor. The other girls had warned Wenna that the loathsome creatures scurried from sleeper to sleeper, pawing at exposed flesh and occasionally biting. Scared witless, Wenna reached out for the stick she kept constantly beside her bed, brought the blankets even higher to her nose and fought to stay awake until the attic became silent. And yet she felt so sleepy, her eyelids so heavy.

She felt a brief pressure on her shoulder. Her eyes flew open and she squeaked in alarm. A dairymaid held a flickering candle to her face.

"Best ee gets up now, Wenna." A distant church clock pealed the hour. "Four o'clock, milking time. Don't do to upset Farmer Pullin." Wenna sat up and panned about the attic watching for the rats.

Other dairymaids had risen from their beds and were now dressing and wheezing at the accumulated dust. Wenna rubbed at her arms as she stood up, wearily parting herself from the dampness that festered in her bedding straw. Feeling a draught, she looked up above her head and gaped at the icicles dangling from the frame of a small broken window. Straightening and brushing at the clothes she lived and slept in, she cursed the horrendous luck that had brought this overly long cold spell to the Cornish peninsula.

Wenna followed her companions down the rickety stairs, out into the muddy yard and across to the dairy barn. The gunny-sacking rags about themselves were poor protection against driving snow and the chilled wind howling across the heath. Her chest heaved behind a deep racking cough as the damp air attacked her lungs.

They entered the dairy barn, which groaned against the wind, loose clapboards flapping noisily against the timber frames. Wenna went to her assigned cow and pulled a three-legged stool alongside the animal. She caught the attention of the girl at the next animal. "You were away from your bed again last night, Emily." Wenna worried; her voice had grown so hoarse over the past week. Her throat was now constantly sore.

Emily, a pale, sad-looking girl with hollow eyes, gave her a frightened look. "You won't tell the master?"

Wenna shook her head. The sharp smell of Emily's unwashed body hung heavy in the air and the sight of fleas swarming in her thin calico dress had Wenna shiver. She began to draw rhythmically on the cow's udder. "But he's bound to find out one of these nights." She paused in her milking. "Was it a man?"

Emily scratched at her lice-infected hair while considering whether to reply. Wenna smiled to encourage the girl. Reassured her secret would be safe, Emily contorted her mouth into a grin which failed to reach her eyes. "You know who 'twas." At Wenna's shake of the head, Emily went on in whispered tones: "'Twas Abel Bunnity. We met down in the old hay barn. I know 'tes wrong but when I gets the gin inside of me I feels like a different woman. 'Tes the only thing worth havin' when ye're stuck in a place like this."

Wenna shook her head sadly. She had taken a particular dislike to Abel Bunnity. The field worker was always dirty, uncouth and, more often than not, drunk. Soon after her arrival at Farmer Pullin's farm, he had offered her gin in return for the use of her body. She had barely resisted the urge to hit him.

"Did you lie with him?" she asked, already knowing the answer and keeping her eyes focussed on the milk bucket.

"Of course I did." Emily stopped her work, drew back her chin and fixed Wenna with a stern reproach from beneath lowered eyelashes. "Don't ee be lookin' at me all moral-like. Why else would any man buy gin for the likes of me? I ain't no beauty, am I?"

"I don't judge you, Emily. I only feel sorry for you." Wenna continued with the milking, a bout of depression settling inside her. Was this the only future she could expect? A daily round of constant degradation. "You know he'll never marry you, don't you?"

Her companion leaned in her direction, giggling childishly. "Reckon as how ee will when ee knows I'm havin' a babby. Got to marry me then, ain't ee?"

"Oh, Emily!" Wenna breathed out long and low to avoid another bout of painful coughing. "Not that."

Emily bent to the task of pulling at the cow's udder. "Tedn't so bad. I had a babby once before, but its father ran off to sea and the babby died. But this one'll live, I can tell. T'will be all right in the end."

"I hope so, Emily, for your sake." Suddenly, Wenna hated Abel Bunnity even more. How could an unwanted pregnancy ever be all right for the girl? Bunnity ... Killiow ... One was as bad as the other, rarely doing the right thing by anyone. Wenna released the udder, calming herself with a deep breath.

She switched to another cow and bent again to the pitiful task of drawing off what little milk Farmer Pullin's animals had to give. With the last cow milked, she followed the other maids back across to the farmhouse for breakfast.

Farmer Pullin, a small-framed, sallow-skinned man with a thin covering of white hair, sat at the head of his meagrely laid kitchen table. His face was pinched and lifeless in the dull candlelight. Through narrow-set eyes, he eyed each of the farm workers as they arranged themselves in some semblance of rank.

Wenna sat at the far end between Emily and an old, consumptive woman who each morning turned some of the milk yield into butter. Gruel – a thin grey liquid ineffective in staving off hunger or cold – was put on the table and a small portion of stale bread was passed amongst the farm workers.

"'Tes a rare cold day, master," commented a cadaverous-looking man half way down the table. Beside him, Abel Bunnity nodded in agreement, his mouth working noisily around a chunk of bread.

"Not so cold as you can think of escaping work." Farmer Pullin narrowed his gaze at the man who'd spoken up then cast a glance around the table at each person in turn. "I wants the old barn repaired and you can all be workin' at it."

"'Tes right slippery out there, master," the same man said, his head lowered over his bowl.

Farmer Pullin snapped a penetrating stare from his gruel to the speaker. "Then you'd better be careful, hadn't you?" He went back to eating then paused to speak again: "At least you all has work to go to. If them union agitators had their way, there'd be barely a farm in Cornwall that could afford to employ you. 'Twas because of the union riots my machinery were destroyed. Don't you forget that!"

All eyes turned, reproach evident, to the man who'd been responsible for Farmer Pullin's bout of moral indignation. No one else dared argue with their employer, so Pullin went on: "An' another thing." He leaned forward settling both elbows on the table, while one forefinger pointed at the ceiling. Wenna sighed out of frustration at his usual pose when on the subject of unions. "There's been talk of some folks hereabouts wantin' to form a union. If any of you lot has anythin' to do with it, you'll be off my land straight away."

"Unions edn't illegal." Abel Bunnity sniffed and grabbed at the uneaten chunk of bread on his neighbour's platter. He snapped it into his mouth before the man could complain.

"No." Pullin stared Bunnity down until the young man sank back in his seat. "But by God, they should be!" He slapped the table hard, startling the women near him.

Wenna settled her nerves and ate her breakfast slowly and deliberately. She, alone, understood the farmer's problems. The last to finish her meal, she followed the others back across mud-coloured slush to the old barn. Stamping their feet to keep the circulation running, they grouped together to study their task. Many of the barn's wattle panels were broken or missing and the foundation sagged to one side.

Farmer Pullin hurried in behind them. "Get to work, all of you, or I'll deduct an hour off yer wages."

"Old miser," Emily whispered under her breath.

"But he's right." Wenna spotted a group of women, who were languidly mixing a concoction of lime and cow dung to plaster the walls, and approached them with Emily shadowing her. "He can't afford to pay us to do nothing when there's sharks like Ralph Killiow on the lookout for cheap land."

Emily pulled at Wenna's arm. "Know somethin' about it, do ee?"

"Maybe." She had told no one here of her past life. It was none of their business.

At mid-day they returned to the farmhouse for a meal of worm-ridden cheese and more bad bread. At the sight of the food, Wenna's stomach revolted but she ate it all nonetheless. She had to fight off the cold. The other workers accepted the fare as normal at Farmer Pullin's table.

With the meal finished, they all rose to return once more to their labours in the barn. Just as Wenna was about to walk out into the cold air, Pullin called to her. "Mistress Lanyon. Wait here one moment. I wants words with you."

She winced. Had she unknowingly done something wrong? She nervously approached the farmer. "Sir?"

Pullin eyed her suspiciously while scratching at his stubbly chin. "I been watchin' you closely these past few days. You been here all of two weeks now, ain't you?"

Wenna lowered her gaze to the ground. "Yes, sir. Is my work not satisfactory?"

"'Tain't that. 'Tain't yer work I'm worried about." He breathed deeply, blowing out his pallid cheeks while he considered his next words. "When you came here, you said you'd been workin' on another farm."

"Yes, sir."

"That don't ring true. What were you really doin'?"

"Farming, sir, like I said," she insisted, keeping her time in Tregonissey to herself. It would only complicate the matter.

Pullin pointed to her feet. "Farmin'? With boots and clothes like your'n?" He shook his head in disbelief. "You'm the only worker here with leather boots even if they are old an' worn. An' I know you wears a silk spencer under that dress. Where did you get them? Didn't steal them, did you? You haven't got the law after you?"

"No, sir." Wenna drew back her shoulders. "My mother owned the spencer. She died some years ago. My father bought me the boots one Christmas when he had some money to spare." She swallowed hard. "He owned the farm where I was brought up."

Pullin frowned. "Owned it, you say? Yer father owned a farm? Where was it?"

Wenna hung her head in dejection. Why was it necessary to reveal her past? "Near Penmarith."

"That'll be close by Squire Killiow's estate. Why don't you still work yer own land?"

"It was sold, sir ... I sold it. My parents are both dead."

Farmer Pullin's manner changed abruptly, as if an unusual mellowness in his character had come to the fore. "Sold to the old squire, did you?"

"No, sir. I sold out to Mister Ralph Killiow, the squire's son."

"The squire's son? Ain't you heard, maid? The old squire's dead. Mister Ralph Killiow's squire now."

Wenna hid her mouth behind one hand. "I didn't know." She quaked with dread; there would be no stopping Ralph Killiow now.

"Sold willingly, did you?" Pullin sounded almost sympathetic.

"No, sir. Mister Killiow and I parted on bad terms. I was pressured into selling." She bit at her lip, fearing his reaction now that she'd admitted to a dispute with the new squire.

The old man's earlier expression of surprise turned into one of sadness then foreboding. "That's bad news, maid. In that case you'd better keep out of the way when the new squire comes up here."

"He's likely to come here, sir?" she gasped, wrapping her arms about her waist to stop a sudden onset of shuddering. The cold hand of fate was reaching out towards her yet again. She wailed inwardly. Would it never stop?

"Oh yes." An old man's tremor took hold of Pullin's face muscles, distorting his sallow cheeks. "Squire Trevance's the squire round here but he's no longer interested in the land now that he's livin' in Bath. Killiow's buyin' up all the land he can get his hands on." His eyes turned liquid with sadness. "I never thought he'd show an interest in us, this far from Penmarith. But now he's tryin' to get hold of my farm. When he does, he'll be puttin' us all off the land unless I can afford to lease it back from him."

Wenna slumped her shoulders. "I'm sorry to hear that, Mister Pullin. I really am."

"'Tes the way of it, maid. And there's nawt much I can do about it."

"I don't know what more to say to you, Mister Pullin."

"Just heed what I tell you. I been expectin' Squire Killiow or one of his men to come by here these past few days. You best keep out of their way." Pullin turned away, instantly dismissing her.

"Yes, sir," Wenna replied to his back and hurried outside to the barn where most of the workers had assembled. A couple of them cast enquiring glances at her but she ignored them. She had no intention of sharing what had passed between herself and Farmer Pullin.

A few men tamped the ground with their boots in the swirling snow, pointing and arguing over an area of damaged roof thatch in imminent danger of collapse. Despite her intention to keep out of it, Wenna couldn't help following their exchange.

"It'll come down soon," one snapped. "Mark my words."

"Reckon master should get Thatcher Penwarne to fix that." The man who'd spoken up at the breakfast table shook his head at the extensive damage. "Don't reckon as how we can do it."

"That thatch was alive with adders last summer," another chipped in. "You won't catch me up there."

Abel Bunnity surveyed the roof from different angles then came back to the others. "I can fix it, I reckon." At the labourers' mutters of disagreement, he added: "I'd do it if master would give I a shillin'."

"Don't be daft, young Bunnity," an older man snapped. "What do ee know about thatchin'? Just because yer uncle was a thatcher before ee took to the drink. I'll tell master –"

"What will you tell me?" Farmer Pullin came up behind the group, startling them.

Bunnity turned to him. "We reckon that roof needs fixin', master, or it's goin' to fall in under the weight of snow up there."

Farmer Pullin eyed the damaged thatch. "For once I reckon as you're right. Can any of you repair it?"

"A shillin' says I can, master." To Wenna's dismay, Abel Bunnity was the first to take up the challenge. To guarantee his shilling he went on: "There's a few reeds stacked round the back of the dairy barn. 'Twould be a lot cheaper than bringin' in Thatcher Penwarne."

He licked his lips, his mind seemingly on the gin he would buy with the extra shilling.

The farmer studied the impulsive young man, gauging whether the shilling was worth the risk. Then he nodded. "All right, Bunnity. Go on an' fix it."

Wenna watched Bunnity walk away proudly while a deep sadness seeped in her heart. She sought Emily inside the barn, amongst the women mixing up the wattling compound, and took up position next to her. "Abel's out to make a shilling by repairing the thatch."

"His uncle were a thatcher." Emily's confident response told Wenna she wasn't the least bit concerned. Wiping an arm across her dripping nose, the girl added: "Abel knows how to do it."

Wenna grabbed a paddle and began stirring the wattle mixture. "But he isn't a thatcher," she pointed out, hoping Emily would see the danger. The young dairymaid remained impervious. Wenna sighed. Determined Emily should gain from the farmer's shilling, she suggested: "You could ask him to use the money to buy extra food for you. You'll need it now."

"More likely ee'll buy more gin an' get hisself roarin' drunk." Emily laughed; a hollow laugh that no one noticed. A shuffling noise from above told them the thatching repair was under way.

"Yes. I imagine he will," Wenna sighed following the sounds coming from the roof.

Emily sat back on her haunches. "I knows how to look after meself, Wenna. I done it before."

Wenna paused, giving the girl an enquiring look. "And when Farmer Pullin finds out?"

The pregnant girl waved aside the possibility. "I'll worry about that when the time comes."

"It won't be easy –" Cries of alarm from outside the barn followed a long, piercing scream, which ended with a dull thud.

The startled women dropped their work and rushed outside to investigate.

A group of men stood around, gaping at the crumpled form of Abel Bunnity, his limbs lying at odd angles and a pool of blood forming about his head. The muddy snow turned slowly pink.

As the women got closer, the oldest of the men muttered: "Ee fell, daft bugger." Wenna caught Emily's arm, holding her back from a closer view of Abel's body. "His foot slipped an' ee just fell," the man added.

"Help him!" Emily wailed, wrestling away from Wenna's grasp and slumping to her knees beside her baby's father. But the labourers stood in a ragged semi-circle, mouths agape at the motionless and grotesquely bent body.

"No point," the oldest man said. "Ee's dead fer sure."

Farmer Pullin came running across from the farmhouse. He knelt over the body and felt for the boy's pulse. "He's had it," he snorted. "Silly fool. Should've been more careful."

Emily pushed the farmer aside and embraced Bunnity while the others looked on, shocked. No one spoke as the two bodies lay in the grey slush, one motionless and the other heaving rhythmically in her wailing grief. Wenna felt Emily's despair. She bent over her to ease the young dairymaid away from Bunnity.

"Poor bugger. At least ee won't go hungry tonight," someone said behind her in hushed tones. Wenna tended to agree.

She hugged the girl's shoulders while Emily, her dirty fingers spread wide across her face, moaned. Death was a way of life in this poor rural community and Abel Bunnity had drawn the short straw sooner than expected. It could have been any one of them. Wenna stifled a sob. One day, it would be her turn.

"All right," Pullin pointed at the nearest man, "Get the body moved away. The rest of you get back to work."

"What are ee doing here, woman?" Darkness had fallen, and Wenna was the only one left in the barn, milking by the light of a weak, flickering candle. She spun round to face the speaker at the open barn door.

Pengwidden stalked in, face harshly set and teeth clenched tight. Ralph Killiow's henchman brushed angrily at his thick oilcloth cape, frozen with snow and ice. A cold shiver of fear ran through Wenna's body.

She rose from the milking stool and thrust her shaking hands into the folds of her apron. "I work here."

"But master told ee to leave Cornwall."

"He did." Wenna stared ahead beyond the cow. The animal turned its head in her direction as if wondering why the milk no longer flowed. "This is as far as I could walk before I had to find shelter. Farmer Pullin offered me work."

Pengwidden approached her, his earlier hostility mellowing into apparent compassion. "Sorry, Mistress Lanyon. Master will want ee away from here and ee'd better go now. Master won't want ee stirring up more trouble for him."

"But I'm not –"

"Don't argue, Mistress," Pengwidden spoke evenly, almost apologetically. "Just pack yer things and be on yer way."

Wenna wiped a weary hand across her brow. Dear God, would the torment never cease? "But I work for Farmer Pullin."

"This ain't my doin', maid. Master will be comin' up here in a day or so. Please, go now as far as yer feet will take ee before master gets here."

Wenna sought Pengwidden's eyes. "Your master really does mean to make me suffer, doesn't he? And you do his bidding." He blanched as the accusation hit home.

What was the point of arguing? She sidestepped around Pengwidden and trudged towards the farmhouse without looking back. She raised a glance to the attic window. She had no belongings up there to collect but what of Emily? She so wanted to hug her friend and wish her well with the baby. Just then snow began falling heavily once again, the swirling flakes illuminated by a dull yellow light escaping from the farmhouse windows.

Hushed voices reached her from behind, and she recognized Farmer Pullin's voice. With a surge of hope, she turned around. She'd ask for her meagre wages before she went on her way.

Pengwidden and Farmer Pullin were in deep conversation in the lee of a hay barn. Wrapping her arms about her chest, Wenna stepped through the slush towards them.

Pengwidden noticed her. "Best ee be off straight away, Mistress Lanyon."

Wenna ignored him, closing in on her employer. "I only ask for my wages before I'm gone, sir."

"Wages?" Pullin hunched his shoulders. "Are you leavin', then?"

"She has to go," Pengwidden said sadly. "Squire would want it."

Pullin glanced at him, mouth open ready to respond. He gulped and slowly compressed his lips. Like Wenna, he recognised the henchman was a mere labourer but one who held the power of a squire behind him. "Best she goes, then." Without further ado, Pullin turned his back and walked away, shoulders slumped, hands dug deep into his pockets.

"Please, sir." Wenna stumbled after him.

He glanced over a shoulder. "You'll get no wages from me. I only pay workers who stay here." He stalked into the barn. Wenna turned away, fighting her distress.

Pengwidden shook his head and followed the farmer. Alone in the semi-darkness, Wenna wiped at her cheek.

Outside the farmyard wall, the heathland lay hidden behind a heavy curtain of snow. Beyond that, the solid blackness of night enfolded the land. She took in a deep breath while gathering her will to survive. Damp, cold air attacked her lungs once more and she coughed, wincing when yet another deep pain stabbed inside her chest. She needed a place of warmth, but where would she find it this late? She turned towards Golant village with no firm aim in mind, just a hope that she would find shelter, somewhere out of the cold and the dampness.

With darkness hampering her, she felt her way along the hedgerow, stumbling in deep potholes filled with snow, twisting her ankles. No matter how tight she pulled her gunny-sacking cloak about herself, the cold and damp always found a way in.

The village church bells drifted across the meadows, a ragged peal of six being pulled in erratic time. Few villagers would attend evensong this cold a night. Even the bell ringers would likely slip away to the warmth of the local inn to drink off their exertions. Wenna paused to catch her laboured breath. The church tower was faintly visible as a dark cone against the night sky. She urged on towards it eager for warmth.

Seeing the light inside, she crept quietly into the porch and listened to evensong still in progress. The unenthusiastic singing and the squeal of a worn-out organ drifted out from the church. Racked with aching tiredness, Wenna sought out the sheltered side of the porch and waited for the service to finish.

Half an hour passed before a rumble of boots on the hard stone floor announced the service had ended. She hurriedly left the porch and hid behind a stone memorial, pulling her sacking over her head to keep the snow at bay. The vicar came out first, stamping off towards the vicarage, his eager steps likely leading him to a warm supper. The parishioners followed in ones and twos; a straggly band of hardy worshippers who would soon be sitting in front of their own fires. When she was sure that all had left, Wenna crept inside the church.

She slipped into the rear pew and curled herself beneath her sacking. Sleep came to her only after hours of agonising depression. Eventually, she dreamed of Crabtree Copse Farm and her own fireside. Her mother sat by the fire with hot soup bubbling in an iron pot and flames licking at the bottom. A door slammed.

"What's going on here?" a deep, angry voice bellowed, startling her awake.

Wenna sat up, blinking against the first tinge of daylight forcing its way through stained glass windows.

"I said, what's going on here? Who are you, woman? Answer me. Have I seen you before? Are you from round here?"

Wenna immediately recognized the vicar, his heavy-set, sagging jowls throbbing with indignation and over-indulgence. "I'm sorry, sir." She slowly got to her feet. "I was lost. I came in here to escape the snow."

The vicar frowned and his bushy eyebrows became one. "What on earth do you think this is? A workhouse? Be off with you this minute!" He grabbed her gunnysack and pulled, coaxing her to speed up.

"But, sir –"

"No arguments! This is a house of God and you should respect it as such. Get out of here now. What will people say when they gather for matins? The likes of you sleeping in our church!"

Wenna hobbled away, her eyes misting. She opened the outside door to snow still falling heavily. Only an occasional shaft of dim light found its way between heavy clouds.

Fourteen

Such was his anger that, given just one chance, Kit would have killed Ralph Killiow without a moment's regret.

Tired and impatient, he had explored the snowbound countryside to the north and west of St Austell and he now headed east in the direction of St Blazey with wind-driven snow obscuring his vision. He pressed on until, by mid-day, huge drifts blocked the road.

Only a few miles from Penmarith, he reined in his horse. It would be so easy to return to the warmth of his new home. Should he turn around and pretend Wenna's fate was not his responsibility? Just as his father's slaves were not his responsibility? Just as the curse was not his responsibility?

He could not – *would not* – give up.

Determined to find Wenna at any cost, he urged the horse on around the drifts while the snow grew heavier and the wind blew colder. His teeth chattered and his exposed skin turned numb but he rode on, at times, seeing barely ten feet ahead. On a hill beyond the Port of Par, he reined back once more, allowing his horse a much-deserved rest. Steam wisped about the animal's flanks.

At the whinnying of another horse some way ahead, Kit pricked up his ears. Shielding his eyes with his hands, he peered into the gloom until he spotted another rider approaching, hunched beneath an oilcloth cape. He called out to the man but the howling wind caught his words and dragged them away. He waited patiently until they were barely a horse length apart. "Hello! Have you come far?"

"Reckon I have," the rider replied with a dark, suspicious look.

Kit eyed him warily. Hadn't he seen the man somewhere around Penmarith? Determined to find out, he clicked his horse forward, blocking the path. "I've met you before."

"P'raps."

A sudden recollection filled Kit's mind. "You work for Squire Killiow! You were manning the manor house gate a few weeks ago.

You and another guard stopped me from seeing Squire Killiow."

The henchman bared his teeth and urged his horse ahead, but Kit grabbed at the reins. "Where have you come from?"

"None of your business, Mister Vanson."

Kit pulled the horses abreast and glared at the rider. "I'm looking for Miss Lanyon, from Crabtree Copse Farm. Do you know what happened to her?"

"If I do know, I can't tell ee." The man jerked back in his saddle, freeing his reins from Kit's grasp. He backed off then urged his mount around Kit's horse, but his animal stumbled in the deep snow.

Kit let out a sharp, profane curse. He wasn't going to let the man ride away, not when information was being kept from him. Still cursing, he goaded his horse forward and grabbed again at the other animal's reins. "Where is she?"

"Can't say." The henchman jerked backwards violently, freeing his whinnying horse. "Master would kill me if I told ee."

Now positive that the rider knew Wenna's whereabouts, Kit jumped from his horse and yanked him to the ground. Before his opponent could rise, Kit pushed aside the man's cape, grabbed his arm and held it tight, seething with fury. "You'll tell me where Miss Lanyon is and what's happened to her."

"Leave off!" The man roared, fighting to free himself without success. "Ee'll pay for this."

"Really?" With his free hand, Kit bundled a tight fist and held it at the ready against the man's face. "There's no one here to witness what happens, and right now, I aim to thrash you to within an inch of your life unless you tell me what you know."

"Master will teach ee!"

Kit fixed both hands on the man and shook him. "Your master ain't here to help you. So speak up. Or else." He released one hand to bundle it again into a fist.

A flurry of snow settled on his opponent's face as Kit wound himself up for his first blow. He cursed again then held himself in check. Damn. This was an unequal contest; he was acting out of pure hatred for a different man.

Killiow's henchman began to whimper. "All right, all right. I'll talk." He let out a long breath and wiped at his nose. "I saw her." He coughed and quickly added: "But I don't know where she be now."

Kit released his grip, allowing the man to regain his footing. "Where did you see her?"

"It was a couple of days ago. She was workin' up at Pullin's Farm over by Golant way. Master sent me over there to assess the farm for purchase. I didn't expect to see the maid."

"She might still be at the farm?"

The man shook his head grimly. "Not any more, she won't. She left."

"Where did she go? Tell me before I make a real mess of your face."

"I dunno," the man said, shrugging and throwing up his hands.

"You haven't seen her since?"

"No. I stayed the past couple of nights at Pullin's an' she didn't come back. Dunno where she be now."

Kit thrust at the henchman's chest, sending him reeling buttocks first into the snow. He swung back onto his horse, looming over Killiow's man. "How will I find the farm?"

The man struggled up. Glowering, he shook off the snow from his frozen hands then pointed the way. "Take the road to Golant an' turn off before ee get to the village. 'Tes a mile or so beyond that."

"Good." Kit sniffed. Without further ado, he set out along the snow-drifted lane.

An hour later, he rode onto a barren hilltop where the wind whipped at him hard, taking his breath away. The horse laboured heavily, and Kit found his own strength sapped by the biting coldness but he could not stop here, he had to continue until he found Wenna. After a further hour's difficult riding, he came upon the snowbound farm buildings and rode into the yard, relieved.

Anxious at seeing no one, he dismounted, cupped his hands around his mouth and called out: "Anybody here?" Receiving no reply, he clumped wearily towards the farmhouse. The door opened as he was about to rap on it and the lean figure of the farmer appeared, framed ghost-like in the doorway. Kit eyed him wearily. "Is this Pullin's Farm?"

The farmer peered at him through beady eyes. "What if 'tes?"

"I'm looking for a young woman called Wenna Lanyon. I was told she worked here not long ago."

"Maybe so." Farmer Pullin eyed him defensively. "She left couple of days past. I dunno where she's gone to."

"Why did she leave?"

"Squire Killiow's man told her she had to go."

Kit gritted his teeth, suddenly wishing he had carried out his threat to thrash Killiow's henchman. "Do you know where she went?"

"No. She might have tried the church down in the village. Vagrants always head for the church. Vicar soon throws them out, though."

Kit frowned. "She's become a vagrant?"

"Dunno." Scowling, Pullin backed into the house and shut the door with a heavy thud.

No longer sure now whether his anger was best vented on Pullin, the henchman or himself, Kit returned to his horse before his emotions again took the upper hand.

He rode back along the lane, heading towards the village. Finding the church, he dismounted and spied a trio of figures standing around an open hole in the ground. He trudged along a narrow path through the graveyard.

A gravedigger leant on his shovel, briskly rubbing his hands together. Next to him, a portly vicar recited rapidly from his prayer book, his words sending puffs of condensation into the chill air. The third figure stamped his feet opposite the gravedigger. All seemed in a hurry to get on with the interment, likely anxious to get back into the warmth of their homes.

Out of reverence, Kit waited in the background, rubbing warmth into his hands. Soon enough, the vicar closed his bible, swished a rapid sign of the cross over the grave then hurried away towards the vicarage. Kit negotiated his way around the gravestones to intercept him.

"Excuse me, sir," Kit called out. When the vicar glanced over his shoulder, Kit gestured for him to stop.

The cleric kept walking, but Kit easily came abreast of him. "Yes?" the man responded testily.

Kit fell into step beside him. "I'm looking for a young woman who may have passed through the village recently. Her name is Wenna Lanyon."

"We don't have many strangers. Not at this time of the year." The vicar jerked his head towards the still open grave. "She was the last vagrant woman to arrive in this village."

Kit's stomach lurched. Dear God, he was too late. "Who was she?" he gasped, struggling for breath.

The vicar shrugged. "She called at the poor house and died during the night. Probably from the cold, but the beadle wanted her buried quickly in case she was diseased. If you want to know any more about her …" He motioned to the third figure still standing beside the open hole while the gravedigger shovelled ice-hard dirt into it. "Ask him."

Kit struggled for the right words. "You've seen no other strangers here?" He had to ask, for Wenna's sake, for his peace of mind. But the vicar had already dismissed him, striding purposefully towards his vicarage. Frustrated, Kit turned away and chased after the well-wrapped beadle who was now retreating from the half filled grave.

Kit slowed beside him. "Pardon me, sir." The beadle inclined his head but kept up his plodding pace. As if Kit was interrupting an important engagement, he hissed: "Yes?"

"The woman you've just buried. Who was she?"

"Why do you want to know?"

"She could be a friend. I'm searching for a young woman who may have come this way." Desperate to convey how important his enquiry was, Kit grasped the beadle's sleeve. "Her name. Tell me her name."

"Don't know. She gave no name at the poor house."

Kit suppressed the urge to shout in exasperation. Determined he wouldn't be put off, he probed with one more question. "What did she look like?"

The beadle frowned. "Big heavy woman. Grossly overweight. Looked like she'd never done a decent day's work in her life. Typical peasant."

Kit let out a loud sigh of relief. It wasn't Wenna.

With no further reason to linger, he took a meal at the village inn and had his horse fed before setting out along the single lane leading towards the coast. The weather grew worse, the snow even deeper.

The horse struggled, but Kit dared not dismount for fear of being unable to continue on foot. Within a short time, the outline of the path became quite lost and only his instinct told Kit where the original track lay.

Another day, another search until twilight gave way to full darkness. It became too late and too cold to be on the road.

Kit opted to stop at Fowey when he discovered an innkeeper with a loose tongue and a wide knowledge of strangers in the area. He lingered at the inn, tucking himself into a dark corner of the taproom where he listened to the raucous banter of local fishermen while he cleaned a plate of pork. Satisfied, he washed the food down with a jug of mulled ale.

Nearby, the locals chattered in a curious sing-song manner, their voices laughing or bellowing as if they hadn't a care in the world. Already, he was beginning to understand their broad Cornish accent.

With his tankard empty, he crossed to the bar, bought another drink and slipped a guinea piece into the innkeeper's outstretched hand. "I'm looking for a young woman called Wenna Lanyon."

The old landlord quickly pocketed the coin. "Lanyon, do ee say?" He scratched his stubbly chin. "Not round here. There ain't no Lanyons round here. But there be some over at Cawsand way."

"Cawsand?" Kit queried, mouthing the word with exaggeration.

"Oh 'ess. There's Lanyons in Cawsand. Mebee yer young maid's gone to them."

"Maybe. It's worth a try." Kit leaned across the bar. "How do I get to Cawsand?"

"Reckon 'tes about a day's ride." He cast a glance to an iced-up window. "Mebee more in this weather. That'n if you've got a good horse. Or ee might get passage on a boat."

"You know of any boats headin' that way?" Kit asked, knowing his horse was reaching its limit.

"Oh 'ess. There's always boats going' Cawsand way." The innkeeper winked and tapped his trouser pocket, which jangled with change. "Fer a price."

"Where might I find one?"

"You'm not from round here?"

Kit shook his head. "Complete stranger."

The innkeeper jerked his head into the heart of the noisy drinkers. "Best ask fer Cap'n Ned Carter. Tell him I said you was want'n a passage."

Kit nodded his thanks. Tankard in hand, he picked his way towards the dozen men sitting around a table heavily burdened with ale pots.

"Ned Carter?" he asked, scanning round the group.

"Mebee. Who'm askin'?" A grizzled face, pockmarked with old smallpox scars, studied him from the depths of a grey mass of matted hair and long side-whiskers.

"Name's Kit Vanson. I'm aimin' to get to Cawsand. The landlord said you might be able to give me a passage."

Carter gave him a curt nod. His eyes took on a quizzical expression "Why're ee goin' to Cawsand?"

"I'm searching for a young woman called Wenna Lanyon."

"Lanyon?" The old seaman snorted. "There be Lanyons in Cawsand, but I can't bring to mind any Wenna Lanyon. What do ee want with her?"

"She's in some sort of trouble, and I want to help her."

"A maid in trouble, eh?" Carter smiled broadly then added in a mirth-filled voice: "There be enough of them in Cawsand. Feelin' guilty about it, are ee?"

Kit ignored the innuendo and pressed on. "Will you give me a passage?"

Carter gauged Kit steadily, took a deep draught from his pot and wiped his mouth with a dirty sleeve. "It'll cost ee a guinea." At Kit's acceptance of the price, he added: "Come aboard at dusk tomorrow. Dusk, mind ee, an' not before."

"What's your ship?"

"The *Maid o' Trevisco*. As fine a brig as you'll see in these waters."

"Suits me." Kit strode away with a feeling to watch his words carefully around this group.

He secured a room at the inn for the night and spent the following day asking around Fowey for news of Wenna, but without success. Just as dusk was falling, he reached the quay where a dinghy waited ready to row him out to the river estuary where the *Maid of Trevisco* lay at her mooring. Within minutes of him climbing aboard, the crew raised anchor and the two-masted brig set sail.

Kit found Ned Carter at the bow, his face tense and alert, his hands clasped behind his back.

"Dusk you told me, Captain, and dusk it is." Kit waved a hand towards the dark waters. "Any reason for sailing at night when the tide ain't exactly favourable?"

"None o' your business." With his gaze sweeping the black shoreline, Carter reached into the pocket of his long coat and withdrew a clay pipe. Still intently staring at the shore, he fingered the bowl before pushing the pipe back into the same pocket.

"Good cargo, is it?" Kit queried.

"Mebee." The word came out terse, dismissive.

Kit took the hint. The captain wouldn't divulge any information on his cargo and that didn't bode well. Carter was hiding something. Kit paced across the deck to where the helmsman stood, easing the boat into the English Channel waters. The northerly wind caught the sails, and Kit confidently grasped a bulwark as the brig heeled over. While the deck was well aslant, he breathed deeply at the familiar smell, the salty tang drawn in from the open sea. A whippy spray blew over the bow, and the *Maid of Trevisco* danced across the rippling water. She was a fine ship; built for speed.

Keeping out of Ned Carter's way, Kit tracked the now vague coastal outline as it passed down the port side. He tasted the sea on his lips and old memories returned, happy memories. He bent forward to counteract the bow lifting on a wave and smiled as the vessel surged forward when she swept over its crest. Leaning over the gunwale, he listened to the wind whistling in the rigging and the spars, the sound of water gushing past the hull. It was good to feel the heave of a moving vessel beneath his feet. For him, time slowed until he noticed the helmsman ease the brig back in towards the coastline.

Kit sniffed at the smell of land, looming on the wind from out of the darkness. "Is this Cawsand?" he called out to the helmsman.

The sailor pointed into the darkness. "Yonder."

Kit stared over the gunwale at the shore. The dark silhouette of land blended seamlessly into the night. Ned Carter eased in beside the helmsman as the brig sailed into the black waters of Cawsand Bay. The captain swung his head from side to side as if giving the helmsman a signal. Tension rose perceptibly as the vessel lost way, and other sailors appeared from out of darker crevices, to stand on deck with an air of taut expectancy about them.

When the *Maid of Trevisco* was brought to anchor with the sails still set, Kit felt quite uneasy; it took little imagination to guess what Carter was up to. The crew hurried to pull open the hatches while the anchor chain was still unwinding.

"There's boats comin' out from the beach," a lookout called out.

Kit panned the shore and quickly found two dark shapes that began to emerge from the night.

Ned Carter turned to him. "They's comin' fer the goods. You can ride ashore in on one o' they."

Kit studied the approaching crafts. "Are you sure they're coming to fetch the cargo, Captain?"

Carter eyed him with undisguised suspicion. "Why?"

"I figure these are from a man o' war."

The *Maid of Trevisco's* captain ran to the side of the vessel, peered at the shapes and cursed. "Coastguards. Cut the cables!"

The deck became a sudden frenzy of activity. The panicked crew hurriedly threw the hatches back in place and cut the anchor rope. But, before the brig could gather leeway, one of the coastguard boats had ran beneath her stern, the crew attempting to board. The warning cries of the coastguard men battled against belligerent shouts from the brig's crew. One of Carter's men leapt from a hatch and hurried to the side with a musket. In the confusion of the boarding attempt, the second long boat came alongside meeting no resistance, and the coastguard men swarmed aboard unimpeded.

Kit cursed himself for taking the voyage.

Without doubt, the *Maid of Trevisco* had dropped one cargo of contraband in Fowey and was delivering a second to Cawsand. Probably French brandy. This was no time to get caught on board a smuggler's vessel. He raced to the bow of the brig, took a deep breath and dived into the sea.

He hit the icy water hard, knocking the breath from his lungs. Breaching the surface, he gasped then swam strongly towards the closest shore. Sooner than he anticipated, he was in shallow water and stood up, shivering uncontrollably.

He staggered onto a long, shallow-shelving beach, wading amidst a line of breakers. Shouts and gunshots carried on the breeze behind him. Heaving from aching lungs, he headed inland, anxious to keep clear of all human contact until he discovered who was friend and who was foe. Moments later, his feet sank into cold wet grass.

His shivering got worse as the night air cooled his wet body, and he cursed himself again for taking passage with Ned Carter. He should have known any Cornish boat heading out on an imperfect tide had to be up to no good.

"Who's that?" A man's voice rasped from nearby.

Kit crouched down not responding.

"Cap'n. Is that ee? Cap'n Carter?" the voice persisted.

"No. But I've come from the *Maid of Trevisco,*" Kit replied. He had no choice but to seek shelter or else he'd surely die.

"Who are ee?"

"Never you mind." Kit rose and trudged towards the voice. "Just get me out of here and back to Fowey. I've had enough of this for one night."

Fifteen

Daylight lit the bedroom from behind half-drawn curtains when Beth awoke at Tregover Farm. Not good enough, she berated herself; she would have to rise much earlier, if she was to fit in with farm life.

A door opened on the ground floor, and Jimmy Rudge called out: "I'm goin' to see to the cows, Jen." He then began to whistle the furry dance melody out of tune.

"Best ee bring the eggs in first." Jenny shouted back.

"Won't be a moment," the boy replied.

"An' be sure to wipe your boots when ee comes in this time. Don't bring any more of that mucky snow into me kitchen."

"All right, then."

Beth smiled to herself with contentment. Beside her, Clem slept peacefully, his straw-coloured hair nudging into her neck. The brothers were alike in so many ways, each with a dangerous past. Perhaps Clem and she had been destined for one another all along. She grinned to herself, recalling details of his masterful lovemaking.

One thing still puzzled her. Why had Christopher sent him away from their home in Alabama? Clem had admitted to being a heavy drinker and consorting with bad women. But so had many other men. He had touched not a drop of alcohol since arriving in Penmarith and that seemed out of character. Could he have been guilty of worse behaviour? Had he perpetrated a crime? She studied Clem's face. No, that was most unlikely. It just didn't add up.

Christopher must have been wrong.

Clem slept on as she crept from his bed. Naked, she ran quickly down the passage on the balls of her feet, stirring up the cold air as she bustled into her own room. Her shift remained behind, hidden somewhere beneath Clem's bedclothes. Recovering it would surely have woken him. Inexplicably, she could not find her stockings while she donned her clothes although she recalled wearing them while working in the house yesterday. She finished dressing hurriedly without them and smiled as she stepped down the creaking stairs. Her father would have been shocked that she wore no stockings beneath her dress.

In the warmth of the kitchen, Jenny was scrubbing the wooden table, much as she had once done every morning at Studmore Manor. Her pregnancy was now noticeable, but she worked on with a firm arm honed by years of drudgery.

"Good mornin', me lady." The maid dropped the sort of curtsey she had habitually practised at the manor.

"Good morning, Jenny. It would be best if you called me Miss Killiow in this house." Curbing her embarrassment, Beth smiled at the girl and changed the subject. "Where's Mister Vanson's breakfast? I'll take it up to him."

"Ee don't have to do that, me lady ... Miss Killiow," Jenny protested. "I can take his breakfast upstairs. 'Tes my job to take it up to him."

"But not any longer, Jenny." Beth scanned about the kitchen, drinking in the warm domesticity: the lime-washed walls, the scrubbed table, the iron range wafting out its warmth and, hanging from the oak rafters, bunches of dried herbs for use in times of sickness. She beamed with satisfaction. "This isn't the manor. I have to start pulling my weight like everyone else."

"If ee say so, me lady."

Beth piled a wooden plate with hot kidneys, eggs and bacon. When that seemed vaguely inadequate, she set a jar of ale and a hunk of bread on the tray. Was this the sort of breakfast a country farmer expected every morning? Having spent her life being waited on by servants, she wasn't sure. She shrugged quietly and carried it up to Clem's bedroom.

"Wake up, Farmer Vanson." She set the tray on an oak cabinet beside his bed and pulled the curtains fully back. Ha! Peeking from beneath a crumpled heap of Clem's clothes were her stockings.

He sat up, rubbing his eyes. "Beth, that you?"

She sat on the edge of the bed and stroked his cheek before letting out a bubble of laughter. "What other women would come to visit you in your room?"

He yawned and stretched his arms. "What hour is it?"

"It matters not." She leaned closer and pecked him on the cheek. "Eat your breakfast. You must recover your strength, and then we can get to work looking after your brother's inheritance."

She caught a sparkle suddenly invading his eyes. "We could …"

"Tonight, Clem." She smiled, sealing her promise with a kiss, and left Clem to eat.

Her appetite had deserted her and, back in the kitchen, Beth picked at her breakfast. Probably the excitement of the last few days. Elbows on the table, she cradled a cup of tea between her hands and watched Jenny working. In a moment of curiosity, she asked: "Are you happy living here with Jimmy?"

"Course I be happy, me lady." Jenny slid a mound of bread dough into the oven then glanced at her. An unmistakable glow crossed the girl's face. "How could I be anythin' but happy when Jimmy's got work, we both got a place to live an' we'll soon have a babby of our own?"

"Is that all you want from life, Jenny? A home, a husband and a family?"

"What else is there, me lady … Miss Killiow?" Jenny straightened herself and patted her tummy.

Beth nodded. What indeed? "I believe Mister Vanson plans to let you have use of a farm cottage."

"'Ess, me lady. We're goin' to get it in proper order when the spring comes. Mister Vanson says we can move over there when ee's sorted out the bad business with yer brother, beggin' yer pardon for saying it." Embarrassed, Jenny busied herself pulling down a tangled loop of onions from a hook beside the door and carried them to the table.

Beth stood up, somewhat envious. "You're a lucky woman, Jenny, to have a good husband and a good employer."

"'Ess, me lady." Jenny beamed out her inner happiness.

Clem entered the kitchen shortly after. When Jenny's back was turned, he winked at Beth wickedly, and she blew him a kiss in return.

"Where's Jimmy?" he asked.

"In the barn, sur," Jenny replied, gingerly chopping the onions. "Mister Vanson said as how ee had to take good care of them animals. And Mister Padder is out there with my Jimmy."

"Quite right too. I think I'll give them a hand. What will you do, Beth?"

"There's enough work here to keep Jenny and me busy this morning." She grew serious. "However, I need to go back to the manor this afternoon."

Clem jerked his head upright, none too pleased. "Why?"

"Don't get the wrong idea." Beth grabbed at a greasy pot and dunked it into a bowl of dishwater. "I don't have sufficient belongings with me. I'll need to fetch more clothes." She scrubbed at the pot and let out a squeak as she broke a fingernail that had never been in dishwater before she came to Tregover.

"I'll buy you new clothes," he offered.

She laughed then examined the broken nail. "A nice idea. But it would be easier for me to collect what I already own. Will you ride over there with me?"

"I sure will. Don't you try on goin' without me." He winked again and hurried away to his work.

At midday, Beth and Clem ate a meal of cold mutton at the kitchen table with the servants. Ralph would have been horrified at the idea of her sharing a table with menials, but Beth allowed a small secret grin to creep around her mouth. She was eating with people she liked while Ralph was probably alone in his fine dining room. Broken nails and dishwater would not deter her from enjoying life at Tregover Farm. After all, she might one day become a farmer's wife. There was no certainty, of course; it would depend upon Clem.

The need to be sure of her feelings dictated she could not yet broach the matter with him, but the thought alone was exciting.

Nervousness crept up her spine as they rode out shortly after the meal was done. How would Ralph react? Would he be sufficiently sober to allow her freedom of movement inside the manor?

Heavy, black-grey clouds had broken up to reveal glimpses of ice blue sky. The snow was crisp underfoot, and hooves generated a satisfying crunch at each contact with the ground. At the outskirts of Penmarith, they both laughed at children slipping and sliding on the frozen surface of the village pond while others tumbled in the snow-filled banks, shouting and screaming with delight.

"It reminds me of when we were children," Beth sighed. "Ralph and I would play in the grounds of the manor and sometimes father would come out and join in the fun. We had such a good life then. Who'd have thought either of us would end up like this."

"Things change. Folks change. 'Tis no problem as long as you don't lose sight of your memories."

"Did you have a happy childhood, Clem?"

Beth waited patiently as he took a moment to compose his reply. "It weren't like this, for sure, but I guess we had us some fun. Swimmin' in the river in summer. Learnin' to ride as soon's we was old enough. I guess 'twas when we got older that things started to get out of hand. When Kit left home, our pa went a mite miserable and he came down hard on Pasco 'n me. That's when I started to rebel more'n I did before. Guess I caused some trouble."

Her heart tightened as she glanced at his lowered head. "That's all behind you now, Clem."

"Sure." But he gave her a haunted glance.

They rode through the village and on to where the countryside bore a mantle of alien isolation, as if the rest of the world was left behind. Easing their horses through the deep, treacherous snow, they continued in silence until their destination came into view. Despite the cold, a sharp afternoon light bathed Studmore Manor, giving it an unreal presence.

They urged the horses round to the cobbled yard and dismounted at the stables.

"We'll go in through the rear entrance," Beth said, leading the way. "Maybe Ralph won't see us."

Mrs Trevose let out a cry of pleasure as they crept into the kitchen. "Oh, my lady. 'Tes so good to see you again."

Pressing a finger against her lips, Beth shushed her quiet then whispered: "I only left a few days ago."

"Even so, my lady, the place ain't the same without you."

Beth responded with a silent shrug, opened the door to the overlong, dark passage and almost walked into Binner, letting out a sharp breath.

The servant stared at her with a mild air of surprise, drawing back his shoulders and tugging at his blue jacket. "The master is in the library, my lady," he announced somewhat pompously. "Shall I inform him you're here?"

"We'd better speak to him," Clem said, coming up behind Beth. Setting a hand on her shoulder, he added: "He'll wonder what we're up to if we don't."

She agreed reluctantly, disturbed by a sudden shiver of fear.

When she and Clem entered the room, Ralph seemed oblivious of cold draughts infiltrating around the library window. Her brother was lounging beside a blazing fire reading *The West Briton*. He then lowered the newspaper to his lap. "You've come back?" he asked in a surprised tone.

Beth kept her expression cold although her brother caused her such intense unease. "No, Ralph. I simply came to collect more of my belongings."

"I see. Making the final break with your past?"

Beth eyed him warily. Ralph appeared unusually sober, a worrying sign. When he was drunk, he was invariably violent. When he was coldly sober, his cunning became dangerous.

"Mister Vanson accompanied me. I'll pack my things as quickly as I can, and he'll escort me away again."

Killiow rose and levelled his gaze at Clem. "By rights, I should have you thrashed. You and that damned brother of yours."

"Ralph, please. No more violence, for my sake. I came only to collect what rightfully belongs to me. I'll leave again without any trouble."

"That man's brother struck me!" Killiow hissed between gritted teeth.

Beth stepped lightly forward and pressed her hands persuasively against Ralph's chest. "We want no more trouble." She lowered her tone. "It's past. Let it be."

"Expect me to forgive him, do you?"

"No. But we haven't caused *you* any trouble over father's death." She left the rest unsaid and Ralph gruffly backed away. His gaze oscillated between the two of them as he digested the situation. His eyes narrowed into slits and Beth shuddered. What was going on inside that devious brain?

"Very well." He turned to a polished mahogany side table and poured heavy measures of rum into two tumblers. "Out of courtesy to me sister, I'll offer you a drink." He marched up to Clem and thrust one glass into his hand.

"I'd rather not," Clem began, anxiously holding the glass at arm's length.

"Refuse to drink with me, would you?" Killiow snarled and drew an insulted expression across his face. "Think you're a better man than me, American?"

Clem sighed in frustration. "If you insist." He lifted the glass to his lips.

"Just to show no hard feelings," the squire said gruffly. "Seeing as it was your brother who attacked me."

Clem took one small sip. "I'll take this one glass with you, Squire Killiow." Giving Beth's brother a curt nod, he lifted the glass again, downing the rum in one gulp.

Beth swung her gaze to Ralph's cunning stare then at Clem. Something was wrong here. "Be careful, Clem," she warned him. Her unease intensified. Had she led Clem into an impossible dilemma?

Her escort turned to her and winked. "I'm used to a tot of rum. Had more'n a few in my time so don't you worry about me."

But she did worry.

She worried because her brother was in an apparently benevolent mood and that made her suspicious. Ralph was many things; a true gentleman, he was not.

She rushed up the stairs to her one-time bedroom and pulled open cupboard and drawers. Clothes and finery tumbled out onto the floor as she decided what she could carry away with her. She gathered up an armful of belongings, bundled them into her biggest carpetbag then pulled them out again because the bag couldn't contain it all. She would have to be ruthless in what she left behind.

A gentle chime had her glance at the mantle clock above the empty fireplace. Half an hour had passed, and she was still not finished. She began to fluster. Her jewellery. She could not leave her treasures behind or Ralph would surely sell them. She threw the lot untidily into a valise. Soon she'd be ready, just change into her grey riding habit and she would ride away with Clem.

Must hurry.

The carpetbag and valise were both now overly full. She looked at the remainder of her belongings, frustrated; so much would be useful at the farm. Then she remembered the old tin trunk. She dragged it out and packed it tightly. She would ask for one of the servants to transport it to the farm later. Finally, she was ready to leave.

Someone knocked hesitantly on her bedroom door. Mrs Trevose came in slowly and bobbed her head. "Beggin' yer pardon, my lady. I was wonderin' how young Jenny be gettin' on now that she's married."

At the interruption, Beth sighed, picking up her two bags as a sign of her intentions. "She's very well, Mrs Trevose. I'll tell her you were enquiring."

But the cook hung in the doorway, seemingly anxious to talk. "She were such a skinny young thing. I hope as how she carries the babby well."

"Believe me, Mrs Trevose, Jenny is absolutely blooming."

"I felt so sorry for the poor mite, goin' off like that."

"Mrs Trevose, I really must go now." Beth edged closer to the door.

"Yes, my lady." The cook shot her a hurt expression as Beth pushed past and rushed back down the stairs to the library.

She dumped the two bags outside the library door and paused to adjust her habit. A loud raucous laugh reverberated from inside. It was Ralph. He was laughing. Panic seized her.

Beth rushed in and took in the scene at a glance. Her brother, the new Squire, stood with his coat tails to the fire, his hands behind his back. He was laughing, but his lips were curled back like a wild animal about to lunge for the kill. Clem sat alongside the fire, a full glass of rum cradled in his hands, his eyes glazed over and his cheeks flushed.

He waved a hand at Beth. "Here she is, Ralph, the Lady of the Manor." To her dismay, his voice was heavily slurred.

"Yes, the whore of Studmore," her brother added quietly, grinning to himself.

Clem picked it up and frowned, then he grinned tentatively. "That right, Ralph?"

A bolt of horror ran through Beth. She cast around the room, fearful at how much Clem might have drunk in her absence. A half empty bottle rested on a side table by his seat. Another bottle, quite empty, lay on its side on the floor. Binner must have brought another bottle while she was upstairs.

"We must go, Clem." Beth hurried across the room and offered her hand. "Quickly."

"No, not yet. We don't have to hurry us none." Clem ignored her gesture and took a deep gulp of rum then wiped a backhand across his mouth. Almost immediately, Ralph poured another measure into the glass with a wicked grin on his face.

Beth tensed, palpitations rising in her chest.

Ralph turned to her. "Let the man have a drink with me, Beth. After all, it does no harm to drink with one's friends."

Beth clenched her hands into tight fists now understanding her brother's tactic. "Friends! You're no friend to anyone, Ralph."

"You wrong me, Beth." Ralph's even-paced voice with a touch of melodramatic pathos angered her even further. He held no drink in his hand and his filled glass sat on the mantelpiece, quite untouched.

"Please, Clem." Beth knelt down beside him and grasped at his sleeve, bunching it between tightly clamped fingers. "We must go. Now!"

Clem threw back his head. "Shut up, woman," he snarled, annoyance glistening in his eyes. "Don't presume to tell me what to do." He grabbed her hand and thrust it aside with a powerful movement.

Ralph laughed. "That's the way, Clem. Don't stand for any nonsense from me sister. Never let a woman get the better of you."

Beth glared at each of them in turn. Realisation reached her brain like a cloud pulling back from the sun. So this was why Christopher had sent his brother to sea. The man, who had been so good to her in bed, was rapidly becoming as foul as her brother.

She stood up and gritted her teeth. "All right, Clem Vanson. Stay here, if that's what you want. I'll not wait around to see you make a fool of yourself."

Clumsily, Clem threw out a hand to her and missed wildly as Beth stepped back. "And good riddance to you."

She pulled the door tight shut behind her, deeply hurt. A couple of minutes passed while she composed herself before grabbing her bags and hurrying out to her horse. She rode away, urging the horse too fast through the clogging snow. Happiness, that wonderful experience of the past few days, was gone from her heart. Would she ever find a new peace at Tregover Farm?

Trudging slowly into the farm under the weight of her baggage, she said nothing of the reason for Clem's absence to Jimmy or Jenny. Instead, she told them he would be late home because of business in Penmarith, and she hated herself for lying on his account. That night she climbed the stairs with a heavy heart, shuffled into her own bedroom and purposefully locked her door before she undressed. Once in bed she lay awake, listening for sounds announcing Clem's return.

Long after darkness had fallen, a horse ambled into the farmyard. A loud, drunken curse followed the thudding sound of Clem falling from the saddle. She heard his scuffling in the crisp snow until a door slammed. Beth pulled her bedclothes tighter around her neck. He was inside the house.

His footsteps scraped on the stairs, stumbled along the landing then his bedroom door creaked open. Moments after, he crashed back onto the landing and stopped outside her room.

"Beth," he commanded in a heavily slurred voice. "Open this ... this door, woman. Don't you ... know who I am?"

She held her tongue. It was now so clear why Christopher had sent his brother to sea, away from a life of debauchery in Alabama. Clem was an inveterate drunk.

Christopher had been right after all.

The room was still dark when Beth blinked open her eyes. The tail end of a dream mingled with the live noises that had woken her. She sharpened her senses to angry voices outside the house and cattle bellowing.

A dull rattle of her door handle accompanied the hushed tone of Jimmy Rudge calling to her. "We got trouble, me lady. There be men outside there, an' they be after the cattle."

Beth grabbed at her cape as she ran to her bedroom door and unbolted it. She pulled on her boots, threw the cape around her shift and followed Jimmy downstairs. Jenny waited in the kitchen, her eyes wide with fear.

"For heaven's sake, Jenny," Beth snapped. "Go back to your room. We can't risk you being hurt."

The pale-faced girl gasped with relief. "Yes, me lady … Miss Killiow." She curtsied and hurried to the stairs.

"Where's Jacob Padder?" Beth asked.

Jimmy pointed to the door. "Ee went outside to see what was goin' on."

Beth frowned. "Let's hope he's not been hurt." She grabbed a lantern and opened the kitchen door. She stepped outside and edged cautiously across the yard towards the cattle barn, the lantern held out high in front of her.

Stopping some yards from the barn door, she gaped at dark figures flittering in the shadows inside the building. Deep voices were arguing, and dim lights danced in the cold air. She hoped a firm authoritative voice would stop them in their deed.

"You there," she shouted. "Whoever you are, leave those animals alone."

A stout figure carrying a shielded lantern came out of the barn's darkness and shambled towards her. At first, he was only a hazy shadow but, as he came close up, Pengwidden's familiar features drew into focus. He stopped a few feet from her and glowered. In the dimness behind him, two more intruders held Jacob Padder captive.

"You," she gasped, her heart full of vexation. "What are you doing in this barn?"

"Never you mind, Mistress Killiow. Get back in the house." Pengwidden's voice was strangely slurred. He took another step forward and, before she could dodge him, he pushed her backwards.

"How dare you," she cried as she staggered then regained her balance. "Leave this farm at once!"

"Master gave orders we was to take no truck from ee." Pengwidden advanced on her again. At a warning shout from the kitchen door, he halted abruptly.

"You heard the lady." The reedy voice came from Jimmy Rudge, his thin body outlined by light from inside the farmhouse. "Leave her alone."

Pengwidden laughed derisively. "Get back inside the house, boy. Before ee gets hurt."

"Leave or I'll shoot this pistol!" Jimmy took aim.

Pengwidden laughed again, a drunken, irresponsible laugh. With a suddenness that caught her totally off guard, he lashed out with his fist and caught Beth across the cheek. She slumped to the ground.

A sharp pain stabbed through her head and distorted sounds screamed past her face. Nearby, her lantern fizzled out, leaving her confused and dizzy on her back in the freezing snow. Her head throbbed. Her eyes refused to cooperate. The cold razed through her body. What was happening to her?

Footsteps scrunched towards her. "I told you to leave her alone," Jimmy bellowed menacingly.

Beth sat up and shielded her eyes as another lantern moved across in front of her, carried aloft by a manly outline. She panned around and dim shapes moved in a semi-circle around her and Jimmy.

"Time someone shut ee up, boy," Pengwidden barked.

A pistol shot cracked.

Beth shuddered from the effects of concussion and crawled to her knees, expecting the contents of her stomach to come up. A moan from nearby had her raising her head. She blinked before her focus sharpened on Pengwidden.

He was on his knees grasping at his right shoulder.

"Hold onto me as best ee can, mistress." Jimmy wrapped one arm about her waist before she was aware of his close presence. He helped her to her feet.

Her head was still spinning, but she caught the smell of the smoking pistol in Jimmy's other hand. She pressed her fingers against her aching brow and looked about.

Her brother's henchman thrashed about in the snow, gasping and shouting for assistance. But the other men held back, gaping and shaking their heads at the turn of events. They had not expected armed resistance. In the confusion, Jacob used th opportunity to escape and run towards Beth.

Eventually, Pengwidden found the strength to rise to his feet, groaning from pain and clasping at his wound. The other men began to withdraw, muttering.

"Come back here," Pengwidden roared thickly as a dark stain grew on his coat. When they ignored his order, he stumbled towards them, cursing his foul luck.

Beth swayed on her feet, shivering in the appalling cold. Taking her weight between them, Jimmy and Jacob eased her towards the house while the pain in her head intensified. Still clasping at her forehead, she glanced at the gun still in Jimmy's other hand. "Where did you get that thing?"

He tossed it aside and used both his arms to support her. "It's their own pistol, me lady. One of them dropped it when they attacked Miss Lanyon at Crabtree Copse Farm." Beth shook her head, confusion hitting her hard.

They had attacked Wenna at her own farm! Dear God! If only she had known such things were happening, she could have done something about it. Slowly, her thoughts fell into more coherent order. Ralph was behind everything. He must have planned it all when he sent Clem back here, drunk as a lord and in no condition to protect the farm. Maybe he had plied Pengwidden with the same rum when he sent him out on a raid to steal Christopher's cattle.

"Well done, Jimmy. I think you've just saved your master's farm from the sort of ruin Miss Lanyon suffered." A pity his brother was lying drunk in his bed. Anguish overwhelmed her, but it was more for Clem's weakness than for her brother's wickedness.

Sixteen

Early February 1838

A capping of snow still topped the distant hills and Kit groaned. He pulled his cape tighter against the cold wind while his horse trudged along the road into Plymouth town in pure mud.

Yesterday, he'd ridden over frozen ground covered with crisp snow. Today, a thick quagmire clutched at his horse's hooves. Kit hung his shoulders.

He had exhausted all avenues in his search for Wenna and found no trace of her. If he met failure here, he would have little option but to return to Penmarith and try to console himself that he had done his best.

His best? No, never. Failure could never be his best.

He urged his horse down the muddy length of Union Street, circuiting a band of drunken revellers, mostly sailors recently paid-off. More sailors congregated outside an inn close by where the road widened at the corn exchange. Kit clicked his mount on into Lockyer Street then Citadel Road, where carriages clattered past, indiscriminately splattering a foul mix of mud and steaming horse dung against unwary passers-by.

Finally, he came onto the cobbled quays and wharfs at Sutton Harbour where flocks of gulls circled overhead while others cried sadly from the rooftops. He rested his mount, gazing up and down at the familiar outlines of so many ships lying alongside and anchored in the approaches. He breathed in the reassuring salty smell of the sea and, suddenly, he had an overwhelming urge to be out there on one of those ships, all set to cross the oceans of the world.

Should he now admit Ben Worth was right? Should he give up all thoughts of farming and return to the sea? He could sell Tregover and forever remain far from both the slavery in Alabama and the devious landowners in Cornwall. But he knew, even now that guilt would surely go with him.

He panned around the harbour and brought his gaze to rest on a group of smaller boats: fishing ketches, revenue cutters and a Brixham trawler, nudging the shore in Coxside Creek. They lay lethargically against the wharves and quays below Teats Hill. Away to his right, half hidden by a misty drizzle, larger ships lay at anchor in the vast expanse of Plymouth Sound. His gaze caught a naval steamship sitting at anchor just beyond the mouth of the harbour. Then he fixed onto uniforms, a group of Royal Navy sailors mingling untidily with the fish market crowd. One boat out in the Sound, a small revenue cutter, was beating its way upstream against the tide.

Tired and soaked, Kit turned his horse towards the town. Passing through the dingy backstreets behind the quay, he by-passed the Admiral Nelson and other cheap lodging places. His seafaring days were now behind him and a visit to his old haunts would serve no useful purpose. Instead, he took a room at the Botany Bay Inn near the top end of the town, well away from the harbour. While he could not avoid mixing with seafaring men in Plymouth, he could minimise the contact.

Later that evening he sat before a warm fire, savouring a tankard of mulled ale. The landlord, a one-armed giant of a man, served him a plate of cheese and pickles. Kit nodded his thanks to the scarred face, which looked like the result of an old powder-scorch wound.

"What ship are ee from, sur?" His scars quivered when the landlord spoke.

"No ship." Kit reached for a piece of cheese. "I'm from a place called Penmarith. I've got a farm there."

"I know Penmarith." The landlord beamed, easing himself into a seat opposite. "Me an' me brother once worked there on Squire Killiow's land."

Kit eyed him expectantly. Filled with a brief moment of hope, he dropped his chunk of cheese and folded his arms on the table. "Then perhaps you know Miss Wenna Lanyon?"

But the landlord only screwed up his scarred face. "Can't say as how I do. We was only young lads at the time and we spent most of our days workin' in the fields. Then we got thrown out of work so me brother upped an' went off to sea. Haven't seen him since."

"But you're not a seafaring man?" Kit waved around at the establishment. Disappointed, he occupied himself by moving pieces of food around the dish.

"No." The landlord sat down and held up the useless stump of a limb. "Lost most of this arm when I took to punt gunnin' in the winter. That's when me face got burned."

"I heard tell of them boats," Kit said, wrapping his hands around his ale tankard. "Men get killed with such weapons."

"Too many." The man's bad breath wafted over Kit as he answered. "Puny boats with heavy guns is bound to be dangerous. But they can shoot a pound of shot a distance of seventy yards. I was wedgin' in the black powder with oakum when the damned thing fired unexpected an' took me arm off."

"I'm sorry for you." Kit had seen worse accidents at sea but he didn't mention it for the sake of upsetting the man.

"You're not a local man, are ee?"

"No, I'm from America."

"America, ee say?" The landlord leaned back in his seat. "And what would a Colonial man be doin' livin' at Penmarith?"

Kit shrugged his shoulders. "My ancestors came from there. My father left many years ago and built up a plantation in Alabama."

"Alabama?" The landlord's eyes widened in surprise. "Why damn me, if I didn't have a seafarin' gent from Alabama sittin' right there in that seat. About a week ago, it was." He nodded his head vigorously. "I remember it on account of ee said ee was born in Birmingham, Alabama, an' I told him how a good friend o' mine came here from Birmingham, England."

Kit pricked up his ears, his interest aroused. "What was his name, this seafarer?"

"His name? Can't quite recall. Cap'n of a schooner, ee was. Name of …" The landlord screwed up his face in deep concentration. "Worth! That's it. Cap'n Worth."

Suddenly elated, Kit sprang to his feet, upending his tankard. Ben Worth. Here in Plymouth! "Is he still here? At this inn?"

"Not at the Botany Bay, ee ain't. But if his ship's still in port, ee's bound to be on board. Ee said as how ee was moored at Union Dock in Millbay. Said ee'd be there a while yet."

Excitement stirring his limbs, Kit took a step towards the door with the intention of racing down to the waterside, greeting his old friend and sharing a few jars while they talked over old times. Then common sense kicked in, and he came to an abrupt halt. At this time of night, the dockside would be a dangerous place. If thieves didn't waylay him, the navy press-gang most likely would. Curbing his impatience, he returned to the table and righted his tankard. His appetite had returned.

He slept more easily that night and breakfasted early the following morning. With few people milling about the streets at that hour, he collected his horse and cantered down to Millbay Docks. The snow of the past few weeks had turned to sleet, dulling the noise of the gathering activity around the shore. Out in the Sound, the naval steamship was turning to catch the morning tide. Women in clogging wet clothes huddled around the fish shambles. Kit's nose caught the decaying odour of fish, carried along the quay on gusts of wind.

He veered his horse away and continued along the waterside until he recognized a familiar vessel. A smile came unbidden to his face and a lump arose in his throat at the sight of the beautiful three-masted schooner – the *Tamarith*.

Many times he had sailed aboard her out of New Orleans, New York, Newfoundland, Bristol or Cape Town. And many times he had returned having gained in stature and experience. Ben was the only captain he ever addressed on first name terms; a privilege he had earned through hard sweat, good seamanship and trust built up on dangerous voyages.

He shouted to a figure on deck. "Is Cap'n Worth aboard?"

"Depends who wants him. And why," the sailor replied.

"Tell him it's Kit Vanson. He'll remember me."

The seaman slouched away and, shortly afterwards, a white-haired figure in a black jacket came up from the forward companionway.

"Ben! Hey Ben!" Kit ran up the gangway.

"Kit." Ben Worth laughed throatily as they clasped hands with the warmth of old friends.

"You ain't changed none, Ben."

"Well, neither have you, boy. You sure are a welcome sight." Ben's slow Southern drawl brought back instant memories of happier times and Kit's heart tightened. "Come on down to my cabin. You an' me got some real talkin' to catch up on."

Kit followed him down the companionway into a familiar cabin infused with comforting warmth and homeliness. Just as he remembered it.

"You'll take a tot with me?" Ben didn't wait for an answer. He opened a cupboard fixed above his desk, pulled out two tumblers and a bottle of Jamaican rum.

Kit sank into a seat and grinned broadly. "Reckon I will at that, Ben."

"It sure ain't the first time we've drunk together, and God forbid, it should be the last." He thrust a glass into Kit's hand and raised his own in salute.

"Amen to that, Ben. What brings you back to Plymouth again?"

"Necessity, boy. Pure necessity." The captain sipped his rum and smacked his lips. "Got us a broken mast when a storm hit the South West Approaches. This here was the nearest port we could make, what with the wind threatening to turn us over, an' all. We've gotten our repairs almost complete and we'll soon be ready to put to sea."

"You've a cargo?"

Ben's face broke into a wide grin. "Now, did I ever sail without a cargo?"

Kit laughed, and a vague feeling that he had lost something since leaving the sea lingered in his chest. "Not in all the time I knew you."

"What about you, Kit?" Ben raised his brows quizzically. "You ain't plannin' on signin' on with us, are you?"

"No, Ben." *But how dearly he wanted to.* "Put the thought from your mind. England's my home now."

"Is it working out?" The old sailor eyed him. "Or did things turn sour?"

Kit sipped at his drink. "You're a sly one. You see through everyone, don't you?"

"And you don't hide your feelin's too well, boy. Are you still aimin' to make a go of it?"

"That's what I told you, Ben. The day I left this ship."

"I remember. Said you'd give it all you've got." Ben grinned then his face broke into frown. "But you're not happy are you?"

Kit hesitated. "No, not at this moment," he replied with an intensity that kept his voice almost to a whisper. He gave himself a mental shake; he wasn't prepared to abandon Wenna. "But I have to stay here and see things through. If I run away from the trouble I've found here, I'll never be able to live at peace with myself again."

Ben studied him then breathed aloud in a way that cut through the seriousness of Kit's words. "Sounds mighty philosophical. I sure hope you know what you're doing."

Kit shrugged his shoulders. "Well, I'm not sure I do and that's the truth of the matter."

"Anything I can do to help?"

"Not a thing." Kit cradled his glass in his hands, lowering his gaze. It was time to change the subject. "When do you leave here?"

"First week in March. We're short of men, but there's a hiring for hands later this month. The Newfoundland trade starts in March, and I reckon I can pick up some extra cargo from it. Enough to pay for these repairs and get us back home."

"All legal?"

"If I can pick up a legal cargo, I will." The rest was left unsaid.

An hour of chatting passed before they climbed back on deck where a cold drizzle had set in. Kit took the old sea captain's hand and shook it firmly. "It's been real good to see you again, Ben. Real good."

The captain nodded. "Look, Kit, you know my plans. If you change your mind and you want a berth on this ship, you just let me know. You hear now?"

Kit gave him a curt nod.

"You can mail me a message. I'll send one of my men to the post office daily to check. Don't you forget now."

"I won't forget. I promise."

Kit rode away into the town and occupied the remainder of the morning by calling at banks, notaries, inns and shops to enquire about Wenna. In desperation, he even sought out the local brothel. But no one could reveal any news of her. In the afternoon, he repeated the entire process with different establishments. He stayed one more night in Plymouth and, lying awake in his uncomfortable bed, resigned himself to failure. As a sop to his feelings, he told himself that Wenna might have returned to Penmarith. He did not believe it, but he had searched long enough and now had no other sensible option than to return to Tregover.

On the final morning, he took an early breakfast at the inn before collecting his horse. He cursed himself as he climbed into the saddle. Maybe he had brought dishonour on Wenna simply by taking an interest in her. But then a surprise question sprung to his mind. Suppose he had found her, would he have married her – thereby proving the power of the curse?

He had no doubts about the answer.

He rode out of town along Union Street, past the post office where he stopped long enough to discover that letters from St Austell arrived at half past four every morning. If he decided to take up Ben Worth's offer, it would be relatively easy to send a message to him. But he knew deep down that he couldn't do it. He had an obligation to his grandfather to rebuild Tregover Farm and, more than that, he had a moral obligation to remain, in case Wenna returned.

The road out of Plymouth became ever more difficult as the rain grew heavier. Kit had been riding for almost an hour when something unusual on the road ahead caught his notice. From a distance, it looked very much like a bundle of old clothes someone had tossed away, and he would have guided his horse around it had the animal not spooked and stumbled in a deep mud hole. Kit dismounted to check the horse's fetlock. Satisfied that the animal had not been injured, he crossed the road to the pile of rags with the intention of kicking them out of the way for other travellers.

But the clothes covered the body of a woman, a young woman with long, dark hair.

"Wenna!" He reached out to touch the body. "Wenna," he sighed loudly, his heart aching.

He gently lifted the body, turning the woman's face towards him.

It was not her.

Thank God it was not Wenna because she was stone cold dead. Her skin was a greyish blue, icy to the touch. Already she had stiffened, the feel and smell of decay oozing about her.

He set the body down reverently on the side of the road and hung his head in desperation. Could this also be the end that Wenna had found? Was she also a corpse on some lonely road? Tears fell from his cheeks as he mounted his horse, praying for Wenna's safety.

The morning after Kit had arrived back at Tregover Farm, he rose early, determined to work in the main barn. Hard, manual labour might just help his air of frustration. He sat at the kitchen table and watched Beth prepare his breakfast. She kept her back towards him, but Kit picked up on her occasional sniffing and wiping at her nose. Since Jimmy and Jenny were in the barn milking the cows, Jacob was out in the five acre field, and Clem was still abed, he vowed to get to the bottom of the problem.

"You'd better tell me what's been goin' on."

"Going on?" she said, but she didn't turn around. Instead, she bent her head towards the pans on the Cornish range.

"Don't play games with me, Beth." He wiped a hand across his forehead, feeling a rising headache. "I can see things ain't right here."

She wiped her hands on her apron and turned around. She kept her eyes averted and her teeth chewed at her lower lip.

"Out with it, Beth."

She crossed the room and sat at the table opposite him. Curbing an insipient tear with the flick of a hand at one eye, she slowly, carefully, related the events of the night the farm had been attacked.

"You did well to hold those men off."

Beth shook her head. "It was Jimmy who really frightened them off. He found a gun and shot one of Killiow's men after he knocked me down."

"Shot him?"

"Only wounded him." She sighed. "Ralph won't make anything of it as long as his man wasn't killed."

"Jimmy did that? Reckon that boy has more guts than I gave him credit for." But Kit worried more about his brother. "What about Clem? How did he cope with the attack?"

Beth turned away and gulped. She seemed to need a moment to compose herself then glanced back at him. "Clem was drunk in his bed. He'd been drinking with Ralph." She gave him a sad look. "We went over to the manor to recover my belongings and … well, Ralph supplied the drink and Clem …" Her eyes glazed over with tears. "I'm sorry, Kit."

Hell, Clem was on the booze again! Kit pounded a fisted hand on the table. "I just knew that boy couldn't be trusted." He jumped to his feet, enraged.

Beth hurried round the table and laid a hand on his arm. "I'm sorry to tell you this, but you had to know. And I feel so bad about it because I was really getting to, well, to be honest, I was getting to love him."

"Love him? That boy don't deserve the likes of you, Beth." Kit stormed towards the stairs. "Damn me, if I don't give him a good whipping."

Beth rushed after him and caught his arm. He gave her a pained look, hoping she could see the anguish haunting his soul. But what was the point of taking out his anger on her? Clem was the villain. He patted her hand, and lowered his voice. "I'm sorry I shouted, Beth, but I beg of you not to interfere." When she released him, he took the stairs two at a time to Clem's bedroom and hammered on the door.

A muffled voice called out: "What do you want?"

"Clem. You open this door now. You hear!"

Kit waited while the bed creaked and padded feet reached the door. It squeaked open slowly and his brother stretched up to his full height, shame-faced and contrite.

"Reckon she told you about me, then?" Clem's voice was even but muted in awkward embarrassment.

"Reckon she did." Kit forced himself into the room and shut the door firmly behind him. "And I reckon you still ain't learned your lesson. You got drunk and you left Beth to defend the farm alone."

Clem hung his head low. "I'm sorry, Kit. I really am. It won't happen again."

"You bet it won't, Clem. You know why?" Kit advanced on his brother, a firm finger jabbing at his shoulder. "Cos I know where there's a ship that'll take you back to America. Right now I figure you ought to be sailing with it."

His brother gave him a hopeful glance. "You won't give me another chance?"

"You don't deserve another chance. By God, I'll write to Ben Worth this very day and have you signed on to sail with him."

Seventeen

"Help me. Please." Wenna clasped at her aching chest and hoped the passing rider would have the compassion to stop.

But he gave her a look of contempt, muttering: "Filthy wretch." Then he urged his horse on along the Bodmin Road.

Wenna leaned against a tall yew and bent her head, fighting back tears. She went into a coughing spell; a deep racking noise, which brought up thick mucus laced with blood. The pain in her lungs was growing worse. She spat out the mucus and drew her sleeve across her mouth.

The fever rarely left her now. She wished she could rest, just a little longer, but she could not stay here in the open, if she were to survive. Dragging her feet, she pushed on.

In the late afternoon, she reached the hard cobbled streets of Bodmin town. Thick mud caked her feet, now wrapped in nothing but torn sacking. A week ago she had sold her boots to buy food. Three days ago she'd sold her dress and now she wore a pauper's garb, roughly cut from sackcloth.

Tired and shivering, she hobbled through the sombre streets, hunching her shoulders and avoiding eye contact. Townspeople observed her with such pitying expressions. Would the local beadle have her flogged as a vagrant? Would Killiow's henchmen find her here? Pray not. She no longer had the strength to run away.

Raised voices filled the air as she shuffled down a steep hill, following a trickle of chattering townsfolk. Laughing and bellowing, they spoke of a hanging and headed towards the town gaol in the hollow at the bottom of the slope. Wenna followed the flow to where a babbling mass swarmed outside the gaol entrance.

The internment buildings rose up dark and brooding but – the thought made her tremble – could it be better than roaming the street on sacking feet? She was tempted to glance up at the lines of barred windows. Indistinct faces of prisoners looked down, surveying a scene in which any one of them might soon take part.

On the edge of the crowd, Wenna shifted her glance to the gallows platform and gasped. A corpse dangled from the gibbet.

"You'm too late to see the hangin'," a wizened old crone told her while rubbing her hands with glee. "Should've come earlier if you'd wanted to see her swing."

Wenna felt no joy at seeing someone swing and wished she had not come here. "Who was she?" she asked, feeling as though the words were choking her.

"Martha Wormwold." The old hag jabbed a pipe stem at the victim. "Killed her husban', so they say. Mind you, most decent folks think ee deserved to die after the way ee beat her." She cackled, stuffed the pipe in her mouth and shuffled away.

The sightseers gawped noisily at the still oscillating, broken-neck corpse while Martha Wormwold stared back at them with bulging, sightless eyes. The rope creaked and her thin, pathetic body began to sway harder on a sudden breeze, revolving on the rope like a grotesque child's toy. Her distended tongue protruded from her mouth like a last defiant gesture.

Feeling faint and nauseated, Wenna turned away and struggled towards the centre of the town. She hid in a dark alley between two houses and took a small sliver of cheese from her pocket, biting into it then chewing it slowly. It was the last of her food. She choked on her tears because she had nothing left to sell.

Except her body.

At the thought, her head began to swim. She reached out to steady herself, determination surging within her. She must find somewhere out of this cold, damp air. Anywhere. Then improper thoughts came into her wandering mind again. Bodmin had more than one brothel. Places where she might earn enough money for food and, maybe, medicine for her chest. But did she have the courage to take that final step?

Why not? Ralph Killiow had already stolen from her all trace of dignity. She was bound for hell anyway. Her only alternative was to throw herself at the mercy of the workhouse. Which would be the worse humiliation: the brothel or the workhouse? It was an interesting question to tax her mind while dying of starvation.

If she went to the workhouse, she would be dependant on the support of the parish for the rest of her miserable life, destined for a pauper's grave and probably quite soon. If she went to a brothel, she would have the chance to earn her food by fair barter, her body for money. And what was the point of worrying about morality when she should be thinking only of staying alive?

She choked. What would Christopher think of her sinking to such depravity? Likely they would never meet again, so his opinion mattered not. But she would always remember him with affection.

In the meantime, she had no other option. She would go to one of the brothels.

The rain turned heavy once more. She huddled into the darkness of the narrow alley, but it provided little protection. After a while, she moved on, a tight cough racking her chest. She raised her sleeve to her mouth and blood soaked it.

Darkness fell as she staggered along Fore Street; the rain turning to biting sleet around her. She turned along another narrow alley where rainwater washed the sewage along in one stinking sludge.

The Bodmin streets and alleys were almost empty now. And yet … and yet the muffled sound of singing drifted lightly on the breeze. She paused to listen, to locate its origin.

She spied an old woman, ill dressed and dirty, shuffling into a thatched cottage that was incongruously hemmed in on either side by two-storey buildings. While the door was open, the hymn singing flowed out into the street like an anthem of warmth and comfort.

A rousing Methodist hymn it was; the sort they never sang in Penmarith parish church. But Wenna recalled her father humming it from time to time.

I feel Him in the land,
Where the power of His hand
Guides me as I follow on His way.
When I'm feeling tired and cold,
It's His loving hand I hold.
Yes, He's with me in the night and day.
The singing rose to a crescendo with the final chorus.
Power in the land!
Power in the land!

There is power in the hardy land.

Wenna sniffed back a tear. Strange how those poor people who owned so little managed to inject such gusto into their hymns, as if they actually had something joyful to sing about.

If she could look inside the cottage, she would doubtless see dissenters, people like Arthur Pengorse holding a prayer meeting. How she hated that man, almost as much as she hated Ralph Killiow.

The singing faded into an indistinct murmur. Wenna shuffled closer, and the singing stopped entirely. Muffled, as if from afar, a strident voice rose from amongst the others.

That voice. Didn't she recognise it? Then the pain in her chest grew and became almost too much to bear. She forgot about the voice and leant against a wall for support.

When her pain subsided, her mind drifted off into a bout of hallucination. Worn out, she glided down on the cold, wet ground and closed her eyes. Recognise the voice? Surely not. She had never attended a Methodist service.

She might well die here on the cold street unless she could make her way to the brothel by nightfall. If only her legs would carry her. If only she could walk just a little farther.

Vivid dreams came to her as in sleep. Dreams of her mother and the precious few years they had spent together. She could see her again, see her quite clearly, hear her calling out. Wenna reached out to embrace the image, but her arms fell back into her lap, limp. After a while she slipped over onto her side and numbness crept up silently through her body.

The vision faded insidiously into greyness until voices nearby crept into mind. Alarmed voices. And the booming timbre of a man speaking to her, only inches from her face.

The voice; there it was again. She ought to recognise it, if she could just open her eyes and see his face. If she could just …

Someone picked her up in one swoop and carried her. Strong arms … A man's comforting words … A woman's voice. Time passed, lost in total darkness. Then warmth enveloped her. She sighed aloud with thanks and her nose twitched at the comforting smell of wood-smoke.

With heat now seeping into her body, she groped about where she lay. It felt like a dry, comfortable bed. Adding to her confusion, someone slipped a soft pillow beneath her head.

Time passed her by; she was unable to measure its passage. She came to often, but would quickly fall back into periods of light sleep.

At the first real awakening she was aware of, daylight blinded her. She snapped her eyes shut against the glare of sunlight and then eased them open, slowly, shielding them with a hand. She lay on a straw mattress stretched out on a compacted earth floor in front of a warm fire crackling in a small hearth. Glancing about the tiny room, she rested her gaze on a grey-haired woman calmly knitting in a rocking chair, the only furniture apart from the mattress.

"You'm awake, then?" the woman said, dropping her knitting on her lap.

"Where am I?" Wenna eased herself up on her elbows, but the effort brought a racking cough, and her head began to swim. She closed her eyes.

"Never you mind where ee be, me 'andsome. Lie there an' don't try to move. I'll bring ee some hot broth." A shuffling sound told her the old woman was leaving the room.

Wenna opened her eyes when she returned with a steaming bowl. "Don't try to sit up, me lovely, I'll spoon it into ee where you lie." Then the woman squatted on the floor by the bed.

Wenna creased her face into a questioning look.

"Four days you've been unconscious." The woman shook her head while she slowly spooned the hot broth into Wenna's mouth. "They all thought ee was goin' to die, but the pastor prayed for ee. We all prayed for ee. God must have heard them prayers."

"What pastor?" Wenna croaked. Then a sudden recollection rose from the back of her mind. The voice.

"Why, Pastor Pengorse. 'Twas him who found ee right outside me cottage. Out there, lying in the dirt and wet, ee was. Half conscious. Reckon ee would have died that night, if the pastor hadn't spotted ee."

Pengorse! A spasm of alarm hit her. Pastor Arthur Pengorse had saved her from almost certain death, how could fate be so cruel?

"And who are you?"

"Ellie Mounter. Most folks round here call me Old Mother Mounter." The woman smiled and her thin, cracked voice conveyed warmth.

"You're very kind, Ellie Mounter."

"Ah, 'tes no more than the pastor asked me to do." Ellie dismissed Wenna's thanks with a wave, adding: "Most concerned, ee was."

Saved by Pastor Pengorse. She shook her head at the cruel irony as a wave of exhaustion swept over her.

She slept on the floor by the fire in what had once been a child's bedroom at the rear of the cottage, but it no longer had a bed just as Ellie Mounter no longer had a child. The baby had been taken years ago by the same typhus that took her husband.

Wenna was woken hours later by voices within the room. Ellie and a man were chatting in hushed tones, as if afraid she might hear their discussion. Firelight bathed them both in a flickering orange light. She stirred and the visitor turned towards her.

"Thank God you're still with us, Wenna," Arthur Pengorse beamed as he knelt beside her, shrouding her hands in his.

"Ellie Mounter said you found me," she whispered hoarsely, suppressing her frustration. "Thank you for helping me."

"It was a miracle, Wenna. God brought you to this house. It's Him we must thank." At her blank look, he explained: "Ellie Mounter's cottage is a safe house where I preach The Word."

"I thought they –" She went into a coughing spell, throwing back her head while her lungs heaved seeking breath. "I thought they had a warrant for you," she said once the coughing eased.

"They do. But they must catch me first." He winked at her then released her hands and rose to his full intimidating height. "Now lie still and don't talk. Your lungs are diseased and need time to mend."

After giving specific instructions for Wenna's care, he left the cottage, and the room seemed strangely empty without him.

"This will do ee some good." The old woman came to her with a poultice. With Wenna's help, she eased open her shift then tucked the warm medicated substance against her chest.

Dear God, how her breasts had shrivelled. Not just her breasts, her whole body was thin and wasted. But she sighed with relief as the poultice sent a warm glow through her pain-racked lungs and induced a welcome sleepiness.

Days passed in a haze; she simply drifted through them, carried along inside a warm cloud of safety. In her more lucid moments, she called up memories of Crabtree Copse Farm and, inevitably, images of Christopher Vanson. Did he still hold out against Ralph Killiow? If things had turned out different, they might have enjoyed a warm relationship. But such dreams were mere fancy; she and Christopher were unlikely ever to meet again.

Ellie Mounter tended her with care and compassion, but her recovery was agonisingly slow. While she lay weak and helpless in the tiny bedroom, Pastor Pengorse conducted his illicit services in the adjacent parlour. Wenna would prick up her ears and listen to his followers singing and praying, and the pastor's booming voice, which echoed through the entire cottage.

His visits were mercifully short. Being as much a wanted man today as the Tolpuddle dissenters had been nearly four years ago, he could ill afford to stay too long in one place. Always, at the end of a meeting, he would visit her, kneeling and praying briefly beside her.

"What will you do when you are well again," he asked one evening after his usual prayer.

"I have no plans." However, deep inside her she was certain she had no option but to return to the streets.

"Do you remember how I once told you that I would one day have need of a wife? A woman like you to help me in my work."

She remembered it, and anger surged in her heart. He had claimed she was without hope of finding a husband. In hindsight, he had been right. Horribly right.

"I still want you, Wenna." He clasped her hands, and she closed her eyes in despair. "I still want you to be my wife."

She turned her head away from him, hiding a light shudder of revulsion. "That's an honour you do me." If he caught her shudder, she hoped he would attribute it to the cold. When she had composed her thoughts, she darted a glance at him. "I'm not fit to wed any man."

He stared into the glowing fire. "I cannot promise you a life of luxury," he said, seemingly oblivious of her protestation. "Far from it. However, I can promise to love you and, with God's grace, we will not starve."

"I believe you, but I cannot wed any man." Tears trickled down her cheeks as fond images of Christopher Vanson came to her. "I'm reduced to being nought but a vagrant." She dared not give voice to the rest of her distress; the abuse she had suffered at the hands of Ralph Killiow. She could not tell him the real reason she was no longer fit to become any man's wife.

In a sudden burst of anger, he added hotly: "You must not think like that." He grabbed at her hands. "You are Wenna Lanyon, the one-time proud owner of Crabtree Copse Farm. You are a fine woman for any man."

How could she tell him, a man of God, of her dishonour? The words would not come to her lips and what good would it do anyway? Meanwhile she would delay the answer and get some rest. "I must think on it," she mumbled, exhausted by the stress of his forceful proposal.

"Yes, of course." He rose to his feet, looking satisfied with her answer. "Think about it and tell me in due course that you will marry me."

For all that she had despised him for so long, she was ashamed of her dishonesty. She hoped he would forget the subject, at least until she was well enough to leave Ellie Mounter's cottage. Well enough to move on to some place beyond his influence.

Three days later, he spoke on it again.

"The more I see of you, Wenna," he said, eyes shining with love, "the more I am attracted to you. Have you come to a decision?" He breathed deep then choked out: "Will you marry me?"

"I am still thinking about it," she replied, lowering her gaze. "Please give me more time."

His face cracked with puzzlement and clearly expressed disappointment. She had hurt the feelings of the man who had saved her life and felt oddly guilty.

A few days later she was well enough to leave her bed and sat at the back of the parlour where the pastor conducted his services. No more than a dozen people stood crammed into the small room, but it seemed like more.

They sang with such enthusiasm that Wenna wanted to join in but her lungs were weak and the singing pained her. She resigned herself to listening and following the sentiment of the words.

The gathering fell silent when Arthur Pengorse began his sermon. She expected him to raise his voice in fiery invective against the rich employers who oppressed the poor working people of Cornwall. She expected him to threaten hellfire against the landowners. He didn't. Instead, he preached about love for all mankind, tolerance towards others. Surprised glances spread like wild fire within the audience.

"What about the employers, pastor? Do ee think we should be tolerant towards them?" one follower called out.

"Yes," Pengorse replied evenly. Then a sparkle came to his eyes. "As long as they do you no harm. The moment they hit out at you, you are bound to fight back." His tone carried just enough censure to draw the audience in. Calls of approval greeted his reproach to the landowners; it was what they expected from him.

"What about those who practise false religions, pastor? What about the Catholic Emancipation Bill, do ee support that?"

"Of course."

Wenna tensed as a heavily loaded silence fell upon the gathering. Murmurs of disapproval followed with looks that claimed: 'How could a Methodist preacher support such a bill?'

A disbelieving voice spoke out from the back of the congregation. "But ee don't 'old with Popery, do ee, Pastor?"

Pengorse raised his hands to heaven, and a hush fell over the assembly.

"No, I do not hold with Popery. I abhor the teachings of that church. But, my friends, it is criminal to persecute any man for his religious belief. Any man! I hold this as my basic truth." His stare went from face to face urging all to consider his next words as gospel. "The Catholics are persecuted for their beliefs just as we, dissenters, are persecuted for our beliefs. Is it right that a man can lose his employment because he is seen entering a Wesleyan Chapel, or because he is known to have visited a priest? No, my friends, it is wrong."

He paused, and a buzz of doubt ran round the room. The pastor scanned his audience, as if drinking in the potency of their complete attention. "We are no less dutiful subjects of His Majesty because we are Methodists. The Establishment Church has only one aim. And that is to grind us under with the power of their money." The congregation shouted their approval, and he beamed back at them.

Wenna smiled at the power of his oratory skills. He bent their thoughts to his own and easily carried them along. He had them in the palm of his hand. He was essentially a good man with other people's welfare at heart regardless of who they were. She didn't hold with the way he raised the workers into revolt, but she had to admire his motives. Maybe she had judged him wrongly. Maybe he was not such an ogre after all; he was prepared to care for her when her only alternatives were the workhouse or the brothel.

In a moment of enlightenment, she gulped out loud. It was not such a difficult decision. She did not love him and probably never would. But she would wed him because she had no alternative.

Eighteen

Kit brooded at his bedroom window, facing out onto a cheerless new day. After the heavy snow of mid-winter, February had finally surrendered itself in rain. Gale force winds were opening the skies, drowning the countryside and changing frozen paths into shimmering liquid mirrors. Trees swayed alarmingly in the copse alongside Tregover Farm, their branches creaking and groaning as if in pain.

Wherever he looked, he imagined Wenna. She was down there on that muddy road, laboriously tramping away from him, a ragged sack clasped about her body. She stood, shoulders stooped forward, in the copse at the farm boundary, sheltering beneath an overhanging oak. She lay in the middle of a distant field, a soaked, lifeless body.

And it was his fault. He had brought the Vanson curse into her life.

He wiped lingering dampness from his eyes, dressed and hurried down to the parlour where Clem sat in uneasy silence, reading a penny novel. His wicked brother had all this comfort while Wenna had nothing.

Gritting his teeth, Kit drew back his shoulders and coughed to attract Clem's attention. "I've spent some days thinking about what's to happen to you. It ain't gonna be no act of vengeance."

"Reckon you've just cause to take revenge on me." Clem spoke without lifting his head.

"Maybe." Kit bent towards the fire and rubbed heat into his hands. "But I won't. I wrote a letter to Ben Worth. Sent it yesterday."

Clem lowered his book, put it aside on an oak chest and stood up. He nodded philosophically. "Seems like you had no other choice."

Kit noted Clem's eyes were bloodshot, his face ashen. "That's right." He crossed to the window, keeping his back to his brother. Did the truth of his anger show in his voice? He hoped not. "I gave it a lot of thought and I figure this is the only way. The *Tamarith* sails in March."

"Sure." Clem's brief reply held an air of resigned acceptance.

Kit fell into silence, still unable to face him.

"You two want some breakfast?" Carrying a tray of food from the kitchen, Beth had pushed open the door with her hip.

She had taken charge of the domestic side of the farm almost as if she belonged here. Kit inwardly cursed Clem for treating her so badly. She was a good-looking woman, potentially a good wife for any man. Maybe, in time, his feelings for Wenna would wane and then he might look towards another woman. A woman like Beth. He quickly shook the idea aside, how could he think such a thing? Wenna was in his thoughts every moment of the day.

Clem's gaze shifted to Beth, enquiring, almost pleading for her forgiveness. When she refused to respond in any way, he turned to study the rain streaming down the window glass. "There's someone comin' down the lane towards the house. Woman by the looks of her. Don't recognise her. She sure does seem upset though."

Beth investigated, the tray still in her hands. "That's Jenny Tinder's mother. And her struggling down here in this weather, what on earth is the matter? I'll go and speak to her." She set the breakfast tray on the table and hurried away to the kitchen, wiping her hands in her apron.

Minutes later, Jimmy Rudge bounded into the room, wide-eyed and agitated. He stared at Kit, anxiously wringing his hands together. "Jenny's ma just called at the house, sur. She's right upset. Mistress be tryin' to calm her down."

"What's the matter?" Kit asked calmly.

"There's real trouble up at her cottage. I think ee better go up there, beggin' yer pardon, sur."

Kit stood fast. "What business is it of mine?"

Jimmy's lip trembled. "There were a union meeting, and the constable came an' arrested Jenny's father an' old Jacob Padder."

"Arrested Jacob?" Now that *was* his business. "What union meeting?"

"Trade union, sur. Old Jacob and John Tinder were formin' a trade union. They were recruitin' new members at the cottage."

Kit gaped at Jimmy then found his voice. "Jacob Padder? A trade union? I know nothing about this. Why in tarnation didn't he tell me?"

"Said ee wanted to get it all formal and ship shape afore ee approached ee, sur." The boy kept his face averted from Kit's searching gaze. "Thought ee might have stopped him if ee came to ee first."

Kit reflected for a moment. "I see. Tell me, Jimmy, does Pastor Pengorse have anything to do with this?"

"Dunno rightly, sur. Jacob an' John Tinder both been to the Pastor's meetin's in the past. Reckon as how ee put the idea in their heads in the first place, but ee ain't been seen round here for some time now."

"All right, Jimmy. I'll go to the village and do what I can."

"I'll come with you," Clem said, reaching the door first.

Kit nodded in approval. With Clem cold sober, his support could be useful.

Heavy rain still pelted the earth as they saddled up two horses and set out along the rough lane towards Penmarith.

The Tinders' unkempt thatched cottage stood alongside a narrow track running between the Cross Keys Inn and the apothecary's house. Outside, a group of bedraggled labourers peered in through the tiny windows while others sheltered beneath the overhanging thatch.

Kit dismounted and called to them: "What's happening?" They turned to him with a wall of surly expressions. No one replied so he hurried into the cottage with Clem at his heels.

John Tinder and Jacob Padder stood in one corner of the tiny room; their haunted gazes revealing they were aware of the gravity of their situation. Sitting behind a small table with his stave of office prominently displayed in front of him, the parish constable wrote on a sheet of paper with exaggerated deliberation.

"Roskilly!" Kit crossed the room in two long strides and banged his fist on the table, determined he would create a firm impression.

Thomas Roskilly jerked back his head, startled. "What be ee doin' here, Mister Vanson?" The village constable gaped at him then recovered. "Ee got no business here. Get out right now."

A hairsbreadth away from outright rage, Kit leaned over the table, nose to nose with the law officer. "No. I will not get out." He pointed to the two men cowering in the corner. "What's the meaning of this?"

The constable rose to his feet, an angry flush running through his jowls. He slipped his thumbs into his waistcoat pockets and drew back his shoulders. "These men be in my charge, and I has a warrant for each of them. They'll go to Bodmin with me."

Kit could barely control his outrage. "Why?"

Thomas Roskilly picked up a legal looking sheet of paper, pointed to a seal by the signature at the bottom and shoved it into Kit's face. "I has a warrant for Jacob Padder. It do charge him with swearing an oath to a trade union and incitin' others to the same felony." Roskilly slapped the paper back on the table and reached for another. "An' this be a warrant for John Tinder. It do charge him with holdin' illegal meetin's here in his cottage."

"Who issued these warrants?" Kit asked, not recognizing the seal.

"The magistrate, Mister Nancarrow."

A long exasperated sigh escaped Kit's lips. Nancarrow. Of course! A distant cousin of James Frampton, the magistrate behind the arrest of the Tolpuddle men in Dorset. Nancarrow wouldn't think twice about stamping down on a union. A dull pain reasserted itself from behind his eyes. "These people just ain't learned yet, have they?"

"Now don't ee go causin' trouble, Mister Vanson. I only be a doin' me job an' so be the magistrate."

"That's a matter of opinion." Kit breathed out heavily. "Who brought this matter to the attention of Nancarrow?"

Roskilly stalled, frowning and biting his lip.

"Well?"

"It were Squire Killiow. He went to Bodmin an' persuaded Mister Nancarrow to sign the warrant. The Squire be most anxious to stamp out any trade union nonsense in this village right from the start. Squire can be most persistent when ee puts 'is mind to it."

"I bet he can. But trade unions ain't illegal. I've learned that much about your laws since I came here."

"No. But swearin' an oath is. Padder put his name to a seditious document and swore an illegal oath."

"Heaven's sake, Roskilly! I learned about that particular Engish law when I was at sea. It was designed to put down mutiny amongst sailors, not to prosecute farm labourers." Kit turned to Padder. "Did you swear an oath, Jacob?"

Padder shook his head sadly. "No, sur."

"Or sign an illegal document?"

"Course not, sur."

"Quite." Kit's temper surged as he returned his attention to the constable again. "Show me this seditious document."

Roskilly reached out and picked up yet another paper. "This be what ee signed. I has to take it with me to Bodmin an' show the magistrate."

Kit took the paper and read it.

<u>*The Initiation Oath of the Penmarith Friendly Society of Labourers.*</u>

I do swear to you, before Almighty God, and this loyal lodge that I will not work with any illegal man or woman but will do my best endeavour to attain just wages for all. And I most solemnly swear to keep inviolate all secrets of this society. Nor will I ever write, or cause to be written, anything connected with this society. So help me God and keep me steadfast in this obligation. And I further promise to do my best to bring all legal men into this order. If I should ever reveal any of the rules of this order, may a sword be plunged into my soul and send me to eternity, and may I be disgraced in every lodge in this country.

By my hand.
Jacob Padder

"You mean the magistrate hasn't yet seen this?" Kit said, slapping one hand across the page.

Roskilly shrugged his shoulders. "The Squire got hold of it an' gave it to me."

Kit swore beneath his breath and held the paper up to Roskilly's face. "How in hell's name did Killiow get hold of this?"

The constable threw back his chin, eyeing Kit from beneath a heavily creased brow. "I don't know." Roskilly's tone turned suddenly defensive, sloughing off his officious posture. "It ain't my business to know."

Kit fixed him with a dark glare. "It will be your business, if you're found to have been part of a felony."

"Felony?" Roskilly blinked then narrowed a suspicious stare at Kit. "What felony?"

"Conspiracy to gaol an innocent man!"

"What do ee mean, sur?" Jacob Padder cut in, shocked and upset by the proceedings.

Kit swung round to his farmhand. "Jacob, did you sign this document?"

Padder grasped his hat into a tight ball in front of his chest. "No, sur. How could I?"

"Of course, you couldn't." With one step, Kit crossed the tiny room and held the paper in front of him. "Have you even seen this document before?"

"No." The old man shook his head emphatically. "Don't know anything about it, sur. Honest."

The constable reached out for his stave, his sole instrument of authority and waved it in the air. "I've had enough of your interferin', Mister Vanson. Just 'cos Padder says ee didn't sign the oath, don't mean ee didn't actually sign it. The jury has to decide that, don't they?"

"Not in this case." Kit swung round to the table, grabbed Roskilly's quill pen and then pressed it into Padder's hand. "Jacob, write your name on the back of this document."

The old labourer's hand shook with distress. "I can't, sur. You know that."

"Just do it, Jacob." Kit insisted irritably, and stabbed a finger on the page. "Put your mark there."

Padder took a hesitant step towards the table. He looked at Kit, and with his employer's encouraging nod, he scribbled the back of the page with a spidery cross then stepped back.

Gritting his teeth in frustration, Kit held up the paper in front of the constable. "See! That's Jacob's mark, and I'll swear to it. The man is quite illiterate. There is no way he could have put his signature to this document."

The constable's expression became confused. "But someone put Padder's name to it."

"Right. And whoever did it committed a felony. I suggest you take this piece of news back to Squire Killiow. Show him the evidence.

After that, I don't expect to hear any more about it."

"Oh no, I can't do that." The constable shook his head vigorously. "I has to take this man into Bodmin. Both men go into gaol this night and appear before Mister Nancarrow tomorrow. That's me duty whatever ee do say about it."

"In that case I'll take this document back to the squire myself. And God help whoever wrote this!" Kit pushed the paper inside his jacket and stormed out of the cottage, Clem hurrying after him.

The rain still fell heavily as they mounted their horses and headed through the narrow gap between the apothecary's house and the inn. At the junction with the road, a carriage pulled up in front of them. Kit's horse bucked and threatened to unseat him.

"Out of me way," the carriage driver roared. "Where are the prisoners?"

"What prisoners?" Clem shouted back while Kit still soothed his horse.

"The union men, where are they?"

Kit shook his fist at the eager driver. "Damn you!" Waving a hand at Clem, he kicked his horse's flanks. "Come on, you, we need to have words with your drinking friend!"

Fury filled Kit's head as they rode. Damn that English Squire and his bullying. Damn the whole system that allowed him to get away with it. Killiow was no better than … than a white thug on an Alabama plantation. Where was the justice in this world?

Outside the manor, he reined back and leapt to the soggy ground. "I'll go in and see Killiow. You wait for me and be ready to leave in a hurry."

Glancing left and right to ensure no guard was about, he raced to the front door. Still breathing heavily, he thrust it open and stormed inside. He found the new squire lounging in his library, his feet stretched out before a roaring fire and a brandy glass in one hand.

Killiow jerked forward and swung his head around to the door. "You? What do you want here?" His pockmarked cheeks bristled red beneath his whiskers.

Kit advanced on him, clenching his fists. "My man, Jacob Padder. He's been arrested on evidence supplied by you."

"Forming a trade union, so I was told." Killiow fell back into his chair and sipped at his brandy. "Influencing some of me own workers. Had to be stopped. Now get out."

"I will not get out!" Kit pulled the paper from his jacket pocket. "If Jacob committed a felony, he would have to be stopped. But he did nothing illegal."

"He signed an oath. Just like those damn Tolpuddle rogues."

Kit thrust the paper at Killiow. "No, he did not. This is your evidence, isn't it?"

With a deeper flush running up his neck and filling his cheeks, Killiow sat forward. "You've no business to be holding that. I told the constable to give the oath to Nancarrow."

"Lucky for you I stopped him. This is a forgery. If this comes out in any assize court, you'll find yourself in serious trouble."

The squire's eyes blazed. "Nonsense! Padder's name is at the bottom. See for yourself."

"Padder is illiterate," Kit hissed out, emphasizing the last word.

"Lots of men round here are illiterate." Killiow lowered his gaze to his glass. After a moment's reflection, he rose to his feet. "Typical peasants. Can't read a book to save their lives but they can at least sign their own name."

"Not Jacob. All he can do is make his mark." Kit allowed another long, powerful silence to reign then he turned the paper over and displayed the spidery cross. "Like that one."

Killiow stared at the page, his cheeks quivering. Cursing, he turned on his heels, kicked at his chair then threw his glass into the fireplace where it smashed into tiny fragments.

Kit slipped the paper back into his pocket. "I suppose you thought this would be seen only by the magistrate and the judge, and they wouldn't question it. Luckily for Padder and Tinder, *I've* seen it and it doesn't fool me."

Killiow sighed loudly in defeat. He swung back to face Kit. "No one else knows about this?"

"Few enough know about it at the moment." Kit fixed his warning gaze deep into Killiow's eyes. "But I could easily change that. You know what the penalty is for a felony like this. I suggest you write a letter to Mister Nancarrow attesting to an error and I'll take it straight away to Bodmin." When Killiow didn't move, he leaned deliberately closer. "Now!"

Killiow's glare seemed set into stone as he walked around his desk. "You, Vanson, are a pain in the backside. One day I'll have great pleasure in dealing with you." He let out an angry snort then picked up his quill pen. "All right, I'll give you the letter you want, and a pox upon you."

With hopes of securing the men's release, Kit and Clem urged their horses back to the cottage, but the carriage, the constable and the prisoners were gone.

"What now?" Clem asked, reining back on his horse.

"I have to get Killiow's letter to Nancarrow but I don't know how to find him."

"Beth will know." Clem turned his horse in the direction of the farm and urged the animal forward with a couple clicks of his tongue.

"You're right. Thank God for one decent Killiow." Kit swung his mount in his brother's wake.

They arrived at Tregover muddied and soaked. Beth hurried out to meet them, a shawl covering her while she listened to their plan.

"I'll go with you." Her sharp tone indicated her determination. "Damn Ralph for his stupidity."

"Can we get there in daylight?" Kit asked.

"With fast horses." Ignoring the rain, Beth turned away. "Wait for me while I saddle up."

"In this weather?" Clem queried at her back.

Beth glanced over her shoulder while breaking into a run. "Yes, if it helps that old man."

"You're one hell of a good woman, Beth," Kit called to her. She smiled back at him then entered the barn. He cast a dark look towards his brother. "Too good for some."

The boggy road to Bodmin delayed the party more than they expected. Frequently, they had to slow their horses and guide them around mud-filled potholes and washed-out tracks. Darkness was fast looming when they arrived at the magistrate's residence.

"I'll go in alone." Kit swung down from his steaming horse. "We don't want to frighten Nancarrow with a deputation. You two take shelter in the Barleycorn Inn." At their silent nod, Kit knocked on the front door and a servant opened it.

After explaining he had business with the magistrate, Kit waited in the marble hallway while the man sought Nancarrow. Moments later he returned.

"He will see you now, sir." The servant escorted him into the library where the magistrate, a small-framed man with a receding hair line peered up at Kit through myopic eyes from behind an ornate desk.

"Well, what have you come to see me about?" Nancarrow barely concealed his irritation while a deeply furrowed brow framed his eagle eyes.

Kit reached for the letter. "I brought this letter from Squire Killiow. It's about two men accused of sedition."

"Give it to me."

The magistrate grabbed the letter as soon as Kit was close enough. He adjusted his spectacles, and read it through. When he had finished, he peered at Kit with a sombre expression. "This letter came directly from Squire Killiow?"

"Yes, sir. I hope you'll see fit to act upon it immediately."

Nancarrow leaned back in his seat. "Where are these men now?"

"I've reason to believe they're in the Bodmin gaol already. The constable was a mite too eager to have them locked up as quickly as possible."

"If that is so, it does seem they should be released." The magistrate gave Kit a curt nod. "But, you know, this union business really must be stopped."

Kit clamped his lips tight together, forcing back any comment. All that mattered was getting Padder and Tinder released. He waited patiently until the magistrate signed the release orders, offered a perfunctory word of thanks and hurried from the house.

Satisfied he had thwarted Killiow's scheme, he rode through the muddy streets to the inn. The church clock rang out the half hour after five, and his stomach plummeted; he had so little time to complete his rescue.

Beth and Clem stepped out from beneath the inn's overhanging storey, clutching their cloaks tight at their necks as rainwater poured from the roof above.

Kit patted his leather saddlebag. "I've got their release orders."

Beth ran to the side of his horse and grasped his hand. "Well done."

"I'll get our horses, Kit." And Clem was gone, hurrying into the narrow lane to the stables.

Kit smiled down at Beth. "Reckon your brother lost this one." Then he turned serious. "But he really did go too far this time."

She stared up at him with rain streaming down her cheeks. "Ralph will stop at nothing. One way or another, he has to be stopped."

"He will be, Beth." Kit patted her hand in reassurance. "He will be." He looked up as Clem arrived on horseback, pulling on the reins of Beth's mount.

They rode away in silence until they came to the dark walls and the thick wooden doors of Bodmin gaol. A woman's body swivelled from a gallows in the road outside. A vile stench reached out, defying the cleansing action of the heavy rain.

Leaving Beth in the shelter of nearby trees, Kit hammered on the door until a gaoler eased it open. After a brief remonstration and a waving of the release papers, he and Clem were allowed entry. The gaoler ushered them deep inside to the block to where Jacob Padder and John Tinder were confined.

A turnkey held aloft a flickering lantern and unlocked the door. Kit crept inside the cell, covering his mouth and nose with his kerchief. He gritted his teeth at the sight of the two men sitting in shadow on the cold floor, their heads already shorn, while four other men sat on filthy straw beds that lay on the stone flags.

"I've come to fetch you, Jacob. You too John Tinder."

Padder looked up through bloodshot eyes. "Fetch us, sur?"

"You're free. Both of you." Kit jerked his head towards the door and Padder rose unsteadily to his feet. Just then the old labourer came in range of the flickering lamp, and Kit's stomach tightened in knots. Already, his skin was pale and wrinkled.

Padder gave him a grateful look. "Thank God for that, sur. Don't reckon I'd last too long inside here."

"No. I guess not. And the man who should be in here is most likely drinking brandy in front of a blazing fire." Kit took the old man's arm and eased him towards the door. "No justice is there, Jacob?"

"No, sur. But little we can do about it."

"Don't count on that, Jacob."

Nineteen

Arthur Pengorse seemed barely able to believe what he'd heard. "You will be my wife?"

"Yes." Wenna's reply came out hesitant, impeded by lingering doubts.

In contrast, an immediate expression of joy lit up his eyes. "You will never regret this," he beamed. He took her hands in his, kissing them lightly and tenderly. "I promise you shall have my undying love."

She harboured no reciprocal feelings of love, only guilt. How could she give her affections to Pengorse when her thoughts continually returned to that young American at Tregover Farm? Her decision was purely a matter of survival. She might end up in prison with her husband, but at least she was less likely to die of starvation on the street.

Suppressing those recurring, painful images of Christopher Vanson, she begged Pengorse: "Could we wait until I'm fit again before we wed?" He nodded with a look that told her he was in the mood to grant her any wish. In the meantime she had to recover from her illness and that meant remaining a little longer in Ellie Mounter's cottage where it was warm and comfortable.

Daily, the old lady wagged a finger at her while declaring her opinion of the union. "A young thing like ee should be lookin' for a steady young man of yer own sort. Mark my words, this union will bring ee nothin' but pain." But Wenna simply smiled and accepted the words as a measure of her concern.

No longer confined to her bed all day, Wenna often spent her time in the parlour, a lighter and airier room than the tiny bedroom. She was there when the village constable called on another grey, damp morning. Ellie led him into the parlour, her lips clamped tight together in a clear sign of apprehension.

Jeremiah Meyrick touched his forelock as he spied Wenna warmly wrapped beside the fire. The squat man with a bushy moustache and a protruding stomach carried his wooden stave with him. This was no ordinary visit; it was a sign of official business.

"Mornin' young lady. Sorry to bother ee," he said apologetically. "Just a spot of business with Ole Mother Mounter, here."

"What's it all about, Jeremiah?" Ellie wiped her hands on her apron, a deep frown across her brow.

The constable hung his head sheepishly. "Well, it be like this. Stories are spreading about the town an' I has to ask ee some questions."

"What about?" Ellie had lowered her voice to a hush and, sloping her shoulders, she played on her age.

He sighed, looking uncomfortable. "About these meetin's ee been holdin' in this cottage."

"But those are just prayer meetin's. Why, yer own mother comes to them. Ye're not goin' to tell me I been breakin' the law with yer own mother here in me cottage."

"There's been stories."

"What stories?" The old lady suddenly came to life again, thrusting out her chest and crossing her arms. "There's no law to prevent me holding prayer meetin's in me own cottage."

"It ain't that, exactly." Meyrick stroked his moustache nervously then his shoulders drooped. "Rumours say Pastor Pengorse been preachin' at these meetin's. An' there be a warrant out for him."

Wenna felt the blood drain away from her face. What would happen to her if her future husband were arrested now? But Ellie gave no sign of alarm.

"Stuff and nonsense," she blustered. "Has anyone actually seen him here?"

"Well, not as I've actually spoken to. At least not so as they've actually admitted to it. But –"

"But nothing." Ellie jutted her firm chin. "If yer own mother won't confirm Pastor Pengorse has been here, ye've no reason to accuse me of any crime, have ee?"

"S'pose not. But I had to ask ee. Ee do see that?"

Ellie gave him a curt nod. "Be off with you, Jeremiah Meyrick. Go an' speak to them trade union people what be causin' all the trouble.

An' don't ee be a botherin' us simple folks again."

She bundled the constable from the cottage, her shouts of annoyance following him out into the street. She came back into the parlour with a bleak expression across her face. "I'll have to get word to the pastor not to come here tonight. They'll be watching the cottage for sure."

"How did they find out?" Wenna asked.

"Dunno, me 'andsome. But don't ee worry your pretty little head about it."

Wenna was unable to sleep that evening. She lay by the bedroom fire, wrapped in a warm shawl, while muffled voices bubbled and droned next door in the parlour. Later, when the last visitor had left, Ellie came to settle her for the night.

"Arthur didn't come. Right, Ellie?" How strange to be calling him Arthur, as if he were a close friend. Or a husband. But how could she continue to call him Mister Pengorse?

Ellie knelt and tucked a blanket about her. "I got word to him. There be some good folks round here and they found him a safe place to hide. Ee's over at Lostwithiel this night."

"What will happen to him now?" Wenna cast an imploring look at the old woman.

"I dunno, me 'andsome. Nowhere be safe for him round here now."

Wenna clutched the blanket close about her chest. "The warrant's been out for him for some time now and yet he seems able to stay on the run."

"Not much longer, ee won't." Ellie rose to her feet. "Best thing ee can do is to leave Cornwall for good. That's what I do say. Nowhere in the whole county be safe for him any more."

Wenna chewed at her lip. "I know him, he's stubborn. He won't leave Cornwall. He'd never give in like that."

With a knowing nod, Ellie sighed. "Bein' on the run by hisself is one thing, but ee'll have to start thinkin' different when there's two of ee. Best thing Pastor Pengorse can do is to flee from Cornwall and take ee with him."

Wenna sought the glowing embers of the fire. Flee from Cornwall? It might be their best option, but where would they go?

Two nights passed without word from Arthur. Ellie said nothing about it, and Wenna kept her thoughts to herself. Late on the third night, just as Ellie was clearing away their evening meal, someone rapped impatiently on the cottage door. Ellie shared a worried glance with her then left the room to see who it was. Moments later she returned with the pastor. He was heavily cloaked, his hat pulled low over his face.

Wenna struggled to her feet, dizziness still dogging every move. Arthur crossed the tiny room with giant strides and clasped her tightly to him.

"I was afraid for you." She pushed away from the embrace and sank back weakly onto her mattress.

"You mustn't be." He reassured her with a grin. "They won't catch me, but we must leave tonight."

"Tonight!" Her outburst triggered a bout of coughing, and Wenna clutched at her chest.

"There is too much risk in staying here any longer."

"Where will we go?" she croaked.

"Friends are waiting with a carriage out on the main road. They'll take us to Lostwithiel and we'll be married there."

"Married!" Wenna shivered, and the room grew cold around her. She had not expected the commitment to occur so soon. A resurgence of her doubts seeped into her brain.

Ellie had stepped lightly into the room behind him. "She still ain't well enough, Pastor." But Arthur ignored the old woman's comment, focussing on Wenna with an enquiring look.

Wenna nodded. She had to do this; she had to go with him. What other option was open to her? She forced a weak smile to her lips. "Very well. I think I'm recovered enough to get to Lostwithiel. We'll be married this night, Arthur."

"It won't be entirely legal in the eyes of the law, as I dare not have a registrar present," he said, apologetically and added: "But in the eyes of God we'll be man and wife."

Wenna held back her deeper fears, her private doubts. "We can put the legal matter right at a later time."

He kissed her lightly on the cheek while she held her breath in anticipation of something more demanding. But he seemed content with the one kiss.

Ellie sharpened her voice, ordering him to leave the room and eat in the scullery at the back of the cottage. Then she turned the same brusque tone onto Wenna. "Ee'm a fool, girl. And I reckon ee knows it." She shrugged her shoulders and said no more as Wenna dressed.

When they were both ready to leave, Ellie Mounter held Wenna close and whispered in her ear: "If ee'm ever in trouble, me 'andsome, just ee come back to Ole Mother Mounter."

Wenna hugged her tight then pulled back to brush away a meandering tear. "I will. I won't forget you Ellie. Thank you for all you've done for me."

Arthur left the cottage first, striding down the street at a pace Wenna could never hope to match. She followed a few minutes later, wearing a poke bonnet with its flaps curled round to conceal her face. She shuffled and stumbled, her legs ready to crumple beneath her. Her breath came in short, exaggerated bursts, condensing in the night air like the desperate gasps of a hunted animal.

Part way along the road, her head began to spin, and she mustered all her waning strength to continue. She must not dally here, for fear it would delay their escape. She staggered on, and at the next corner, she stopped again. Arthur came to her, creeping from a nearby shadow and grabbed her arm.

"Quickly." He hugged her tight against his huge frame and helped her to walk on. "Spies are watching the cottage. We must hurry away from here."

Their carriage stood at the end of a dark street, the horse pawing the cobbles impatiently. The driver sat quiet, head bent, a smoking pipe gripped between his teeth.

Arthur paused to scan the merging, dimly lit streets before hurrying her across the last open space. He bundled Wenna into the carriage. She sank down on the cushions, more exhausted than she'd ever been. The carriage moved off immediately, the wheels rattling noisily on the wet stones. Wenna closed her eyes and set her head on Arthur's shoulder. Dear God, the pain in her chest was taking her breath away.

She registered little of the journey, drifting in and out of consciousness until Arthur woke her. "Wenna, we've reached Lostwithiel."

A small-framed, spindly man pulled open the carriage door and, at an unseemly pace, hurried them into a chapel alongside a whitewashed cottage.

Ignoring formalities, he studied Wenna. "So, you're the woman who's to marry the pastor?" At her nod, he eyed them both warily, as if they were from some far-off land, and then called to his wife. Wearing a perpetual worried look, he married them with his wife and the coachman as witnesses.

"Preacher Pengorse, you and your wife can't stay. Not now that there's two of you. Too much risk of being seen. Farmer Pidgin says you can use his hayloft, if you wants to, but you can't stay here."

"Thank you anyway, Preacher Ranlegh." Through tight lips, Arthur added coldly: "The hayloft will be enough."

Growing weakness made Wenna's head spin. She hung onto her husband's arm as they stepped back out into the cold night air. They followed the preacher across a small field to a barn set well back from the road.

"It's up there." Preacher Ranlegh indicated a rickety stairway and a door into the barn's upper level.

"I thank you again, friend." Pengorse waved him off then he gathered her in his arms and carried her up the loose wooden steps to the hayloft.

Fighting against nausea, she wondered how she would cope when Arthur sought the satisfaction of her body that night.

Daylight crept across Wenna's face and wakened her. She lingered on a straw palliasse while watching her husband at a small window, his back towards her. Her head ached and her hands shook. "Where will we go now?"

He turned but kept his eyes averted. "There are people who will shelter us in Polperro." He stared at some distant point, as if unable to face her. "There's a lot of support for me over there. And we'll be safe for some time. But we must make our way to Polperro on foot."

She forced herself to sit up. "I brought some food from Ellie's cottage." She reached for a small package in the fold of her dress. She opened it gingerly to reveal a chunk of hardened cheese. Her stomach heaved at the thought of eating it and the headache magnified. Lying back, she studied her new husband, noting how he avoided contact with her eyes. His face was firmly set with deep furrows across his brow, and his teeth were clamped together as if he was upset. She had done her best to satisfy his sexual urge. Maybe his many worries were weighing heavily on his mind. Was something other than their obvious plight troubling him, something he chose not to speak of? "I'll do my best for you," she said, "but please don't go too fast."

They left early that morning, heading south towards the coast. At first Wenna kept up with her husband, but within an hour she lagged well behind. Weak, cold and plagued with bouts of dizziness, she strained to place one foot in front of the other, stumbling over the uneven ground. Her effort caused the headache to worsen.

Recognizing that she was about to give up, Arthur gave her hope: "We'll stop soon. I have friends not far from here. They'll give us food and allow us to rest a while."

They took refuge at a farm worker's cottage near St Winnow with the intention of begging only a meal. Wenna was grateful when the family urged them to stay the night, giving up their own bed for Pastor Pengorse and his new bride.

The next day they continued their journey south and that evening they stopped at Fowey where Arthur led a prayer meeting in a cattle shed. Wenna lay in a dark corner, her chest heaving, each breath sending a stabbing pain through her lungs. Exhausted, she fell asleep even as her husband preached.

The following morning, she had difficulty rising from her straw bed. Did Arthur not see the deterioration in her health? The evidence grew clearer by the day. Pain constantly stabbed through her chest, and when she coughed as she often did now, traces of blood stained her thick phlegm.

Two nights later they took shelter in a barn near Polruan. Village lights twinkled barely half a mile away, but Arthur dared not approach it, unsure whether they would find shelter and protection.

A strong wind blew throughout the hours of darkness. The barn roof shook and rattled above them, and the cold wind infiltrated the building, catching Wenna's chest. She coughed constantly, the pain hitting her worse than before. Knowing she could not go on like this much longer, she visualized Ellie Mounter's warm cottage and wished they could be there again. Ellie had warned her that they should flee the county. How could there be any doubt now? She'd been right.

Another day passed. By nightfall, they had found a safe house in Lansallos where they were given shelter by an old couple who fussed over Wenna as if she were their own daughter.

They lay in bed that night in a small room at the back of the cottage, and Arthur spoke above the rumble of waves breaking against the cliffs not far off. "Tomorrow we must leave early."

"Can we not stay a while?" Wenna turned a mournful gaze at him. He wrapped his arms about her while strangely avoiding looking into her eyes.

"No. We cannot impose further here. Ralph Killiow has some influence in this village, and these people know what will happen to them if I'm caught in their cottage."

"Whatever you say, Arthur." She was too weak to argue and was soon fast asleep.

During the night she awoke with a racking pain through her chest. She coughed and her lungs locked tight, refusing her attempts to breath. In a fit of panic, she reached out and woke up her husband.

He sat up quickly. "What is it? What's wrong?"

"I can't … breathe … properly," she croaked. "Help me … sit up."

Arthur helped her to a semi-sitting position, and she coughed again in an effort to clear her lungs. This time the pain hit her badly, and for the first time, she cried out in agony.

She wanted to die.

It would be such a simple way out of the problem: to sleep forever. But her breathing eventually returned to normal.

Arthur set her back gently on the bed and lay beside her with one arm about her shoulders. After some minutes, he rose to light a candle and lay back beside her, staring up at the bare roof.

"You need help, Wenna. And it pains me that I cannot give you that help."

"By morning I'll feel better," she whispered.

"Maybe. But you've been ill for some time, and it does you

nothing but harm to be living like this. Mother Mounter warned me this might happen. She was right, but I didn't listen to her."

Wenna nestled closer for warmth and mentally grasped at his change of heart. "I need just a few days to rest."

"No, you need more than a few days. Much more." He spoke clearly, almost angrily. "You look so pale and you are so very weak."

"You said we must move on tomorrow. But can we not stay just a while longer?"

"I think not." He turned away, his body tensed and stiff beside her. After a lengthy silence, he swung his head back to face her again, and she detected an air of resignation in his manner. "We're a few miles from Penmarith. We could be there in a day or two. Two days at the most, Wenna, and we could be at Tregover Farm. Whatever the American thinks about me, at least he'll not turn *you* away."

Wenna's spirits lifted enough for her to smile weakly. "Christopher Vanson? Yes, I'm sure he'll help us." A strange glow built deep inside. A feeling of warmth and homecoming.

"I'll not ask him for myself, Wenna. The risk would be too great, if I were to hide out on his farm. But I'll ask him to give *you* shelter. I know that … that you and he have a friendship to fall back on." His voice turned suddenly sour. "I suspect it was once a very strong friendship."

What did he mean by a strong friendship? She and Christopher had been friends, but no more. Nevertheless, her heart went out to him for his decision.

Early the next morning, he wrapped her in a blanket and carried her across fields and heath towards Polruan. They spent the night at a farm beyond the village. The following day, a boatman took them across the river to Fowey, from where Arthur carried her on the last leg of their journey. All the time she nestled her head against his chest while pain racked her body.

They had to stop many times to rest, but eventually she recognised the familiar landscape around Penmarith. They kept to the woodland paths where they were less likely to be seen, but these paths were all known to her.

She slept a while beneath a hedge and her husband woke her from a lingering dream of her home. "Almost there, Wenna." He gathered her again into his arms.

She raised her head as Arthur carried her over the brow of a hill. Tregover Farm was spread out below, just as she remembered it. A distant figure strode across the yard. Was it Christopher Vanson? For a moment, her heart leapt.

"I'll leave you here." Arthur lowered her to the ground, propped up against a tall oak. "While I go for help. There may be people watching the farm, and I will need to creep in quietly. Someone will come for you soon." He smiled in a way that held little warmth then he crept away towards the farm.

A light, drifting feeling took hold of her head, and soon after, she fell into a faint.

Twenty

"Your friend, Mister Vanson, has persuaded me to leave the country." Arthur sat beside her, clutching at her hand. Wenna sensed a deep hurt behind the way he spat out the words, 'your friend'. She now lay in a comfortable bed with a warm fire in the bedroom grate but could find no feelings of comfort in her husband's presence.

"Leave England?" She had been prepared for him to flee from Cornwall but not this.

"It's best for all of us." He squeezed her fingers but kept his face inclined towards the door, as if he did not want to look at her.

She digested his words with misgiving. "When will you go?"

"Soon. Vanson says he'll fix things for me. I swear by God, I'll find a way to send for you, Wenna. You can be sure of that."

She nodded, and her heart filled with dread.

Shortly after, he left her to go downstairs. In his absence, she twisted in the bed but found no comfort. The pain in her chest had subsided in the past few days but not enough to eradicate her unease.

Christopher had offered shelter for both herself and her husband, but Arthur had refused the offer for himself. While she lay in a warm bedroom, her husband spent much of his time hiding in a barn, out of sight of Killiow's spies. When he came into the farmhouse to visit her, he acted strangely, as if he suspected a conspiracy.

A light tread set off tell-tale squeaks from the worn stairs. Moments later, her bedroom door creaked open. Christopher slipped quietly into the room, just as he did every evening when he arrived back from working in the fields. Weary creases radiated from the corners of his eyes, and he kept his focus on the floor.

He sat on a hard chair across the room, putting the maximum space between them. He spoke with a dull, abstract tone about things that were of no interest or concern to her. Eventually their conversation dwindled into nothing.

She brought to bear all the charm of a smile she could muster but it wasn't enough. A well-defined slope marred his broad shoulders, as if her marriage to another man upset him. What reason could he have for not accepting her as the wife of Arthur Pengorse? Unless he cared about her too much.

If only he would look at her, acknowledge her. "Christopher …" she began then paused. She had not at first intended to use her illness as a subject to recapture his attention but, with all casual conversation now exhausted, she decided to reach out to him. "You know that I'm still very weak and I can't fight against you."

He frowned, glancing her way. "Fight against me? What on earth are you talking about? You don't have to stand up to me."

"I think I must, Christopher. Just so long as you keep this barrier between us. You must know I need your help badly. Now that Arthur has agreed to flee the country, I must get well enough to travel after him. But that may take months, and I'll need your support in the meantime."

He shrugged his shoulders. "We'll take care of you, Wenna. You've nothing to fear on that score." His voice was so calm, irritatingly calm.

"Yes, I know that." She softened her tone. "But it's not just a matter of food and shelter. I also need your approval and your friendship."

His eyes flashed. "Please!" he said roughly, rising. He marched to the window, adding over his shoulder: "Don't play on my emotions this way. It isn't right."

"Why won't you look at me?" she asked forlornly. "Is it because I married Arthur?"

He swung round in a flash, and his steely eyes met hers with an intensity that sent a quiver running through her spine. "It was no legal marriage! You didn't go through the proper procedures."

"We're wed in the eyes of God."

"You think so? Damn that preacher. You don't love him! I know you don't. I see it every time you look at him. Do you know how much I cared about you? Do you?"

Hurt flooded her mind until her eyes were liquid pools. "How could I have known? We spent so little time together, how could I have known that you had tender feelings towards me? Besides, it would never have come to anything."

"Why not?"

"There is a reason, Christopher." She interlocked her fingers, twisting and untwisting them until they ached. "A good reason. One that you don't want to know about."

"Tell me." He took a giant step towards her.

"I can't."

"Tell me!" He bent over her, his eyes blazing, frightening her.

"All right then! I'll tell you." She lifted herself up in the bed and glared back at him. Then her nerve left her and she lowered her eyes. "Ralph Killiow attacked me at the manor. He –"

"He raped you." The look in his face frightened her. "Dear God, I knew it!"

She sank back into the bed, twisting her head away from him. Now she wished to God she hadn't told him.

Suddenly he was at her side, arms reaching out for her. "Oh, Wenna, I swear to you I'll kill that man. With my own hands, I'll kill him! Was it the reason you turned me away that day?"

She shrunk away. "I was too ashamed to face you ever again. I didn't know you cared, all I knew was the way I felt towards you."

"You felt the same for me?" A haggard expression flickered across his face. "You cared?"

"It no longer mattered after I was dishonoured. I was no longer fit for you."

"No longer fit? Oh Wenna!" His face turned bleak. "This is my fault. Don't you see? It's the Vanson family curse."

"The curse?" She frowned. How odd that he should think his family curse was to blame. "How could you possibly imagine that? That's just silly superstition, Christopher. It means nothing. Killiow is to blame, not you." She stifled a sniff. "But it matters little who is really at fault, it was enough that I was dishonoured."

Christopher sat on the side of the bed. "You think that would change things? How little you understand."

Wenna's heart beat wildly. He meant what he said; his love had been there all along, and she had not seen it.

"Whatever Killiow did ..." Christopher stumbled over his words,

"… doesn't alter how I feel about you. Can't you see that?"

They remained unmoving in a deep silence broken only by the pelting of rain on the window panes. What passed between them was more powerful than words.

"I should have come to you before I sold the farm." She shook her head with a sad wistfulness. "I should have asked for your help. I can see it all now. But I messed it up, all the way along."

"It's done now. You're the wife of Pastor Pengorse, and there's nothing I can do about it because neither of us would ever resort to anything dishonourable." The bitterness in his voice could not be mistaken; a hand grasped her heart and squeezed.

The edge in his voice spoke of a raw, bleeding wound that ate at him, and his words brought more tears to her eyes. He was quick to see it and hid his expression of bitterness.

"Do you blame me?" she asked.

A startled look spread across his face. "Dear God, Wenna, I don't blame you. How could I ever blame you? As for that blackguard Killiow …" He left the rest unsaid.

He returned to the window, his shoulders sagging. She waited in silence. Would he say something she could accept as another affirmation of his love for her? She longed so hard to hear him say it again. The silence stretched. "If only I'd known how you felt, Christopher."

He swung round, frowning. As if he'd come to a decision, he crossed the room, sat beside her on the bed and wrapped his arms about her. She inched her face closer to his.

Tantalisingly close.

"We mustn't let Arthur know," he said. "You've given yourself to him, and he's your husband; whatever the law may say and whatever you and I may feel for one another."

He was right. But the intensity inside her would not subside, and when he gazed into her eyes so forlornly, she leaned her head forward that last inch and kissed him. He returned the kiss, tenderly at first, and then with passion. And all the wrongs of her life, all the pain and hurt flew away like doves fluttering up into a clear blue sky.

The bedroom door squealed open, and Wenna squeezed her eyes tighter, desperate to prolong the kiss.

"Wenna, what are you doing?" Arthur's voice was sharp, accusing. Like a well-honed knife, it sliced keenly through the tense atmosphere. She stared, wide-eyed at her husband standing dumbfounded just inside the door.

Christopher leapt up, swinging around to face him. It was the first time she had seen the American look so deeply uncertain and at a loss for words.

"What is the meaning of this?" Arthur crossed the room and towered over the two of them.

Wenna swung her gaze from one man to the other. Which of the two was the more perplexed? "Arthur," she said weakly, but no other words came to her lips.

"How could you?" Arthur began then threw out his hands helplessly. "How could you do this to me?"

She couldn't find an acceptable explanation. She breathed low and shallow then said: "It was no more than a warm embrace between friends. Think what Christopher has done for me. For the both of us." Dear God, she had lied to a man of the cloth, her husband.

"Do you take me for a fool? It was more than that!" Arthur shook a fist at Christopher. "You don't need to tell me what he's done for you. I know it already. Damn you both."

Embarrassment and shame washed over her in floods. She closed her eyes, and when she opened them again, the two men were staring at her. Christopher eyed her with a mixture of anguish and shame. Arthur had a glaring look that was both ugly and frightening. Then it hit her; her husband loved her with an intensity she had never expected from him.

Christopher spread his hands wide, as if he was protesting his innocence. "You misunderstand –"

"No, I think not." Arthur dismissed him with a wave. Her husband's face creased with a deep withering look. In the silence that followed, he redirected his expression to her, and she shrank back against her pillow because he was right. "Perhaps it's well that I'm leaving the country. I think it best if I leave this house as soon as possible. There are others who will give me shelter; people I can trust." With that, he swung on his heels and stormed out of the room.

Kit sat in a dark corner of the parlour, his long frame overshadowing his writing desk, a candle flickering beside him and Pengorse standing at his shoulder. Their eyes had never met since the confrontation in Wenna's room, and Pengorse offered no word of interruption while Kit wrote the letter of introduction to Ben Worth. During the entire time Kit wrote, he was aware of the pastor's hands, flipping over and over again, as if Pengorse was inspecting them, as if he had never seen them before.

Was it possible he now understood that all his union talk had brought nothing but trouble? Or – most disturbing of all – was he visualising again Wenna embracing another man?

His letter complete, Kit leaned back in his chair and handed the folded paper to Pengorse without looking up. "This will introduce you to Captain Worth." An uneasy silence passed between them. How could he face the preacher without betraying his turbulent inner emotions?

Ben Worth had once told him the human species existed for the sole purpose of reproducing itself, nothing more than a deeply ingrained primitive urge. At the time, Kit believed him because it explained why Pa had acted in such beastly ways. Pa was weak and had given in to his urges while Kit had long suppressed them to ensure the Vanson curse could not continue through him. But with insight he now knew Ben was wrong; human life was far more than biological reproduction. And Kit's emotions were beyond suppression. He loved Wenna and ached for her more than he could admit to anyone.

"The *Tamarith* sails from Plymouth early in March. Show him this letter and you'll be guaranteed a berth."

"And you'll take care of Wenna until she's fully recovered?" Pengorse's words were stilted and without feeling.

This time Kit searched out the preacher's face. "Yes, of course." Surely Pengorse must see the conflicting emotions on his own face. "I give you my word that I will give you no cause for concern."

Pengorse scowled and narrowed his eyes suspiciously. They were filled to overflowing, first with bewilderment then naked anger. He turned his head away as if the sight of Kit offended him. "You knew my wife before we were married."

He had stated a fact as if he did not expect an answer, but Kit felt obliged to respond. "Yes. I met her the first day I came here." He tidied away his writing implements. "She gave me shelter at Crabtree Copse Farm when I was lost and caught in a snow storm."

The pastor whipped around and glowered back at him. This time his eyes were even more intense. "Did you sin with her?"

"Did I what?"

"You heard me. Did you sin with my wife?"

Kit jerked to his feet, resentment burning through his veins. "I did not! How dare you suggest such a thing?"

Pengorse drew back as if regrouping for another verbal attack. He shook a forefinger at Kit. "Someone did. When I went to her on our wedding night, I discovered she was not pure. Someone has sinned with her."

With understanding quickly replacing his anger, Kit breathed out long and loud. "You're right. But why don't you ask Wenna about that?" Pengorse stared back at him, his shoulders shaking with suppressed emotion and, amazingly, Kit began to feel just a little bit sorry for the man.

"Not now. She's suffered enough. I don't want to hurt her further while she's ill. But I will find out the truth." Pengorse raised his thick finger higher, aiming it directly at Kit's face. "If you are lying to me, I will find out."

"Pastor Pengorse, you are one damned fool." Kit faced the big man square on. "Your wife has had more than her share of troubles, more than you realise. I'll tell you what she has obviously been afraid to tell you. Ralph Killiow is the one who dishonoured her. When she went to him to sell her farm, that blackguard kept her prisoner overnight. He attacked and raped her." In the silence that followed, neither man moved.

Slowly at first, Pengorse's shoulders began to heave with rising emotional turmoil that quickly boiled into something intense and gut-wrenching. He covered his face and a sudden flash storm of howling ripped apart the silence. "Nooo …"

Kit turned away, embarrassed to see the man's pain. He let some time elapse. The pastor's huge hands still covered his face while he sobbed pitifully. "I'm sorry," Kit said. "She was too ashamed to tell you."

Pengorse drew a deep breath and wiped at his eyes and cheeks. "When I get my hands on that man, I swear that I'll –"

"Kill him?" Kit obliged, knowing the word was blasphemy for a preacher.

Pengorse nodded. "Thou shall not kill, says the commandment. But I would willingly go to hell for what that evil man has done."

"You'll do nothing of the sort." Kit folded his arms across his chest. "What you've just said was my own sentiment when I first discovered the truth. But it ain't gonna help Wenna or anyone else, if we pick a fight with Squire Killiow."

"By The Lord God, I swear that vengeance will be mine," Pengorse growled, his fist raised towards the ceiling. "Vengeance will be mine!"

Kit patted him on the shoulder. "Save it, pastor. That ain't the way of a man of the cloth. Best thing you can do is make your way to Plymouth soon as possible and wait for that ship to sail. There'll be a better life for both of you in the New World."

The preacher gave him a questioning look, and Kit nodded in confirmation.

"You're right, Vanson. Maybe I have misjudged you, even if I did see you holding Wenna in an unseemly manner. But now I'm forced to trust you to look after her and see that she comes to no harm. Until the day when she's well enough to follow after me."

The implications were unmistakable. Any betrayal of that trust would not be forgiven.

Wenna leaned over the landing balustrade, straining to overhear the conversation in the parlour below. A steady drone of voices drifted up to her, rising and falling as tension flowed and ebbed between Christopher and Arthur. An outburst erupted from one man and then the other, startling her. To her frustration, the words remained indistinct. Finally, the conversation seemed to be over, and she returned to the bedroom wondering what had transpired below.

She lay prone in the bed, shivering with cold while a clammy sweat soaked her face. Like one who had resigned herself to premature death, she was physically drained.

An hour or more passed before Beth came to see her, gently

closing the door and crossing the room with a flickering light above her head. She sat gently on the edge of the bed, putting aside the candle to take Wenna's icy hands in her own. Tears trickled down Wenna's cheeks and she shook her head to dislodge them.

"Poor dear, you look like you need someone to talk to." Beth drew her kerchief and offered it to Wenna. "What's happening between Christopher and Arthur?"

Wenna sniffled and wiped her cheeks. "Trouble, I'm afraid. The sort I hoped would never happen in this house."

"Want to tell me about it?"

"I feel so wretched. It was all my fault." Wenna gulped. "I embraced Christopher and Arthur surprised us. He must know that I care for Christopher, and he's a jealous man, Beth."

"Most men are." Beth patted Wenna's hand. "I understand the problem now, so let's not talk further of those two. They can sort out their differences for themselves. Tell me, what do you think of Clem?"

"I know nothing about him. How can I judge him?"

"Do you think he looks pleasing?" Beth tilted her head in query, but to Wenna, she seemed to be in another world, visualizing a man for whom she clearly had strong feelings.

"He's a handsome man, for sure." Wenna's voice held no enthusiasm.

"That's what I think. A handsome man for sure." Then Beth's smile faded. "But he has a weakness for drink, and that'll be his downfall. He's not like Christopher, is he?"

"You like Christopher, don't you?" Wenna hesitated then forged ahead. "You feel something for him."

"How could I fail to like him? Yes, of course I like him."

Wenna turned her head to one side and closed her eyes, pretending exhaustion while needing to shield herself from the pain surging in her heart. "Will you marry him?"

"Now there's a question to be asking a lady." Beth rose up and stepped lightly to the window. Wenna held her breath, waiting for her answer with baited breath. "I'll tell you the truth." Beth paused, and Wenna gulped. "I like him rightly enough, I like him a lot, but no, I won't marry him because I don't love him."

Neither spoke for a while. In the silence between them, Wenna was beside herself with the love she held for Christopher. She wanted him unwed, and her immoral selfishness shocked her to her core. She recovered enough with cleansing breaths to change her focus to Beth and her happiness. "What about Clem? Do you love him?"

"Ah, yes. Clem." Vocal signs of Beth's inner emotions rose to the surface: sadness, helplessness and hope. "You're perceptive, Wenna. But he's not yet ready to marry me or anyone else. And I won't tie myself to a man who isn't ready to commit himself. I won't wed a man who has a serious weakness in his character and won't face up to it. We need time."

Wenna cast her gaze at the windowpane. Outside, in the complete darkness, rain still fell heavily, reflecting her mood. "What do you think will happen to Christopher, if neither of us is to marry him?"

"Who knows?" Beth smiled at her with understanding in her eyes. "Perhaps someone suitable will learn to love him as much as you."

"Yes, perhaps so."

"Of course so," Beth said, but Wenna saw the strong doubt lingering in her eyes.

Twenty One

March 1838

Kit encouraged his horse slowly across the narrow, rickety bridge adjacent to his farm while he admired the dawn shaking off the orange glow on the horizon, replacing it with a vague hint of weak sunlight.

The rush of water beneath the bridge had him pausing at the middle. He stared down at the old millstream, running in full flood as if anxious to escape this place. Up in the moorland hills, the snow melted and fed the river with the violent energy needed to thresh and retch its way towards the sea.

Kit clicked his tongue and, with his horse continuing to the other side, he called to his two companions to follow.

Clem was next to cross and quickly caught up with his brother. "'Tain't right for Beth to be riding that old nag all that way to St Austell, Kit. She should be riding' in some sort of style. She bein' a lady."

Beth reined the mare beside the two men and gave Clem a brooding look. "I can handle any horse of Kit's. Been on horses all my life. And who was it who rode with you to Bodmin to rescue old Jacob?"

"You heard the lady." Kit looked over the tired animal and grimaced. "But I figure we'll do better next time. I've set Jimmy and Jacob to repair an old landau I found under wraps in one of the barns."

"Just don't seem right," Clem muttered and hurried ahead, turning in the saddle. "She's a real lady. And ladies ain't used to bein' abroad this early."

"Gotta get to St Austell before other employers take the best men." Kit glanced at Beth, just in time to catch her wry grin. She put a hand to her mouth, but Kit caught her insipient laugh nonetheless.

She had told him earlier that morning that she wanted to tag along because Wenna now spent more and more time out of bed, and needed new clothes. She would have preferred to shop in Truro but, in her opinion, St Austell was a reasonable second best. She had laughed when Jenny told her: "I wouldn't go to S'nozzell, me lady. 'Tes too big an' noisy."

Clem offered no explanation for joining the party, and Kit asked for none. Maybe he simply wanted to be near Beth, or perhaps he grew tired of idling away his days before joining the *Tamarith*. His behaviour had improved markedly of late, sufficiently for Kit to have misgivings about sending him back to sea. Nevertheless, he refused to change his decision. He expected a letter any day from Ben Worth letting him know the schooner was ready to sail.

They followed the lane parallel to the bubbling millstream until a leat branched off from the main river, diverting the fast running water towards an overshot mill wheel. As they rode through Penmarith village, more sunlight broke through, clearing the clouds entirely when they reached Mount Charles on the outskirts of St Austell.

In Farmer Greep's field, opposite the Duke of Cornwall Inn, canvas tents housed a variety of public amusements. Adults and children mingled amongst tawdry peep shows, toy stands and the inevitable display of medical miracle cures. Cornish wrestlers attracted an audience of braying young men, egging on their favourites.

Amongst the public gaiety, an endless succession of heavily laden wagons clattered through the streets, carrying slippery white loads from the china clay works to the north of the town. The wagons, each pulled by up to four heavy horses, lumbered on towards the busy port at Charlestown, leaving an untidy legacy of clay mingled with horse dung along the road.

The streets were busier than usual because of the hiring fair and extra constables kept the peace, each man carrying a long polished wooden stave as his badge of office. Kit led his party to the Red Lion Inn at the centre of St Austell town where they dismounted, left the horses at the stables and tackled the streets on foot.

They walked by an alley where a group of specially hired policemen hid themselves to avoid any unpleasantness. Kit shook his head. "Money not properly earned."

Beth hung back in the lee of the parish church, opposite the Temperance Hotel. "This shopping is a woman's job," she told Kit, kissing him lightly on the cheek. She gestured in the direction she intended to take, avoiding all eye contact with Clem. "I'll meet you at Fanny Gloyn's dress shop later. It's half way along Trinity Street."

Kit pulled at Clem's arm. He noted how his brother had clenched his hands as Beth sauntered away, drawing other men's attention. "We've work to do, brother."

"Sure, Kit." Despite Clem's easy answer, his face had remained dark with sadness.

They picked their way through the crowds to the far end of Fore Street where the unemployed farm workers stood about waiting for their hire. They looked them over and chose ten suitable men; four to work on the long meadow while the rest would clear the ten-acre field.

Kit gathered the farmhands together. "You'll be properly hired when you get to Tregover one week from today," he told them, wary that some might not actually reach the farm if alternative employment presented itself on the way. He gave them directions to the farm before letting the men drift away.

"I figure that's enough to get us started." Kit turned to Clem. "We'll hire more men when we're ready to get more land cultivated. Now, how about a meal at the Red Lion?"

"Food, yes. But no drink, Kit." Clem shook his head emphatically. "I ain't touched a drop of liquor since that time Killiow made a fool outa me. And I ain't gonna risk hurtin' Beth again even if I am obliged to leave the country soon."

Kit raised his eyebrows at his brother's declaration. "Well, you sure got it bad for that little lady. Pity you already gone and messed things up between you."

Clem's face dropped. "Reckon she'll ever forgive me?"

"Most women wouldn't. Can't tell with this one." Kit shook his head, thinking how Beth had him confused most of the time. He slapped his brother's back. "Hell, Clem, why don't you ask her?"

"'Fraid she'll tell me to take myself down to the Fowey River and drown myself."

Kit gave him a pointed look. "She's good reason to do just that."

They walked back through the town towards their expected

meeting place with Beth. Part way along Fore Street, Kit set a hand on Clem's arm. "D'you hear that?" He inclined his head and pointed back towards the Bodmin Road.

"Soldiers," Clem nodded. "Should be no bother to us."

Kit pushed his brother into the next narrow alley. "Jacob warned me about these men." At Clem's confused look, he explained: "They beat up the town at hiring fairs. It's their way of recruiting men into the regiment and they can be a mite overzealous." Kit pressed himself against the alley wall and glanced back into Fore Street.

"Sure don't look like a very friendly bunch," Clem observed as the soldiers came into view.

A platoon of the Cornwall Regiment marched through the town, pushing aside women and children who strayed into their path. The recruiting sergeant grabbed at any young men within reach, thrusting them into the arms of his foot soldiers with no heed for their cries of protest.

"Reckon we can get back to the dress shop from the other end of this alley." Kit clasped at Clem's coat and led him away from the main street.

They turned into a side lane near the Bull Ring and then into Trinity Street, where they found the small dress shop. Beth stood outside with her hands tucked into her sleeves, an impatient look on her face.

"Thought you'd be a mite longer selecting clothes," Kit remarked casually.

She flapped a hand at him, saying: "Never mind that. I've more important news for you." She waved them closer until they were within reach of whispered conversation. "I've seen Pastor Pengorse."

"Where?" Kit gritted out. Surely the man had more sense than to show himself in public.

"Where do you think? Here, in St Austell!" She pointed in the opposite direction from which they had approached her. "He was skulking down that alley over there with his face half hidden. But I knew it was him as soon as I clapped eyes on him."

"What in tarnation is he doing here?" Sensing trouble, Kit's heart sank.

"You think I'm a mind-reader, Christopher Vanson?" Beth shooed him towards the alley. "Come on, we have to find out what he's up to."

They grimly walked into the stinking alley, Beth and Kit taking the lead with Clem protecting their rear. At the bottom end, they emerged into a wider courtyard with a recently built Wesleyan chapel dominating one side. Singing percolated out from the building.

At first the sound was no more than an indistinct muffle, but as they drew closer, the tune became clearer. A prayer meeting was underway. A group of late arrivals to the meeting drew open a side door, and the full force of the singing wafted out into the alley.

Kit began shaking his head and, once started, couldn't stop. That hymn. The tune – those words – he knew them. He ground his teeth on recalling a rich baritone voice singing inside his barn. The chapel side door was left wide open, and Kit signalled Beth and Clem to stop and listen.

I feel Him in the soil,
In my daily work and toil.
I glory in the strength of His command.
In the rain and in the snow,
He's beside me as I go.
Yes, I feel Him in the hardy land.

The voices rose to a rousing crescendo in the chorus.

Power in the land!
Power in the land!
There is power in the hardy land.

The singing stopped and the deep-resounding voice of the preacher poured out through the door. Kit waved Beth and Clem to stay put while he stepped inside, searching for sight of the orator. Pengorse was mad to preach in St Austell on one of the busiest days of the year. Kit moved his head from side to side, cursing silently at the worshippers blocking his view. Anxiously, he backtracked to the front entrance and peered along the main aisle.

A brightly painted message of hope adorned the far wall: *'Oh Worship The Lord In The Beauty of Holiness'*. Beneath it, Pengorse leaned across a lectern with his finger raised towards God. Hellfire and damnation were the themes of his sermon, and his words echoed round the chapel like rumbling thunderclaps. His eyes glistened as if he were enjoying himself.

Kit hurried back to where Clem and Beth were waiting. "That damned idiot."

"What do we do about him?" Beth asked.

"I dunno." Kit balled a fist and hammered the other palm. "Need time to think."

"We can't just stand around here. We'll look suspicious," Beth pointed out.

Kit agreed with a nod. "Let's go and eat at the Kings Arms while we consider things."

"Hang on there, brother." Clem caught Kit's sleeve. "What about Pengorse? We can't just leave him in there."

Kit whipped around to his brother and glowered. "You know something better to do with him? He's put himself in danger, and I ain't gonna walk in there and join him. Not 'til I've thought about it."

Beth went back to Clem and placed a hand on his arm. "He's right, Clem. Let's think carefully about this before we do anything. We don't want to get ourselves caught up in problems of Pengorse's own doing." She regaled him with half a smile, and he capitulated instantly.

The Kings Arms Hotel was almost filled to capacity, and they had to jostle their way through a heavy throng before finding a vacant table set in a bay-window alcove at one end of the packed dining room. Outside the half open window, the St Austell town band started a ragged, out-of-tune melody. Inside, the babble of voices, the jingle of glasses and the laughing shouts of customers and serving girls made conversation difficult.

"This sure makes you appreciate the peace and quiet of the farm," Clem said, leaning across the table to make himself heard. "Reckon we had to go as far as New Orleans to find this sort of crowd back home."

"*This* is my home now. Leastwise, as far as I'm concerned." Kit signalled to a harassed serving wench who looked no older than her fourteenth year. She pushed and elbowed herself into the bay window space, jolting heavily against the back of a well-dressed man at the next table.

Lurching forward in his seat, the customer spewed out a mouthful of ale then swung round to her. "Idiot," he roared.

Kit, Clem and Beth all gasped.

Ralph Killiow.

Killiow's tirade ended abruptly when his gaze found their group. His expression turned to thunder. "Why, 'pon me life. If it ain't me own sister." His eyes blazed and his whiskers quivered. "Damn me if I can't enjoy a meal without being cursed with the presence of me wayward sibling."

Tightness gripped Kit's innards. Fuming at her brother's verbal abuse, Beth half rose to her feet, but Clem held her back. "Ignore it. He's only baitin' you, Beth. Look at his ruddy cheeks. He's been drinking for some time."

"Ha!" Killiow raised his ale pot towards them and jeered: "Here's to any man who can hold his drink with me. There's some who certainly can't." He then winked at Clem.

Fuming, Clem kept his head low.

Kit leaned towards the Squire. "We came here to eat in peace, Killiow. Let's not cause any trouble in the town with so many people looking on."

Killiow pushed back his seat with a loud clatter and struggled to his feet. "Trouble? You dare accuse me of trouble?" The background noise in the room faded away as diners noticed the confrontation, but no one spoke out. The squire wobbled unsteadily before leaning across the bay window table, resting his knuckles on the surface. Scraps of food soiled the front of his coat, and Kit grimaced at the stench of alcohol on his breath.

The inexperienced serving wench hastily backed away, terror rippling across her face.

"You dare accuse me of trouble?" Killiow raised one hand and jabbed a thumb at his chest. "Me!"

Kit held his temper, refusing to be drawn into a brawl while Beth edged closer to Clem, clutching at his arm for safety. "Leave us alone, Ralph."

Killiow belched loudly and sneered at her. "No. I'll not leave you alone. And you want to know why? I'll tell you why." A silly expression flittered across his face, suddenly replaced by a dark scowl.

He stabbed an unsteady finger at Clem's shoulder. "Because I saw that man there kill my father!"

Gasps of shock erupted amongst the diners. Chairs clattered as people rose to their feet to better witness the confrontation. In the confusion, Kit spotted one of Killiow's cronies push his way out of the room.

"Him," Killiow shouted, playing to the crowd and jabbing again at Clem's shoulder. "I came into me own father's bedroom and saw *him* with a pillow across me father's face." He added in a falsetto squeak: "I tried to pull him away but then me sister held me back."

"That's a lie." Clem rose to his feet and turned to the diners. "A damnable lie!"

Now the centre of the crowd's attention, Killiow pointed accusingly to Beth. "And *she* helped Vanson do the foul deed. Me own sister. In fact I do believe he only did it for her. She whores for him, the filthy little slut, just like she whored for so many others."

Uproar suddenly took hold in the room; cries of disgust, anger and revulsion filled the stifling air.

Kit remained seated and met the gaze of the customers nearest him. "Squire Killiow is drunk. Please take no notice." He turned to Killiow. "You don't know what you're saying."

"Drunk, you say? Ask your brother the meaning of the word. What judge is going to believe a man who can't hold his drink?"

Just then Kit spotted Killiow's crony returning and pushing his way towards them, a constable tagging behind. "Time we left." Kit urged Beth and Clem to their feet.

"Arrest those two," Killiow bellowed when he spied the constable. "That man killed me father and that woman aided him!"

The constable barged his way to the table, clutching his stave in one hand and frowning. He switched his attention between Killiow, Beth and Clem. "Well now, be that true, then?"

"Of course it ain't true." Clem waved a hand at Killiow. "The squire's drunk and don't know what he's doing. Don't you know who this here lady is?"

"Reckon as how I do at that." The constable touched his forelock. "Good day to ee, ma'am."

But Killiow was in full spate, pointing his podgy finger at Clem.

"You have a duty to arrest that man. Vanson's his name and he's an American drunk who forced his way into me home and killed me father."

The constable breathed deeply as he weighed the possibilities before clamping a firm hand on Clem's shoulder. "I think you'd better come with me, Mister Vanson. Just 'til we get this all sorted out, like."

"Wait a minute." Rising to his full height, Kit grasped at the constable's arm to ensure his complete attention. "Do you have a warrant for my brother's arrest?"

"No." The constable was taken aback. "Don't have any warrant. But Squire Killiow do say –"

"Never mind what he says." Kit released his hold, satisfied that he'd injected enough doubt into the man's performance of his duty. "There's been no crime committed on these premises, and you've seen my brother do nothing wrong in this town. You've no reason to arrest an innocent man."

"Ain't seen no crime, 'tes true." The constable pulled at his jaw, perplexed. "'S'pose by rights me an' the Squire could go an' see the magistrate. But ee be away in London at present. Won't be home until tomorrow afternoon. We can't get no warrant issued 'til then."

"Then you can come back when you have the warrant. In the meantime, unhand my brother."

"But Mister Killiow says –"

"Mister Killiow is obviously drunk. Do you want to be held responsible for the wrongdoing of a drunken man?"

The constable studied Killiow, dithered, and in his indecision, he released Clem. Kit released his pent up breath; mayhem could so easily escalate inside a hotel.

"Outside. Now!" On an impulse, Kit un-ceremoniously pushed Beth and Clem towards the exit.

"Stop them," Killiow roared while Kit glanced over his shoulder. "They're getting away!"

"Can't do that." The constable crossed his arms as if shedding all responsibility from the situation. "Ain't been no crime here."

"But he killed me father! Do you doubt me word?"

While the argument continued, Kit bustled his party out from the building, pausing briefly when they were in the busy street. He quickly took his bearings then led the group away at a fast trot.

"That was a nasty business," Beth gasped as she struggled to keep up with the two men's pace. Clem took her arm and helped her along the uneven cobbles.

They turned into a relatively quiet side street and paused again to catch their breath.

Leaning back against a stone wall, Kit made a snap decision. "We can't stay here in St Austell much longer. Not with Killiow in that state of mind. But there's still the post office and Pengorse to deal with. Clem, you and Beth see if there's a letter from Ben Worth. I'll try to get to Pengorse without being seen."

"What you gonna do about him?" Clem asked Kit.

"I'll figure that out when I see him."

"Take care, brother."

Kit gathered himself. "And you keep a sharp look out for Killiow. It's you and Beth he's after."

"Don't worry, I don't aim to let the little lady come to any harm." Clem smiled meaningfully. "See you at the stables in about half an hour."

"Right. And for heaven's sake, Clem, do make sure you take care of Beth this time."

Kit approached the chapel, walking against the flow of the congregation ambling away towards the centre of the town where the men would likely seek entertainment and drink, and the women would look on with disdain.

He circled round to the rear of the now quiet chapel and discovered a windowless door standing ajar. He pushed it fully open and stepped into a poorly lit room where two men were in deep conversation. Both glanced up as he entered. One was Arthur Pengorse.

"Mister Vanson." The pastor rose and thrust out a hand in greeting. "How is my wife? Is she with you?"

"No, she ain't with me." Ignoring the hand, Kit firmly closed the door behind him and turned to the pastor with a penetrating stare. "What in hell's name are you doin' here, on a busy day like this? Don't you have the sense to keep your head down until you can get out of the country?"

The other man stepped forward, old, frail with long white hair. "I don't know who you are, friend. But you don't have any right to talk to our preacher like that. Pastor Pengorse risks a lot to come here and preach to us, and we thank him for all he does for us."

Kit stood firm. "So he's been preachin' here. But it just ain't safe for the pastor to stay. Squire Killiow's in this town right now and he's in a foul mood. You got some safe place for your preacher to go?"

"Forgive my friend." Pengorse turned to Kit. "Vanson, I got here without any trouble and I'll make my way back to Plymouth, without any trouble."

"Like hell you will. You know what Killiow would do if he got his hands on you?"

Pengorse grasped his lapels and pushed his shoulders back with a proud air of defiance. "Squire Killiow doesn't know where I am."

Kit shook his head at the preacher's misplaced pride. "Well you better be sure he doesn't find out. He's already made ludicrous accusations against Miss Beth and my brother. Says they killed the old squire."

Pengorse's stance collapsed. "That sounds bad."

"You're a damn fool to take chances preaching in public at a hiring fair. The roads out of town are gonna be busy all day. Where you gonna go until it's safe to leave? Tell me that."

"I'll find somewhere."

Kit massaged his now aching forehead and forced himself to breathe easily. He glanced around the room and came to an instant decision. "The St Blazey Road won't be quite so busy as the rest. Make your way out there. Meet us where the Trevisco Road branches off, and we'll take you back to the farm for tonight. Wenna would never forgive me if I left you here while Squire Killiow's in town."

"I can take care of myself," Pengorse protested.

"No, you can't. You don't have the sense to take care of anything or anyone, pastor. You mess things up for everyone you come in contact with. Now, just do as I say!" Kit stormed out of the chapel and slammed the door shut behind him.

He paused to gather his breath then hastened back to the main street in deep thought. They might all be gaoled if Pengorse was caught in their company, but it was a chance they would have to take. For Wenna's sake.

He hurried into the stable yard where Beth and Clem were already mounted up with Kit's horse in tow.

"You saw him?" Beth asked.

"Yeah. He's comin' back home with us." He climbed into his saddle, knowing she could see the sour look on his face and hear the disgusted tone in his words.

"Wenna will be pleased. But if he's seen ..." Beth's voice conveyed outright fear.

"The letter you was expectin' arrived." Clem pulled an envelope from his jerkin and passed it across to Kit. "I guess that's gonna be my orders to leave England. Right?"

"Possibly." Kit opened it and scanned it quickly. A few days ago Ben Worth had sailed the short distance from Millbay Docks to Sutton Pool where he had picked up a full cargo and was now ready to set course for Newfoundland. The *Tamarith* would leave Plymouth tomorrow on the early morning tide.

Early tomorrow.

"What does it say?" Clem asked.

"We'll talk about it when we get home." Kit pushed the letter into his coat pocket and swung his horse away.

He led at a steady canter with Beth and Clem riding side-by-side a few paces behind him. At the inn courtyard at Mount Charles, the platoon of the Cornwall Regiment stood in an untidy group, watching them pass. Kit glanced sideways, fixing on two men standing beyond the main body of soldiers, facing the inn's open doorway. Ralph Killiow stood, head bent, in earnest discussion with the recruiting sergeant. Kit quickened the pace, drawing into the cover of a heavy crowd oozing from the fair in the field opposite.

Once past Mount Charles, he relaxed marginally. The clouds grew darker, the wind rose, and he pulled his coat tighter at the first sign of dampness in the air. He raised one hand to signal a halt at the arranged meeting place farther along the St Blazey Road.

Kit figured that it would take Pengorse some time to walk to the meeting place, but he was wrong. The pastor darted out from the cover of a small copse and slipped into the shadow of their mounts. At a sign from Kit, the party trotted on with Pengorse jogging along beside them. Farther down the lane, Kit stopped and allowed the pastor to climb up behind him.

They rode on in silence. The first drops of rain began to fall when they were still an hour from home but no one commented or complained. Within minutes, a heavy downpour soaked them and continued until they came once again into the farmyard.

Twenty Two

Dusk turned into night and long grey shadows evolved into full darkness. Pain still racked Wenna's chest, but something was going on downstairs, and she intended to be in the thick of it. Arthur had stayed with her long enough to tell her why he had returned to Penmarith, but he seemed anxious to return to the discussion down in the farmhouse parlour.

Near the glowing fire, she eased herself into a dress Beth had loaned her, her muscles stiff and sore. It would have fitted her a few months ago, but now it hung loosely from her thin body. Remembering how Arthur had studied her with a long, puzzled look before leaving the bedroom, she crept out into the semi-darkness of the landing, lit only by stray light from the passage below.

A low buzz of voices echoed up the stairs from the parlour, no more than a succession of vague drones. She shuffled to the banister rail and leaned over to catch the rumble of men arguing, and the occasional high-pitched squeal of Beth adding her opinion.

Wenna trudged down the stairs and, before she entered the parlour, she stood for a long moment with her eyes closed, blotting out that nagging pain in her lungs. Then she pushed open the door.

Candlelight and a blazing fire lit the room. The cheery glow was unmatched by an argument that ceased abruptly when she entered. Bright yellow patches chased shadows fast about the walls while the four occupants of the room sat close together around the hearth, swinging their heads towards her in unison.

Arthur jumped to his feet and threw out his arms to her. "Wenna! You shouldn't be out of bed."

"Something is wrong here, and I'm well enough to be told what it is." She pushed aside her husband's helping hands, staggered across the room and slumped down onto the wooden settle next to Beth. She sensed anxiety as she sank back uncomfortably against the hard backboard and clutched at Beth's arm. "Tell me what's happening."

Worried looks darted from face to face.

Beth broke the silence. "We didn't want to tell you everything, Wenna, because we didn't think you were up to receiving bad news."

"I'm used to bad news. My life has been built on bad news. Tell me what the problem is and what you're intending to do about it."

Clem coughed to hide his discomfort.

"You know," Christopher began, "that we bumped into Ralph Killiow in St Austell today?"

"Yes." Her heart went out to him, but she struggled to keep her feelings hidden.

"He was drunk." Christopher paused, as if dragging the words from the very depths of his soul. "And he publicly accused Beth and Clem of killing the old squire."

Wenna sat bolt upright, and another pain shot through her body. "But it's not true! No one would believe that."

"Killiow can't prove it," Christopher breathed deeply, "but if he makes the accusations to a magistrate there's bound to be a trial. And suppose he brings his cronies into court to lie on his behalf? There's no guarantee what the outcome might be."

"What can you do about it?" she asked Christopher.

"I've already made arrangements for Clem to sail on a ship from Plymouth. Your husband will sail on the same ship. She leaves …" He tailed off and stared at her.

"Yes?"

"The ship sails early tomorrow morning." Christopher gave a dismal glance at each of them in turn. "We have to get Clem and Arthur over to Plymouth tonight."

Wenna stared across at her husband, but he averted his gaze from her. How strange that she should feel no great hurt when he was leaving so soon. She wished she did. She wished she could feel that she was about to endure a great loss because that would give meaning to her marriage. "Oh," she replied, as if it were a matter of little importance.

"We were discussing what I should do," Beth broke into the conversation. "Christopher is in favour of me leaving the country with Clem and Arthur."

Wenna turned to Beth. "And what do *you* want?"

Beth drew in a long deep breath as she considered her reply. "I feel that this is tantamount to running away from the problem and I never ran away from anything in my life."

"You left the manor to come and live here," Pengorse pointed out in a calm, persuasive voice.

She nodded. "But I'm still here to face up to my brother. I don't believe he can convince anyone I'm guilty of such a charge as this."

"You know your own brother better than any of us, Beth." Christopher rubbed at the knots in his neck. "Now that he's made public these damnable accusations against you, he won't let it drop. He'll have warrants issued for you and Clem."

"As Wenna says, no one will believe him. I think the risk is small. I see no reason for Clem to leave either ... unless *you* force him to go, Christopher." She darted a gaze in Clem's direction and something indefinable to Wenna passed between them.

"Perhaps." Christopher compressed his lips. "The magistrates might believe *you*, Beth. But you have to remember that Clem's a foreigner as far as they're concerned. They'd have to make a choice between an English squire and an American drifter with a proven alcohol problem. Any magistrate would be bound to favour Killiow. Do you want Clem to take that chance? Do you want the whole business to end up in an assize court anyway?"

Wenna understood now why they had omitted her from the discussion. With argument and counter-argument, they were getting nowhere. Her tiredness increased just as the pain in her lungs became more acute.

"Maybe ..." Arthur began. All eyes swivelled round to stare at her husband. "Maybe you've all got it wrong. Maybe you're failing to see what this is all about. Maybe you're badly underestimating Squire Killiow's real intentions." He pursed his lips as he seemed to consider his argument. "Maybe he doesn't intend that this business should ever go to an assize court anyway." He paused and scanned about the room. "After all, that would leave him open to counter-accusations from Clem and Beth that he was the real killer. I doubt that he wants anything like that to come out in court. In my opinion, he has other plans."

Uneasy silence settled over the gathering, broken only by the crackling of the fire. Christopher exchanged curious glances with Clem then turned to the pastor. "Carry on, preacher."

"Look at it this way." Arthur drew himself erect in his seat. "Killiow has made public accusations, which are lies, but could conceivably be true in the eyes of a magistrate or the public at large. Suppose there were now to be a physical confrontation between Clem and Killiow and, in the course of that confrontation, Clem was to be killed. Would it not be a reasonable justification for Killiow that he was attacked by the same person who killed his own father? And that Clem's death was a matter of self defence?"

"Surely not!" Beth began. But, as realization hit her, the words tailed off into nothing.

"Would he really kill again, Beth?" Christopher asked.

Beth remained silent. Wenna guessed that in Beth's eyes, the question needed no answer.

Her husband waited for the implications to sink in before he continued. "Killiow would never tackle Clem alone, and he doesn't have to. He has dangerous hired men to do his dirty work. I think Clem is in as much danger of his life as myself. I think it's vital he should leave the country with me before Squire Killiow has the opportunity to confront him and, perhaps, kill him or, more likely, have him killed."

"But what would Killiow gain from such a senseless killing?" Wenna asked.

"As long as Clem's alive, Killiow must constantly look over his shoulder in case the truth about his father's death should come to light. With him dead, the risk is eliminated."

"Not true." Beth spoke up with bravado and all turned towards her. "I was with Clem when my father was murdered. I saw the same thing Clem saw. Killing Clem doesn't eliminate the risk, far from it."

"Then, madam," Arthur intoned with great meaning, "perhaps you also are in grave danger of your life."

A tidal wave of weakness washed through Wenna. She steadied herself against the armrest while Beth, sombre, nodded. "You could be right, pastor."

Christopher rose to his feet. "It occurs to me that Squire Killiow has to act soon if he's to do anything at all. He's made his accusation and he can't afford to wait for people to forget it."

Beth swung her gaze around the gathering. "I agree. His story will be implausible if he doesn't follow it up immediately." She focussed her attention on Christopher. "Where will Clem go when he sails on this ship?"

Wenna looked at Clem, registering his hurt expression because Beth was unwilling to ask *him* the question. He withdrew within himself and stared down into his lap.

"Back to America," Kit provided. "Our brother, Pasco, manages a cotton plantation in Alabama. If you went with Clem, he might even be persuaded to settle there once again."

Beth's expression clearly conveyed the misery that had come over her. "Could I go with him?"

Christopher leaned forward and patted her hand. "Beth, give him the opportunity to ask you."

The ensuing silence was long and awkward. Wenna knitted her fingers together, wishing them both a happiness she could never enjoy in her own life. This was the moment of decision between Clem and Beth. The sort she had faced back in Ellie Mounter's cottage when she had been obliged to choose between Arthur and continued starvation. Pray God these two choose wisely.

Arthur rose from his seat and came to her. "I think it would be best if I help you back to your bed, Wenna. We must leave these people to their own deliberations."

He eased her to her feet and took her arm. As they left the room, Wenna was aware of Christopher's stare following after them. Half way up the stairs, she turned back at the sound of the parlour door closing. Christopher was also leaving Beth and Clem alone.

Out on the landing, she pulled on her husband's arm, allowing Christopher to catch up. "When do you leave, Arthur?"

"This evening some time. Mister Vanson is making arrangements to take me to Plymouth."

Christopher paused beside them. "We must be away soon, Wenna. The *Tamarith* sails on the morning tide. We must get Arthur to Plymouth tonight. I've sent Jacob Padder over to Trevisco to find a boat heading up the coast to Plymouth. It would be quicker and safer than riding over the heath on a night like this."

"What will happen to me?" she asked, afraid the group might meet trouble and Christopher would fail to return.

"You must remain here until you're fully recovered. Then you may follow your husband to the New World."

"I see." Except that she did not want to travel to the New World, she did not want to follow her husband. But her choice was firmly cast and she was obliged to follow that choice until the end of her life. "Thank you, Christopher, for all that you are doing for my husband. We're both indebted to you."

He averted his eyes. "It's the least I can do, you know that."

She did and, in another way, she didn't. But this was not the time to question his words or her heart. She allowed Arthur to draw her into her room, leaving Christopher standing in the flickering lamplight on the landing, silently watching as her husband closed the door behind them.

The bedroom held an eerie feeling. Rain beat against the window, and the only light came from the fire glowing in the grate. A draught lifted the curtains ghost-like against the black night outside.

Arthur remained with her, seemingly deep in thought, while she removed the loose dress, pulled her warm nightdress over her chemise and climbed back into the bed.

When she was settled, he came to her bedside and stood over her, his hands pressed together as if in prayer. "Even though I will not be here, I will be constantly praying for you, Wenna. You have no idea how much love I have for you, and what great lengths I would go to for you." Strangely, he avoided looking at her. He left the room with no sign of affection in his face or his manner, as if his words belied his thoughts.

Half an hour later Beth hurried into the room. She closed the door carefully behind her before looking straight into Wenna's eyes. "I'm going, Wenna. Leaving tonight." Her voice held the same excitement as her eyes. "Just think; it'll be a new life in the New World. Me and Clem together."

"I'm glad for you, Beth." But Wenna could not wipe aside her deep-rooted distress for her own future.

The fugitives each came to her room to bid her farewell. Christopher alone stayed away. After an hour or more the house became quiet. Then voices outside broke the silence. Wenna climbed from her bed and stood by her window peering out into the gloom.

The horses' hooves clattered on the cobbles as the restored landau rattled out of the yard. She shaded her eyes from the lit candle beside her, straining to see Christopher, but she made out only dark, indistinct shapes at the driving seat. She tried to imagine Christopher at the reins, with Clem beside him while the others hid beneath the raised hoods, protected from the driving rain.

When the coach was gone, she heard the kitchen door slam shut; Jimmy Rudge had retreated out of the rain. His footsteps pounded on the stairs until he reached the attic.

Wenna returned to her bed and dozed for a while, unable to fall into a deeper sleep while her mind dragged back thoughts of Beth, Clem and her husband. She would be faithful to him, she was quite determined about that, but it would be difficult while living in the same house as Christopher Vanson. So very difficult.

She wasn't sure how many hours passed before an outside noise invaded her barely conscious brain. She sat up startled, not sure at first what had disturbed her. Had she been dreaming? More sounds split the night air; horses' hooves clattering on the cobblestones, raised voices, carriage wheels creaking. She jumped at an excessive banging on the kitchen door and a booming voice demanding: "Open up. Immediately!"

Not recognizing the deep bass voice, she rushed to the window and peered down into the yard. Lamps swung unsteadily, a moving mass of horses whinnied and shuffled around a dark carriage stopped in the middle of the yard. Horsemen dismounted, the blades of their swords reflecting flashes of light.

Soldiers! Wenna's stomach churned and nausea rose in her throat. Christopher had escaped with the fugitives in good time.

Wenna struggled into her dress while Jimmy Rudge's footsteps rushed down the attic stairs. Moments later, he hammered on her bedroom door. "Mistress?"

"Yes, Jimmy."

"There be soldiers outside."

"Find out what they want, Jimmy, while I dress." She coughed and a sharp pain shot across her chest. "I'll be downstairs in a moment."

"Should keep them out, mistress."

"Do as I say, Jimmy."

"Yes, mistress." The boy's footsteps continued down the stairs. The kitchen door opened, someone bellowed and Jimmy Rudge shouted in reply. Her stomach worsened, tightening in knots. Was that Killiow's voice? Dear God, she hoped not.

The noises in the yard faded. A moment's respite followed then a terrible thump echoed throughout the house. She wished the sound was only furniture being knocked about in the kitchen and not an attack on Jimmy.

Wenna held herself tightly about her waist to ease away a feeling of dread then stepped slowly out onto the landing. Cautiously, she tackled the stairs, grasping the rail so tight her hands ached while angry voices wafted up towards her. She staggered into the kitchen then gasped at the turmoil.

Chairs were knocked over, the table pushed aside. Jimmy Rudge, still in his nightshirt, was held firmly in the grasp of two soldiers dwarfing him, his hands pinned tight behind his back. He kicked and fought against his captors but was powerless to escape. He stopped struggling the moment he saw her.

"I tried to stop them, mistress," he said, his eyes wide with fear.

"All right, Jimmy. I'll deal with this." Wenna drew back her chin and scanned around the room, searching for the officer in charge.

The men were splattered with mud from their ride and all were soaked by the pounding rain. Armed with Baker rifles, they wore long-tailed scarlet coats over scarlet jackets and dark grey breeches with two red stripes. Their helmets had brass combs with black horsehair manes. Dragoon Guards.

Wenna cringed at the realization.

Those men belonged to the platoon barracked in Bodmin – the notorious precaution against further union trouble.

The officer in charge stepped forward with an angry look about him, as if he resented the nightly outing in such unpleasant weather. He saluted half-heartedly. "Madam, you will tell Mister Christopher Vanson and his brother, Clement Vanson, to come down here immediately."

Wenna drew herself erect. "What business do you have with Mister Vanson?"

"If you try to obstruct me mission, I will order me men to go upstairs and fetch them both from their beds. Get him down here. Now!"

"I can't. Neither of those two gentlemen is at home this evening."

"Where are they?" he barked.

"They went to the hiring fair in St Austell early this morning and they haven't returned since."

"Liar." The officer swung round to his sergeant. "Have your men search the house and bring them both down here."

The kitchen door swung back on its creaky hinges, and a dark figure stamped into the room. With a violent jerk of the head, the man knocked off the hood of his cloak. Wenna gasped at the sight of Ralph Killiow in an ill humour.

"All right, Miss Lanyon," he snapped, hitting a riding crop angrily against his breeches, "where are they? All of them."

"Who?" She coughed as the pain in her chest intensified.

"Don't prevaricate, woman." Killiow pushed past the officer, and more soldiers spilled into the kitchen behind him, taking the opportunity to escape the rain. "Where's the Vansons and me sister? And where's Pengorse?"

Wenna clutched at her chest, knowing she couldn't give him an honest answer, but she could try to buy the fugitives time. "What do you want with them? You have no right to come here like this."

Killiow suddenly whipped his riding crop upwards until it stopped tight under her chin. She recoiled, but a soldier blocked her way, his soaked uniform dampening her dress.

"Don't tell them, mistress," Jimmy called out. "Don't tell them!"

Wenna glared at Jimmy, and he went silent. He'd made things much worse for her. Now Killiow would for sure know that she was hiding their whereabouts.

Killiow swung on his heels. "Get that boy out of the room. And get out of here the rest of you! Miss Lanyon and I will have a talk together. She *will* give me the answers I want." He lowered the crop, tucked it between her legs and slowly pulled it upwards, rucking up her dress.

Wenna clenched her fists to hide their shaking but stood her ground. She had to buy more time.

The dragoon officer raised an eyebrow and signalled his men to hold their positions. "That's not right, Mister Killiow," he said firmly. "There's no cause for that."

"Damn you, Lieutenant!" Killiow roared, but kept his eyes focussed on Wenna. "Do as I order you. I intend to find out where these miscreants are, whatever it takes. I've had me way with this wench before, and I'll do it again, damn her eyes!"

"No!" Wenna lashed out suddenly, pushing the crop aside then knocking the squire backwards. "You violated me once before, Mister Killiow. But now there's nothing you can do to me that will make things worse. I'll die before I talk to you."

Killiow quickly recovered his stance then sneered. "You might have to." He swung round to the troops. "Fetch me the servant girl. She'll be here somewhere, probably in one of the attic rooms. Bring her down here. We'll get answers out of you one way or another, Mistress Lanyon."

Four soldiers left the room, and Jimmy began to struggle once again, protesting at Jenny's involvement, until Wenna signalled him with another glare to hold still.

Minutes later, a soldier stood Jenny before Killiow, holding her firmly from behind. In nothing but her chemise, Jenny's mouth hung wide open, her eyes wide and staring.

Jimmy cursed the soldier and when this had no effect he turned, frustrated, to Killiow. With a low growl, he tried to leap at the squire but he could not escape the dragoon holding his arm.

The soldier shouted warnings and strengthened his hold on Jimmy by jacking up the boy's arm. He forced it higher, higher than the arm should physically go behind the boy's back. Jimmy cried out, a long shriek of agony.

"You ready to shut yer mouth boy?" the soldier snapped.

"'Ess!"

The soldier released his grip and Jimmy took to cursing beneath his breath.

"I told you to shut yer mouth." The soldier raised a fist and brought it down across the side of Jimmy's head.

"I don't know nuthin'," Jenny whimpered in a small, weak voice. "Honest, I don't."

Killiow brought his riding crop up against the girl's distended stomach. "So this is the result of your whoring." He spat at her. "This is an obscenity. This ... this *thing* shouldn't be allowed to live!" He brought the crop back into a striking position.

"No!" Wenna rushed towards the girl and stood before her, spreading her arms as a protection. "No. You mustn't do this!"

Killiow smiled, a cruel smile of satisfaction. He lowered his riding crop. "Then you'd better talk, woman. Tell me where I'll find the Vansons and me sister. And maybe you also know where Pengorse is. If you refuse to speak, you know what will happen." He raised his weapon once more.

Wenna cast pleading eyes at the lieutenant who turned away, his face flushed with embarrassment. When he didn't act, hatred filled her. "Can't you stop him? You can't allow him to do this!" She moved towards the officer, arms outstretched, begging him to intervene.

Before the officer could reply, Killiow suddenly swung the crop towards Jenny, diverting his aim at the last moment so that it stung her across her breast. She screamed in pain and fell back against the soldier behind her.

Jimmy cried out at the sight of the inhuman abuse against his wife. Cursing all the more, he struggled against his captor until the soldier hit him across the side of his head and the boy slumped to the floor, unconscious.

"Jimmy!" Jenny tried to rush to him, but the soldier behind her held her firmly in check. She slumped back against him, her body heaving as she whimpered silently.

"Stop it!" Wenna rushed at Killiow, her arms flailing. He brushed her aside roughly and aimed his crop at her face, in warning.

Slowly, he swung his weapon round to Jenny's stomach. "Talk, Miss Lanyon. Or else, next time I'll aim lower."

The background noise and all commotion stopped instantly, as if it had been snuffed out like a candle.

"All right!"

In the brief respite, Jenny wept with relief.

"All right." Wenna croaked as the bile rose in her throat. She swallowed hard then glared at the squire. "Let the girl go, and I'll tell you what you want to know." Deep in her heart, she hoped that Christopher had enough head start.

Leaning threateningly towards her, Killiow narrowed his eyes into slits. "Don't even think about giving me any lies. In fact, I think it best if you come with us and show us where they are."

"You don't need me." She shivered. Such a trip might likely be the death of her.

"You'll come with us or I'll shoot you in just the same way I shot your father."

Wenna staggered back, clasping at her chest and allowing her mouth to fall open in shock. Then confusion set in. "How can that be, you … you weren't there?"

"My dear young woman," he pulled out his pistol, "'twas I who pulled the trigger. Even I can brave the cold in order to see justice done."

"Justice?" Wenna's eyes filled with tears.

Killiow shrugged. "He was a criminal trying to escape the law. Someone had to stop him. I was within me rights to shoot him."

"No!" Panic mixed with utter hatred for this vile man filled Wenna's entire being. Her mind began to swim. She forced her eyes wide open and stared at the lieutenant, seeing a look of shock registering across his face.

But he did nothing.

How could these men allow a squire to arbitrarily mete out justice outside of an assize court? "You must stop this," she implored the officer.

He squirmed uneasily. "We have to obey orders, ma'am."

Twenty Three

"Don't spare the horses, Kit. I've a feeling the hounds of hell will soon be at our back, with Killiow leading them on." Sitting tight beside Kit, Clem grasped the landau's handrail as it bucked and bounced along the winding road from Penmarith to Trevisco.

Kit silently agreed with his brother. With darkness covering their flight, he raced the horses as fast as he dared while the incessant rain churned the surface into thick clogging mud which accumulated on the horses' hooves and splashed the sides of the bouncing carriage. The wheels slipped often and, at times, were perilously in danger of skidding off the road.

Clem held up one hand across his face to protect himself from the cold, stinging rain. "Ain't like this back home in Alabama."

"It rains, even there," Kit growled and ground his teeth tight together. Dealing with this damnable weather was not paramount in his mind, but was he doing the right thing for Clem and Beth? Especially Beth. How would she cope with the demands of living on a Southern plantation where the wealth of the owners depended on the backbreaking labours of coloured slaves? It would be hard on her. But at least both she and Clem would be safe from the clutches of her evil brother.

Coming to the top of a rise, Kit eased up on the reins, scanning the darkness ahead until the faint lights of Trevisco flickered into view. He urged the horses on one last time and breathed a sigh of relief when their destination came into closer view. He clapped a hand across Clem's shoulder then pointed to a dark shape moored alongside the quay. "Reckon Jacob found us a sailing barge."

"Don't look too big from here," Clem muttered.

"Big enough." Kit eased the landau into Trevisco's cobbled streets. He cast a glance at the nearby river. It ran fast, swollen with the last of the melting snow in the hills pouring down through numerous tributary streams.

"Kit, watch out!"

At Clem's warning, Kit returned his attention to the road ahead where a figure had ran into the street and was waving at them. Despite a heavy cap hiding his shaven head, Jacob Padder became discernable in the reflected light from nearby buildings.

"That way," Padder directed them towards the quayside and broke into a run alongside the coach.

Slowing his team of horses to a gentle trot, Kit guided the carriage round a sharp bend onto the quayside and halted the landau alongside the clay vessel that would take them down the coast to Plymouth. Throwing aside the reins, he clambered down.

Padder tipped his forehead out of habit. "The barge be waiting for ee, sur."

Kit stared out towards the sea, picking out white-capped waves close inshore, dimly lit by the quayside lamps. "We'll be able to leave immediately?" he asked Padder.

"Oh, 'ess." The old man pointed along the quay to where the barge owner awaited them, clothes sodden, shoulders hunched, and hands jammed into his pockets. "Name's Tilleyman. Reckon ee's anxious to be away."

"How much payment does he want?"

Padder called out an exorbitant figure.

"He's a pirate!" Kit cursed under his breath, but what alternative did he have? He tapped on the carriage door. "Hurry, all of you."

Tilleyman anxiously waved them towards the vessel. A strong wind blew the rain almost horizontally, right into the faces of the anxious party of fugitives while they ran across the last of the cobbles.

Hearing a reverberation of hooves, Kit glanced back towards far end of the quay. Padder had turned the landau around and was now heading back to the farm.

The vessel's owner threw Kit a keen look. "The tide be flowin' fast now. 'Tes goin' to be dangerous 'til we get clear of the shore."

Kit returned the look with a glare. "You're being well paid for this. Just get us to Plymouth on this tide."

The bargeman sniffed, spat into the muddy water and signalled a crewman to cast off.

Kit joined Clem on the open aft deck while Beth and Pengorse sought shelter below. Sniffing in the salty taste of the sea, Kit almost welcomed the prospect of rain in his face and a heaving deck beneath his feet.

The big sails were unfurled and, as they caught the full force of the swift-moving water, the barge eased away from the quay. Clem grinned. "Looks like we're gonna make it."

"Don't be too sure." Kit pointed back along the road they'd come from. A dark mass of movement came slowly into focus.

Horses and riders.

The barge turned out into the tidal waters, making agonisingly slow headway against the heaving waves. Clem and Kit looked on helpless at the riders cantering onto the lighted area of the quay with a resounding clopping of hooves. What had been a dismal grey outline quickly became the jackets and plumed helmets of a platoon of Dragoon Guards.

Clem's shoulders slumped. "Guess they must be after the pastor and me."

"Looks like Killiow's called out the men billeted at Bodmin." Kit shook his head sadly. "That's a sign of his desperation. Three of you fleeing the country, and he has to call out a whole platoon of dragoons."

His brother slumped out of sight, on the nearest stack of rope. "His freedom depends upon silencing me. And what better plan than to have a fugitive shot by Her Majesty's soldiers."

The barge listed, its sails abruptly caught by wind escaping around the nearby headland. Within minutes it was ploughing gainfully away from the shore, rapidly leaving Trevisco behind.

Kit sighed, relieved that Clem had escaped a gaol term or worse, and happy for the new respite the fugitives had gained. He leaned over the deck rail and scanned back along the Trevisco road. A black carriage swept over the bridge, pulling up behind the dragoons. Moments later, the barge swung again, tacking into the wind, and Trevisco was lost to sight in the enveloping darkness.

"Best go below, Clem," Kit said. "Reassure Beth. I'll stay out here on deck."

Clem hesitated. For once he seemed uncertain. "I sure do appreciate what you're doin' for me, brother. And I figure I probably ain't worth the effort anyway."

"That's a matter of opinion, Clem." Kit managed a wry grin. "Beth thinks you're worth it, though only God knows why. I owe her a few favours. You go on down there and comfort her."

The boat lurched, and Clem reached out, grabbing a rope to steady himself. "You won't regret this. By heavens, I promise you that. I know I've done some bad things and I guess I've made life hell for a load a people, but I promise you, I aim to change my ways an' do some good."

"Beth knows that?"

"Reckon she does, an' all." Clem slipped away while Kit stood on the deck, staring into the darkness behind them and keeping watch.

Would Clem change his ways? Kit had no way of telling except to give him the opportunity to prove it.

Pengorse emerged onto deck, looking worn and tired, as if carrying a greater burden that the rest of them. He stumbled towards Kit and grasped the handrail. "It may be weeks or months before you hear from me. Don't let Wenna worry unduly. I mean to keep my word to her. She'll be able to join me as soon as I'm all settled."

"You can trust me, pastor." Kit looked him in the eye. "I'll take very good care of her."

Pengorse gave him a curt nod. "I believe you will. But remember she's my wife." He held eye contact a moment longer than necessary, as if he were administering a threat.

"I never forget it, pastor. Every time I look at her, I remember that she's your wife."

Pengorse stared at him long and hard, a look of distrust still covered his face when he stumbled back below deck.

Kit remained on deck while the hours passed. The deck bucked and tilted but that was good. It brought back happier memories. The water was still choppy when they entered Plymouth Sound, the roll of the open sea replaced by a closer and sharper chop. He scanned the shore relentlessly. For now, there were no worrying signs, but how long would it take Killiow and the dragoons to ride to Plymouth over the muddy heath?

Yawing uneasily in the darkness, the barge swung into the pull of the incoming tide running into Plymouth Sound, and clawed its way east towards Sutton Pool until it finally nudged into the quay wall.

The fugitives hurried ashore where a steady, annoying drizzle still tingled against their faces. Scurrying figures came and went from inns, warehouses and tall-masted ships all along the wharf, littering the slippery quayside. Voices echoed around them, but no one seemed interested in the small group beside the insignificant-looking clay barge.

Tilleyman was next to last ashore. Chewing on his unlit clay pipe, he held a hand out to Kit for his payment.

"Where do we go now?" Pengorse asked, his eyes darting from side to side, as if in expectation of being thwarted at this last moment.

Pocketing the money with one hand, Tilleyman pointed with the other to a three-masted schooner a short way along the wharf. "That's your ship. The big one over yonder."

Kit immediately recognised the graceful lines of the *Tamarith* and felt a surge of admiration.

"Look at how her hull's low in the water. She's fully loaded." Tilleyman turned to Kit. "Reckon she'll catch the next tide."

Kit nodded then hurried the group towards the *Tamarith*. So far so good, but they were not safe yet. The next tide was hours away, and in the meantime, it would take very little imagination for the new squire to deduce that the barge had taken the fugitives as far as Plymouth.

Ben Worth waved to them from the deck, and Kit raced up the gangplank ahead of the others, grasping at his friend's outstretched hand.

"Ben, I knew you wouldn't let me down."

"You'd do the same for me, Kit." The sea captain's weather-beaten face smiled warmly. "When I got your message, I hoped you might be willing to sail with me again."

"Not this time, Ben. I'm still aiming to make a go of that farm."

"Ah." Ben Worth nodded. "The optimism of youth."

The rest of the group joined him on the deck, and Kit introduced each one to the ship's captain. Ben Worth shook their hands then beckoned one of his officers to shepherd them down to their cabins.

"I'll take care of them." Ben assured Kit once they were alone again on deck. "You can be sure of that."

"I don't doubt it, Ben. How soon can you sail?"

"Next tide. Six hours – maybe five if I cut things fine. You coming down to my cabin for a drink?"

"No. I'll just stay on deck until you sail. Just in case, you know."

"I know."

For the next few hours, Kit crouched by the companionway, alternately dozing and listening for the tell-tale sounds of approaching soldiers. The noises of quayside activity fell away, and hope rose inside Kit's chest with each passing hour.

Maybe they would succeed. At least they had given it their best, just as he was given his best shot to making the farm work.

How many weeks had passed since that cold night he strode away from the *Tamarith* and found Killiow attacking Wenna in the Admiral Nelson? The ship lay at a similar berth, the same ghostly sounds echoing along the wharf; disembodied voices mixed with the myriad creaks and groans of ships at rest.

So much had happened since then, so many misfortunes. Was he to blame – responsible for Wenna's plight? Or was the curse no more than superstition? If only he could be sure.

He dozed for short periods, jerking awake at any insignificant noise nearby. Shortly before dawn, he jumped to his feet at the clatter of horse's hooves on the nearby cobbles and ran to the gunwale. A mud-caked carriage rattled slowly along the wharf, halting one hundred yards or so beyond the *Tamarith*. The coachman climbed down, his movements tired and slow. He walked along the cobbles, studying each vessel in turn. Then he returned to the carriage and drove it back along the wharf.

This time the coach – with two flickering lights burning at the front end – stopped directly opposite the *Tamarith*. Shimmering lantern light from an inn opposite the wharf held the whole vehicle in broad silhouette. Kit waited, hands tightly clenching the handrail. But no one emerged from the dark interior, and the coachman remained on his front box, silently waiting.

Minutes passed, long and ominous. A distant drumbeat grew steadily, sharpening into the thunder of many horses' hooves on cobblestones.

A sharply bellowed order split the air, and a troop of Dragoon Guards paraded into view, halting behind the carriage. The leading officer dismounted and marched to the carriage door. He saluted then spoke to an occupant before returning to his men. Drawing back his shoulders, he snapped out another sharp order, and the soldiers dismounted in unison.

Kit's stomach twisted in knots. Would the soldiers march directly to the *Tamarith*? Or would they search every ship in the harbour? Either way, Clem and Pengorse were in real danger.

The schooner's deck heaved gently on the rising tide. Just an hour more and the *Tamarith* would put to sea, on its way to Newfoundland and then south to New Orleans. Kit crept two steps backwards and couched behind a barrel lashed to an eyelet on deck. He had to warn the others, but how could he reach the companionway without being seen? He peered above the level of the gunwale.

The carriage door opened, and a figure stepped down into the quayside light. Ralph Killiow swung his gaze up and down the wharf. He whipped around, jabbed a fist at the carriage door and barked out an explosive order to step out. A dark shadow moved inside the carriage, and Kit focussed on the shape.

The figure appeared at the coach door. Kit held his breath as the woman stepped down gingerly onto the cold, wet cobbles.

Damn that evil squire.

The slender form bent against the night air was unmistakable. Wenna wore a dark cloak but her head was bare and her long, black hair became quickly plastered against her face by the drizzling rain. She coughed as the cold early morning air seeped into her chest, the sound of her hacking bouncing across the water. Kit winced at the pain she must be enduring.

She stumbled on the uneven ground, but no one moved to help her, and Kit gritted his teeth, half-jerking to his feet to protest at her rough treatment. But what would revealing himself accomplish? Reluctantly, he crouched back behind the barrel, silently cursing.

The lieutenant in charge of the dragoons stood erect and impassive despite the drizzle and beckoned to a perky sergeant major. After receiving instructions, the sergeant major dispatched his men into teams and directed them along the wharf towards the line of tall ships.

The soldier's voice blasted out, sharp and clear. "Search every inch of space on these ships. I'll lash any man who lingers. At the double!" Kit winced in dread.

The line of soldiers, mud-spattered, wet and miserable, spread out and advanced. Marching across the cobbles, they unsheathed their swords and walked up the line of gangplanks.

Cries of alarm greeted them as they boarded the ships, but the dragoons pressed ahead. Three soldiers strode up the gangplank of the *Tamarith*, a dour-faced corporal followed by two privates. Kit crouched even lower behind the barrel in the darkest recess, hoping they would make only a cursory search. The *Tamarith's* officer of the deck blocked their path, arguing with them, but the corporal roughly pushed him aside and ordered his men to search below. The dragoons clambered down below decks.

One chance to escape capture seemed open to Kit. He was alone, separated from the fugitives, and in the dim light, he could pass himself off as a sailor. Dammit, he *was* a sailor. He pulled back from his hiding place and removed his coat. Then he positioned himself lazily against the gunwale, picked up an untidy rope and began to coil it while waiting to see what would happen next.

He flinched when angry and insulted shouts wafted up from the companionway. Tension oozing through his limbs, Kit dropped the rope in an untidy heap to pick it up and recoil it again until Ben Worth stumbled on deck and stormed down the gangplank, waving his fists and protesting loudly. But Killiow and the lieutenant remained unmoved.

More angry cries drifted up from below deck and moments later a sorry group came up the rear companionway. "Lieutenant!" The corporal marched to the side of the ship and called out to the officer on the quayside. "Here they are." He grasped Pengorse's arm and pushed him up against the gunwale.

"Get them down here. At the double!"

"Yes, sir."

A lumbering line of figures shambled down the gangway to the wharf, the corporal in the lead, Clem behind him. Pengorse and Beth followed while the two privates brought up the rear.

"Capital!" Killiow clapped his hands in elation. He took a step forward and inspected the little gathering. "Where's the other one? The other Vanson. The ringleader."

"This is all, sir." The corporal saluted his officer briskly.

"No, it ain't." Killiow beckoned Wenna to come forward and took a pistol from his belt.

At the sight of Killiow pressing the pistol close against Wenna's temple, Pengorse growled and cursed loudly. Two soldiers quickly took hold of the preacher.

The lieutenant raised a hand to Killiow in weak protest, but the squire ignored him. "Vanson! Come down here or I'll blow this woman's head from her shoulders!"

Kit let out a long, resigned sigh. It was all over. They had failed. Many risks he was willing to take, but not with Wenna's life. He crossed to the gangway and strode down to the quay, fuming.

Clem and Pengorse looked on with despair, each guarded by two dragoons. Beth and Wenna stood either side of Killiow. Beth's face showed an incensed expression while Wenna looked tired and dejected, her face deathly white.

The new Squire of Studmore Manor pulled at his whiskers, evidently pleased with himself. "Sorry to have to spoil your little journey."

"Wasn't going anywhere," Kit replied. "What made you think I was?"

Seething, Beth grabbed her brother's s arm. "You'll never get away with this, Ralph. I know too much about father's death."

Killiow swung round on his heels and repositioned his pistol against his sister's neck. "Whatever you may think you know about father's death ..." His words trailed off, allowing for a long pause, as if to torture Beth and ensure she would take seriously the meaning of his next words. "Forget it."

Clem suddenly pushed aside the soldiers watching over him, catching the men off guard, and took two paces across the cobbles to bring him face to face with the squire. "Leave her alone, Killiow. Would you threaten your own sister?"

Startled by Clem's audacity, Killiow blinked and stepped backwards, lowering his pistol. In the same moment, the sergeant major sprang forward and aimed the tip of his sword at the back of Clem's neck. "Stand back or this blade goes right through you."

Clem froze. Quickly recovering from the threat, he turned to face the sergeant major. He stared into the soldier's eyes and leaned towards him until the point of his blade pressed tight against his coat. "Would you protect a man who threatens a defenceless woman?"

The soldier was taken aback by Clem's affront. In that moment, Clem took the advantage and whipped round again, grabbing at Killiow's armed hand. But the sergeant major reacted fast and swung his sword in an arc across Clem's back, cutting a deep swathe across his coat. Clem arched his shoulders back in pain, staggered then dropped to his knees.

"Clem!" Beth reached out towards him, staring at the speed of his blood mingling with the water on the cobbles. "No!" she cried out horrified.

Kit leapt forward towards his brother, but his captors grabbed at his arms and held him in check. Only yards away, Beth sank to her knees to cradle Clem's head in her lap.

With no more than a scowl of satisfaction, the sergeant major sheathed his sword.

"Let me go. I ain't got no gun." Kit raised his hands to show he was unarmed, shook off the soldiers restraining him and moved closer to Clem.

Killiow once again raised his pistol towards Wenna. "Don't try anything else, Vanson, or this bitch will die."

He was barely two yards from Killiow and yet he could not risk attacking him. Kit gritted his teeth and glared at the squire. It was all over. He let out a loud curse that rent the air. Killiow had won.

Then, behind him, a loud voice bellowed: "You heathen!"

Kit swung around in time to see Pengorse fling aside his captors with one mighty heave of his arms. He sprang at Killiow, grasping the squire in a powerful bear hug. Arms trapped by his sides, the squire shouted for help and struggled to shake himself free, but the pastor held on and squeezed tighter.

"Help me!" His wide eyes sought the dragoons within reach.

Both the sergeant and the lieutenant raised their swords and advanced.

"No!" Kit raised a hand at them. "You'll risk killing one of them. Might be the squire." Privately, he wished Killiow dead, but he had a hunch it would be better done by Pengorse. The pastor was already certain of imprisonment, possibly hanging. Best he was allowed to choose his own end.

"God's vengeance be upon you," Pengorse bellowed and he pivoted swiftly on his heels, putting his captive between himself and the soldiers. "The vengeance of the Lord is mine." He dragged the fighting squire steadily backwards across the wharf, all the while keeping his gaze firmly focussed on Wenna.

Kit gaped as he recognised a wide gamut of expressions chasing one another across the pastor's face: his understanding of what he was now doing, his love for Wenna and, most of all, his pain at the thought of losing her.

Pengorse's voice rose like an anthem. "Though I walk through the shadow of the valley of death I will fear no evil."

Turning his attention to Wenna, Kit felt deep pangs of sorrow at her confusion. Was she wondering what vengeance her husband spoke of? Then her look of confusion began to slip away and an expression of horror took its place. Did she, like him, begin to understand why Pengorse spoke of the valley of death?

Wenna threw her hands to her face as full enlightenment suddenly took hold. Her lips silently pursed into the shape of the word 'no'. Then her eyes begged for comprehension. Why? What was Killiow to Arthur Pengorse? Wicked, yes, but not worth dying for, unless … unless he had somehow discovered the truth. She turned towards Kit, and the answer was there in her eyes. She finally understood that her husband knew of her rape. He was about to administer his own private justice.

Powerless, Kit could only look on as the drama was played to its terrible end.

Despite his arms tightly pinned to his sides, Killiow still held on to his pistol but was unable to use it for any purpose. "Help me," he roared at the soldiers.

The sergeant and the lieutenant again approached, but Pengorse had Killiow locked as a shield in front of himself. After a struggle, the squire finally succeeded in bringing his pistol to bear and a loud report echoed across the wharf. The shot flew wild and the two men staggered closer to the water. Still, Pengorse kept his gaze locked on Wenna.

Waves of admiration rose in Kit's heart for the man he had once so despised. Pengorse was thinking only of her to the very end. As he looked on, he detected determination in the preacher's eyes. Pengorse nodded to Wenna. In his heart, Kit knew that action was a last goodbye.

Teetering on the edge of the quay, the pastor switched his attention to Kit, casting him a look that was startling in its intensity, a look that demanded fulfilment of a promise to take care of his wife. It was a promise Kit could not refuse. He nodded to the preacher, and Pengorse closed his eyes as if relieved.

Killiow threw back his head with a groan of agony and panic as Pengorse, eyes still shut, choked the breath out of him. Both figures began to topple. A last gasp erupted from Killiow before they both tumbled towards the dark icy waters.

A splash cut through the night air.

The dragoons stumbled around in surprise and shock while Kit ran to the edge of the wharf. A dark eddy swirled around where the two men had sunk into the depths.

Quickly recovering from their horror, others came alongside him, crying out in alarm. Astonished voices bubbled along the quayside, growing in volume as the minutes passed and no one came to the surface.

Suddenly, like a ghost from the dead, Killiow's cloak surged upwards and floated on pockets of air trapped within it. For a few minutes it danced on the water and then began to follow the tide.

"Throw 'em a rope!" a soldier called out.

"Who to?" a seaman replied. "No one there to grab it."

A soldier jumped into a nearby dinghy and pulled away. He circled around the area where they had gone under. After a time, he shouted to the watchers: "Nothin' here!"

Kit negotiated his way back through the onlookers across the cobbles to where Beth helped Clem into the Killiow family carriage.

She had managed to stem the blood loss but it was clear the wound needed the urgent attention of a surgeon.

Determined there would be no more mistakes this night, Kit marched up to the lieutenant of dragoons. "There's been a tragedy here, and I hope you'll have the sense not to make things worse."

The officer gave him a puzzled look. "I don't understand."

"A man is injured by the hand of one of your soldiers and two others are likely drowned. And you had a part in all this." Kit jerked his head towards the coach. "Now, you must allow us to take my brother to a surgeon immediately. He's in urgent need of surgery."

The lieutenant stood to attention, the habit of a lifetime of soldiering. "I have my orders, sir. I must take these people into custody."

"Show me your orders, Lieutenant." Kit glowered at him.

The lieutenant frowned. "Sir?" But he nonetheless reached into his tunic and brought out a single warrant.

Kit inspected it in the light of a lantern. "This, Lieutenant, is a warrant for Pastor Pengorse. Show me your warrant for the arrest of my brother."

The lieutenant folded up the paper. "I've only this warrant for Arthur Pengorse."

"Is that all?"

"Yes, sir." The lieutenant's smart demeanour dropped further. "We didn't have time to collect a warrant for your brother. We arrested him on the say-so of Squire Killiow."

"But Squire Killiow is no longer with us." Kit gave him a pointed look. "So, Lieutenant, you arrested my bother with no authority whatsoever. Release him immediately."

The soldier flared his nostrils. "I don't know about that, sir."

"Lieutenant, you have no warrant to arrest anyone except Mister Pengorse. Yet one of your men has deliberately attacked and injured my brother." Kit leaned closer to the officer. "This was done in the presence of Miss Elizabeth Killiow, the daughter of the late Squire Killiow. You get my drift?"

"No."

Kit released a sigh of frustration. "If Ralph Killiow is drowned, Miss Elizabeth Killiow becomes the rightful heir to the family estates.

A lady with influence. And there is no one to accuse her or my brother of any offence. Now do you understand?"

The officer's shoulders slumped. "I think I comprehend your reasoning, sir."

"And?"

The lieutenant gulped. "And I apologise for the injury your brother sustained. An unfortunate accident, I'm sure you'll agree." At Kit's nod, the officer turned on his heels and mustered his soldiers.

Kit held his hands on his hips as the lieutenant gave the order to mount. Within minutes, the dragoons were riding off in the direction of the Plymouth military barracks at the Royal Citadel. Shortly after, the squire's black carriage clattered away from the wharf in search of a surgeon in Plymouth town.

Kit found Wenna sitting on a bollard. She shivered violently when he clasped her in his arms. She was so cold. Would she suffer a relapse? He sincerely hoped not.

"It's all over now," he said softly.

Tears flowed down her cheeks, and she made no attempt to stem them. "He knew, Kit. I swear to you he knew what Killiow did to me."

He put his fingers lightly to her chin and tipped it so that he could look deep into her eyes. He hoped she would be able to see the love reflected in his own eyes. "Yes, he knew. And he died in order that you might be able to live without the shame of it."

"He died because of me?"

"Because he loved you and he saw that he was the only person who could wipe away the source of your pain. The only one who could remove the threat of Killiow from your life."

She sniffled and wiped at her eyes. "Will God look kindly on him?"

"I reckon so."

"God bless him," she whispered.

Kit nodded. "He surely will. Come, I'll take you home."

She suddenly threw her arms about him and her body shook as she sobbed against his chest.

Twenty Four

April 1840

The night had been unusually cold. For Kit, it had seemed unending as if his own future was dependent upon what happened in the hours of darkness.

He stood at the kitchen door and stared out, shivering in the cool air of dawn. An orange glow lit up the horizon, silhouetting the small copse where he and Wenna had picnicked only a week ago. Heavily pregnant, she had sat back against a gnarled oak with baby John in her lap while he stared out across the fields and counted himself a lucky man.

There were still times when he kept his worried thoughts to himself but they became fewer with the passing years. On occasions he wondered if Wenna still grieved for her first husband; the one she had never loved.

Ralph Killiow's body had washed ashore days after the confrontation in Plymouth but no trace of Pengorse was ever found. Soon after his marriage to Wenna, rumours came to Kit that the pastor had been seen in the Methodist circuits in remote parts of Cornwall, and he steeled himself against the possibility that Wenna might yet be taken from him. The passing of time had eased that anxiety, and he came to accept that his marriage would survive.

His memories in full flood, he didn't hear Clem come up behind him and he started when a hand fell on his shoulder.

"Beth knows all about these things," Clem assured him. "Most women do. And that old midwife told me she's delivered dozens of babies round here."

Kit turned and sought his brother's eyes. "It's taking a hell of a long time." He ran his tongue round his parched lips. "Wenna had such a bad time when John was born, you recall?" Then he cast a fond gaze to the heart of the kitchen where Jenny Rudge held baby John on her lap while her own two toddlers played at her feet.

As if she sensed his stare, Jenny's gaze came up to meet Kit's and she smiled, the smile of a woman content in her simple domesticity.

"Me and Beth figure on havin' lots of kids when we're married." Clem sounded positive, as if relieved that Beth had finally agreed to marry him. "She wants a son first off, so's he can be the next Squire of Studmore."

Kit nodded. The responsibility of raising a son would be good for Clem. He had been off the booze for so long now. He deserved a stable marriage, and Beth would make one hell of a good wife. But had Clem forgotten the implications of having a son? Was he man enough to support his offspring when he came up against the family curse?

And what of John? What of his own firstborn? How would he cope?

Pursing his lips, Kit turned away and closed his eyes. In time, he had come to understand that his love for Wenna was all that mattered, not the painful experiences preceding their marriage. Nor the legacy of his father's misdeeds. And yet, in a perverted sort of way, those past experiences bound him to Wenna far stronger than their emotional love.

As for John ... Kit drew back his shoulders. He would help his son through the problem of the curse when ... *if* it ever arose. Maybe Clem was right; maybe it was just superstitious nonsense.

He jumped at a sudden rush of activity on the floor above. Clem reached out and squeezed his hand tight about Kit's arm.

A baby's cry floated down through the upper floorboards, a ragged burst of lusty noise.

"She's done it, Kit!" Clem released his grasp and then slapped his brother on the back. "By golly, boy. You'm a pa again."

Kit took a halting step forward, dazed and momentarily unthinking. His head whirled. His limbs were weighted like lead. Pray God the birth had gone well.

A door opened upstairs, footsteps rattled across the landing, down the stairs. Kit stared at the passage door, unable to take a step towards it.

Beth burst into the kitchen, her eyes and cheeks glowing. "It's all right, Kit. They're both all right." She paused abruptly and threw out her arms to him.

"Wenna? You're sure?" The words choked in Kit's throat. He had another child and yet his first thought went to his wife.

"It's all right," Beth assured him then wrapped her arms about him. "Wenna has a healthy little boy."

A boy, a healthy boy! When Beth released him, Kit wiped at a keen dampness dribbling down his cheeks. He turned away and covered his face, forcing composure back into his brain. With difficulty, like focussing on something from a great distance, he slowly turned his attention back to Beth. "You're quite sure Wenna is all right?"

"Quite sure." Beth took his hands in hers. "You can see for yourself in a moment." Then Clem clapped a hand across his shoulders.

"What you gonna call him, brother?"

Kit rubbed his brow, relief washing over him. "Edward. We decided, if we had another son, we'd call him Edward."

Clem reached into a cupboard for a bottle of good brandy. "A good choice. A noble English name. Reckon you should drink a toast, brother. To your wife and your new son."

A drink? Kit's brain froze at the sight of his brother uncorking the bottle and reaching for a goblet. "Clem," he called. "Are you sure?"

"I'm damned sure *you* need a drink, brother." Clem turned on his heels and winked mischievously as he held out the goblet to Kit, eyes twinkling with merriment. "But you know I ain't up to drinking a toast to anyone. I'm figurin' there'll be no booze on the table when Beth and me get wed."

Kit smiled with relief and took the drink. "Make it real soon, Clem. Real soon."

The End

Also by David Hough

A Tangle of Roots

Beneath the dark canopy of impenetrable tropical forests Fayzella dreams strange dreams of a white-faced man and woman.

Then she escapes the brutish depravity of primitive clans and enters a man-made jungle ruled by the pale-skinned creatures of her dreamlife.

She finds herself thrust into another nightmare … facing demons of prejudice, sin, lies and intrigue to untangle the twisted roots of her past.

Fayzella's quest to discover the truth of her life sweeps from Stone Age to Computer Age. It will haunt you long, long after you have reluctantly turned the last page.

ISBN 978-1-904492-51-1

"This book touched me beyond imagination. It touches every emotions a reader could possibly feel. I recommend it to anyone who likes to read stories that are strong, captivating and very real."
N Lessard

"Mr Hough has succeeded in creating a soul-stirring novel. Whether you're a father, a mother, or someone's child you will not put this book down once started.

Don't miss this extraordinary emotional journey. I promise you won't be disappointed."
Carole Spencer

BeWrite Books
www.bewrite.net

Coming Soon
Spring 2007

King's Priory
by
David Hough

King's Priory Manor is a house of secrets. Some are so terrible they affect the lives of the Portesham family through each successive generation. Within the manor's ancient walls, Colin Portesham finally discovers what happened to his grandfather, sixty years ago in wartime.

Why did his grandfather kill a fellow officer? What happened to poor, brain-damaged Aunt Lucy in a Nazi death camp? Slowly, the secrets that plague Colin are revealed. But the truth is so terrible it leads to the death of a member of the family.

Worse is still to come. The truth also foretells of further horrific family tragedies. A young woman must die and someone Colin loves must suffer an accident. Is there anything he can do to hold back the hand of fate?

ISBN 978-1-905202-66-9

BeWrite Books
www.bewrite.net

Also Available from BeWrite Books

Magpies and Sunsets by Neil Alexander Marr
ISBN 978-1-904492-29-0

Redemption of Quapaw Mountain by Bertha Sutliff
ISBN 978-1-904492-38-2

The Cuckoos of Batch Magna by Peter Maughan
ISBN 978-1-904492-46-7

Matabele Gold by Michael J Hunt
ISBN 978-1-904492-35-1

The African Journals of Petros Amm by Michael J Hunt
ISBN 978-1-904492-57-3

Whispers of Ghosts by Ron McLachlan
ISBN 978-1-904492-62-7

Plato's Child by Ron McLachlan
ISBN 978-1-905202-06-5

Death in Malta by Rosanne Dingli
ISBN 978-1-904492-92-4

The Bad Seed by Maurilia Meehan
ISBN 978-1-905202-12-6

BeWrite Books
www.bewrite.net

Printed in the United Kingdom
by Lightning Source UK Ltd.
114434UKS00002B/1